ALSO BY CHRISTA WOLF

Divided Heaven

The Quest for Christa T.

Patterns of Childhood

No Place on Earth

Cassandra

Accident: A Day's News

What Remains and Other Stories

The Author's Dimension: Selected Essays

Parting from Phantoms: Selected Writings, 1990–1994

Medea

In the Flesh

One Day a Year

CITY OF ANGELS

CITY OF ANGELS

OR, THE OVERCOAT OF DR. FREUD

CHRISTA WOLF

TRANSLATED FROM THE GERMAN BY DAMION SEARLS

FARRAR, STRAUS AND GIROUX   NEW YORK

Farrar, Straus and Giroux
18 West 18th Street, New York 10011

Library of Congress Cataloging-in-Publication Data
Wolf, Christa.
    [Stadt der Engel, oder, The overcoat of Dr. Freud. English]
    City of angels or, : The overcoat of Dr. Freud / Christa Wolf ; translated from
the German by Damion Searls. — 1st American ed.
        p.   cm.
    ISBN 978-0-374-26935-7 (alk. paper)
    I. Searls, Damion.   II. Title.   III. Title: City of angels or, The overcoat of
Dr. Freud.
PT2685.O36 S6713 2013
833'.914—dc23

                                                        2012018515

Designed by Jonathan D. Lippincott

www.fsgbooks.com
www.twitter.com/fsgbooks • www.facebook.com/fsgbooks

10   9   8   7   6   5   4   3   2   1

So, for authentic memories, it is far less important that the investigator report on them than that he mark, quite precisely, the site where he gained possession of them.

—Walter Benjamin, "Excavation and Memory"

TRANSLATOR'S NOTE

Italics (except for emphasized words and titles of books, movies, and so on) indicate words and phrases in English in the original.

CITY OF ANGELS

No writer can reproduce the actual texture of living life.
—E. L. Doctorow

TO COME DOWN TO EARTH

was the phrase that came to me when I landed in L.A. and the passengers on the airplane clapped to thank the pilot for flying it across the ocean, approaching the New World from the sea, circling for a long time above the lights of the giant metropolis, then gently touching down. I still remember how I decided to use that sentence later, when I would write about the landing and the sojourn on a foreign coast that lay ahead. Later: Now. That so many years would pass in dogged attempts to reach the sentences which were to follow, to reach them in the right way, was something I could not foresee. I decided to fix everything in my memory for later, every detail. How my blue passport caused a stir with the wiry red-blond *officer* who was rigorously and carefully checking the papers of every arriving visitor; he flipped through its pages for a long time, studied every single visa, then picked up the invitation letter from the CENTER, under whose auspices I would be spending the following months, a letter certified and authenticated many times over; finally he looked straight at me with his ice-blue eyes: *Germany? —Yes. East Germany.* —I would have found it hard to give him any further details, because of the language barrier too, but he decided to ask a colleague for advice over the phone. The whole scene seemed familiar—how well I knew the feeling of tense excitement and the sense of relief too when he finally, having no doubt received a satisfactory answer to his question, stamped the visa and slid my passport back across the counter with a hand covered in freckles. *Are you sure that country exists? —Yes, I am,* I said curtly, even though the correct answer would have been *No* and I had to wonder, during my long wait for the luggage, whether it was really worth it to travel to the United States with the still-valid passport of a no-longer-extant country just to confuse a young redheaded immigration official. That was one of the acts of defiance I was still capable of then, acts which, it occurs to me now, become fewer and fewer with age. And there the word stands on the page, mentioned in passing, as is only fitting: the word whose shadow flickered across me for the first time then, more than a decade and a half ago, and has meantime grown so thick and dark that I have to worry about its becoming impenetrable before I can fulfill the duties of my profession. Before I have described, that is, how I hauled my bags down off the baggage carousel, loaded them onto an oversize luggage cart, and headed for the EXIT in the middle of a confusing crowd of people. How, having barely set foot in the terminal, something happened that according to all the earnest pleas and warnings from experienced travelers I should never have let happen: a giant black man came up to me, *Want a car, ma'am?*, and I, inexperienced creature of reflexes that I was, nodded yes, instead of resolutely refusing the way I had been told to. Already the man had snatched the cart and set off with it—I would never see it again, or so my alarm system told me. I followed after him as quickly as I could and there he was, in fact, standing outside on the curb of the access road where taxis were rolling up, bumper to bumper, their headlights dimmed. He pocketed the dollar he was entitled to and handed me over to a colleague, also black, who had gotten himself a job waving down taxis. He too discharged his duties, stopped the next taxi, helped me load my bags into the trunk, likewise received his dollar, and turned me over to the skinny little driver, an agile Puerto Rican whose English I couldn't understand but who obligingly listened to mine and, after studying the letterhead with my future address on it, seemed to know where he was supposed to take me. Only then, when the taxi started driving, I remember, did I feel the mild night air, the breath of the south, which I recognized from an entirely different coast where it had come over me for the first time like a thick warm towel—at the airport in Varna. The Black Sea, its velvety darkness, the sweet heavy scent of its gardens.

I can still, today, feel myself in that taxi, with chains of lights racing by on either side and sometimes streaming into handwriting—world-famous brand names, billboards in garish colors for supermarkets, for bars and restaurants, outshining the night sky. Words like "orderly" would be out of place here, on this coastal road, perhaps on this whole continent. Very softly, and quickly repressed again, the question came to mind: What had actually made me come here?—just loud enough for me to recognize it the next time it announced itself, already more urgent than before. In any case, the scaly trunks of the palm trees glided by as though they were reason enough. The smell of gas and exhaust. A long drive.

Santa Monica, ma'am? —Yes. —Second Street, ma'am? —Right. —Ms. Victoria? —Yes. —Here we are.

For the first time, the illuminated metal sign affixed to the iron fence: MS. VICTORIA HOTEL, OLD WORLD CHARM. Everything quiet. All the windows dark. It was a little before midnight. The driver helped me with my luggage. A front lawn, a path of stone slabs, the smell of unknown flowers that apparently gave off a scent at night, the weak light of a gently swaying lamp over the front door, a doorbell which had, stuck behind it, a piece of paper with my name on it. *Welcome,* I read. The door was open, I should go right in, the key to my apartment was on the table in the hall, *second floor, room number seventeen, the manager of the* MS. VICTORIA *wishes you a wonderful night.*

Was I dreaming? But unlike in a dream I didn't lose my way, I found the key, took the right stairs, the key fit in the right lock, the light switch was where it was supposed to be, in the blink of an eye I can see it all before me: Two floor lamps lighting a large room with a cluster of armchairs opposite a long dining table surrounded with chairs. I paid the taxi driver, to his apparent satisfaction, with the unfamiliar money that I had luckily exchanged in Berlin before my departure, thanked him in an appropriate way, and received, as was proper, the answer: *You're welcome, ma'am.*

I examined my apartment: Aside from this large living room there was an adjoining kitchen, two bedrooms, two bathrooms. What a waste. A family of four could live here comfortably, I thought on that first night, then later got used to the luxury. A welcome note from someone named Alice lay on the table—she must be the employee of the CENTER who had signed the invitation letter, and it was probably she who had also thoughtfully left me bread, butter, and a few drinks in the kitchen. I tried a little of everything and it tasted foreign.

I worked out that back where I had come from it was already morning, so I could call without waking anyone up. After a few failed attempts with several *overseas operators* trying to help me, I managed to get the telephone in the tiny cabinet next to the front door to work, I dialed the right numbers and I heard, behind the white noise of the ocean, the familiar voice. That was the first of the hundred phone calls to Berlin in the next nine months. I said I had made it to the other side of the globe. I did not say what I was asking myself: What was the point? I did say I was very tired, and it's true, I really was, a strange, foreign tiredness. I looked for a nightgown in one of the suitcases, washed my hands and face, lay down in the bed, which was too wide and too soft, and didn't fall asleep for a long time. I woke up early, out of a morning dream, and heard a voice say: Time does what it can. It passes.

Those were the first sentences I wrote down in the large lined notebook that I had taken the precaution to bring with me and had placed on the narrow end of the long dining table and that quickly filled up with my notes, which I can now refer back to. In the meantime, time has passed, the way my dream laconically informed me it always does—which was, and is, one of the most mysterious processes I know and one that I understand less and less the older I get. The fact that rays of thought, looking back into the past and looking ahead into the future, can penetrate through the layers of time strikes me as a miracle, and the telling of stories partakes of this miracle, because otherwise, without the benevolent gift of storytelling, we would not have survived and we could not survive.

For example, it's possible to let such thoughts flit through one's head and at the same time flip through the packet from the CENTER I discovered on the table in my apartment the next morning: *"First Day Survival Information"* for new arrivals. It listed the nearest grocery stores, cafés, and pharmacies, described how to get to the CENTER and its rules of operation, and gave its telephone number, staffed twenty-four hours a day, of course. It recommended restaurants and also bookstores, libraries, scenic drives, museums, amusement parks, and guidebooks, and last but not least impressed upon the unsuspecting newcomer the proper behavior in case of an earthquake. I conscientiously reviewed all the information and also studied the list of my fellow scholars, from various countries, who would be my colleagues for the next six months, who would develop into members of a friendly community, and who have since scattered to the four winds again, or in other words, back to their various native countries.

I could not let myself get sick or get too stiff to move. I then went to the bathroom I had decided to use, the smaller one, and climbed into the shower, whose head, unlike in Europe, was attached to the wall, so that special techniques were necessary to reach my whole body. To the accompaniment of music I could not understand and news I could not understand from the local radio station in Los Angeles, I assembled my breakfast with hand movements I was already used to, but out of components that to some extent I was not used to: muffins (well, why not?), a strange muesli mix, and orange juice, which, after a few failed shopping efforts, seemed the most reliable. It was only when it came to coffee that I still had to experiment—I had to find someone who understood Germans' taste in coffee and could recommend which brand out of the dozens of tins on offer at PAVILION came closest to it. (In the GDR, it had almost caused a revolution when the government, to make the expensive "genuine" beans last longer, expected the population to accept an undrinkable coffee blend; when the workers' protests started to approach the threat of strikes, they immediately took it off the shelves.) Bill, who had lived in the apartment before I did and then moved in with a friend, had left behind various exotic spice mixtures for me, as well as an impressive array of bottles: olive oil, balsamic vinegar, good whiskey, California wine. On his last day in the city, he went out to eat with me at the Italian restaurant on Second Street, and introduced me, with affectionate irony, into the customs of the old MS. VICTORIA and the young CENTER. It's the damnedest thing, he'd said, there is nowhere you can work on the history of *good old Europe* better than here in the New World. They collect everything that has to do with the old country, it's like they're possessed, as though they wanted to preserve at least a copy of Europe in case it ever ceased to exist, because of nuclear war or some other catastrophe. Bill was working on the history of Catholicism in Spain and France, and calculated for me the thousands of human victims that the various pushes to Christianize those countries had claimed. In every colonization, he said, the first thing to be rooted out among the conquered in order to take away their identity was their religion, their beliefs. Aside from that, the conquerors had a pressing need, however implausible it may sound, to insist that not only their weapons and commodities but their worldview and beliefs were superior. It stemmed from a deep-seated inferiority complex. Oh, I know that, I'd said, and Bill, the Englishman, had given me a searching look: You're going through that now over there, aren't you? He hadn't insisted I answer. Sometimes, in the evening, when I had drunk a glass of wine from his stock, I clinked glasses with him in my thoughts.

So, many times, I set out in the morning through the blossoming front lawn of the MS. VICTORIA, full of unfamiliar plants and with a small bitter orange tree in a circular flower bed in the middle, whose fruits I saw ripen. The cars here, extraordinarily wide, crept carefully up to the intersections and politely stopped even when there was no little green man on the traffic sign to permit pedestrians to WALK; they rocked gently back and forth on their suspensions; friendly, well-dressed, carefully coiffed female drivers or chic male drivers in dark suits with ties and collars signaled the pedestrian to go ahead, with nonchalant waves of their hands, so I crossed California Avenue without hurrying. Did I even notice the trees still with gaudy red blossoms in November, in December? I was spared autumn leaves and gray foggy days that year, but also denied them. Did I already miss them?

I can call up the CENTER before my mind's eye whenever I want. At the time it was housed in an ordinary multistory office building, which has long since been replaced by a spectacular postmodern complex high above the city. So: a wide flight of stairs outside, leading up to a series of columns, through which I saw myself walking every day in the giant reflective glass double doors. I always opened the same door from among the six possible options, and stepped into the massive lobby, where there was always the same man stationed at always the same place, day in and day out, a doorman or guard who greeted favorite visitors with an outstretched right arm and a friendly snap of his fingers, and whose watchful gaze roamed over the spacious area the lobby opened up into on the right, where the First Federal Bank had its windows. This bank, to which I had already several times entrusted my biweekly checks and which had assured me of its gratitude for this act of trust both verbally and in writing, had for its part, however, expressed little trust in my financial seriousness—for I had not yet received the *ATM card* that would put me in a position to get *cash* from the machines. The ladies behind the bank counters had seemed extremely distressed and were forthcoming with reassurances, while in me the impression was reinforced that they, or their invisible superiors above them, were intentionally delaying the issuance of this crucial piece of plastic because they wanted to be reassured first that this customer's account, though small in scope, would nonetheless continually increase and pose little risk of suffering a precipitous collapse. Still, I sometimes had to laugh when I thought about how different the grounds for suspecting me were in the various societal formations I lived and had lived in.

In any case, I didn't veer off toward the bank windows but went straight to the elevators and noticed, not without satisfaction, that the doorman (guard?) greeted me for the first time with the gesture reserved for only those of the countless visitors to the building he had admitted into the inner circle of those who belonged there. *How are you today, Madam? —Oh, great!* —There are degrees of comparatives and super-latives for every level of well-being.

I took the second from the left of the four elevators, as always, and admiringly observed the young lady on the *staff* who stood across from me, ultrathin in her tight-fitting suit, with a swan made of gold paper, a gift, on her palm, and wafted up to the higher spheres, the eleventh floor, to which I never once strayed. *How are you today? —Fine*, I heard myself say: a sign that new reflexes were forming, because a very short time be-fore, even yesterday, I would have had to dig around in my brain for an appropriate quick answer that might well have come out as *Pretty bad* (and actually, why would that have been my answer? I'd have to think about that more later). But by then I understood that nothing was expected of me except to carry out a ritual, which suddenly no longer seemed dis-honest and superficial, but almost humane. Elevator syndrome.

As always, I got out at the fifth floor, where the black security guard already knew me by name and spoke it while handing me an envelope that had been left for me; where I automatically reached out for the correct hook in the little locker to take my *Identity Card*, complete with my photograph, and attach it to my lapel—a further important sign of my belonging there, and in the end that's what it was all about.

I sometimes walked up the two flights of stairs to the seventh floor, and sometimes, when my joints hurt too much, took the elevator. My feet knew the way between the shelves in which photographs of all the works of art from every century and every continent were archived; it no longer happened that I tried to open a wrong door with a wrong key. So I opened the door to my office space and was already so blasé that I no longer had to go up to the large window first thing every morning, with a feeling of something like reverence, to look at the Pacific Ocean stretched out behind Second Street and a line of houses and a row of palm trees. The phone. It was Berlin, the city had melted down into a single voice that I had to hear every day. That wanted to remind me of the Baltic Sea. The Baltic, well. I am fond of it and always will be, and I know that I cannot endure sublime landscapes over the long run, the Alps and such. But still, the feeling that there's nothing all the way to Japan but this endless expanse of water! Were my feelings exaggerated?

I put down the bag in which I was carrying around the bundle of papers that had come to me two years before, after the death of my friend Emma, and that burned away at my soul (I am not overstating it): the letters from a certain L., about whom I knew nothing except that she had lived in the United States and must have been very close friends with my friend Emma, and the same age. I had come here because of these letters, among other reasons, nurturing the illusion that it must be possible here to find out who this "L." actually was.

I walked to the middle of the *office*, waving, as I walked past open doors, into rooms where my colleagues sat at their computers, when they were not off somewhere in the rambling building, in the library or the archives, following some trace, or meeting with other scholars in the city. I sometimes envied them for their clearly delineated projects and disciplinary identities: they could state their field immediately: history of architecture, or philosophy, or art and literature, or film studies, there was even medieval literature, and every one of them could name the topic of study they were here to advance just like that. Whereas I was plunged into embarrassment whenever anyone asked me about my work plans. Was I supposed to admit that I had nothing in hand but a bunch of old letters from a dead woman and I was simply curious about their author, who must have lived in this city years ago when she wrote them to my likewise dead friend Emma? And that that was why the invitation I had received from the CENTER came at such an opportune time? And that I would now take advantage of the privilege of being an author of literary books, someone who couldn't be questioned too closely about her project? It seemed highly likely to me, though, that my plans were destined to fail. Even now, the coincidences that in the end brought this project at least to a successful and happy conclusion seem unbelievable to me. If I may use those inappropriate words, "successful" and "happy," just this once, as an exception.

For me, incidentally, the least embarrassing of my evasive actions (that maybe no one else recognized as such) were those directed toward the two department secretaries, Kätchen and Jasmine. Kätchen was middle-aged, somewhat nondescript in appearance but expert and experienced in all matters pertaining to the CENTER, absolutely reliable and discrete and versed in the technological skills that I often had to avail myself of, especially at the beginning, and finally, as we all appreciated very much, sympathetic about all the hardships and difficulties that a member of our *community* might encounter. The other secretary, Jasmine, blond and young and slender and supple and a delight to the men's gazes, was in charge of our bodily well-being, for sending and receiving the mail, and for all affairs outside the building, such as arranging meetings with other people in the city, including invitations to this or that restaurant from this or that *scholar*, since the department staff felt responsible for making sure that the new arrivals felt at home in this foreign country as quickly as possible.

I took the mail out of my cubbyhole, Jasmine handed me a few newspapers, and Kätchen said that no one had gotten back to her yet about the information request she had put in to the city and university *libraries* for me. But it seemed unlikely in any case that there would be a complete index there, or anywhere else, of the German émigrés who had found refuge here in the thirties and forties. Although, said Lutz—my much younger countryman, an art historian, who was working at the copier nearby—although the totally impossible is possible here, where else if not here? He immediately provided an example: how he had found a photograph of a painting by the long-forgotten and recently rediscovered painter he had chosen as his object of study right here in the archive, as simple as that, after all the archives in Europe had reported it as lost. Well, good, I said, a little sheepishly, but I don't even know the name of the person I'm looking for. I don't know anything except one initial, probably from her first name, L. Yes, well, Lutz said, in that case it certainly is an especially difficult situation. He would be at something of a loss himself, he said, while we walked to the lounge, where it was time for tea and the others would be gathered as well.

In the lounge, where a gigantic glass wall let in the California light unfiltered, drawing your gaze to the Pacific Ocean and the course of the sun in its great arc from left to right, a sight that took my breath away every time and that since then I see in my mind's eye more often than any other sight from that year—there they sat, each one behind the newspaper from his or her country of origin. Benevolent habits began to develop. *Hi!* I said, and *Hi!* came back from behind the newspapers. People already had their regular seats, and mine was, accidentally or not, between the two Italians: Francesco, working on architecture, and Valentina, here for a short stay to conclude her work on a classical sculpture in the CENTER's famous museum. She had laid out my cup, put the thermos of tea within reach, and also the German newspaper they subscribed to here. I thanked her with a glance. She was looking especially beautiful again with her brown curly hair and her patchwork jacket combining every color; as always, whenever we ran into each other, she beamed delightedly at me. So I poured myself some tea, unfolded my newspaper, and read whatever seemed worthy to report on in Germany three or four days ago. I read that a colleague of mine, who had had to abandon our country a few years before its collapse but was nonetheless someone of rather the same convictions, was now revealing himself as a radical critic of everyone who had stayed in the GDR rather than leaving in horror as he had. I read that he had criticized the "Revolution" of the fall of 1989 for being peaceful. Heads needed to roll, I read, and we had been too timid and cowardly. It's someone whose head wouldn't have been in danger anyway who's writing that, I thought, and I noticed myself starting an inner debate with this colleague of mine.

I remembered—and I still remember today—your relief when, on the morning of November 4, 1989, around Alexanderplatz, the marshals approached you in high spirits with orange sashes on which was printed: NO VIOLENCE! The previous night, at a meeting you took part in, the rumor had been spread that trains with Stasi people disguised as workers had been sent to the capital to provoke the peaceful demonstrators and give the armed forces an excuse to attack. A kind of panic gripped you, you called your daughter and told her she couldn't bring the children with her to Alexanderplatz, but they had already drawn their banners—MAKE SCHOOL MORE INTERESTING! and HELP US GORBY!—and they could no longer be kept away. You went over your speech again, word by word. None of you talked about it but you all thought about the Tiananmen Square massacre in Beijing. The idea that you all might have fallen into a trap, by being too naive, too carefree, weighed heavily upon you, but the more demonstrators streamed up out of the subway stations onto the square, raising their banners and signs, forming a protest march, without needing instructions, the more sure you became that nothing would happen. You couldn't know, none of you could know, that companies of the People's Army were stationed on the roofs of public buildings along Unter den Linden, with live ammunition. In case of emergency. In case the demonstrators left the agreed-upon route and broke through to the Brandenburg Gate, the border with the West. Or, what you learned only later: that one of the sons of one of your colleagues was up there in uniform, lying on the roof, while her other son marched in the demonstration down below.

But would the soldiers have fired? A few months after that day, when the borders had long since been opened, the euphoria had passed, and reality—which apparently is always necessarily disillusioning—was gaining ground, you were walking home in your neighborhood with heavily loaded shopping bags when a young man ran after you and begged you to have a coffee with him and his two comrades, all officers in the National People's Army, out of uniform. You sat with them at a sidewalk café, it must have been the first warm days. Until the fall of the Wall, the three of them had kept watch over the border with the West, but now that they were no longer needed there they had been withdrawn, to be transferred to the Polish border, which they absolutely did not want, they had their families and apartments or little houses here in Berlin, and anyway, the number of troops was being cut. What was going to happen to them? When after all they were among those who had made sure that no shots were fired at the Wall on the night of November 9. They said that they, a captain and two lieutenants, had not been able to reach a superior officer to receive instructions when the crowds started streaming toward the border crossing and that they had collected all the ammunition from their unit so that nothing could happen. You asked them why they had done it. They said: A People's Army can't shoot at the people. —Good for you, you said. —And now that's all the thanks they would get in return? —I'm afraid so, you said. —In that case they would be the ones who lost the most in the reunification, they said.

The lounge. I was elsewhere for a few fractions of a second; memory outraced the light. I would photocopy my colleague's article and put it on the shelf in my apartment with the other clippings and photocopies, a pile that quickly grew, that I would send back over the ocean, by air freight, to add to the other, similar, but far bigger piles at home, useless things that collected dust but that I might be able to use someday to shore up a memory that I otherwise couldn't trust. Couldn't trust anymore. In case of emergency. Even though I was well aware that the power of memory supplied by these newspapers was at best an artificial substitute for my real work.

Francesco was groaning over his Italian newspaper. The politicians are ruining us, he said, those criminals. My country is drowning in corruption. I showed him my article and he read it shaking his head. Has everyone gone crazy, he said, I hope you don't take that nonsense to heart. I didn't tell him what I took to my heart. He said how much he hoped that he would live to see another revolution someday. How he imagined that one's sense of life, so crushed by our day-to-day existence—and more crushed the longer it goes on—would be permanently changed by such an experience: inspired, he should think.

I forced myself past my reluctance to talk about those days, a reluctance I didn't fully understand myself. I said yes, having lived through and taken part in that, one of the few revolutions in German history, removed every doubt I had had about whether staying in that country, which so many people had left with such good reason, was the right thing to do. Now I was even happy I had stayed, in fact. But some defect I seem to be afflicted with, I said, prevents me from feeling the proper mood during so-called historical events. On that November 4, for example, I said, a day for high spirits, in the middle of my speech in front of the hundreds of thousands standing on Alexanderplatz, I felt the cardiac dysrhythmia I was well acquainted with overtake me, which the doctors absolutely refused to connect with psychological experiences, so I had to be taken to the nearest hospital in one of the ambulances standing ready at the edge of the demonstration, where everything was ready for admitting numerous patients. I, however, was the first and only patient to be taken there, and was seen by a team of doctors and nurses who thought I was a vision, since they had just seen me fresh as a daisy onscreen. So I lay there on an ER cot for the rest of the event and waited for an injection to take effect.—So much, my dear Francesco, for one's sense of life. We laughed. I promised to join the outing that Francesco had arranged for the following day, to an installation of modern art.

Pat and Mike, the young Americans with their Clinton buttons pinned to their shirts—assistants in our department—were brooding over the weekend's *New York Times*, which saw declining prospects for the Democrats in the upcoming election. *If Clinton doesn't win I'll have to leave the country*, Mike said gloomily. —*Why?* —They both worked at a Democratic election office every night and they explained to me how hard it was for liberals, never mind people on the left!, to find suitable jobs in recent years, how stale and demoralizing, denunciatory too, the environment was in government offices; the same in the universities, how you had to gauge whom you could talk openly with, and young people like them would have had absolutely no prospects if they hadn't conformed to the point of denying who they really were. You probably don't hear much about that abroad? —You're right, we don't, I said.

But then we all gathered for the spectacle of the sunset over the Pacific, a ritual that was never planned but was usually observed. The sun turned its decline and fall into something special, a climax we wouldn't have thought possible, and we mutely watched the performance until it came into someone's head to say: *God exists.*

The light! Yes, the light, that's the first thing I would say if someone asked me what I miss when I think back to those months. The endless streets, fringed with palm trees, that seemed to run right into the ocean, like Wilshire Boulevard, which I drove up and down so many, many times. And, yes, the MS. VICTORIA would come to mind too, which I gradually fell in love with, once I understood that it was a magical place. It did not come as a complete surprise that the earthquake that struck Los Angeles a few years after we all left damaged the old, somewhat ramshackle Spanish-style building to the point where it was uninhabitable. It wasn't so easy to figure out *"how it worked"* but you had to take it with a certain sense of humor, and what other house or apartment could you say that about? I have kept some of the announcements that the invisible hotel manager regularly slipped under our doors, mostly warnings, for example: We should make sure that the front door remained closed at all times. We should never, under any circumstances, open this door for unknown persons, because we were surely all in it together when it came to the common goal of security, especially in these times, the nature of which Mrs. Ascott did not further specify. Not one of us had set eyes on the manager yet but a picture of her was already taking shape in our minds: that of a strict, middle-aged woman in a gray suit with her hair tightly pulled back. Obviously, to keep things running smoothly at the MS. VICTORIA we had to follow her instructions, for instance organizing a system in case—as happened rarely, but occasionally—a late visitor arrived at the door (which was supposed to remain inexorably closed to him). Depending on age and gender, the visitor could receive a roof over his or her head for the night from Emily, the American film studies professor who lived upstairs from me, or from Pintus and Ria, the young Swiss couple who lived downstairs, or from me.

It turned out that it was easier to smuggle in people than animals. One day a large sign, NO PETS! appeared on the hallowed front door and Mrs. Ascott, its author, took the prohibition against house pets fiendishly seriously, as I learned from Emily, who had not been allowed to bring even one of her beloved cats with her.

I had still not yet seen her in person, our Mrs. Ascott, and when one day I saw a frail old lady get into the giant white Cadillac that, to our annoyance, constantly blocked half of the entrance to the garage, I would never have dreamed of suspecting that she was Mrs. Ascott, who in the end did bear the title of "Manager" and so, I thought, had to be at least fit enough to be able to carry out her duties, and clearly was, since the cleaning staff, mostly Puerto Rican, who cleaned my apartment and changed the sheets and towels twice a week, one woman and two men, worked on Sundays too, and when I asked the woman, a black woman with short frizzy hair, a stout bosom, and wide hips, if that was really necessary, she rolled her eyes and said in her rough, labored English that Mrs. Ascott was "*not good.*" As a result, I decided to reply to the monthly questionnaire that the management gave out, in which we were asked about the quality of the cleaning staff, by checking the box next to "*excellent*" every time without exception. Yes, *excellent* cleaning of the *living room*, the *bedroom*, the *bathroom*, and the *kitchen*, Mrs. Ascott. If only you knew how little I cared.

TELLING THE STORY FROM THE END

can be a disadvantage too—you run the risk of pretending you know less than you really do, for example with respect to Mrs. Ascott, whom of course I inevitably did meet one day, if "meet" is the right term for our first encounter. One morning, a gaunt female creature with disheveled white hair, wrapped in a floral-print dressing gown, darted out of the apartment door across the hall from mine and down the stairs in front of me. I recognized the Cadillac driver and she crossed the somewhat dusty Spanish colonial–style lobby with light, swift footsteps and made a beeline for the short Mexican gentleman sitting at the little table like a bank teller who acted as concierge: "Mr. Enrico," liked and appreciated by all the residents of the MS. VICTORIA. To my amazement, he stood up as the strange lady approached him and received her instructions, not exactly obsequiously but still with his full attention. This could only be Mrs. Ascott. She gave me, when we finally encountered each other in the hall, a distracted look from her watery blue eyes and I heard for the first time her exaggeratedly friendly "*Hi!*" uttered in a high, shaky voice, and I got the impression that this hotel manager did not have the slightest idea who this person coming up to her in her hotel was, or what was going on under the roof under which she was responsible for maintaining order.

I can't prove it but I don't think it is altogether impossible that the reason I have refused all invitations over the past few years to return to that city again was not least because I did not want to see the MS. VICTORIA as a half-destroyed ruin or as a new modern building. I imagine that it's the same for Europeans who had been to New Orleans: they don't want to visit again after seeing the city flooded on television, its poorest residents wading chest-high through contaminated water. But I'm probably deluding myself about that.

Before I move on to introduce some of the people who were important in giving my stay a certain excitement and suspense, I need to remember how I spent my time when I wasn't traveling, alone or with colleagues, to explore the city and enjoy what it had to offer. Since I did not want to discuss in any detail my actual insane project—tracking down the L. whose letters to my friend Emma I was carrying around with me—I had to pretend to be working on something else, so I sat in my office for several hours a day, like everyone else, my door stayed open like everyone else's door, and I proceeded to document my days faithfully and exhaustively on the little word processor there, a BROTHER, which I had unnecessarily brought with me because I considered it a transition to working on a computer and I hadn't yet worked up the courage to try actual computers, which were, of course, made available to everyone there and used by all the others. The fact that I was the oldest was generously taken as an excuse for my shameful deficiency in technical abilities, which I did eventually overcome later. In any case, I always sat diligently in front of my little machine and quickly realized that the time I had at my disposal was barely enough for these detailed daily reports. They, the reports, are now piled around me on various makeshift tables, but I turn to them as aids to memory less frequently than one would think. Incidentally, I also wrote out aphorisms, reflections that seemed to have nothing to do with the daily chronicle. For example, I just now find, typed in capital letters:

```
YOU CAN CHANGE THE CITY BUT NOT THE WELL. THAT IS AN
OLD CHINESE PROVERB I HAVE COME TO LOVE, BUT IS IT RE-
ALLY TRUE, DOES IT ACTUALLY MEAN ANYTHING? AND DOESN'T
IT CONTRADICT THE WATCHWORD THAT SECRETLY ACCOMPANIED
ME HERE, WHICH SEEMS TO BE: DISTANCE.
```

People are mysterious, the voice on the telephone said, and if we could exchange family sentences like that then it must be going well for me in general. Of course I'm doing well, why wouldn't I be? And so why "distance," and distance from what?

A crisis is supposed to have its advantages too, at least that's what people who aren't in crisis at the time tend to say. The main advantage of a crisis, allegedly, is that it throws those afflicted with it into doubt. For example: The age-old fact that things occur and are felt and are thought simultaneously but that all those things cannot be put down simultaneously on paper in linear writing suddenly rattles me so much that doubt in the realism of my writing grows into a total inability to write.

Why haven't I mentioned yet the three well-behaved *raccoons* that I got to know long before I met Mrs. Ascott? They were a bit creepy, the way they crouched on the flagstone path in front of the entrance to the MS. VICTORIA, staring fixedly at me with their round, brightly circled eyes and making no move to retreat at all until I scared them off by clapping my hands.

You must be thinking about staying here, said Francesco, our Italian. I was sitting next to him in his extravagant, quintessentially American, wood-paneled cabriolet, the fulfillment of a childhood dream of his, and we were driving after a quick early sunset on one of the freeways, a long, long drive east to see an installation by an artist Francesco called "famous." I hadn't heard of the artist, had simply joined the other *scholars* in the underground garage of the MS. VICTORIA where we split up into three cars. I just went along, the way I always went along when the opportunity arose, because the city, the monster, was exerting a pull on me that I didn't yet want to admit. And now Francesco shocked me with his assumption, or suggestion, that I stay.

Me? Stay? What gives you that idea?

Most of us think you'd be stupid not to. If you went back now. To that German witch's cauldron.

You think I should emigrate?

For a while. We're living in the city of émigrés after all.

Did they really know me as little as that? Or did they see my situation more realistically than I did myself? I could never have predicted how often people would continue to ask me Francesco's question. And how rumors of my possible staying would spread.

The rough poetry of the freeways in the evening light. Francesco merged delightedly into traffic while he tried to explain his purchase of this extravagant car as the result of cravings he had caught like a disease, as a young man, from an overdose of American movies. I looked at Francesco's profile: jet-black, slightly unruly hair over his forehead, a big straight nose, all very masculine. Ines, sitting behind us, let out a sound that might have meant doubt, or displeasure, but also a certain deliberate willingness to let him have his way. She was the most beautiful of the scholars, in my opinion, with a face cut like a jewel and a mane of gorgeous black hair.

Rush hour. We had to become one with this thousand-eyed creature of legend in two equal parts, five lanes each, racing toward each other and then past each other, seemingly missing each other by a hair's breadth; had to attune our spirit to the other parts of this creature driving along in front of us, behind us, to either side—a creature that ruled us all and cruelly punished every individual movement, every mistake, as we saw shown on television night after night. Auto bodies wedged into each other, passengers driven away from a scrap heap in a state of shock or carried away on stretchers, wounded or dead and covered with a white sheet, rejected as useless failures too weak to pass the test of strength that we, I thought, exposed ourselves to artlessly, carelessly, for no good reason.

The steady motion we were embedded in had a hypnotic effect and put me into a slight trance, in which Francesco's words reached me only in muffled form: The installation we were driving to see was very, very modern, but this damn college we were driving to, it was so far outside of town, he hadn't realized that. He had turned on his headlights a long time before; the ogre Traffic hurtled toward us with its countless lights. Only now did downtown appear on our left, a fata morgana, towers of light in bizarre forms. To think, Francesco said, that none of that existed twenty years ago, Los Angeles was flat as a pancake, in terms of buildings I mean. But it was easy to have that impression today too, I thought, when downtown had slowly orbited past us and the flat cityscape stretched out on both sides, reminiscent of allotment gardens sometimes, with only the columns of the palm trunks sticking up with their disheveled fronds of leaves. Look at the space they have for development and construction—Francesco spoke like an architect.

It had grown completely dark. Ines wondered if Francesco hadn't perhaps missed the exit after all, Francesco denied it, annoyed, and then Ria and Pintus passed us in the left lane, the youngest scholars in our group, recognizable from their snazzy cherry-red car and Ria's little leather cap. She made gestures of despair over the endlessness of the drive. Then suddenly the name of the exit we were looking for appeared on the road sign over our heads and Francesco had to quickly get to the right lane, had to hope that the other drivers would let him cross all the other lanes. They did—they almost always did—Americans don't let out their frustrations while driving, they have guns at home for that, *you see*, one American woman would explain to me later. EXIT ONLY, we could hardly believe it, we were on the right street, found the right turn-off, and ended up on a dark campus. We drove around looking for the right building until we saw Pintus and Ria get out of their car in front of one with the entrance lit up. The other car was parked there too, with our other four road warriors: Hanno, the passionate Parisian intending to write a seminal work comparing Paris and Los Angeles; Emily, the one American in our group, constantly irritated by her sharp features that we all admired as much as we did her deeply intelligent essays on American film; Lutz, my countryman from Hamburg, who had admitted to me that he was coming along just to be polite, these so-called modern pieces were not his thing, while Maya, his wife, in the loose clothing she always preferred, showed up wherever there was something new to her and in the end knew more about Los Angeles than any of the rest of us. The gang's all here, someone said.

We went in. A student was waiting for us, a girl with Japanese features who led us down convoluted passageways, partly constructed out of fencing, to the object of our long drive, the famous installation: a square room made of hastily put up walls of the lightest possible material, with big gray blocks piled up on two opposite sides to create surfaces to sit or lie down on, which the viewers were to do in order to direct their gazes up at the dull red, indirectly lit walls, up to the ceiling, where a twenty-square-foot rectangular hole was cut, for the sky that was the actual event of this installation—you were supposed to crane your head and look at the deep black night sky until you *saw* something. With this piece, the artist was trying to teach his audience how to see, Francesco explained. Lutz, a specialist in nineteenth-century art, could not suppress a groan. Okay, said Pintus, who spent most of his time with medieval literature, we'll see. The mockery in most of the people's faces was clear, restrained only by the presence of the Japanese student, who remained perfectly unaffected by it. Then Ines said: A bit hard, this seat, and Ria complained that we wouldn't even see the stars. She took off her little leather cap and pushed her way into a corner. Only Emily, whose area of study was fantasy films, stayed quiet and attentive, as though expecting something extraordinary.

Okay. I lay down on one of the gray blocks and looked up at the opening in the roof. After a time, the blackness began to undulate, it seemed to me. The nothing that nothings, I said. Silence. We all seemed to be calming down, but what does that actually mean, I asked myself. Francesco might for a short period of time stop feeling threatened and guilty about Ines's dissatisfaction with their life together and be free of the stress that usually forced him to brag and strut around. Ines, during this same short period, would gain so much confidence that she would no longer hold Francesco responsible for failings she saw in herself and that no one else saw in her. Ria would not have to keep throwing her leather cap into the ring and Pintus would not have to keep running off to be the first to fetch it—a pattern that both of them must have been tired of; they separated later, as I heard only recently. At the time my thoughts turned next to Hanno, who might have felt free of the pressure to demonstrate his cosmopolitan superiority with polished phrases and elegant clothes.

And me? What about me?

Meanings gradually dissolved. The dark rectangle of sky sucked me in, it reminded me of the square Lion Gate of Mycenae, behind which darkness lay in wait for the vanquished, the final darkness my night-dark rectangle of sky gave me only a weak foretaste of, but it carried me off, the senses vanished, the senses vanish, I thought, they go inside me, why not, deeper, still deeper, the final darkness, wished for, yes, wished for sometimes, to free me of the compulsion to have to say everything. Never to go down into that well again, no one can ask that of me, but then who says I have to go in the direction others ask me to go in—*richten*, a beautiful word, I love these words with equivocal meanings: *sich richten*, to go in the direction, or to conform; in the passive, to be condemned or judged; *das ist richtig*, that's right. *Gerechtigkeit*, Righteousness, thou word of thunder. Deeper. Still deeper. Sucked into the vortex, spit out. Silence. The silence is greatest in the eye of the hurricane. Now to let go. Groundlessness, a fathomless fall.

Hey, wake up!

I wasn't asleep!

It sure looked like it. Did you dream, at least?

I think so.

We're off to get Chinese. You in the mood?

In the mood for late-night Chinese food? I was always in the mood, I remember. The platter with the various dishes spun around in the middle of the big round table, pushed by our hands. They were right: this was the best Chinese restaurant in the whole enormous city. It was almost midnight, we were the last customers, we sat at the table that would become our regular table. This simple local restaurant's owner and his diminutive wife served us with absolutely unchanging, impenetrable politeness, the little smile that could be either welcoming or stand-offish, and a finesse we Europeans could never hope to match. That is how it would be every time, that's how it was, whenever we would decide to undertake the long drive out to this out-of-the-way restaurant, whenever we undertook it. We praised to each other the various dishes we'd ordered, we tasted everything, we drank red wine, we were in a good mood.

Then Pintus had the unfortunate idea to ask me, in English for some strange reason, probably out of embarrassment: *What about Germany?*

I had learned to be afraid of that question. It always meant the same thing: How can you explain, to yourself and to us, the photographs from Germany that the newspapers are full of here—the asylum-seekers' residences in flames, the anti-Semitic slurs spray-painted on buildings' walls, the president with eggs thrown at him during a demonstration against racism. Then all the pointedly questioning gazes would be directed at me and would make it impossible for me to say simply: I don't know either. I can't understand it myself. It is almost exactly as surprising to me as it is to you.

But maybe it all turned on precisely that "almost." Because didn't you have to be prepared for anything since the day you stood in front of the graves of Bertolt Brecht and Helene Weigel and saw the gravestones defaced with the words "Jewish Pig"? But prepared for what, exactly? That the people from this slightly dreary small town in Mecklenburg that had always just sat there quietly would, one fine day after the fall of the Wall, the TURN, head out to the secluded barracks compound that was always strictly fenced off, occupied by Soviet troops, and surrounded by rumors—rumors that were confirmed after the withdrawal of the Soviet troops: yes, it's true, right here in our immediate vicinity there had been nuclear rockets stationed—that all these peaceful people, then, would go out from their little town and occupy the compound for days and nights on end, because it was now supposed to be turned into a makeshift camp for foreign asylum-seekers and not, as they all (meanwhile unemployed) had hoped, a tourist center for the region and its paradisiacal landscape. Could I have imagined that they would live in tents, as they had not done since their childhood and their service in the National People's Army? And that their wives would bring meals in insulated lunchboxes to the peaceful, fragrant, early-summer forest? Did they sing in the evenings? I wondered. Which songs? I would have loved to know that.

The residents of this small town insisted they didn't hate foreigners. They only wanted to draw attention to their own desperate situation and prevent further loss of jobs, the wanton destruction of the economy. When they withdrew from the barracks and returned to their homes, they apparently planted small green birch trees in front of their houses. I had to imagine how pretty the single long street of that small town would have looked, decked out with green birches—it was otherwise so joyless, or primped up recently with a few garish advertising billboards—and how sad this prettiness would have been. And how sad the nights might be in the little rooms where the TV was on all day and the husband did not come home from work but rather from the allotment garden or the bar or the bench in front of the house where he could now sit all day long and read the paper, which only made him more furious and more dispirited, since he read there—and still reads there today, which I couldn't know when we were sitting at the Chinese restaurant and I was supposed to tell the others what was happening in Germany—he read and still reads today the unemployment figures of around 20 percent, and even those are calculated with a formula that makes them look better than they are, and I wondered, and also said: I wonder how we can stop superimposing one false signal on another. Why, for example, I said, while the round platter with the Chinese dishes spun around in the middle of the table, why didn't anyone talk to the people in that small town, why didn't anyone ask them what they actually wanted, why did they let it get to the point where they were pilloried as xenophobic? No, I heard myself say, no, I don't believe it. The reporting in your media is one-sided, as though asylum-seekers' residences in flames are all that exists in East Germany anymore. That's what people here expect from the Germans. But the repetition you're afraid of won't happen. We won't allow it.

And who is this "We"? Francesco asked, an echo out loud of the question I had already silently asked myself.

Anyway, said Hanno, the Frenchman eager to compare, that's not a single country's problem, or even a single region's. The real question is: How sturdy and solid is the floor our civilization stands on? How many lives with no prospects, shattered and senseless, can it bear the weight of before it cracks somewhere or other, splits at the joints?

And then?

Back then I was much more sparing with the word BARBARISM. Today it's on the tip of my tongue. The stitches that held our civilization together, that kept it from falling into the abysses that yawn beneath it, have rent asunder: disasters well up, towers fall, bombs are dropped, people blow themselves up.

Signals on a multitrack tape running in an endless loop in my head—the words on one of its tracks would be spoken without my willing it. Cut, cut, I couldn't use and didn't want this material, thoughts that were off the record or rather that I thought were off the record, while a sound film was showing continuously on one of the other memory tracks—sounds of the city, the terrible sirens of the police cars present day and night, wailing like grievously wounded animals as they pursued their victims. Or the short, shrill bursts of a car alarm when anyone came too close to a sanctified car. Or fire trucks. They raced past, howling, in their whole incredible childlike fire-truck beauty, always directly toward the fire and the cameras that were always there already to bring the bodies of the burned and maimed and the screams and tears of the bereaved to the TV screen in my apartment, they faithfully laid every single one of the daily murder victims in this monstrous city at my doorstep the way a naughty cat brings home every single mouse it catches. At first I let it happen, I took it upon myself as an exercise of duty to watch, what did I care about these unknown dead, until one evening I surprised myself, in the middle of an outburst of despair from a mother whose small son had fallen into a usually harmless creek during the recent downpour and been carried off and drowned, by pressing the red OFF button. This little gesture made me realize that I had arrived, and that the secret hope I had that I might be able to stay aloof from life here had once again proven deceptive.

Then I sat down at the narrow end of the long dining table in my apartment, where I had recently set up my little machine, and I wrote:

And what if all my busy activity, meant to look like damn hard work, is nothing more than an attempt to silence the tape running in my head? But I can't yet know what depths within me are going to be plowed up here or maybe on the other hand paved over.

The telephone took the trouble to admonish me from across the ocean: You're completely free to write whatever you want! So just go ahead, what could happen? —Yes, yes. —You shouldn't defend yourself, you should just say how it was. —Yes, yes. Defend? At first there were only these individual words, treacherous and revealing.

Then I tried to fall asleep, in the bed that was still too wide but not too soft anymore now that Mr. Enrico had put a board under the mattress, as my spine urgently required. I could not fall asleep, I could not banish the image of Brecht's defiled gravestone, I could not stop recalling lines of poetry:

> Considering you are
> threatening us with guns and cannons
> we have now decided to fear
> bad life more than death.

Up on stage actors dressed as the Paris Communards, down in the audience you, the young, enthusiastic faces of your generation, who were not destined to experience the fate of the communards, their failure, you were all utterly sure of that and scornfully laughed at all doubters, I thought, and I could see in my mind's eye the faces growing old in an instant, old and pinched and used up, worn out, disappointed, betrayed. And timid, calculating, stupid. Cynical. Skeptical and desperate. The usual. We alone were going to be spared that fate. What hubris.

Cut to another time. Was it not here, half a century ago, in this city, a few miles from this very room where I lay unsleeping, that Brecht, the émigré, gave his Galileo—who would then come face-to-face with us, who were young then, in the shape of the actor Ernst Busch—that he imposed on his Galileo an indomitable pursuit of the truth? Nobody can go on indefinitely watching me drop a pebble and saying it doesn't fall. Oh, Brecht, we can indeed, almost every last one of us can. And while we despised your Galileo for finally abjuring himself, the pebble was still falling, before our eyes, it fell and fell without end and we did not even see it. If someone had pointed it out to us, we would only have said: What pebble?

But you saw it, didn't you, the flower seller who meddled in the fate of a nation. It was in the fall of 1989, she stood on the street and handed out fliers she had made herself, and you knew the expression on her face from the faces of the actors who played the communards: a bright face bursting with hope and resolve, there is that too, you thought, you didn't want to forget it, even if the historical moment that brought forth such faces was terribly short, and actually already over. To have lived through it, you thought, made everything worth it. And the flower seller said the same thing, with the same words.

At some point I fell asleep and found myself in one of those gatherings in dreams that are actually high courts, in this case the large lecture hall at the university. Again your name was called, you heard the sharp voice say the word "document," you were supposed to comment on the loss of your Party document, which had fallen prey to a department-store thief together with your whole briefcase. The sacred trust of every comrade, which he has to carry with him always, but at the same time has to staunchly protect from loss. Did you realize that this loss leads one to draw certain conclusions about your relationship to the Party? You hesitantly admitted it while secretly contesting it. Did you not know what comrades went through during the time of Fascism to safeguard and preserve their Party documents? And the misuse that the Class Enemy could put them to if the documents should happen to fall into their hands? I do! I heard myself scream, as I woke up. I recognized the feeling of hopelessness and suppressed revolt that even back then, forty years ago, had long since haunted me.

Party reprimand. You shouldn't take it personally, the comrade who had spoken against you most sharply in the proceeding told you later. How else were you supposed to take it then? It was a matter of principle, you heard, and that was clear to you too, and you would have been the first to deny that your pregnancy played any role at all at the hearing. Every individual has to bow to principle. Severities were unavoidable.

I take the little red booklet out of its box and page through it, through the many pages with visas and entry and exit stamps. I won't throw it out, it will go back into its box with the other papers that have become invalid. I wait for my feelings to be stirred, in vain. When did the feelings that were once attached to these papers become invalid too? This whole range of divergent, contradictory, mutually exclusive feelings? That have faded over the course of the years. But what does that mean, I cannot help asking myself. Hasn't my whole store of feelings faded? Been depleted? Will it be able to supply enough feeling for life to last the rest of my life?

I dashed to my little machine in my pajamas and wrote:

There are several strands of memory. Sense memory is the most lasting and reliable. Why is that? Do we need it especially urgently for our survival?

One part of the urge to tell stories is the destructive urge, of course, which reminds me of the destructive urge in physics that I read about in the newspaper, under the headline "Beaming for Advanced Students." Quantum physicists have apparently succeeded in making atoms "whisper something to each other" over a large distance: "transferring the original superposition state of Atom A to Atom B," whatever that means. What interested me most was the statement that, in so doing, the physicist "destroys the original condition." This information helped to ease my conscience, since storytellers too have to destroy the "original condition" by coldly observing people and transferring whatever seems to go on between them onto unfeeling paper. But this destructive urge, I tell myself, is counterbalanced by the creative urge that brings new people and new relationships about out of nothing. Whatever was there before has to be wiped out.

Night after night, I remember, I sat in front of the TV when *Star Trek* was on, permitting myself the excuse that I had to improve my English even though I secretly knew that it was really my need for fairy tales and happy endings that kept me in my seat. For I could be certain that the Star Trek crew would bring the noble values of Earth dwellers into the farthest galaxies, prevail over every enemy, no matter how dreadful, and not get hurt in the process.

The telephone. Finally, a voice I had been waiting for for days. *How are you, Sally.* Then a strange, dark voice came out of the phone, which said: *My heart is broken*, and that was literally true, as I realized when I saw Sally face-to-face, in her little house far from the center of the city, in a neighborhood that was hard to get to. There was no way to comfort her, no way to help, nothing to say, and I also had to keep to myself my shock at seeing how much she had aged, how gray her hair had gone, and that she had let her short, stylish haircut grow out and run wild. How long would it last, she asked, and she meant her obsession with her loss. It lasts, I said, while I stood next to Sally in her tiny practical kitchen and watched her cut tomatoes and grate cheese, at least two years, and I remembered when a Prague friend had told me that. It was in 1977, a decade and a half before; it was on the way from Hradčany to the Old Town, on a cold, gray, windy day in early April; Prague Spring lay far in the past, the Prague friend had experienced the plummet into hopelessness more than ten years earlier, while you knew what it meant to be without hope only since the previous fall, 1976, the worst year. During a horribly cold December you had stood on a street in Berlin in the dark, in front of a lit shop window, stared at the toothpaste tubes and detergents, and understood in a flash: This is what pain is. You did not want to believe your friend when he said you had to endure it for more than another year. Two years! you said at the time, in disbelief, and the argument I had with him made me realize how long I had already spent in that pressure tank. According to this chronology, Sally still had six more months to go. It's so humiliating, she said, and I said, Yes, I felt that way too. Sometimes, I said, careful to stick close to my own personal experience, the turning point comes suddenly, *you know*, overnight. You wake up and you're free.

But Sally couldn't hear me, she was still stuck in the pressure tank. She said she had always thought that if it ever happened to her, if her husband ever left her for another woman, she would be able to be magnanimous to him. But she couldn't do it. No, she couldn't do it. It's not just any man, *you see*. It's Ron. It's like a compulsion, she has to take every last advantage of his guilty feelings, do you know what I mean? He has everything he wants—a career he's happy in, money, a beautiful young woman with tattoos all over, he is free to do or not do whatever he wants, and as for me, Sally said, mixing the salad, I always oriented myself to what other people wanted from me. You, Sally? I said. Now don't exaggerate. I described the impression I had of her when we first met, years ago, at that college up north: an attractive, very thin young woman, confident, athletic, cheerful, busy, strange in interesting ways, an inspired dancer full of original ideas, a lecturer at the college where I was going to teach *creative writing*, and a committed feminist.

Oh, Sally said, if only you knew. And I thought: Yes, if only we knew the truth about each other. If only she knew what kind of tape recording I have running in my head all the time; if only anyone knew that I was thinking: Where does this compulsion come from? The need to cling to people and ideas and things that destroy us? I thought, while Sally said: Did you know I spent ten months in a Buddhist monastery? There was a nun there who really looked out for me and tried to guide me onto the path of loving-kindness and self-acceptance, I think she genuinely liked me even though I was sure I was a worthless piece of garbage that Ron could just throw away. She brought us together for meditation and explained to us, in her friendly, steady voice, that everything we had, however little it was, and all the daily activities she held us to, and our psychological and spiritual condition in that moment were exactly what we needed to help us become humane, awake, and alive. As though we had sought out precisely what would lead us to a fulfilled life. But the nun didn't help me either. We could choose, she assured us, Sally said, mixing the salad dressing, we could decide to become the world's greatest experts on anger, jealousy, and self-deprecation or to become extremely wise and sensitive to all of humanity by knowing ourselves just as we are. But I didn't want to know myself. I wanted revenge on Ron. I didn't want anything else.

This was the first dinner party she was hosting alone, Sally said, and now she wasn't sure if the meat was cooked properly. How do you like it, *rare* or *well done*. I said *medium*, she gave it ten more minutes, then the four of us sat down at the small round table in her brightly colored *living room* and it tasted delicious. We could not avoid—and I didn't want to avoid—talking about the *riots* that had spread from the black neighborhoods and shaken the city six months earlier, and that the whites were still talking about, half fearfully and half dismissively. Would they happen again? I asked. *Sure,* said Al, the sociologist. But next time the police will be prepared and they'll nip any hint of unrest in the bud. Maggie, who taught school in a poor neighborhood, said that the riots hadn't changed a thing in South Central L.A. There were simply too many people there with nothing to lose, she said, and the whites for their part just tried to repress as fast as they could the fact that they had stood outside the doors of their houses in their rich neighborhoods, trembling, and had seen the city burning.

But you know about that, Al said, and at first I didn't know what he meant.

Your *riots*, he said.

You call them riots? You mean 1989? Some people called it a revolution. Our peaceful revolution.

Al knew the Leninist definition of revolution: The historical moment when the lower classes do not want to live in the old way anymore and the upper classes cannot. Maybe. But if we're quoting Marxist theory: Isn't revolution a step forward toward a more advanced social formation? Well? Can we say that in your case? A step forward from socialism to capitalism?

They let me take a while before answering. Then I said: For a few weeks, we could feel that history was going our way. The future looked like the one that a lot of people had longed for and none of us had ever seen. And that we had all had a hand in building.

Maggie said she would like to experience that someday. It might restore her faith in life as a whole, a faith that seemed to be inexorably vanishing at the moment. It was as though the air were leaking out of a container and leaving us, every human being, stuck, airless, and power-less, with a substitute life as the only option left to us.

I know, Sally said. Don't I know it! She put in a video. *It's about my job*, she said. Her job was working with at-risk youth. We saw and heard on the video how she interacted with them. How she asked cautious questions, how the young people talked about their lives and their grim fates: abandoned by their fathers, neglected by their mothers, growing up in gangs in run-down ghettos, addicted to drugs, stuck there at the edge of criminality and often drifting over that edge. The girl with the afro whom Sally took to the theater, who sat next to her and started cry-ing because she realized that this play was about her too. Sally came right out and told her: You were abused as a child. How the girl, for the first time, could say yes, so that Sally dared to ask more: By a close relative? —Yes. —By your father? —Yes. Yes, yes, yes. —She's in therapy now, Sally said, and smiled for the first time that night. She's mad at me now, she has to cut out her mother in herself and she's practicing on me.

You don't realize how strong you are, Sally, I said when we said goodbye. How her smile went out like a candle when I said it. How she said: But I'm about to quit that job. I can't take it anymore. It's like scooping up water with a sieve.

And you? she asked me when we were standing in front of the door of her little half-house with a narrow flight of stairs leading down to the street. What are you here for, really? To get some distance? To forget? What do you want here?

I'm looking for someone, I said. A woman whose name I don't even know. Well, good luck, Sally said. And we laughed, near midnight on one of the quiet outlying streets of Los Angeles, in the gentle air of Cali-fornia, under the Big Dipper, now overturned and standing jauntily on its head.

THE BLIND SPOT

I wrote on my little machine back home: Maybe it is our task to take the blind spot that is apparently in the center of our consciousness, which we therefore cannot notice, and gradually make it smaller and smaller, in from the edges. So that we gain a little more space that is visible to us. Nameable. But—I wrote—is that what we want? Can we want it? Isn't it too dangerous. Too painful.

When my thoughts were going around in circles I jumped up and went out to Second Street, in the late afternoon light, into the multicolored crowd of people drifting back and forth as evening approached, to see and be seen, to sit outside at the little restaurants and eat hamburgers, Italian pasta dishes, Mexican tortillas, Japanese sushi, and gather around the many performers putting on their shows. And, in the middle of this lively crowd, unnoticed by everyone, as though invisible, the *homeless people* drawn to this gentle climate like little splotches of color that didn't match. I would have to learn to suppress my tears when one of them said, in an abject voice with a slight singsong to it, *Have a nice day* after I'd given him a dollar, or, even worse, *God bless you.* My sympathy came cheap. How would it help that *homeless* woman with the mouse-gray felt hat if I sat down next to her on the bench in front of the discount clothing store, where she always was with the shopping cart from PAVILION that held a few discolored items of clothing, empty bottles, several plastic bags filled to bursting, and a wool blanket, all her belongings, her survival kit—she pushed it around with her, she didn't want any money, she shook her head and pointed at the bottles she had picked out of the garbage cans whose deposits she lived on. I remember that I felt inferior to her, guilty, due to my unearned life of luxury; she was probably as old as I was, early sixties, life had left its marks on her, white curly hair poured out from under her cap, she had grown fat and shapeless from the low-quality food she was forced to eat, she confidently stretched out with her bundles on the bench that no one challenged her claim to and struck up a conversation with the *homeless* woman on the bench across from her. I heard her raw voice, slang I couldn't understand, though I picked up a few words here and there, "children," "family," I saw the woman gesticulate wildly and laugh a loud hearty laugh with her mouth wide open, revealing bad teeth. This woman, I said to myself, doesn't kowtow to anyone, she is beyond every kind of conforming or compromise to fit in with other people: if that is what freedom means then she is free, free of possessions too, with only the barest minimum a person needs. She did not have to fearfully protect and defend her wealth, she took nothing from anyone, she took no part in the exploitation of natural resources, she is innocent, I thought, while the rest of us are guilty, because we don't want to pay the price demanded of us.

And so the tape player in my head started up again, while I ate my grilled fish and salad, while the people drifted by in front of me, darkness approached, and I went back to the MS. VICTORIA, which, I had to admit, mildly amused, had among all its other virtues the fact that it would have made an ideal location for a thriller, I thought, crossing the half-dark hallway and climbing the narrow steps to my apartment: everything a little dark, everything a little creepy, and, as if to furnish proof for my feeling, there was actually a bulging wallet right in front of my door with a lot of checks inside and credit cards embossed with the name of their owner, one Mr. Gutman, Peter Gutman, who must have lived in the building. I had to decipher his apartment number on the badly lit and almost illegibly scribbled list on the front door in order to ring his buzzer. He lived a floor above me. Luckily he answered, but I couldn't think of the English word "wallet" so I informed the bewildered Mr. Gutman that I had found *something* of his.

What did you find?

Something, Mr. Gutman. Please, come down.

He came downstairs. So that is how I first saw him, in the half-dark, on the stairs. He was a very tall, angular man, whose clothes seemed to hang negligently on his limbs, with a tall, bald, egg-shaped head, I couldn't help thinking *egghead*, a typical egghead, and how strange that I hadn't yet run into this striking person in the MS. VICTORIA. He was happy to get his wallet back, *"wallet,"* oh yes, that's what it's called, another word learned. He hadn't noticed it was missing. He politely asked if I would care to come upstairs with him so that he could repay my kindness with a drink. No thank you, I surprised myself by saying, I'm too tired. I'd be glad to another time.

Later he would tease me about this first rebuff and I would laugh at him for having stubbornly continued to speak English with me even though he must have known from my first sentence that I was German. But you know why I couldn't shift into German from one word to the next, he said. There is always a barrier between the two. Unconscious. Unwanted. And anyway he had gotten used to hiding behind the second language he had grown up with.

Then I told him—this was weeks later—what obsessively occupied

my imagination when he went back upstairs and I went into my apartment and sat down with a margarita, my favorite drink, in front of the
new episode of *Star Trek*: I had spun a thriller plot around his mysterious person, invented a business card that had fallen out of his wallet
and that I hadn't returned to him. On it, I imagined, stood the address
for a lawyer's office, a reputable address in Beverly Hills—Malrough &
Malrough, I boldly invented, two brothers, why not—and on the back
of the card I discovered, in Peter Gutman's difficult-to-read handwriting, which of course I had to invent too, an appointment and the note
that he, Peter Gutman, had to call a Pacific Palisades number very urgently to talk to one "Gladis Meadow." What would happen, I wondered,
if I called this Gladis myself. I would surely hear a dark, sympathetic
voice, who would answer the question "Is this Gladis Meadow?"—the
name came to me just like that—with a surprised *Yes*, and I would say
Thank you so much! in a friendly but firm voice and hang up, at which
point I realized with a feeling of elation that with this one phone call,
whether it took place in banal reality or only (but what does that mean,
only!) in my head, I was inextricably entangled in this story taking place
between Mr. Gutman, the dark-voiced Gladis Meadow, and the law firm
of Malrough & Malrough.

Peter Gutman was delighted with this imagined story and would
have liked to keep playing his role in it, and to classify Gladis Meadow
as a real person. What does "real" mean anyway? This was one of the
core questions his philosopher had slaved away at, he said. By then I
already knew that Peter Gutman had spent years toiling over this philosopher, whose name he hardly ever spoke, as though tying him to a
name would be to break a magic spell. Yes, you see, I'd said, but neither
of us knew what exactly he was supposed to "see."

I don't want to jump too far ahead. I will only say that Gladis
Meadow did her part to bring us together and then unobtrusively vanished from the screen.

I ran into Peter Gutman again unexpectedly the next day in the
lobby of the CENTER. He stepped out of one of the elevators and came
up to me, said a polite greeting, and headed for the exit, while I detoured
to the right, to the counter of the First Federal Bank, where I was finally
able to pick up my *ATM card*. An elfin young lady handed it to me with
a triumphant smile, and I understood that only from that moment on
was I a full-fledged customer of this bank, and more: a full-fledged (if

temporary) inhabitant of this city. What was Mr. Gutman doing in this building? Sunk in thought, I took the elevator up to the fifth floor, forgot to return the black security guard's greeting, picked up my bundle of keys from the little locker, went up to the seventh floor, skimmed the nameplates on the doors as I walked past, and dropped into the chair behind my desk. While the question about Mr. Gutman's activities continued to run through my head, I had to figure out at the same time what had so disturbed my walk to my office, it must have been a minuscule observation that had not found its way into my consciousness and only rubbed up and down against my brain like a grain of sand in a shoe rubs against one's foot. Since you were staying in the MS. VICTORIA, I thought your job might have something to do with the arts— this was the next day, we were speaking in German by then, but still with formal pronouns, one step at a time. Or maybe a businessman in some art field. A movie producer? Nope. Museum director going around buying? Hardly. Keep guessing, Peter Gutman said. Consultant, I said. Some type of consultant. Or expert, there are thousands of those. The only question is, in what field. We had our fun.

But where did that nagging feeling in my office come from, the feeling that I should really have known what Peter Gutman's job was? That the solution to the riddle of his person was close at hand? I closed my eyes and emptied my mind of thoughts. A little white card appeared before my inner eye with his name on it, and the card had a border just like the nameplates on our office doors in the CENTER. No, it couldn't be—I jumped up, went out into the hall, and inspected the door of the next office. There it stood: Prof. Peter Gutman, really and truly, I told Peter Gutman later. I was almost sorry that this vexing enigma had such an ordinary solution, would you believe it? I had constructed such beautiful, intricate figments of the imagination about the entanglements I thought you were caught in, and I had decided to avoid you for as long as possible.

Fooled you then, Peter Gutman said, with his serious professorial face. You gave up too soon. There are entanglements galore here. I inspected him closely. Aha, I said. Now we're talking. We were standing by the copy machine in the CENTER's office and a feeling of almost giddy happiness came over me.

Sally called me that night. Have you read the book I gave you? By the Buddhist nun?

I started it, I said. Seems pretty good. But you—did you take her advice to heart?

Oh no! Sally cried. What she wants us to do is the hardest thing of all: let go! Sally couldn't do that, she said, and didn't even want to. She had just started therapy and her therapist encouraged her to calmly take the money Ron offered her—no, owed her—from his mother, an inheritance meant for them both. In the end, they were still married, and Ron's mother had loved her and obviously assumed that they would use her legacy together. But the way things were now—wouldn't people say she was taking a payoff to give Ron his freedom?

You would say that about yourself, I said, but you're the only one who would. I wanted to ask her if she still hoped Ron would come back to her, but I suppressed the question. What Sally believed and hoped was only too obvious, and if this therapist was good she would have to take this hope away from her, and Sally would hate her for it, but I wasn't her therapist, I could leave her her pipe dreams, and I also didn't want her to hate me, I had had enough of being hated.

The nun, in any case, felt that people had a widespread misunderstanding about trying to avoid suffering as much as possible and "*getting comfortable,*" and I had to marvel at this Buddhist nun's insight. I wanted to avoid suffering, of course, I wanted to live "comfortably," of course, which didn't necessarily mean "affluent," not that, Brecht. But yes, in relative prosperity, in circumstances that made it possible for me to work: that was what I meant by "comfortable," and in this world, I told and tell myself every day, that level of comfort is a great and unearned privilege. Suddenly I felt gripped by a kind of curiosity about what this woman thought. She saw it as a much more interesting, more adventurous, kinder, and more joyful approach to life to cultivate your own thirst for knowledge and not worry about whether the results of your explorations will prove bitter or sweet. You had only to realize that you could stand an enormous amount of suffering and joy in order to find out who you were and how the world was. How you work and how the world works—how this whole thing really *is.*

I said goodbye to Sally, sat down at my little machine, and wrote:

```
It's a good opportunity. Why not find out how I really
am, if this nun insists that I can get to know myself
through and through and still like myself. She calls
```

it "*loving-kindness*," which is a problem for me since I cannot translate that into German. Apparently we don't have this friendliness toward ourselves. There is self-hatred, and self-love, and vanity, and on the other side of the coin this nagging sense of inferiority, but not that. It really is strange.

I found a note slipped under my office door at the CENTER. For the first time, I saw the tiny, calligraphically perfect handwriting of Peter Gutman, my mysterious neighbor (he later told me when he had trained himself to write that way), and I read the information that today was the birthday of our mutual friend Efim Etkind, from Leningrad but exiled and stripped of his citizenship, now living in Paris. His number was on the note. So, we had mutual friends? How did he know that? And would items found lying in front of my door be the only way I ever came into contact with Peter Gutman? I went out into the hall again and the door to the next office was closed, as always. Kätchen came in with the latest computer printouts: bibliographical references that the Orion computer system had spit out after being fed certain keywords. Not that you could enter the fateful cipher "L." by itself, although Kätchen had tried, in vain of course. Then, without much hope of success, she had entered the name of my friend Emma, the old comrade who had left me the bundle of letters from L. in her will, and Orion had hit pay dirt, printing out the title of a book that I immediately found in the university library and borrowed (*The Left-Wing Press in the Weimar Republic*, ed. Emma Schulze: Frankfurt, 1932). Emma had never mentioned this book and I doubted that she herself had still owned a copy.

The thought came to me that Kätchen knew what was going on at the CENTER backward and forward. Who is Peter Gutman? I asked her. Oh, him, Kätchen said, he's not around much. Almost never here. This morning I saw him, he picked up his mail and then disappeared again, she said. It's like he intentionally avoids joining us for our teas.

That made sense to me. But why, actually? I dropped off my mail, shouldered my brightly colored bag from the Indian store, and walked to the MS. VICTORIA, sunk in thought. To find out why he was acting so strangely I would have to know something about Peter Gutman's past, I said to myself. I ate, then made myself comfortable in the deep armchair in front of the television, wine within reach, and as usual *Star*

Trek was on Channel 13 and I followed Captain Picard and his crew in shameless delight, given over to the outer-space adventures of the Starship *Enterprise*, where the Picard crew demonstrated that unconditional discipline could go perfectly well with mature humanity ennobled by masculine understatement.

The telephone. Peter Gutman. *What a coincidence!* I said, and then had a hard time explaining why I called his phone call that, after all I couldn't tell him I was brooding about him. He, on the other hand, only wanted to check whether I had gotten the note he had slipped under my office door. Indeed I had. In fact, I had called Paris right away and learned from Efim that he, Peter Gutman, was an old friend of his. And of course I wished him happy birthday. *Great*, Peter Gutman said. But how did I know this friend? he asked, all in English. I answered in English that it was a long story. Then, in flawless German, came the reply: Why didn't I tell it to him? Right now? Why not? He owes me a drink in any case and can't even imagine what might have happened if his wallet had fallen into the wrong hands. Ah, I said. Sounds like top security clearance. But I'm already drinking some wine, I said, still in English. —White or red? —White. —Good, Peter Gutman said. I'll bring another bottle.

I can no longer tell apart the numerous times—more than I can count—that Peter Gutman knocked on my door over the course of the next few months, stuck his polite tall bald head into my room, and settled down into my deep armchair. But I remember the first time very clearly. He accepted my breadsticks, I accepted his wine, and he proclaimed for the first time his thesis that we lived on a luxury liner, here in the MS. VICTORIA and especially over at the CENTER. We went back and forth between the deck of one luxury liner and the deck of the other, even more luxurious vessel, and only in order to take ourselves seriously when we excreted our actually rather superfluous texts. What was it Brecht had said about Thomas Mann? "I say that he is blind; he's not been bought." We can only hope that someone will be able to say that about us someday, Peter Gutman said, in German of course. None of us has the slightest idea if they will, he said. He had not been in my apartment ten minutes, and my apartment was not used to such tones. Aside from the television and occasionally a song I sang softly to myself, it was not used to any sounds at all.

Hello, I said. What's going on here? In German. Now we were both speaking German. Then Peter Gutman made his characteristic, defensively apologetic hand gesture and got to the point: How exactly did I know our apparently mutual friend Efim?

Were you ever in Leningrad, his city before he was expatriated? I asked him. Peter Gutman shook his head.

Or St. Petersburg, as it's called today?

No. Peter Gutman had never been to Russia, he had met Efim at a university in Texas where they were both teaching. Classes on the various stages of German literature—me, the German-English Jew, and he, the Russian Jew, Peter Gutman said. We had a few laughs about that, he said.

So, I began, back when Etkind was still a professor in Leningrad, G. and I took the whole family on vacation to a writer's residence in Komarovo, near Leningrad.

Now I am trying to remember everything I told Peter Gutman on that first evening, and I look in all my drawers for a certain document that could buttress my memory. Once again I realize that I have treated my files that include this document carelessly and inattentively. Lev Kopelev, our Moscow friend, had sent Efim to you and your family: one day he turned up unexpectedly at the residence to get you in his old Pobeda. Then a drive in the direction of the Finnish border, to his dacha, you remember a pine forest, mountain pines. It was late summer. Suddenly Efim whispered: Duck! at which point all your and your family's heads disappeared below the car windows and you drove unchallenged past a military guard with a Kalashnikov hanging diagonally across his chest. They don't need to know that I'm bringing you here, Efim said, and he took you to a wooden house in the middle of the forest, where it was bright and warm and comfortable. His wife gave you a friendly welcome, his two daughters started talking in German and Russian with your daughters. If I remember correctly, there were cookies and tea from the samovar first, later probably pelmeni. I still remember exactly how, in the place where icons and oil lamps hang in old Russian houses, that room had a corner dedicated to Alexander Solzhenitsyn: photographs, books, letters, you even thought you saw something like an altar candle. Do you know him? you had asked Efim, and he had answered simply: We're friends. Which promoted him, as far as you and especially your daughters were concerned, into another category of living creature. The friendship cost him and his family their country—he was accused of concealing Solzhenitsyn's manuscripts and arranging for their translation in the West; it couldn't be proven but everyone who knew him believed that the suspicions were not entirely unjustified, you believed it too, but you never asked him about it, not later either. In any case, he lost his job and then was forced to emigrate. You saw him again in Paris, years later, in an ultramodern part of the city; his apartment was full of mementos and soaked in nostalgia and homesickness, which is what I think his wife died of even though the official diagnosis was cancer.

And as I am calling that all back to mind and a series of pictures is passing before my mind's eye, I find the document I was looking for, in the chest with the copies of our Stasi files, of course, which I open only rarely and reluctantly. It is the only document in Russian among those files—an NKVD report to the agency's German counterpart describing in meticulous detail a young man's visit to our apartment. He had wormed his way into your trust—this is what I told Peter Gutman that evening, in condensed form—by mentioning Efim's name on the phone, so of course we invited him over, and he reported to you that he had studied science in Leningrad (he might actually have done so, on the side), had met Efim by chance in a used bookstore—oh, these Russian coincidences!—where Efim was bringing in books to sell because he had been forced to leave the country, he told us: Efim had told him that in confidence, since they had talked to each other for a while. And then he said Efim had asked him to ask you if he could continue to stay in contact with you from the West, or if that would be too dangerous for you, and you, incurably gullible, insisted that you wanted to keep in touch with Efim and offered him your help.

That is how it stands in the files, in Russian with a German translation affixed with a Russian stamp. You continued to see Efim, on the street in Bloomsbury in London, in a West German city where you both took part in a conference, and on his roof terrace for a Russian meal in Potsdam, the last place he lived. That was after the "Turn." He was full of Russian and Jewish stories, you laughed a lot, but he always wanted to discuss the most serious questions too—he was tormented with an unease about the future that he tried to chase away by indefatigably traveling around the world, giving lectures, teaching. He had heart problems.

He would keel over somewhere or another while he was traveling, you thought. It turned out, in the end, that he died there, where he never in his life would have predicted: in Potsdam.

I never really understood, I told Peter Gutman, how two secret police forces could see such an ordinary event as worth spending their time on.

Well, Peter Gutman said, you probably didn't try hard enough to put yourself into their frame of mind.

We certainly did, I said. Sometimes we knew everything, then we forgot it again, the thing about some insights is that they surface and then, in an unpredictable rhythm, go under again into the "sea of forgetting," now that's a lovely image. Don't you think it's strange, I asked, without even noticing that I had started using the informal pronoun, that our brains don't seem to be built to retain such simple insights? While there are all kinds of stories we can absorb and retain without any problem.

Objection, Your Honor, Peter Gutman said, and the thought crossed my mind that he was from England and that, in the list of fellows, "essayist" stood after his name as his job title.

Why? I said. Stories are preserved for centuries in the great river of narrative, once a story is told it's told. Never again will Achilles be able to be anything other than a hero. Or take Werther. Again and again he will put that bullet into his brain, Goethe himself couldn't stop it now. So what to do? Or rather, what to write, how to write? The fact that everyone dies at the end may be tragic but it doesn't result in a story. Or does it? What do you think?

I don't know, Peter Gutman said. What you're saying is not unlike what my philosopher says about narrative, I'll tell you about it sometime. But first, I have another question: Would you say it results in a story when a theme recurs again and again in someone's life?

I don't know, I said. What theme do you have in mind?

For example, the theme of a wasted life.

Listen, as a well-read person you must be familiar with . . .

Now now. I know all the books, with all their stories, they're of no use to me.

Right, I said. We agree on that.

And that was where Peter Gutman wanted to leave it for the night. He stood up and left. A few minutes later, he phoned. Thank you for a lovely evening. I'm sure you realized I was talking about myself. I am the one busy wasting my life. No, don't say anything now. It did me good to talk.

In the layer of my brain responsible for day-to-day routine, I had stored away the bus lines for Santa Monica and Los Angeles and the information about how to use the university library. I rode without any problem down the endless, palm-lined streets, straight as an arrow, in *Blue Bus Line Two*, always into this unreal light; I looked for the library on the UCLA campus and found it; I entered my reader's card into a computer and after typing in a keyword watched lists of authors and titles scroll past my eyes on the screen of another computer until I came to one which might prove useful for my researches: *Women's Emigration to the U.S.* I pressed the button to order the book and saw that it had been loaned out, only a few days ago in fact. I entered my hold request. Yet another track that led nowhere. The question of why I was actually here seemed to grow more urgent.

I admitted to myself that I had felt a twinge of jealousy when that bundle of letters came into my hands. In the old hard-cardboard suitcase that held my friend Emma's papers when she died was a large brown envelope with my name written in the corner, in Emma's handwriting, and the large letter "L" in the middle, written in thick black marker—the same letter the writer had used to sign all her correspondence. During all those years when I thought I was her closest friend, Emma had corresponded with this L. without saying a word about it to me. Don't be childish, I had to tell myself, don't take it as a breach of trust. Was Emma obligated to tell you anything and everything? Her acquaintance with L. went back far into her past, into the nineteen twenties. Emma was already in the Communist Party and presumably friends with "L." when I was born. The fact that she left me these particular letters was a kind of consolation, and proof of her unqualified trust in me. I also took it as a suggestion to investigate this area of her life she had kept hidden from me. Otherwise, wouldn't she have destroyed the letters before she died?

I was unusually tired and went back to the MS. VICTORIA in the bright light of midday, instead of to my office. I lay down and immediately fell asleep, and dreamed of a dream book I had wanted to write once—a plan that, like so many others, I had not carried out. But now, in my dream, I am holding this dream book in my hands, a lined school-book of A4-size paper between whose pages I had put old banknotes, money invalid since the state in which they had been valid had ceased to exist. Then, to my surprise, the dream continues on the topic of money. A friend, who is already dead, calls me to say he needs Western money for his mother. So we must have still been back in GDR-times, as they say today, I think in my dream, and I say to my dead friend: Recently I even heard someone talk about "East times." But where am I supposed to get West-money so quickly, I ask him, and he says all you have to do is go to a certain office and tell them what you want and you'll get some. So we drive through a desolate city of rubble to a gloomy office building, and at a teller window I am in fact handed slips of paper, but they don't seem to me to have anything to do with money. I anxiously show them to G. and he shrugs his shoulders: Barter system, he says. Now we have to take this "money" that I am convinced is worthless to our dead friend's mother. We drive over rough ground and stop in front of a house that is probably the most desolate of all my desolate dream-houses—completely neglected, one of the gables sticks up into the sky like a stage set, there are isolated flagstones in the courtyard with mud and grass between them. We say: The last rain has done a lot of damage here. Our dead friend's mother comes up to us, totally changed, shattered, with features grown old and indistinct, and wrapped in thick dirty clothes, she who always dressed so properly. Clearly she has been freezing. She leads us into a cold, inhospitable room, we realize that she is terrified by our visit and wondering if we want to spend the night there, we reassure her, hand her the money that doesn't mean a thing to her. Your son sent us, we say, oh yes, she says lightly, he's still looking out for me from the grave. I have the impression that the woman is half-crazy from loneliness, not in her right mind. We are very depressed and we leave her and then see our younger daughter, who tells us that the woman was only pretending to be friendly, she saw through the window how the woman had stuck the "money" in the oven with an evil grin.

When I woke up I felt that the dream, in the guise of a scary fairy tale about an old witch, symbolized the collapse of the East German state, which had ended in the lines of people standing in front of the banks after the new money was introduced, in celebrations in the streets around midnight—champagne, cars driving around honking their horns—to celebrate its arrival. I was half-asleep and the TV images pushed in front of the dream images I still had in mind, whose meaning I wanted to interpret, and they disappeared. I fell back asleep.

That morning I needed to look at L.'s letters, whose existence was the reason for my stay in this place. The red folder was right there on the shelf, next to the growing pile of newspapers—today it is sitting in a drawer where I keep other mementoes of Emma too: photographs from various stages of her life, all since the war—Emma as a woman who loved life, with friends, including me, in her garden—the old tattered cookbook whose recipes she cooked for me, her ancient Party handbook going back to the twenties, copies of court records from the fifties when she spent two years in a prison of the German Democratic Republic due to "unjustified accusations," as it said later in the rehabilitation document. We had talked about that for nights on end.

I missed her. Just then I missed her very much. No one could straighten things out the way she could. I wanted to hear her voice through the words of her friend L. I sat down at the table and opened the red folder: a little pile of stationery, some of the sheets yellowed, in various sizes, mostly in American paper sizes, almost all of them typed and a few written by hand in a sprawling, almost masculine-seeming woman's handwriting that turned, over the course of the more than three decades that these letters spanned, into an old person's handwriting, hard to read. There were no envelopes with a sender's name and address, not a single one, as though the recipient had painstakingly destroyed them. No photographs and no other clues about the sender other than the date on each letter after the place: "Los Angeles."

It was just like Emma: She was never willing to discuss my plan to write her biography but then she left me important material for it, without any explanation or commentary. It must have been a message: Write! What she couldn't have predicted was that I would fall prey to something like an obsession: I had to track down the woman who had sent her the L. letters and solve their riddle.

I still had to overcome a certain shyness when I read the letters. I picked up the earliest pages very carefully, afraid that the thin paper, already crumbling at the edges, might fall apart in my hands. Today I absolutely cannot believe how negligent and thoughtless I was to bring the originals on that long journey instead of having copies made, as I have since, copies that lie in front of me now while the originals are secure in a bank safe.

The first letter: from September 1945. The blue ink on both sides of the paper shows through the page and makes it hard to decipher. I know the first sentences by heart:

Emma, my dear, I hope I am writing to someone who is still alive. That is the most important question we have to ask our friends in Europe. Please, answer as quickly as you can, even though it must still be hard to send a letter overseas from there. I am giving this letter to a young man traveling through Europe as a reporter for a big American newspaper. If you are still living where I think you are, he will visit you there and ask you to give him a letter for me. I have just looked through my old address book, one of the very few things I took with me in my flight from Europe and kept with me through all the stations of my exile, and I was horrified, and sad too, how few names were left that I could send such letters to. The Führer almost managed to do it: make a tabula rasa of our people. Your name, Emma, was always right at the top of my mental list. Through all these dark years it has been with me like a beacon I could cling to: When peace comes I will find you again, and you will be your old self—I never had a shadow of a doubt about it.

As for me, just this for now: I am in good health, within the limits that age and the situation allow, and my circumstances have not changed, neither the external ones nor the internal ones. You will understand what I mean, and will shake your head again, like before, with your mocking grin. Yes, my dear, people never change, and you will probably contradict me, and then I'll tell you the details, and you'll tell me yours too! I embrace you. L.

I knew that Emma, in the fall of 1945, before we had met, was still living in Berlin—she never lived anywhere other than Berlin—but no longer in the house where the young American reporter went looking for her, a rear building in Neukölln that had been destroyed in the bombing, which might have been what saved its inhabitant of many years, who was under surveillance by the Gestapo and about to be arrested again. She had managed to work her way out of the ruins on the night of the bombing and go into hiding in the mass of rubble that the city, almost completely destroyed, had become. Emma almost never talked about that. We sat together so many times in her labyrinthine little house on the eastern edge of the city, a house that had grown, with years of adding-on and building-up, from the bower she had fled to at the end of the war. I took the last letter out of its envelope. It was written in May 1979, not by L. but by someone else, and contained the brief news that L. had died of a heart attack. It was signed with a first name: "Ruth."

I wondered what Emma would say to me. Be reasonable, girl? The mere thought of it made me feel better.

Doctor Kim, whom you went in to see in your socks and whose waiting room had bamboo chairs to sit in, asked different questions than other doctors. He was interested on a deep and fundamental level in the physical pain that brought me to see him. Hip joint, I see, that didn't seem to be the main point as far as he was concerned. Then he raised his thin Asiatic head from the sheet of paper I had had to fill out for him: *You are a writer. What do you have to do to become a good writer?* I felt like I was back taking an exam, I wanted to do well and tried to put myself in the teacher's place to figure out what he wanted to hear. I said I tried to know myself as accurately as I could and then express that. Doctor Kim seemed satisfied. Then he suggested I meditate regularly, I would get to know myself well that way, and I should not be afraid of what I would find there, and not shy away from expressing it. Then I would be able to become the best writer in the world.

To which I could truthfully say that that wasn't my goal, which seemed to amaze him. With a motionless face he stuck his delicate metal needles into my body.

But it wasn't my goal, I insisted to myself when I was back in the bus that rode the whole length of Wilshire Boulevard and picked up the poorer people, the carless people, who apparently existed even in this car city. Was I one of them? It was a pointless question, I could buy myself an inexpensive used car whenever I wanted, if I ever lost my inhibition about driving in this city I found so unfathomable. I tried to memorize the changing passengers: the black mother and her black daughter with little bows in her hair; the disheveled homeless man clutching his bottle and furiously muttering at nobody; a group of white, black, and brown schoolchildren gathered by the door in the middle of the bus and acting stupid like schoolchildren everywhere in the world; a woman whose body, a mass of flesh, completely filled both the seats in one of the short rows. I observed them as I had gotten used to doing. At every stop I noticed how many people walked badly, could get on or off the bus only with difficulty, how many used a cane or crutches, how many had an arm in a sling or an eye patch, and when the bus finally stopped at Fourth Street I took care to get off as light-footedly as I could, as though I did not actually need the handrail, even though the results that Doctor Kim apparently expected from only his first five needles didn't seem to have taken effect. Still, I had heard that a worsening of the symptoms could sometimes indicate that the therapy was working, and I wondered, as I laboriously climbed the steps to my apartment, if I couldn't let myself make use of another one of the pills that Doctor Kim didn't need to know anything about; he had already prohibited other pleasures—*no coffee! no wine!*—since in his view these damaging drugs blocked the free flow of energy in my body, which is precisely what Doctor Kim was trying to bring about.

I was unprepared, then, when the news I did not want to hear came at me from the television, before I could flee the room, all I could do was close my eyes and later flip past the page in the newspaper with a picture of the murder device called an "electric chair." But the man, who had been on death row for ten years since committing murder, was killed by lethal injection. In despair I tried to suppress the picture, but I couldn't. In despair I tried to greet the news of the kidnapping of a female archaeologist in Iraq with composure, so that it would become more bearable. But I couldn't, or only sometimes. I still remember how as I child I sometimes used to lie in bed and wonder how I was supposed to endure hearing about the suffering constantly inflicted on other people, and the fear of being hurt myself, for my whole long life long. I didn't then know, and would not have believed, that sympathy gets weaker when excessive claims are made upon it. That it doesn't grow back to the same extent after you give it out. That people, without realizing it or wanting it, develop protective techniques against self-destructive sympathy.

I headed to the CENTER and crossed the lobby. *How are you doing today? Great, thank you. Oh good.* Four elevators, two on one side and two on the other. I imagined that they were transparent and I saw the glass booths float up and down, keeping the circulatory system of the office skyscraper running, saw the mouths of the people in the booths move in response to always the same questions, always the same answers, saw the elevators stop at the various floors and the young women with their stacks of paper carry their important messages into every cell, every corner of the large building: We're doing great, wonderful, incredible. Couldn't be better. And the same thing all across the country. And my assumption, that smiling all the time must be stressful, was wrong, as I had learned by then. Normal behavior is not stressful.

Now there were letters from the city in my mailbox more and more often, including invitations, a sign that more and more people and institutions had learned of my presence here. One West Berlin colleague, for instance, had apparently flown across the ocean so that here, where no one knew him or his past, he could rail in an article called "Wrong Life Cannot Be Lived Rightly" against those of his colleagues who had not publicly forsworn their leftist errors, as he himself had recently done. He even added that he was certain that his colleagues under the regime in the East could not have led a meaningful life.

I did not know the man personally and wanted to avoid being unfair to him. But I still had to wonder whether he—one of the leftest of the left!—didn't at least know his Adorno: Did he not know that the sentence from *Minima Moralia* he had used as his title, which was now being used throughout the media to bludgeon East German intellectuals, came from the end of the eighteenth chapter, "Refuge for the Homeless," and expressed the impossibility of living rightly under "false"—that is, capitalist—property relations? Whatever the sentence originally meant, it turned out to be an irresistibly handy formulation in this new context.

I sat down at my little machine and wrote:

So what would a right life lived in the right circumstances look like? If our caravan of fugitives at the end of the war had been lucky enough to make it across the Elbe, which we were, after all, trying to use the last strength of our draft horse to reach? Would I have been a different person under the other property relations, the right ones? Smarter, better, guilt free? But why is it impossible for me to want to trade my life for that easier, better one, even now?

Then I had to run away, away from my patient, terrorizing little machine, out of my quiet apartment, a cell with the walls closing in on me—had to escape from the constant monologue in my head to the spot on Ocean Park Promenade with the best view of the Pacific Ocean.

I could hardly believe, and barely endure, that all these people walking past me on Ocean Park Promenade could be innocent, guiltless—that there were such people, the Japanese couple who first took their own pictures in various poses using a timer and then asked me to take one of them trying to hug the trunk of a giant eucalyptus tree, the big Mexican family who had dragged two benches together and were eating *hamburgers* and *hot dogs* out of *recyclable* fast-food containers, innocent, all of them, from the woman dressed in bright Indian colors to the newborn brown-skinned baby. They were guiltless even if some members of their clan might have crossed the border illegally. It wasn't about that. The young people jogging alone or in pairs, some attached to pulse monitors or pedometers, what did I know, some carrying dumbbells just to make things more difficult. One sweaty T-shirt said in black letters DO YOU LIKE ME and there could be no other possible answer but Yes and once again Yes.

Or the group of Russian emigrants that even from afar, from the observation post of my bench, I recognized as Russian: even they were guiltless too. I tried to pick up something of their language when they walked past me, the Russian that my first Russian teacher, a Baltic German woman, had urgently recommended we learn—we graduates from every possible corner of the defeated Greater German Reich brought to a Thuringian small town for no other reason than to learn the language of the victors: Learn it, children, learn it, once the Russian is somewhere he never leaves again. I picked up a few words and did not have the courage to ask them which of the various waves of emigration this family group belonged to. The children, I noticed, shouted words at each other in English.

A wave of memories flooded over me, unleashed by the language, the word "Moscow." The memory of my last trip to Moscow, in October 1989, which left me seriously depressed over the grim news I got from friends about their country's condition.

Before the return flight, at Sheremetyevo Airport, a young woman came up to you and started talking to you in the purest Saxon German.

They, the members of a madrigal choir from Halle, had been on tour in Central Asia for weeks, cut off from all news of the GDR: she wanted to know if you knew anything about the most recent Monday Demonstrations in Leipzig, there were rumors of deaths among the protesters in clashes with the security forces, they were worried about their friends and relatives, could you tell them anything. Yes indeed, you certainly could. The previous Monday, October 9, 1989, you had arrived in Moscow in the afternoon and called home that night, full of anxiety about the fate of the protesters in Leipzig, and you heard what you could now relay: There were hundreds of thousands on the street and nothing happened. And then you felt the same happiness again, the same as this young woman now felt, as she hugged you and passed on the good news to the other members of her choir.

While all of you—a large number of travelers, including many West German tourists—had to wait in the departure hall, someone spoke some soft instructions behind you and the choir assembled and started to sing: "O Täler weit, o Höhen," in many voices, so pure, so clear, so heartfelt. You were the only listener who knew why they were singing and you had to look away and you could not put a name to the feeling in your aching heart. It was not only a farewell from Moscow that was taking place here. And later, in the new era, interrogated over and over again as though for a capital offense about what there was about that washed-up country worth shedding a single tear over, for heaven's sake— what did it have to contribute to the big, rich, free Germany besides scrap metal and secret police files?—you sometimes had to think back to those few minutes at the airport in Moscow. We sang that song for you. And had to think back to the surprised, displeased faces of the West German travelers who whispered the place where this choir came from among themselves and eventually, in the end, applauded enthusiastically. They had liked the song, unable to perceive the painfully joyful undertone in it, and so you kept your silence when people started pestering you with questions and accusations.

At some point, the sentence formed: We loved this country. An impossible sentence that would have earned you nothing but mocking jeers if you had spoken it out loud. But you didn't. You kept it to yourself, the way you were keeping so much to yourself now.

It tires you out, I sometimes had to let it all go and walk back to my apartment and lie down. I started reading Thomas Mann's diaries, which he had written as an émigré here, only a few miles from the MS. VICTORIA, but the book soon slipped from my hands and I fell asleep. We are driving to Berlin on the autobahn, I have the road atlas open on my knees again and I'm looking for the country, the city, we can emigrate to, my companion is talking about speed traps, he knows where they are located, the traffic police have never once caught him speeding, and I say: But it's not the same police anymore, and he says: Yes it is, they've only changed their uniforms, and the new speed limit signs are a trick, in reality we have to obey the old speed limit of 100 km/hr., anything else will be punished. In the left lane, the West German cars race past us as always, they are allowed to, he says, because there are other laws for them. Suddenly we are sitting with our daughters and sons-in-law at Café Kranzler on the Ku'damm in West Berlin, I can already tell what the older daughter is going to tell us, and she says: So, we've decided to leave, why should we stay and put up with this gray life of shortages and cramped apartments. I nod and have the tormenting feeling that there's something wrong with her decision, I can't figure out what it is, and our second son-in-law says, distressed: Well, now you'll probably leave too, and I say: No, that's not necessary. We all have gigantic bowls of ice cream in front of us and we are sad, now it's caught up to us too, I thought when I woke up, and it took me a long time to realize why it was no longer necessary, in fact no longer possible, to leave.

Peter Gutman came by, not for the first time at just the right moment. You seem to have antenna for when you should show up here, I said. He asked what was going on.

I have discovered, I said, that my emotional state is often inadequate to historical events.

An example, please, if you don't mind?

Certainly. The fall of the Wall was a day of celebration, as you know. That's how it will be described forever in the history books.

Yes?

This is how I experienced it: We went to the movies that night, to the premiere of a film about the "coming out" of a homosexual teacher in East Germany—a theme that had never been handled publicly before. The audience was very moved and applauded the filmmakers for minutes on end. In those days, the events in our country were stirring up everyone's emotions. Afterward we went to visit our daughter. Our son-in-law met us at the door and said: Have you heard? The Wall is open.—And what did I say back, totally spontaneously? I said: In that case the Central Committee needs to wave the white flag.

So? Peter Gutman said. Was that the wrong thing to say?

Not wrong. Inadequate. I should have thrown my arms around my son-in-law's neck and screamed: Unbelievable! I should have burst out in tears of joy!

Yes, well, Peter Gutman said.

ALWAYS THESE AMBIVALENT FEELINGS

Ambivalent feelings? I thought. Were my feelings ambivalent when we were stuck for ages in our car on the drive home, at the intersection of Schönhauser and Bornholmer Streets, because the stream of Trabis and Wartburgs pouring toward the Bornholm border crossing did not let up? What did I feel, actually? Happiness? Triumph? Relief? No. Something like fear. Something like shame. Something like depression. And resignation. It was over. I had understood.

If only we always knew what would happen next, I said.

What you are describing, Peter Gutman said, are harmless cases of mistaken feelings. There are worse ones. Fatal ones. My father, for example. Senior postal clerk in Bromberg. What did he feel when Hitler came to power: Disgust? Fear? Nothing of the sort. He felt carefree. Turned a deaf ear to warnings. Until the Gestapo locked him up for a week. Then he understood and brought his feelings around to the way things actually were. He sent his two sons to England the first chance he got and made arrangements for himself and my mother, who wasn't my mother yet since I wasn't born yet. They got out and survived. How many others went to their deaths with their false feelings, their trusting natures.

I said: My mother was born in Bromberg. My grandfather punched tickets for the railroad there. He liked to drink one too many.

So, you see, Peter Gutman said, as though that were some kind of consolation. We both had to laugh.

Later he called me: By the way (that is how most of the things he had to say started)—by the way, my philosopher also expressed his views on the incongruity between objective occurrence and subjective feeling.

I said: I'm sure he did. What did he have to say?

He said that the facts are not always right when confronted with feelings.

I said: You made that up just now.

And he said: Madame! I wouldn't dream of it.

Memory pictures: I was with John and Judy for the first time at the café that would become our regular café, on Seventeenth Street, where you could get a good salad for not too much money. John had written several letters to me at the CENTER, with invitations, and I had answered Yes, I would be happy to meet with him and a group of Jewish friends, "*survivors*" he wrote, or members of the "*second generation*." They wanted to talk with me about Germany. I was afraid of this meeting, but in any case I wanted to meet John and his wife, Judy, first. John, who picked me up for dinner and "took care of everything," as he would later too. *I hope you're doing fine*, he said, as though we had known each other a long time already, and I said, surprising myself: *Not really fine, John.* And he said, another surprise: *I know. But don't worry. You will be fine.*

I knew we would be friends. A married couple, mid-forties, he tall and thin with medium-blond hair combed smoothly back, everything correct; she short with dark curly hair, lively. We sat across from each other for the first time and John almost immediately told me about his family, whose last surviving members he had just discovered in East Berlin, after the German unification: two cousins with wives and children on Karl-Marx-Allee in Berlin, one an engineer and the other an editor at a publishing house, both of whom felt, as John put it, "colonized" by the unification. He spread a large sheet of paper out over the table, on top of the salad plates: his family tree that he had researched over the years and drawn himself. I heard the first of the many reports on German-Jewish life paths that I would hear: that of his parents, who were able to leave Germany at the last minute, in 1939, and ended up in the United States via England, where John was born, and got by for a long time with little jobs here and there. For the first time, I heard that descendants of Jews forced to flee Germany felt drawn to Germany. Their roots are there, after all, John said. He carefully cultivated his relationship with his newfound relatives in East Berlin and collected everything he could find about the unification of the two German states, with passionate interest: he gave me articles on the subject from the folder he carried with him at all times and always kept up-to-date.

He was the first American I'd met here who didn't expect me to make a pious face at the mention of the word "unification."

He and Judy had a shared appointment in the sociology department at the university; their work was on business management and they didn't hide the fact that they found the capitalist economic system perverse, with its striving for endless economic growth, but they couldn't go public with this opinion, they said, not *yet*. Not only because it would endanger their careers but above all because hardly anyone would understand them. "They" had finally managed to convince people, John said, that we do live in the best of all possible worlds, and as long as people believe that, against all the evidence before their eyes, they stay deaf to other opinions. Probably they will only be shaken awake by a catastrophe, and you can't really hope for that. Until then, John and Judy had to use their time collecting convincing evidence, but also, if possible, developing ideas for possible alternatives.

Oh, I know, I said.

Oh, I knew. How many times in recent years, observing the decline of my country, did I recall what Goethe had said when he was old, the lines beginning: "We would not welcome the radical transformation that would be necessary to prepare the way for classical works of literature in Germany." "Literary Sansculottism."

To have to welcome what brings destruction. To be stuck between a rock and a hard place. To learn to live without alternatives. German conditions.

They'd think we were crazy, John said, we have moved so far to the edge of society with our views. Had I already noticed how strong the pressure was here in the States to conform, and how little the people under that pressure even realized it? That daily life in America was the norm for the rest of the world; that it was normal to live for profit and success; that the president is elected by only a third of the citizens while at the same time we are the most exemplary of democracies. That after the collapse of Communism, all of this is valid for all eternity. It would take a long time before the enormous contradictions in the system broke out into the open, but when it happened, they would be at least theoretically prepared for it.

You poor things! I thought, I still remember, half in pity, half in envy. At least they weren't consumed by self-doubt, that must be a great help, I thought. You don't know what lies ahead, I thought. But now we do know it, and we have to admit that we never could have imagined that one day more than two thousand coffins with dead American soldiers would be shipped back from Iraq to the United States without the Americans rising up against it.

Many of the details are blurry now, I obviously can't remember precisely the various phases of the reports from Europe anymore, but I am certain that the articles sent or faxed to me, that Kätchen put in a folder and passed along to me, struck other tones: more impatient, more ferocious, more cutting. I read the newspaper pages with letters from readers: The West German readers had had enough of the East Germans' problems. You could see a real helplessness in them: For heaven's sake, all this screeching about so-called values that they wanted to preserve from a state that had fallen apart, what was that supposed to mean? What can you preserve from a dictatorship?

Gentle, precise, and open, the nun says, typed out on my little machine: I sat for hours a day at the narrow end of my dining table and wrote, which everyone who knew about it thought was industrious hard work, except me, since I knew what hard work was, or would have been. But maybe my idleness too came under the nun's all-forgiving comprehension.

Gentleness is a kind of goodness toward ourselves— I translated the nun's lines into German—precision helps us see clearly without fear, the way a scientist is not afraid to look in the microscope; and openness is the ability to let go and open yourself up.

I want to understand, I have always wanted to understand sentences like that, I now think, years later, years in which absolutely everything has gone against these sentences. The dream I had last night comes to mind: I am with my whole family in a kind of cave and a giant tower, made of iron along the lines of the Eiffel Tower, rises up in an open field before us and slowly tips over to the right, a horrifying sight, and then folds up at two hinges like a pocket knife. We flee in panic, in a crowd of many people doing the same thing, I realize my grandmother isn't there so I run back, the cave has meanwhile turned into a small, rather nice restaurant, my grandmother is sitting there in her wheelchair and looking at me. I think: September 11! and wake up screaming. The start of a new era, I hear a voice say.

The last time I woke up screaming, I remember, was the night after my visit to the small, modest Holocaust Museum of Los Angeles. Two rooms. In one, photos on the walls of Jewish life in Europe before the Holocaust. Family pictures. Documents of the annihilation of the European Jews. Photographs from survivors . . . The second room was empty except for a railroad car, built to look like the cattle cars that took people to the death camps.

I sat down in a nearby café with the museum director, a short, unobtrusive man, still young, with a businesslike look. I knew what he would ask me before he said a word, he too had seen the pictures from Germany in the papers, of course. I beat him to it and said that I couldn't explain the riots against asylum seekers in Germany either. I said that the young people, especially in East Germany, had learned in recent years how hard it is to be weak. He said: But they *are* weak, and they have to learn not to be violent anyway. I thought I perceived in him too the belief that Germans were infected with an incurable sickness, a virus that in better times could pupate or hibernate so that Germany seemed normal like any other country, but which every crisis brought back to life so that it burst out and turned aggressive. The name of this virus was Contempt For Humanity. For a long time I thought it had been defeated in the part of the country where I lived, defeated by Enlightenment. When I spoke that word, I thought I saw in my Jewish interlocutor's eyes something like a sad amusement. Enlightenment! he drawled. Yes, well. This tendency to fool oneself. We were familiar with it too.

Being put on the spot and asked to stand in for and speak for all of Germany was new to me, and I felt how strongly I resisted it. Most of Germany was foreign to me, and not just in a geographical sense. He let me talk, get tangled up, look for arguments, utter protestations. Finally I fell silent. And then, at the end, this unbelievable question again: So you really want to go back there? And my quick answer: Yes, of course. No question about it. What else should I do?

And after we said goodbye and I was sitting on the bus again, I could not get free of the feeling that I had forgotten to say something crucially important. I couldn't think of what it might have been.

I did not go back to the CENTER that day. I sat at my little machine and wrote:

How can the survivors live with it? How can we Germans live with it? It is a burden that gets heavier year by year. There is nothing to work through, nothing to resolve, no sense to find in it. There is nothing but crimes that burst all bounds on our side and suffering that bursts all bounds on their side.

And how long it took us to say "our," our crime. And we clung for such a long time—I clung for such a long time—to the promise held out to us that we were totally different, the absolute opposite of those crimes: Communism, the society fit for human existence, not Fascism.

> The exploiters call it a crime.
> But we know:
> It is the end of crime.

The telephone. Peter Gutman. Night had fallen. Could he read me something? A quote.

Please do. If it's not too long and complicated.

He read: "The storyteller is the man" (my apologies, Madame!) "who can let the wick of his life be completely consumed by the gentle flame of his story."

Hmm. A wonderful sentence.

But?

But I would replace "the gentle flame" with "the scorching flame."

But then, Peter Gutman said, the wick of life would not be consumed, it would probably be charred.

Exactly, I said.

Aha, Peter Gutman said. I understand. Sleep well, Madame.

> People will say about our times:
> They had old iron and little courage
> since they had little strength left after their defeat.
> People will say about our times:
> Their hearts were full of bitter blood.
> And their life ran on worn-out tracks,
> they will say—
> and they will stand on their glass terraces—

And point to the bridges—
And point out the gardens—
And they will see the new city lying at their feet.

These lines ran through my head as I lay in bed. The poet KuBa, Kurt
Barthel, who wrote them once upon a time, believed them too and made
us believe them and was furious when our belief faded, then fell apart
when his own unshakable belief was repaid with mockery and jeers. I
could not agree with those jeers, and still can't. "People will say about our
times . . ." No, KuBa, no, that is exactly what people will not say. And
they also won't say: "Mother of Gori, how great is your son." It's good
that no one says that, I think, and I hold the thin book with the austere
gray cover in my hand, flip through it, and find the lines I am looking for:

> Gori, you cruel one, lost in the gardens,
> Cradle placed in peaceful times.
> Brave humanity, sworn to peace,
> Be like the father of peace in this world.
> Head of the proletariat, brain of the educated,
> Jacket of the soldiers: Comrade Stalin.

KuBa: Someone who died at the right time, I think. Dead and forgotten, or usable now only as the object of mocking disapproval, which he
also deserves. In the little book is printed the year of its publication,
1952, and above it, written in ink, the year you and G. bought it: 1953.

Your university days were over, there was a child to take care of,
finding an apartment for your family was the most urgent task. You
walked down streets of rubble to your job at the writers' union on Friedrichstrasse, where the poet KuBa, in the name and the interest of his
colleagues, occupied an entire floor of the office and gave lectures left
and right to young authors, lectures you had written for him, had his
driver buy him the one suit he needed for official occasions, which didn't
fit him but fit his driver and so was passed on to him. When someone
had no money he reached into his pocket and gave away whatever he
found there. He was proud to be a proletarian and after emigrating to
England he became a Communist, unconditionally devoted to the Party,
one of the truest of the true believers and at the same time most ruthless
and narrow-minded. Today he is known only as the person who rebuked

the rebellious East German people after the Uprising of June 17, 1953: The people had forfeited the confidence of their government. They would have to behave very well in future before their shame would be forgotten. And he is known because of Brecht's reply: Wouldn't it be simpler, in that case, for the government to dissolve the people and elect another?

KuBa dedicated his little book to his friend Louis Fürnberg, his idol and patron, one of the first of the émigrés to return—one memory calls forth the next—Fürnberg invited you to Weimar. Did you know at the time that Weimar, his work at the Goethe-Schiller Archive, was what saved him? In Prague, in his homeland, the Slánský trials would have meant his death. Close comrades of his—mostly Jews like him—were judged to be "traitors"; some were shot.

When did I learn that? And from whom? Fürnberg was curious about you young nameless writers. He told you lots of stories. I can still see him sitting at the piano in his house in Weimar, intoning songs from his agitprop group from the twenties too, songs you all learned by heart, like his poems, and could sing along with him. For example: the

SONG OF THE DREAMERS

When the dreamers take to the streets
to undertake their dreams,
nobody has overslept,
no opportunity has been missed.
Whoever changes the world in dreams
and acts accordingly when he awakes,
he has slept well and dreamed well,
he is our friend.

An ardent Communist. The long path of knowledge began for you with him. Fürnberg, the son of a German-Jewish manufacturer in Karlsbad, now impoverished, had not fled in time before the German troops marched in. They had shattered his hearing during his transport to jail by physically throwing confiscated library books at him, his wife had bribed an SS man with his grandfather's money and bought his free-dom, he and his family had spent their exile in Palestine. For you, he was the author of the youth song "You have a goal before your eyes, / So that you will not go astray in the world," which seemed so much better to you than all the songs that dominated your childhood and adolescence, which were so hard to forget. But Fürnberg was also the author of more profound poetry, and sensitive prose, like *The Mozart Novella*. And today he is forgotten, or else, even worse, only mentioned when someone needs an especially absurd example of Party poetry, because he did write that too, the "Song of the Party," which he wrote despite his doubts—but who knows?—in 1950, two years after Stalin had expelled Yugoslavia, one of the countries the Fürnbergs had fled to and one that they loved, from the international association of socialist states. "For he who fights for what is right, / He is always right, against lies and exploitation." The song of the Party Congresses at which Comrade Stalin was chosen as honorary president, along with Comrade Mao Zedong.

Until one day, a report by Comrade Khrushchev was read out at one Congress, about the cult of personality around Stalin and giving the first hints of his "errors," and comrades who had been in exile in the Soviet Union burst into tears and admitted that they too had lived through some things themselves, knew a lot, but kept silent, so as not to endanger the reconstruction in our country, and then it was KuBa who rushed to the lectern and said that he was grateful to his comrades for keeping such a difficult Party secret for so long. From that point on he considered Comrade Khrushchev a renegade and traitor, while Louis Fürnberg sent a jubilant letter: A thaw! At last we can write again! . . . The exultation betrayed the deep depression in which he and many other comrades of his generation had lived for so long. Not seeing any alternative. And keeping silent. And writing poems like:

DIFFICULT HOURS
Maybe we are destined to be the sacrifice
for a greater goal; if so, we should keep silent,
even if pain and shame bow our necks
as we look on as spectators to this game.

"I felt the touch of death today," Louis Fürnberg wrote on November 23, 1953. When he died of a heart attack, in 1957, aged forty-eight, a large crowd of people joined his funeral procession in Weimar, and you were there.

Other funeral processions rise up before my eyes—too many poets who returned to us from the emigration died within a decade, almost all from "broken hearts," to use the old-fashioned language: their hearts had withstood the pressure for decades, but not the sudden release from the pressure. And so the processions to the Dorotheenstadt cemetery began. F. C. Weiskopf, Bertolt Brecht, and Johannes R. Becher died within four years and were laid alongside Fichte, Hegel, Schinkel, Rauch, and Schadow; Bodo Uhse and Willi Bredel followed soon after. Today flocks of tourists file past these graves, and the graves of those buried there in the decades to follow: Wieland Herzfelde, Helene Weigel, Anna Seghers, Hans Mayer, just to stay with that generation. So many names. So many stories. Who will tell them? Who would still want to hear them? They wouldn't be especially entertaining, these stories, and definitely not without taint or blemish. Wrong turns? Oh, yes. Mistakes? Those too. Heroic deeds? Yes, those too. But not heroic stories—they wouldn't have wanted that. And when the "great cause" fell apart before their eyes, every one of them reacted in his or her own way: with despair, defensiveness, depression, rage, silence, denial, self-deception. And some with dogmatism and insistence that they were in the right.

After one of the stirring assemblies, Willi Bredel laid his arm around your shoulder and said: Yes, now we should probably do a bit more for you young people too. The next chance he had, when you were at a congress in Moscow, he gave you a tour through the Moscow he remembered from his émigré years: That's the Hotel Lux, we all lived there. In the bad time, during the purges, we would call each other up at night to hear if the other person was still there, and when they answered we would hang up without a word. Some comrades weren't "there" anymore . . . And here's the Lubyanka, the NKVD headquarters with the bars on the windows, from here they were sent to the camps and we never heard from some of them again . . . And when Ribbentrop and Molotov signed the Nonaggression Pact between Hitler-Germany and the Soviet Union, we émigrés had to stop our public anti-Fascist propaganda.

You tried to imagine the loneliness they were plunged into. And then? you asked. How did you bear it? —We had no alternative, he said.

That wouldn't happen to you. You were young back then and you sat around together hour after hour, night after night. Your task, you thought, would be to exorcise the demon of Stalin from social life, to get through the conflicts, which were more severe than you predicted, and to not give up. A naive agenda.

—

Even the west coast of America, the sunny land of California, could be drenched in steady rains, I hadn't known that. I stayed in the MS. VICTORIA and saw on TV whole sections of cliffs break off and wash away the coastal road, a few hundred yards away from me.

I walked to my bench in Ocean Park. The rain had stopped, the earth had drunk its fill, the leaves of the palm and eucalyptus trees glowed a contented green. Peter Gutman was already sitting there and he said a casual hello as though we had planned to meet there. He had also been stuck in his apartment for days, he also seemed to need some fresh air. We walked to the Huntley Hotel, went up the glass elevator, saw the coastline get smaller below us, the people on the beach shrink to tiny figures, and found a free table in the round glassed-in restaurant. *Happy hour.* Groups of very young people had occupied almost all the tables and were acting like they owned the place, helping themselves to countless cheap drinks and bites of food from the copious buffet, with not a glance to the landscape below them, the beautiful curve of the Malibu coastline, instead they pranced and preened for each other, yelling and creating a level of noise that made it almost impossible for us to talk. We too drank pitchers of watery margaritas and ate grilled hot dogs and stir-fried vegetables, and we looked through the enormous glass wall at the glorious sunset we hadn't seen for days.

I asked Peter Gutman the question: Can a person fundamentally change? Or are the psychologists right and the basic patterns are set in the first three years, and can then only be filled out, not changed?

For example? Peter Gutman asked.

For example, the risk of always remaining dependent on something: Authorities? So-called leaders? Ideologies?

That, Peter Gutman said, is something my philosopher reflected very deeply on, conveniently enough. He says that we Western men and women pay the price for our life of luxury with the loss of maturity. What we drink in with our mother's milk is the idea that whoever goes against the mainstream will be excluded from the subsistence group.

But is any other system even thinkable?

That's exactly the point: they've made sure that even our utopias stay enclosed in this thought-space. All we can do is wish for more and more of what is. Or less. Or a more beautiful version. Or more rational.

As opposed to what! I cried.

Precisely, Peter Gutman said. And then we're surprised that our proud belief in reason flips around into the worst irrationalism. And we keep moving down the same track, which we call "progress." That's what my philosopher says.

That's why you can't finish your book about him, I said. You keep running up against unthinkable things.

You may be right, Peter Gutman said.

The sun went down and we couldn't keep talking while it set.

We left the restaurant and took the glass elevator down to the darkness starting to descend on Third Street, which had come to life with passersby, artists, musicians, and performers. So is every utopia ridiculous? I asked.

He hadn't said that. At the moment, he found himself disagreeing with his philosopher on the question of revolutions and their function. Whether a revolution is the only way to bring about a utopia.

I said: Maybe they're the most effective way to fool yourself into thinking that utopias cannot be brought about.

You would know, Madame, Peter Gutman said, and did not want to say anything more on the topic. We walked for a while in silence among the crowds of the evening street.

I no longer know if the word "revolution" ever came up among you in 1989, but I doubt it. It would have struck you as too bombastic. The word that did come to occupy the empty space we inherited was inadequate, and intentionally obscured the nature of the "events." The whole process, from the demonstrations to the fall of the Wall to reunification, became known as *die Wende*, the "Turn" or "Turning Point." But what exactly had "turned"? Away from what? What you experienced was a people's uprising that took the form of peaceful demonstrations and catapulted those at the bottom to the top. Assuming that that is what revolutions are intended to do, this was a revolution. When I think about it seriously, it ran strictly according to the theoretical model. Erosion of the old power structure on almost every level: suddenly the actors in the theaters were reciting critical manifestos after performances and no one was there to stop them and call the wildly applauding audience to order; suddenly, for the first time, large numbers of people did not turn out to vote, and groups of civil rights activists spread out to all the voting places, kept a close watch on the vote counters, wrote down the results themselves, compiled them in the municipal districts, compared them with the official tallies, and then told each other and everyone they knew over tapped phone lines: Election fraud! Suddenly you couldn't find anyone who didn't sharply criticize the social conditions, which showed that even the timid and conformist people had picked up a scent: change was in the air.

First, the small private groups, often disguised as reading circles, who made contact with each other, united, led political discussions, developed platforms, approved resolutions, formulated demands. Busily shuttling back and forth from one apartment to the next, people exchanged documents and practiced the ways of conspiracy, under close surveillance from state security, of course. It seemed unavoidable that parties would form, names would be passed along, NEW FORUM, DEMOCRACY NOW. All while the anniversary of the state was celebrated with military pomp and honors. And the government authorities took it as the most serious possible threat when the masses on the street shouted out the slogan: We're staying here!

There is always a *point of no return*, I said to Peter Gutman. But you don't always realize it at the time.

We let ourselves be carried along by the stream of people enjoying the offerings of the street performers and artists. I felt something like envy inside me. It's possible to live like this too. The idea of trying to tell these people, most of them young, acting out their precious selves in the most marvelous masquerades and given totally over to the moment, about the passion with which people on the other side of the globe, decades before, equally young, had sat together day after day, night after night, and tried to talk into existence a future in which man would not be wolf to man—the very idea struck me as absurd. I said something of the sort to Peter Gutman, who replied that he was familiar with such discussions too. With us, he said, they were castles in the air, whereas you had your feet on the ground, we thought: I mean you were living within the new property relations, the ones that are now held against you as crimes and that they're rushing to try to annul. Whereas the real crime is the "toxic money economy," Ludwig Börne already knew that. Even if he didn't know the kind of crimes that new property relations could call forth when combined with totalitarian power structures.

We walked in silence. Hats and caps lay out on the street in front of the dancers, musicians, and magicians, the spectators strolling by were free with their dollars. I stood spellbound in front of a very thin black man who was standing on a pedestal dressed as Uncle Sam, wearing a top hat covered with an American flag and representing a kind of machine-man moving in slow motion in tiny jerks, powered, you couldn't help but think, by some device hidden somewhere within his human exterior, so that I was unconsciously expecting to hear the gears whir. I was fascinated and followed how he jerkily bent his arms, with infinite slowness, then stretched them out again, bent his upper body, straightened it up again, which all took several minutes and required total physical control. The audience applauded wildly. We kept walking, to the end of Second Street, where we bought warm waffles with acacia honey at a stand and ate them there.

When we walked back past the black Uncle Sam, I threw the dollar he had earned into his top hat and turned to go. Now he's waving! Peter Gutman cried. And so he was. The mechanical human moved his right index finger in a jerky wave and a masklike smile appeared on his face. I stepped closer. He reached out his hand to me in slow motion, bent down, hugged me, and I tried to imitate his movements, laughed, and left. Now he's following us! Peter Gutman cried. For the black man had freed himself from his mechanical state and stepped down off the pedestal, and he came up to me with quick steps and the relaxed, supple movements of many African-Americans, he was beaming, he shook my hand again, for real this time, loose, loose, we hugged again, as though the machine-man's embrace didn't count, and then he let me leave, waving after me. And I felt the shock in every bone in my body at this transformation from an artificial creature into a human being, as though that were the unnatural thing, as though a chain had just been shattered and the bonds that had held him for so long been broken.

I felt that something had happened, as though this physical contact was what I had needed, and Peter Gutman seemed to see it in my face. We hurried back to the MS. VICTORIA in silence and parted almost without a word in front of my apartment door. I sat down at the table and wrote, as if taking dictation, what today, paging through my old notebooks, I am amazed to read:

In any case, the time of lament and accusation is past, and we have to get past grief and self-reproach and shame as well, so that we will not keep falling from one false consciousness into another. "The flags rattle in the wind"—whatever colors they bear. So what?

So they rattle, but why did it take us so long to realize that? We have to live following an uncertain
inner compass, without any appropriate moral code. Only
we cannot keep deluding ourselves any longer. I don't
see any end to it, we are digging in a dark tunnel but
we have to just keep digging.

I went to the shelf with the folder of L.'s letters. Her second letter to my
friend Emma was from January 1947. It began with exclamations of joy
that Emma was still alive, and that they were in touch with each other
again. Then she wrote:

> Even if a letter can never take the place of our kitchen conver-
> sations, as I'm sure you'll agree. Do you remember? We sat at
> the kitchen table, the streetcar line ran practically through your
> room, a room and a kitchen was all you could afford, we drank
> coffee substitute, you didn't have a job, the office could no lon-
> ger afford an addiction counselor, but I was still getting by as an
> assistant doctor in the clinic for the poor where we had met. I
> met my dear gentleman then too. Life became precious to me.
> And so it has remained.
>
> So, now the old lady has told you the most important
> thing, that I'm still acting like a silly schoolgirl, and I can see the
> shocked and mocking look on your face. My ambassador, the
> young journalist, has probably told you that I have been work-
> ing as a psychoanalyst for a long time.
>
> And, since I know how curious you are: Yes. His wife, Dora,
> is still there too, they live together as they always have. Don't
> laugh, it's nothing to laugh about.
>
> As I write this everything rises up to the surface inside me.
> I can see you before my eyes. Do you know how beautiful you
> were back then?

Was Emma beautiful? Not when I knew her. When we met her, she
had just finished her jail time in the small town of Bützow in Mecklenburg. Her features were sharp and exhausted at the same time. Still, in
the biggest room of her ridiculous little bower house there was a picture
hanging above an old-fashioned sofa that a painter friend, who later had

also had to emigrate, had painted of her in the late 1920s and that had survived the Hitler era through a series of remarkable adventures. It showed an attractive young woman, confident and provocative. You have to always look out for yourself, child. She was disappointed in me sometimes, she wanted to cure me of my feelings of guilt.

Sally called. Nothing new with her. Her therapist was trying to convince her that what was happening to her was normal. Normal! Sally cried. When the person closest to you betrays you! I was tempted to ask her if she thought "betrayal" was the right word to describe someone's love ending, and if she would want Ron to stay with her even though he no longer loved her. But I suppressed the question. That was the scandal, after all: that he no longer loved her and it was nobody's fault. She couldn't sue his love.

And you? Sally asked me. What are you up to? Have you settled in? How are you feeling?

Without having planned to, without even seeing it coming, I suddenly asked her what the English word for "*Akten*" is. Why do you want to know? Sally asked. I ignored her question and used circumlocutions to describe what I meant until she finally arrived at the right word: *files*, she said. But what do you need that word for? —Later, I said. Maybe I'll tell you later.

I looked it up in my Langenscheidt dictionary to make sure. I couldn't believe that this short bright little word "*file*" could mean the same thing as the dark, threatening German word "*Akten*." So "to lead an *Akte* about someone" is "*to keep a file on someone*"; "to put something aside" is "*to file it away*"—letters, reports, surveillance records, credit statements, whatever. The main thing was that all these words were neutral: a *file number* could be something completely harmless, I told myself, no reason to get sweaty palms.

The break I had given myself, or taken for myself, was coming to an end. I hadn't memorized my file number, which the agency had assigned me. The agency where—as in the fairy tale about the porridge overflowing out of the magic pot until it covers and smothers the whole city—sheet after sheet of paper is brought forth from a dark well and painstakingly archived until they take up many rooms, a whole new building, one space after another, from which in turn spill out their calamitous effects. Copies of the "good" files—called, perversely, "victim files"—sat in a chest at home and still sit there today, and I couldn't help but think about the whole series of containers that had been hidden for years in a crate, before this chest: cardboard boxes tied with string and taped around all the edges and diagonally, document boxes, travel bags, with material, manuscripts, and diaries that "they" mustn't find. If these various containers stayed in their obvious hiding place, it was a sign that you did not think they were in any real danger. This hope was always fragile, and consisted in large part of self-deception, as you knew perfectly well in another layer of your consciousness, and if the delusion collapsed you would have to take immediate action: friends would have to be ready to take in the boxes and bags without asking what they contained, agreements would have to be made about where to take them if they turned out not to be safe anymore with these friends either, code words would have to be agreed on, with embarrassed laughter, it would be humiliating—codes that could be given over the phone in case of emergency to produce behavior the opposite of what we seemed to be asking for. And you were always afraid that you would mix up the code words, since of course you couldn't write down even the most harmless password, that was agreed. None of which is in the files, I thought, that this agency is bringing to light. I have told it to only a very few people. The chest is not empty. I haven't opened it for years.

I sat down at my little machine. I wrote:

TO TURN EVERYTHING UPSIDE DOWN YET AGAIN

```
                                I   know    how
far I can trust my memory, don't I. I can only hope
that I never get to the point where I have to tell all
these innocent people, with their pure, lacuna-less
memory, something about remembering and forgetting.
```

Then I got ready to go out to dinner. A couple in Pacific Palisades, both German professors, had invited me, and this dinner, among all the many dinner parties from that year, remains crystal clear in my mind. A Polish couple fetched me, which I was especially looking forward to. I wanted to ask him, an essayist I admired very much, all sorts of questions about the early sacrificial rites of primitive peoples, I had just read something by him about them. But sitting next to me in the car was a sick, gaunt man, obviously hard of hearing, who had great difficulty breathing and spoke American English with such a thick Polish accent that I could barely understand him. His wife, a frail older lady, sat mutely next to the driver, with an aura of mourning, it seemed to me.

As we drove through Pacific Palisades, I tried to see as much as I could—the well-tended gardens and expensive villas, often hidden behind high, impenetrable hedges. Two white dogs, of a rare, aristocratic breed I had never seen, sprang at the wire fence next to our host's front door, barking furiously, jumping high. One of the dogs was named Willy but he didn't listen to his name, or any other command from his master. Both dogs had to stay outside. I already knew the couple who met us at the door—Marja, a Hungarian Jew, and Henry, the son of a German-Jewish family—from Berlin, where they had spent a semester as visiting scholars. Marja was a bit older than me and we had liked each other from the beginning. The guests who had arrived before us—Gottfried, a director, and his wife, Sylvia—were already standing with champagne glasses in their hands in the front part of the *living room*, furnished with deep armchairs and sofas that were flanked in turn with two floor lamps, as in every American living room. We sat down to the obligatory snacks and dips. Ted was led into the room, a member of the German Department at the university, and presented to me as "liberal and leftist"; his wife, Elizabeth, an anthropologist, dressed and coiffed especially meticulously, did not speak German and was clearly bored when the others shifted into German for my sake.

Finally the last guests arrived, and Marja meant them as a surprise for me, which they certainly were: Svetlana and Koma, Lev Kopelev's stepdaughter and son-in-law. We were friends from Moscow and rushed to hug each other. She was a stately woman, dark-skinned, in a black dress with a black-and-white shawl, a typical Russian woman, I couldn't help thinking. He was bursting at the seams, a man who loved to talk and was thrilled to be able to give a seminar at the university here on the poet Osip Mandelstam. For ten students, he said with a shrug.

Whenever I hear that name I see the book by Nadezhda Mandelstam before my eyes: one of the first books that revealed to you what life under Stalin was like. Nadezhda Mandelstam, who memorized all of her husband's poetry to save it in her head during the decades when it was banned. I thought back to the Moscow gathering that Lev had taken you to one night at his relative's apartment, where we met Koma, who had just gotten out of prison; he had protested on Red Square against the entry of Soviet troops into Czechoslovakia with a small group of like-minded demonstrators. That night they had sat in the apartment and talked about emigrating. It was more than twenty years ago. Since then they had been driven to the four corners of the world; Lev, who by then had had his own citizenship revoked, once said to you at his kitchen table in Cologne: My family is scattered across the globe. But that was later.

On that night in California, with emigrants from various countries, an apparition forced itself into my mind which must have been summoned up while the party continued, while we sat down at the big dining table for rice and *seafood*. The need to fix in my memory someone whose ashes lie in a grave in Moscow and who is vanishing the way the dead do. Lev. Forced out of the country that was his, the country he had fought for as a soldier and among whose enemies he had won friends, because the principle he lived his life by is well described with the obsolete word: humanity. Even if everywhere else, for almost every other person, the term is an exaggeration or mischaracterization, it was true of him. Lev was humane, he couldn't be anything else. It stung me to see, one day, at the Midnight Special bookstore on Third Street, a copy of his book from the autobiographical cycle *To Be Preserved Forever* next to the shrill book by Madonna that had just come out, *Sex*: the expensive, opened copy which some bookstores would let preferred customers page through for a dollar so that they could enjoy the star's naked body in its various daring poses. But together with the twinge of revulsion I felt, I knew that Lev himself would have accepted the juxtaposition with a generous smile.

He was incapable of hate. In the book where he describes the crimes that brought him a sentence of many years and resulted in the gruesome stamp being placed on all his belongings, "Хранить вечно" ("To Be Preserved Forever")—namely, that as a Soviet officer he had spoken out against the violent trespasses of Soviet soldiers against the German civilian population in East Prussia—in this book there is no hate. I wonder if I ever once heard him speak a hateful word. Definitely not on that first evening, when you met at Anna Seghers's place and Lev got into a serious argument with her, whom he greatly admired, about Ilya Ehrenburg's pamphlets calling on the Soviet troops to hate the Fascist enemy. Anna Seghers, the German Communist whom Ehrenburg had helped in Paris when her countrymen in Nazi uniforms were on her trail, defended him, while Lev, the former Soviet officer, refused to condone what he had done. They fought bitterly about it, and at the end gave each other a big hug. That was one of the moments in life you happened to witness that taught you more than a lot of big books.

And Madest Thyself an Idol: The Education of a Communist is the name of the book in his trilogy where Lev tries to justify to himself the false beliefs of his youth. Did you not later share those beliefs yourself? It is not least because of him that you understand how ruthless self-examination is the prerequisite for the right to judge others.

That night I could call up numerous images of him. How he, a big man, trudged around in the small rooms of his Moscow apartment, always packed with visitors who had come to him for advice and support and some of them, no doubt, to inform on him too. How he stomped on the phone: "You little traitor!" How he grimly walked around Moscow with you, taking you to see a painter who was officially not allowed to exhibit—the same day that the reactionary journal *Ogoniok* unleashed yet another campaign against the people close to Vladimir Maya-kovsky who were still alive: Lily Brik and her husband. All Jews, Lev said, himself a Jew. This could get bad. They're stirring up anti-Semitism here again. He seemed anything but furious and filled with hate, more like concerned and sad.

The Soviet Union that expatriated him and his wife, Raisa, to their great sorrow, no longer exists. Lev survived it by a few years. I rummage around a little in my unsorted papers. Yes, there it is: the copy of the journal *Ogoniok* that you brought back from Moscow with you, I kept it.

I could think of nothing that characterized him better than the phone call I received two days after the fall of the Wall: I'm here. —Where? —With you! Can I come see you? Carried away with the euphoria of the masses who were surging back and forth between East and West Berlin even though the border restrictions had not been offi-cially abolished yet, he had gotten into a car and come to Berlin, with-out passport or visa. When the border guards tried to stop him, they were loudly and vigorously instructed by GDR passersby: Surely they did not intend to stop the famous Soviet writer Lev Kopelev? He was allowed through, on the condition that he "leave the country" at the same border crossing. The first thing he wanted to see were Brecht's and Anna

Seghers's graves. He always felt an almost childlike reverence for great writers.

Or a little later: How he had a fall when he was about to appear at the Berlin State Opera, and nonetheless had himself carried out onto the stage to give his speech, and then it turned out he had broken his hip. How he lay in bed in the Charité Hospital in East Berlin, impatient, surrounded by newspapers, letters, and manuscripts, always hard at work, always pushing his assistants to make progress on his book about German-Russian relations, with all his antennas aimed at Moscow, where relatives and friends were relying on his help. They all gathered at Raisa and Lev's kitchen in Cologne, whenever they were "in the West" for a short period or a long one. Raisa and Lev never spoke of their own homesickness.

My last image of Lev: He is sitting in his émigré room in Cologne, at his desk, with photographs of friends and family all around him on the walls—a room transplanted from another country and another time, like its inhabitant. He had held his ground between the two fronts. His like would never come again. The times have moved on past people like him.

It moves on past all of us, I thought, all of us sitting here in a typical American house, eating a carefully prepared American meal in a typical American *dining room* even though, for most of us sitting at the table, very different customs had shaped our ideas of meals and hospitality—Hungarian customs, Scandinavian customs, Russian, Jewish, German—and I wondered if they felt as much like an actor in a foreign play as I did, a play they pretended to know, that they had memorized under penalty of personal destruction if they didn't, whose words they pronounced as correctly as possible, dialogue that would never be their own language. They knew this about each other, and the fact that they knew it was the bond connecting them—more strongly, perhaps, than any bond between natives of a country ever could, they knew that too, and I learned it that night from their looks, their talk, their silence, their gestures. My role was to listen to them and pretend that I understood more of their English, interspersed with fragments of Russian, Hungarian, Polish, than I did.

It was one of those nights I wish I had on tape. They talked about mutual acquaintances, made fun of the quirks of Jewish mutual friends, and of themselves, and of American idiosyncrasies, all in a tolerant, relaxed way. I realized that I was almost the only non-Jew in the group. The conversation turned to how anti-Semitic America had been in the thirties and forties, which I hadn't known: even the richest Jews were not allowed to join country clubs and other associations, Gottfried said, and they couldn't stay in certain hotels, his father had had that happen to him, his father who was a god in the theater world of Berlin.

I was happy to be hearing Russian again. Koma had firm opinions about the new politicians in Moscow. Marja thought the developments in Hungary were simply "terrible": *The outlook to the end of this century doesn't look so optimistic, does it?* The Polish couple was happy and proud that their only son, married to an American, now lived in Warsaw as a consultant for a big company and that his child was learning both English and Polish.

It got more and more lively and fun around the table, we were drinking, we praised the new American wines, it was harmonious and everyone seemed to be having a good time, and still I could feel thick clouds of grief hanging over these people. I was sitting among refugees. All of them had taught themselves not to let their sorrow show—it was buried the most deeply in the features of the old Polish woman—but rather to come to terms with their nostalgia alone, within their own four walls. You have to give America credit: It was the lifeboat for millions of people like these.

Elizabeth turned to me. Then, at last, it came, the question I was waiting for and dreading: *What about Germany? You live in Berlin? West or East? East? Under the regime? You lived there the whole time?*

Yes, madam. Under the regime. Silence around me. I felt that I was the foreigner. That my whole life and all my attempts to explain it converged, for a normal well-meaning American, on the single concept of the Regime, from which there was no escape, the way no beams of light can force their way out of a black hole in outer space.

The group had not noticed anything. They had changed the subject. Gottfried put forward the argument that what had made it possible for National Socialism to cling to power in Germany was not the rabble but the elites. Why didn't Max Planck go with his colleague, his brother, Albert Einstein, when Einstein had had to flee Germany? Counterargument: Max Planck helped a lot of Jews. Gottfried refused to allow it and named Gustav Gründgens as another example. The passionate debate continued.

I felt: Time has stood still for decades for these people. Nothing was in the past for them, nothing had been eased, no pain had lessened, no disappointment had faded, no anger had blown over. The one and only relief they found, if only for a few minutes, was to talk about it sometimes, to tell stories to someone who wanted to know, who listened, who sympathized and agreed that their feelings were right. That night it was I who had to be that Someone, not because of anything specific to me but simply because I was German, and younger. For the first time, I experienced the need refugees have to share, with a German, their neverending bewilderment. I stopped trying to defend myself against it and accepted my role.

The coffee was handed around; Willy and the other enormous, pure-bred dog were let in and walked around between the guests. It was time for anecdotes, of which Gottfried had an inexhaustible supply. He had served as a sergeant in a propaganda unit of the army during the war and was chosen to try to convince Albert Einstein to take part in an anti-Nazi film. The great physicist was eager to help but his accent was so dreadful—for example, he couldn't pronounce the word "such" except as "zootch"—that that was one reason the project never happened in the end. Still, Gottfried had admired the man deeply ever since. He had never met someone like that before and never since. People don't really know what he's like, Gottfried said. They always praise his modesty but that's nonsense: Einstein was never modest. He was just sure of himself. He had said so to Gottfried. All he needed for his work was a pencil and paper, then he performed his calculations and when an equation worked out then he was right and he didn't need anyone else's agreement or confirmation, and if not, then not.

Einstein had explained his theory of relativity to him once. It was while Gottfried was driving him back to Princeton. He should imagine, Einstein had told him, that he was in a closed box, without a window, that suddenly received a push so that he, in the box, was shoved against one side of the box. He might think, out of habit, that it was gravity but it wasn't gravity, only centrifugal force. Something like that, Gottfried said, full of emotion, and at the time, in the car on the road to Princeton, he had understood it. Or thought he understood it, because Einstein was firmly convinced that everyone would understand it. And we, sitting around the table, all thought for a minute that we understood it too.

Henry asked Ted, the German professor, who had said the least aside from me, what topic he was working on at the moment. We would laugh if he told us, he said. He was working with a group of students on aspects of literature in East Germany. Very practical, Henry said. A research field with a clearly marked beginning and end. —Yes, and this is precisely the right time to study it, Ted said, despite the overwhelming public hatred of East Germany. The way the West German media were treating GDR culture and its representatives these days really had only one possible explanation: it stemmed from a need to make up for what they had failed to do in settling their own accounts with Nazi cultural figures. In any case, that is what lies behind this campaign to equate Communism with Fascism. But especially in literature, in Ted's view, there was clear proof of how groundless the equals sign between the two really was. Marja agreed with him and gave examples, named authors and titles. When someone mentioned Brecht, I asked whether, buried in his work, preoccupied with worries about Germany, deep in discussion with colleagues and actors who were putting on his Galileo play—whether Brecht ever really paid attention to his city of refuge, Los Angeles.

Henry had only to walk over to his bookshelf, pull down a volume, and open it to a certain page. "Landscape of Exile."

The oil derricks and the thirsty gardens of Los Angeles
And the ravines of California at evening and the fruit market
Did not leave the messenger of misfortune
Unmoved.

Well, still, I thought. "Not unmoved" . . .

At that moment we all turned to look at the Polish essayist's wife, who had just let out a cry of pain. We crowded around her: Was she okay? No, she wasn't okay, it seemed to be a cramp. She was given some drops and had to be quickly taken home. That was the signal for a precipitous departure for all of us. Henry, who drove me back to the MS. VICTORIA, apologized for the sudden end to our evening. The evening had gone on long enough for me.

I could not fall asleep. I lay in my too-wide bed and couldn't stop the four lines of poetry stuck in my head from calling up other lines from my memory. "It's quite straightforward, anyone can understand it . . . you'll understand it. It's not hard. It's for your own good, so find out all about it." —That's what we did, Brecht, I thought, and it really did look so straightforward, so logical, in fact, yes, inevitable. There was this thing we wanted, a humane society, and all we had to do was dismantle the ruling class's ownership of the means of production, everyone would surely be happy to be able to live each according to his abilities, understanding, and reason. Was that not the age-old dream of humanity? It occurred to me that it was in fact here, in this utterly foreign place, only a couple of miles from the very room where I was now lying in a foreign bed, that Brecht, in his bare house of exile, put his Galileo into the conflict between loving the truth and being prepared to compromise. Oh, how well we knew that conflict! Was there anything in the world that would have brought us, or forced us, to recant? The Inquisition? We would have laughed at the Inquisition!

Finally the pills worked and I fell asleep. Then I was in one of my desolate dream houses, this time a hotel in a state of total chaos. I was on a patio surrounded by pieces of broken furniture. I started to straighten up, hauling all kinds of useless things from one corner to the other, but it didn't get any more organized or habitable. Outside a thick pane of glass was an unkempt, partly scorched bit of lawn where a woman was puttering around. She was pale and expressionless with ash-blond hair, carelessly dressed. She came closer and turned her face toward me, pressed it against the glass, and said, in a tone of giving instructions: Start from the other side! Waking up, I understood the dream: I shouldn't always start from the side of guilt when I straighten things up. But what gave this rather unattractive dream woman the right to tell me that? I was still laughing about it over breakfast.

It was Sunday. I sat down at my little machine and wrote:

What I am writing pushes forward in microscopic steps, against a resistance that pulls away from me when I try to name it.

Perhaps it is only a coincidence that just now a headline from today's paper comes to mind: "The Paper-Thin Veil over Barbarism." That is how a production of *Don Giovanni* struck one reviewer. Recently, another commentator warned the television audience that current events could develop into a far-reaching disaster for all of us. But that we thought that if the atomic bomb hasn't been dropped on us yet then none would go off in the future either.

A scare that keeps repeating itself loses strength, I said to Peter Gutman as we walked down Ocean Park Promenade. Do you remember how we panicked in every bone of our bodies when nuclear missiles were set up on both sides of the German-German border in the early eighties? And here, Peter Gutman said, we started hearing the phrase "Better dead than red."

Peter Gutman had convinced me to come to lunch at one of the nice restaurants. The *homeless people* were lying there again, in the California sun, alone or in groups, on the grassy traffic islands, some of them on padded blankets with the padding spilling out, in a deep, unconscious sleep; we walked past them as though we couldn't see them and tried to avoid the ragged wreck of a man who was always there, trapped in a loud conversation with himself and sometimes, quite suddenly, aggressive to people walking by. I surreptitiously observed all the different degrees of devastation and desensitization on display.

We were talking about the possible end of our civilization. But the bombs had not yet fallen on Baghdad then. The twin towers in New York had not yet been brought down. *"Nine eleven"* was not a date of terror yet.

God bless you, the half-blind black man in front of the door to the restaurant said when we paid him our toll. I only hope, I said, that there is no God and no Judgment Day, because he wouldn't bless any of us fat contented heartless white people, unless he really was only *our* God.

The restaurant was famous for its oysters. We ordered a dry California white to go with them.

Peter Gutman reproached me for constantly getting worked up about the old, well-known problem of the "blind spot." Every single one of our modern societies, based as they are on colonization, repression, and exploitation, has to block out certain parts of its history and deny as much of its present as possible too, in order to keep the self-assurance it needs to live. But one day it will all collapse, if we don't face reality, I said. Yes, well, Peter Gutman said. Sooner or later.

A word wandered through my head like a ghost, not for the first time: IRRGANG, "labyrinth" or "aberration," literally a "going astray." I thought that that would be a good title for a future piece of writing, it would fundamentally lead me in the right direction—no, force me in the right direction—and so then the question arose: Is that in fact where I want to go? Could I want that? The title fit too neatly: it remained a lonely title in search of its text. I knew it was there, that book, written in invisible ink in case it fell into the wrong hands. The writing would appear when held up to a special kind of light, I thought, it had to be not too bright and not too faint, but rather, and still I shied away from the word: Right. Fair. Just. One of those obsolete, discarded words, like boulders from prehistoric times that obstruct the smoothly flowing current of our new language.

Valentina, the Italian who had been at the CENTER for only a short time, got in touch with me and I was glad to hear from her. Her stay was coming to an end and she came to say goodbye. She was sparkling with life. With love of life. She had approached me with a kind of delight that disarmed me. We went to our Thai restaurant. Along the way, little cries escaped her at every new plant she discovered. She thought it was practically a sin to be given so much beauty to look at, she said. She was the type to cry out: *C'est génial!* —What is, Valentina? —*La vita*, she said. *La vie. Life. Das Leben.* And just like that, on humdrum Third Street, we found ourselves in the middle of a whole universe of brilliant, *génial* life. Valentina was a sorceress, though she didn't know it. We ate the sour seafood soup that Valentina loved. I considered her one of those people at peace with themselves, taking pleasure not only in others but in themselves, but now she wanted to tell me something different: how hard it was for her to avoid being dependent on other people and their opinions, for example her husband, to whom she had been too submissive for too long, and now she was in the middle of the long and difficult process of separating from him, and she had shied away from doing it for so long that she had almost lost her son over it, and now her husband had had a terrible accident and she had to ask herself if she had a right to leave him now.

Valentina? Downtrodden? Feeling guilty? I told her I would never have thought it of her and she said I thought other people were like me. Oh, Valentina! But now I couldn't rob her of this illusion too.

Then, without explaining the connection, she asked me: What do you think about death? —What do you mean, Valentina, I asked, to gain time. She wanted to know if death was really the end of everything, if that's what I believed. I do, I said, I remember, more flippantly than I would say it today. I do believe that but it doesn't bother me. Not yet, I thought at the time, and that "not yet" has since turned into a "now."

Then Valentina made an enigmatic face, but she obviously wanted me to ask her directly so that she could say what she believed. The body dies, she said, that's true. It disperses into its molecules and atoms and is taken back into the natural circulation of physical matter. The soul, though, the spirit, the energy, are indestructible, she said, and they are preserved in some form or other. Death has no power over them. I said: But we, you and I, as individual people, won't exist. Valentina admitted that. But maybe that wasn't so important. In any case, she found consoling, from a higher point of view, that something lasted and that it wasn't this solid mass, this clumsy opaque body. She much preferred the vivacious, joyful spirit.

I had no more counterarguments to offer. When we said goodbye, I asked Valentina if I had come across to her as very German. She said, unfortunately, yes: I seemed to her severe, single-minded, and thorough, which are textbook German characteristics, aren't they. And for that matter, my asking her whether I seemed typically German was itself typically German—could I imagine an Italian worrying about whether he seemed typically Italian? We laughed, gave each other a big hug, and had a hard time parting. We never saw each other again.

I still remember very well the time when I would have given a lot not to have to be German. But that's how it is for all of us, said Lutz, the blond Hamburg man from the '68 generation whom I ran into at the office. He, who was so much younger than me, knew this shame at being German? So that was something East Germans and West Germans had in common, not wanting to be German after the war? Absolutely, Lutz said. That's the only way to explain the rage of the younger generation at the time against the older generation.

I wondered, and asked him, if this was common ground that could be expanded and built upon. And, while we're at it: Build what? "A healthy sense of national pride," I read in the newspaper I had taken out of my mailbox. I showed it to Lutz, who snorted: Now, how are two parts of a single population, each of which compensated for a weak sense of self in completely different ways, supposed to produce a "healthy sense of national pride" when they're thrown together? Wouldn't each side have no choice but to put the blame for its own defects on the other side? So that it can gloat over the obvious weaknesses of the other? And to buoy up its own shattered self-confidence? Which was, in fact, what happened in the so-called Reunification.

It was us, after all, the East Germans, who had had to join the side of the eastern peoples after the war—the very people who had suffered the most under us, I said.

I cannot forget how, at the banquet for a delegation from the GDR at a Soviet collective farm, around a table piled high with food, between high-spirited toasts repeated over and over again to your health and happiness and welfare, never accusatory, the conversation was about the son who had been shot as a partisan by the Germans, the brother who had died in the war, the family next door that had been wiped out. And how the leader of your delegation—an old Communist who had acquired his uncompromising loyalty in the class struggle of the twenties and proven it in illegal activities and in jail, and who had meanwhile become a high-ranking, irredeemably narrow-minded functionary—how he burst out in an uncontrollable fit of tears when it was his turn to respond to the toasts of the Russians.

It was that scene which later made it hard for you to endure his rage and his opposition when it was time to speak out against him, sharply and thoroughly. Your petit-bourgeois upbringing has caught up to you, he allowed himself to shriek in your face; you were indulging in idiocy about humanity in place of the proper, class-struggle viewpoint, he was bitterly disappointed in you, you should expect no mercy from him. You thought about his time as a resistance fighter and your own time in the Hitler Youth and wished very much that your opposite views of what would be useful for "us" had not driven you farther and farther apart. You were standing in his enormous office, where you had been admitted with a permit and only after a thorough check by armed guards who followed you with alert eyes all the way to the paternoster elevator and whose comrades, likewise armed, were already waiting for you upstairs, so that they could check your ID against the permit yet again and then point the way through the endless, empty hallways and a series of anterooms that had their intended effect on you. Why did they need all that? Where did this fear, this paranoia, come from? Fear of a population that had done so much to them and whose smaller portion they now ruled. Now had to rule, without being able to rid themselves of their suspicion of this people. A cold fear came over you; you would not have been able to put it into words, not yet.

At the time, the issue was a book you had written whose publication the high-ranking comrade wanted to prevent because he considered it damaging. The book was important to you, it was a test of whether you could continue to live in this country or not. Then he shrieked at you. It went deeper than just this book and you both knew it. You parted, unreconciled, on the long walk to the door you fainted, and when you came to, his frightened face was above you.

I knew that Lutz had not lived through such scenes, and that I would not be able to make them comprehensible to him, even to him.

Doctor Kim did not let up, he asked me with a sanctimonious smile: *Can you cut down on your eating?* and I said yes, I said yes to everything Doctor Kim recommended, but I was not determined to follow all of his reasonable suggestions the way I had been at first, I wanted to be rid of him, I didn't want to restrict myself anymore, I wanted to live how I was used to and how I liked, and I also didn't want to tell him what I was thinking or feeling, but then he got me again after all by asking how my relationship with my mother had been: *Did you love her?* Again I said yes, that she had been a strong woman, I had loved her. Doctor Kim, with his dark face under a black head of hair, in his blue tracksuit, smiled as though he already knew everything I could tell him, and he stuck his needles in my back, hips, and legs. *Relax!* He turned off the light and left me to the stream of memories and thoughts flooding over me.

Mother's life. A strong woman, the strongest in the family, who unconsciously inculcated the message that nature had designed things so that women took charge and directed affairs in times of crisis. She always needed to know exactly which way the wind was blowing and to say it too. You did not grow up with a model for feminine submissiveness, I thought in my warm dark cell. Instead I saw that strength does not exclude goodness, but it goes with severity, against oneself too: not being weak, not revealing your weak points to anyone, adhering to self-mastery to the point of self-destruction. Not telling anyone about the tumor in her breast she had discovered until the family celebration was over, because she did not want to disturb it. Later, you could not help but imagine the growth of the tumor during those lost weeks, again and again, while Mother lay in the hospital, still self-controlled, or while she gave off a strange smell after radiation treatment. When you told her one day, distraught and flustered, that soldiers from the Warsaw Pact states had crushed the Prague Spring, she answered—she who was dying: "There are more important things." But it was important to you, maybe too important, maybe the truly important things hadn't been important enough to you for a long time. I was very tired, I heard the sound of the sea, was I by the sea?

Were you sleeping? Doctor Kim had turned on the light. My face was streaming with tears and Doctor Kim wordlessly handed me a tissue. *Don't worry*, he said. *Be careful*. While I was getting dressed I heard, from very far away, the sound of the sea. A recording. Something Doctor Kim used to help his patients relax.

I left. On Wilshire Boulevard I noticed that I was pain-free, praised be Doctor Kim. I crossed the street to the enormous, conspicuous *drugstore* I had noticed for a long time and now finally wanted to investigate. I appreciatively strolled past the kilometer-long aisles between shelves filled with dozens of cleaning supplies for every imaginable purpose and some unimaginable ones too, all there to make our bathrooms and kitchens and stairwells and floors gleam with germ-freedom. I wandered up and down the narrow aisles lined with perfumes, creams, soaps, deodorants, shower gels, leg and body lotions, shampoos, and hair dyes, again in countless varieties—who in the world was supposed to wash, cleanse, and perfume with all of this stuff and beautify with all these foundations, lipsticks, and mascaras? I thought the contents of all the little bottles and jars and packets in all these *drugstores* would be enough to cover the entire globe with lather and then, cleansed, thoroughly rinsed with ocean water, there would be enough creams and lotions to make it ready for a *party*. Maybe the especially numerous anti-aging products would smooth the deep wrinkles and furrows of our old planet, I thought. But first things first: the products to care for our sensitive furniture, detergent for our clothes and linens. I couldn't help think about how parsley and vinegar, Ata, laundry soap, and soft soap had been enough for my grandmother, a cleanly woman. She washed herself with Palmolive and never in her life had a bathroom. I can still see her, standing in the steam of the laundry room: how she scrubbed the whole family's laundry on a board while Grandfather slaved away over the hot water in a large cauldron over the fire, with an old-fashioned implement that does not exist anymore.

I had asked too much from my joints, of course; I got back into the bus, which had to wait while a big motorcycle rally thundered past in front of us, young riders in black leather outfits, the black woman on the seat next to me shook her head in disapproval, what was the English word for "*Rücksicht*"? no, these young people showed no *consideration* on their mighty machines, but why should they? Why shouldn't they show off their strength and superiority to everyone?

I rode down Wilshire Boulevard, straight as an arrow, toward the Pacific, exhilarated as always by the light that I never, never wanted to forget and that now, even so, I can call up only a pale reflection of. I remembered a large official gathering in one of the grand new cultural offices built next to the big nationalized companies. It must have been in the early sixties. A high-ranking business functionary had given a speech on basic principles and mentioned in his speech that young people were complaining about the shortage of motorcycles, and he had prophetically cried out that you, comrades, you too would very soon be able to supply your youth with motorcycles built in your very own factories! But you, as usual, had to be clever, you had to make yourself jump up and ask for the floor and march to the podium to contradict him: Surely this cannot be our goal, comrades! Surely you do not want to overtake the capitalist countries in the production of trivial consumer goods! You should focus on other values, redirect the desires of the youth toward more important goals. I see, the speaker said, good-humoredly, so you're scared to ride a motorcycle? You crept back to your seat amid the laughter of the auditorium.

I could not help but think about the masses of people, my countrymen and countrywomen, who, in the early days after the opening of the Wall, picked up their welcome money and returned happy from their first visits to the West, with bags and pockets and boxes full of purchases that had been utterly out of reach until then. That was what really mattered, at the core. But what did I know back then?

The lounge slowly filled up, one person after another came in, took some tea, started talking to the people sitting next to them. Even Peter Gutman was there, with his long skull hidden behind a copy of the *Times* and not taking part in the general discussion of electoral predictions until I spoke to him directly and got him to express his conviction that it didn't matter who won since nothing would change the underlying social relations and most people didn't even want them to change: not the members of the ruling and possessing class, from a natural and well-developed instinct of self-preservation, and not the others, since they had successfully been convinced that they already lived in the best of all possible worlds. Or didn't.

At that we all fell silent, until Pintus, of all people—our young Swiss man—hesitantly put forward that he was not a stranger to radical ways of thinking, not at all, he himself had been a member of a Maoist group in Zurich in his youth, but since then he had decided once and for all in favor of more differentiated views. For example, he thought that even incremental change could have an effect. Peter Gutman politely turned to him and asked: What effect? Yes, well, Pintus reflected— his short, spiky hair was sticking straight up as always, and he was wearing his usual jeans and jeans jacket—in any case, new and hitherto unused forces were coming into play that dared to scratch away at the privileges of the elite. Younger critical spirits, he said in German, with his thick Swiss accent, would get a chance. Really? Peter Gutman said. And how long would that last? Until they acquired the same privileges themselves?

He really knew how to kill a conversation. Nor did he return to the topic when we walked back to the MS. VICTORIA together. Suddenly he started talking about how anxious he had been not to let a single word of German escape him in school, even though he spoke German at home with his mother. Who was, by the way, the only member of the family who showed something like homesickness.

What does that have to do with the election results? I asked, as we walked into the MS. VICTORIA past the three alert raccoons and waved to Mr. Enrico, who was extremely happy to see us. Think about it, Peter Gutman said, as we climbed the stairs. He said goodbye at my door; no, no drink today. He seemed to be very tired, and I felt a stir of bad conscience without understanding why.

The *Enterprise* hurtled forth into the unknown universe once again, and I could not understand why I wasn't able to enjoy it as much as usual. Two hours later, Peter Gutman phoned. It seemed to me he had been drinking. Am I bothering you? —No. He said: What did we actually mean by those "Western values" of ours that other cultures were supposed to admire and respect us for? I was taken by surprise and said nothing. Peter Gutman said: Think about it, Madame. But that night there was nothing I wanted to do less.

The next day was overcast, a Sunday, and the television preacher cried, no, shrieked at his enormous congregation: *Your sins are forgiven!* and the congregation gave a loud groan with isolated cries of *Yeah! Oh Lord!* The preacher strode like a lion-tamer in front of the first row, in costume, wearing a handsome purple robe that flowed out behind him, and now he was asking the congregation: Which is the greater miracle? When Jesus says to the cripple, Stand up and walk! or when he says to us all: Your sins are forgiven! Then the famous preacher walked down the center aisle, toward the camera, and spoke to individual believers—to a black woman: What do you think, sister! and to a well-dressed white man: And you, brother, you haven't thought about that yet, have you!— and they could all feel with every fiber of their bodies what had to come next, I felt it too, they all feverishly longed for the saving word that they were about to hear, and wanted to hear from him, since only he, the chosen preacher in his purple robe, standing up at the front again, elevated on the steps next to a giant tree with yellow flowers on the branches: only he could pronounce this word. At last, in a well-rehearsed movement, he raised the Bible up to the heavens and cried: As God is my witness! There is no greater miracle under the sun than the forgiveness of sin!

Yeah! cried the congregation with one voice, tears of emotion streaming over their faces, they burst into applause, the ritual had worked, purification had occurred. On Sunday mornings the streets of American cities are filled with purified men and women silently gliding by in their oversize cars but the real temples, the department stores and supermarkets, do not close for a minute, as though people were afraid that if consumption were interrupted for even a second, if the cycle of money into goods into money came to a halt for even the briefest possible moment, the organism that calls itself society and is on life support would immediately collapse from withdrawal.

I sat down at my little machine and wrote:

The quest for paradise has always and everywhere led
to the creation of hell on earth. Is there an incontrovertible law at work here? That would be worth looking

into. It would also be worthwhile to consider why the belief so prevalent here—that there is a solution to every problem, a remedy for every ailment, a relief for every suffering, a cure for every sickness—creates a feeling of unreality, even uncanniness, and can easily tip over into madness.

I reached for the red folder with L.'s letters. I realized that I always reached for that folder when I needed consolation. The letters were not separated by equal intervals of time—the third letter is dated June 1948. It is one of the longest, most detailed letters in the group, clearly answering questions and responding to opinions that Emma had sent to her old friend. L. writes that she is not surprised that she and Emma are once again puzzling over the same problems, after all, that's how it always was before too.

> Of course your experience in prison and my experience in exile are hardly comparable. But they seem to have at least one thing in common: the feeling of otherness they produced in us. However critical we were, however radically we opposed that society in earlier years, we were part of it—maybe it was especially because of our critique that we belonged to it.
>
> But the moment my train crossed the German-French border in April 1933, this otherness descended upon me, never to leave me again, and it seems from your letter that the exact same thing happened to you when the prison gates shut behind you. We were Outside. If I read your letter correctly—the subtext too, my dear, which is often the main text with you—you too can never shake off this feeling of being a stranger to the countrymen and countrywomen who locked you away and kept their distance from you. I want to tell you right now that this is one of the reasons why I did not go back "home": I knew that I could never be at home again among those people.
>
> But of course you know my other reason: I could never leave this continent without my dear gentleman. I will never be able to leave him. Whatever reasons I try to come up with for why that is: that's how it is.

Did this letter give me the consolation I was looking for? In some ways. The thought occurred to me that Emma's loyalty to her Party, whose errors she recognized and ruthlessly expressed, had to do with her need to feel at home at least somewhere, since everywhere else had become alien to her. Was I too always alien to her?

TO LOOK INTO MY OWN OTHERNESS

was something I had avoided for a long time, until now.

A song came back to me, from a cycle of songs that accompanied you in an especially dark year. You had put on the record multiple times a day. My memory supplied me with the first verse, the melody too:

> As a stranger I arrived
> As a stranger I shall leave
> It was a perfect day in May
> How bright the flow'rs, how cool the breeze
> The girl, she spoke of love
> The mother e'en of marriage
> But now the world is full of woe
> The path ahead all covered in snow

A friend had sent you the record. He felt you needed it. He laconically compared the era in which Schubert had set Wilhelm Müller's *Winterreise* poems to music—the restoration period after the Carlsbad Decrees of 1819, the dark years before the Revolution of 1848—with the restoration period you all had ended up in, which had plunged you into a depression. He was trying to tell you: We're not the first! But you had discovered that already, on your long walks in the area around the hospital, in the forest where both of you had been treated for your psychosomatic complaints with a lot of water and raw fruits and vegetables, but above all by being "taken out of circulation," as the chief doctor put it. No one could imagine today how laboriously, in what tiny steps, against what inner resistance, and over how long a span of time your thoughts had had to struggle. You remember to this day the way the light fell into the sheltered pine forest you were walking past when your friend said: So, now we know: This state is a tool for domination like every other state. And this ideology is like every other ideology: false consciousness. We can't keep our illusions about that anymore. You stopped in your tracks. You asked: What are we supposed to do? Then the two of you said nothing for a long time, and then your friend said: Behave ourselves.

I wrote:

How clear everything is in hindsight. How there is no way, no effort you can make, to see the pattern that underlies appearances when you are stuck in the middle of it. Because the blind spot covers the center of insight and recognition.

I headed out to the coastal promenade and looked out across the Pacific Ocean, where the islands of Japan were floating, far beyond the horizon. I looked for a long time at a big family of African-Americans enjoying themselves in the water, how the women gathered their skirts and ran into the gentle waves again and again, accompanied by delighted screams from the children, I could not get enough of that boy, maybe ten years old, beside himself with joy, hopping and dancing and squealing. We don't have that, I thought, envious. Self-control is a kind of domination too, just over oneself.

From the Santa Monica Pier I had before my eyes the full curve of Malibu Bay, the soft green odorless sea with its white fringe of foam, the ocher-colored sand, the white row of houses in the foreground, the dark green hills farther back, and finally, carefully set apart in a different color, the sharp mountain range jutting up in the background. And up above, unbelievably, flawlessly blue, the sky.

It hurt. Everything hurt. It had come to that point again. Alone and full of fear, I saw on TV the crash of the Israeli plane into two Amsterdam skyscrapers. Peter Gutman knocked on the door; he had seen it too. We didn't want to talk so we sat there together and watched a movie about an important English art historian whom Peter Gutman knew about and who, we now learned, had been a Soviet spy (and a homosexual). Her Majesty the Queen had even honored him with an audience once, in which the conversation turned to propriety and morality, and the scholar had spoken in impressive, moving formulations—

moving for anyone who knew his situation. But then, of course, his cover was blown, he admitted everything, they promised to protect him but then broke their promise and threw him to a public lusting for blood and destroyed his life. To the extent that it wasn't he himself who had destroyed his life; that was a fair objection. It was almost unbearable to see him on-screen in person at the end, an old, broken man, and to watch him respond to the intrusive questions with which they pressured him.

I don't have the stomach for that, I said, and I turned off the TV. I have that reaction a bit too often these days, by the way, I said to Peter Gutman, and I realize it's just a phase I'm in, or the times are in, or maybe it's that the brutality of the times and my oversensitive taste are colliding again, but I turn off the TV or look away when enormous crowds level their curses in Allah's name against us, the whites, or when men in white protective suits collect the dead birds from the Baltic coast. The fact that some—no: most—of it could have been pre-dicted is no consolation. Maybe I don't know what's right and what's wrong anymore. What's good and what's evil. I catch myself feeling pity for the wrong people if I see them as having lost.

Better that than no pity at all, Peter Gutman said. And anyway, ex-cuse me, which of us is the Christian here? If someone strikes you on the right cheek, who's the one supposed to turn him your other one? You move within the core of your system of values, Madame. Don't forget.

And you? An eye for an eye, a tooth for a tooth?

We didn't have a Bible at home. In any language. We were three brothers. Our parents rarely told us not to do something, and almost never made us do anything, except follow certain rules of behavior so that we wouldn't give ourselves away as German on the street. And when boys in school called me a Nazi, I never said anything at home. That was our prime directive: Protect Mother. My father? He practi-cally didn't speak at all after going into exile. He came home at night from his hard, badly paid factory job, we ate, and not much by the way. Then the dishes were cleared and my father spread his books out on the table and got to work on his elaborations of nineteenth-century German literature. He never published a word. I don't think there could possibly be another human being for whom it meant more to be German and who was more deeply disappointed, hurt, and embittered when the Germans kicked him out. I wasn't born yet when the family, already poor enough, had to find their way in a foreign country, and in those circumstances, after the war had started, you can imagine how my parents welcomed a third child.

Silence. Then I said: Do you have a tape recording that runs in your head night and day too?

Oh dear Lord, Peter Gutman said. I'm a champion at that. If you only knew what goes round and round in my head like a broken record, day and night.

Well, what, Monsieur? If one may ask.

You know, always the same thing. That year after year I never accomplish anything except to systematically waste my life. What do you say to that?

Maybe you and I can agree that rhetorical questions do not require an answer.

Okay, okay. As you probably know, I'm almost fifty, Peter Gutman said.

Which I hope we'll celebrate with a good bottle of California wine.

And I'm in limbo like a twenty-year-old. I haven't made a life for myself. Not married. No children, even though I want children. No long-term relationship with a woman, not even a professional career worth mentioning.

Objection, Your Honor.

Come on. Okay, yes! I've been obsessed with my philosopher for twenty years, I pore over his every move, no matter how obscure, even though he himself left behind nothing but fragments. I ask you, do we really need much familarity with Herr Freud to find it neurotic, this unquenchable need to express myself through another, to take refuge behind another person? A person who crushes me. Who has burrowed his way inside me, the same way I've burrowed into him, we are inextricably tangled together. I can't get rid of him and he, perversely, prevents me from finishing the book about him in which I want to find both immortality and the grave.

How. How does he prevent you?

I've thought about that for a long time. I think it's his perfection. The fact that he left behind nothing but fragments is precisely the sign of his search for perfection. He would have seen a complete text as a lie, because it presupposes a complete world. Nothing would have seemed worse to him. And so what made me decide to write my book about someone who never worked his thoughts and insights into a system and never published a book in his lifetime? Wasn't that presumptuous of me? Even more since his basic thought is that our culture will never recover from its deepest fall. We are living in end times.

That was the first time Peter Gutman talked to me at length about his philosopher.

I also asked him that night if it was really true that he had never had a deep relationship with a woman.

No, I have, he said. Just then he was in the deepest relationship with a woman you could imagine. But also the most pointless, as both of them had known from the beginning. She would never leave her husband and children. They had decided just two weeks ago not to call each other anymore. And now he was terribly depressed, had severe panic attacks, and woke up every morning with a feeling of terror.

You didn't let it show, I said.

I've had lots of practice at not letting things show, since I was very young. And now, good night, Madame. Don't brood. That's some good advice from a professional brooder.

He left. I cried. He would never want to know why. Everyone who got close to him and wanted to stay close to him had to abide by a tacit agreement not to force open the *understatement* in operation. I realized that I had fulfilled this requirement against my will up until that point. It couldn't continue like that. I decided that I had to, very carefully, even lovingly, scratch away at the armor he had intentionally built up around himself over the years. You thought you had a man standing in front of you but it was really just armor.

I picked up my copy of Thomas Mann's diaries. Ever since I had driven up to his house with a group of other scholars—1550 San Remo Drive, Pacific Palisades, where by the way there was no plaque about the famous first resident of the house whose entrance we crowded around—and had followed his afternoon walk down to Ocean Park, I read his diaries with even greater interest. I came across the place where he wrote, in his notes for his 1949 Goethe speech:

Nevertheless, if we take into account certain intimate confessions like that in his letter to Frau von Stein at the time of his winter journey to the Harz Mountains: "How deeply I fell in love again, on this dark train, with the class of people they call 'lower' but who are surely highest before God . . ."; if we also take into account what he says in *Hermann and Dorothea* about the inspiring freedom and higher—"higher"!—equality, and the fact that he thoroughly familiarized himself with the theories of the French socialist Saint Simon shortly before the end of his life; then we arrive at strange questions. I am not absolutely certain—it is just a suspicion, but I want to express it— whether Goethe today would be directing his gaze more toward Russia than toward America. I immediately counter this suspicion with Goethe's rejection of despotism. But it is well known that this aversion broke down when he was faced with the phenomenon of Napoleon, and who knows what it might break down in the face of today. The question, after all, is how the act of losing oneself in a crowd of people following well-ordered rules—which was, if not his ideal, then at least his vision— could play out in any circumstances other than under the control of a state and a certain despotism. His bright spirit certainly did not labor under any illusions about the fact that more and more would happen under the new social relations involving the "government-free sphere" that liberalism insists on, and I would not be surprised if he was occupied, even back then, with the question of whether freedom of learning and art might not be better preserved in a state that is not itself the instrument of private interests than in one that depends upon private interests.

Who still asks such questions today? Who would dare to speak them out loud?

Now, more than a decade and a half later, I read similar questions in some newspapers, brought to the surface by a CRISIS that is actually the collapse I was anticipating in a more distant future. Still, the collapse of the banking system, which is in turn the lifeblood of an economic system we are suddenly allowed to call "capitalism" again, is being attributed as much as possible to psychological causes: individual bankers' and executives' unquenchable lust for money. Yesterday I heard that a group of neurological researchers has apparently discovered a gene that is responsible for the greed for money and possessions, through a complicated system of rewards in the brain, so that anyone in the clutches of this gene can do almost nothing to overcome his wild, selfish spirit of enterprise. The way to solve the problem, they said, would be to intersperse bearers of the greed gene with other personnel, accountant types, in the leadership of certain businesses.

What would John and Judy have said about the socioeconomic conditions today, if they could have predicted them at the time? We were sitting in our café on Seventeenth Street again, where we had a regular table and knew the menu and each ordered our favorite salad. The bright-eyed young black waitress knew us and smiled when we came in, which was nice.

John had picked me up. We were going to drive out with Judy for an evening with her friends who had invited me to visit them, most of them members of the "second generation." We would have to postpone our discussion of Thomas Mann, John said. I said that there was another fact almost precisely as interesting as this astonishing passage, and that is the fact that Mann left it out of the final version of his Goethe speech. Maybe he was right not to expose himself to the predictable criticisms, I said. "Communism" would have been the least of the accusations. Did John and Judy know about the scandal around Mann's tour of Germany in 1949? No. In America, they said, Communism was a rotting corpse, deader than dead. Even though hysterical anti-Communism raged just below the surface.

John said that his long-lost cousin living on Karl-Marx-Allee in Berlin was now starting to be interested in Communism again. Not GDR Communism, of course, that wasn't what he meant. He meant the same rational Communism that they, John and Judy, meant too. Oh you dear things! I said, and I thought: Now, that is a big topic, and in treading that terrain we wore down the soles of our shoes and then the soles of our feet too. I thought I could see their eyes, especially John's, shine with the same naiveté that we all must have had in our eyes once. At some point the light would go out in his too.

In the car, Judy explained to me that in her view the descendants of the murdered Jews and the descendants of the Germans who had perpetrated or witnessed the crimes had something in common: Their parents had refused to talk with them about the past. I protested: But it's totally different. In fact, they're exact opposites! Keeping silent about crimes you committed or not being able to talk to your children about the atrocities and humiliations to which you were subjected. They both insisted that these two kinds of silence, so opposite in content, created similar patterns in the relationships between parents and children.

We were driving through a nice neighborhood I had never been to, and we stopped in front of a *middle-class* house on a side street, climbed a short flight of stairs, and arrived at an apartment with all the lights on, furnished like the apartment of a West German lawyer or head-master, where people of various ages were crowded into the room. A delicate blonde in her mid-fifties, the host, came up to us and said, in German: My name is Ruth. Welcome. And added in English: *I was a hidden child.*

The sentence hit me hard. I understood immediately what it meant: a child who had been hidden away from the Germans. It was a dreadful story, one of the many I would hear. When I think back to that evening, I see one person after another coming up to me, glass in hand, and softly talking to me. I saw in their eyes, more than once, the absurd hope that a miracle might occur, somehow, the abyss their life had plummeted into might somehow close, and the never-ending pain might somehow get at least a little easier to bear, if someone shared this pain with them. No, not "someone": a German. Most of them had never been to Germany or—the older ones—never been back to Germany. I was silent. There was nothing to say, nothing to explain, no way to make up for anything. There was nothing to put right—nothing would ever be "right" again.

What about Germany today? The question was inevitable and I was inwardly prepared for it. I remember I tried hard to stay objective. The fall of the Wall. Yes. A historical event that—I hesitated to admit it—was not expected or intended by the demonstrators themselves. I quoted the phrases on banners, phrases that had wilted meanwhile. The eu-phoria of the transitional period. I didn't want to disappoint the people here, who expected to hear that everyone was happy in unified Ger-many. No, there was nothing in their newspapers about disappoint-ments. Nothing about losses. It would have seemed petty for me to talk about them here.

But then there was a lawyer who apparently had German clients. He knew that thousands of former property owners who had lived in West Germany a long time and received compensation for their losses were demanding their land and houses back, where East Germans had often been living for decades, believing in good faith that they had le-gally, properly bought or had use of the property. That's true, I said, and had no choice but to bring up the legal doctrine of "restitution rather than compensation." John was incensed. No one here knew anything about that! Just imagine that happening in another country! I tried to explain that the former owners and their heirs insisted on their claims with the best conscience in the world, because private property was for them one of the highest possible values you could aspire to.

And for you? someone asked. The East Germans? I said we had accustomed ourselves to not considering private property so sacred, and even when we rejected the GDR, many East Germans subscribed to the opinion that the common good should take precedence over profit.

I quietly said to John that these different relationships to property were probably at the root of the "division in the mind" that everyone was always describing. John said: You must not be the only ones seeing your way of life called into question—the West Germans must feel their own ways of thinking about things under attack too. I thought that was a point well worth thinking about.

What was really important for the guests that evening was something else: There was right-wing violence against asylum seekers in the news, especially in eastern Germany. Could I explain that? I half-heartedly tried to explain the circumstances that gave rise to such violence, with many circumlocutions. I saw that no one was convinced.

At the end of the evening, two young people came up to me, a couple: he a German, she an American Jew. They wanted advice. They were planning to emigrate to Germany, where he had the prospect of a good job as a chemist, but now they were wondering if it was irresponsible to take their child to that country. I was horrified. Was I from some barbaric land you couldn't justifiably bring children to? I told them their information was definitely one-sided, and I for one would be happy if they came, but I couldn't decide for them. I evaded the question.

Ruth drove me home. I could tell that she wanted to talk and I didn't know if I wanted to hear what she had to say: Ruth's father, a German Jew who spoke perfect French, was able to flee to Alsace in 1933 with his family and pass as a Frenchman. When the Germans invaded, they had no place to hide. To save at least the child, they put Ruth in a nunnery. No one suspected a Jew in the little blond girl. For months she was a hidden child, abandoned by her parents. And that's what I remained, Ruth said, as we drove down the freeway through a city that was never dark, never slept—even after my parents found a way out for all of us and came to get me. She had stayed a hidden child to this day. Could I imagine what that was like? She had finally stopped blaming and accusing her mother: stopped telling her that she, Ruth, would never have given away her child, under any circumstances. I said nothing.

Obviously, Ruth said, steering her car through an area I knew, obviously she understood exactly the tragic situation her parents were in at the time. My head understands everything, *you know*, she said. But in her deepest core, the wound that her parents' repudiation had inflicted upon her had never healed, she could never forget it and never forgive it. Never forgive her own parents, Ruth said, with tears running down her face. She blames them instead of cursing the Germans who did it to them. It would not have taken much, Ruth said, for her to go crazy from the upside-down world in her head. At first she couldn't accept her own child, her son, she said. Did I have any idea what that meant? Only after a long course of therapy—from a woman who had emigrated from Germany, by the way, who had become her close friend but then sadly died a few years ago—only with her help had she learned to understand what was going on inside her. Now she was a psychologist herself.

Back at the apartment, the first thing I did was reach for the red folder. Never before, it seemed to me, had I so deeply regretted never having met L. I imagined very precisely how she would have looked: striking features showing little effect of age, gray hair combed back, medium-tall at most in stature, not thin and not fat, always in motion. Classically dressed in good fabrics and muted colors, unlike Emma, who cared little about her appearance. Emma must have brought up L.'s predilection for nice clothes in one of her letters, must have called it a "bourgeois relic." L. replied in her letter of February 1949—a month when I was preparing for my final exams in a small town in Thuringia—by asking if Emma had forgotten that her dear gentleman valued that way of dressing in women. "And why," she went on:

> And why wouldn't I give him this little thing when there were other things I had to refuse him? For example, I went to Spain during the Civil War even though my dear gentleman was strictly against it—not because he thought the struggle against Franco

wasn't good and right and necessary, but because I shouldn't put myself in danger, he thought, I wasn't made for a "heroic attitude."

He did not risk a break with me and I went to Spain as a journalist. Then, of course, he greedily read the articles I wrote and collected every one. Later I saw that he had worked my reports into his reflections on the sources of inhumanity in our culture, a topic he was obsessed with and that always dragged him down into hopelessness, more and more, a hopelessness I couldn't share with him and didn't want to.

We lived in great poverty in Paris, by the way, like most émigrés. My dear gentleman lived off his wife, as he so often did later too. She had a job as a cleaning lady for a rich French family and gave German lessons to their sons. Dora is a very remarkable woman, in all those years she never swerved for a second from her conviction that it was her task to keep this man alive. And in all these years she has never once shown the slightest trace of petty jealousy about our relationship. My dear gentleman is bound tightly to Dora, he will never leave her, and I would never want him to.

It was one of the longer letters L. wrote to Emma, typed in faint ink on American-size white paper, rather less hastily, it seemed to me, than many of her other letters. Not for the first time, I now tried, at my long dining table in my California apartment, to read between this woman's lines and pick up a trace of the worry, self-denial, and constant renunciation that love must have imposed on her too. And I tried to imagine the content of those decades-long conversations between her and her "dear gentleman."

And me? Wasn't I, barely twenty years old, already firm in the conviction I had recently taken from certain writings of classic authors? Obviously my conviction was: REVOLUTION. Revolution was the only way to liberate mankind. Your math and physics teacher, a refugee from the east who was stranded in that Thuringian small town just like you—deeply intelligent, somewhat inscrutable, but for that very reason an especially fascinating man, who stood out from the other, fossilized teachers there—had recommended those revolutionary writings to you and noticed, not without satisfaction, how they made you see that the world must be not only interpreted but fundamentally changed. He had accepted citizenship without hesitation, while you decided to join the Party that had just this fundamental change as part of its platform. And then, to make it a typical story of those early years: it turned out later that this teacher, who had been promoted to principal by then due to his incontrovertible abilities, had earlier worked in Goebbels's ministry. He had kept it secret. He was demoted and transferred to a small country school. But even though the news hit you hard, you did not imagine for a moment that he had betrayed his students, had betrayed you, by not believing the doctrine he recommended to you, nor did you think that he had ever believed the insane doctrines of his former masters. He was too smart for that, you thought.

I paged through Thomas Mann's diaries and found the entry I was looking for: March 31, 1949, near the date of L.'s letter. "In the afternoon, an hour-long speech from Churchill in Boston, embarrassing in its falsehood, gross flattery of America's sense of noble victimhood, glorification of the Cold War, trite propaganda against the Russians . . . The whole thing depressing, even if it is exactly as it must be."

I wondered if you had heard the term "Cold War" back in the spring of 1949; I didn't remember. You stayed up late in your basement room, whose window gave you a view of the high thin church tower of the little town and the overwhelming starry sky, working on an essay for a contest. The topic: "Revolutions: Necessity or Historical Excess?" You made the case for "Necessity" and won a prize, and were allowed to go to Weimar for the Goethe Youth Festival, where you saw Lothar Müthel as Mephistopheles and heard Grotewohl, the future prime minister, give a speech under the slogan: "You must rise or fall / Suffer or triumph / Be the anvil or the hammer."

Jena. The old university from whose lecture halls you could look out at the paths Goethe and Schiller used to stroll down together. Your docents traced out the lines of thought from the edifices of these two down to you: Progress and reaction, they have always faced off in the struggle against each other. You can still see yourself sitting with the others around the square table in the seminar room, surrounded by bookshelves, you can hear the young docent talk enthusiastically about Georg Lukács, whose theories made you see that what mattered was Realism, what else was there, and you and the class enthusiastically drank in his arguments and could not imagine how anyone could judge literature differently.

You and G. read Remarque's *Arch of Triumph* at night—this book, of all books, was the first of the hundreds you have read together since. You had borrowed it for a few days, you both gulped it down and forgot to categorize it as Progressive or maybe a little Reactionary after all, it was deep in the heart of winter, the two of you walked down ice-cold, badly lit streets late at night across the Saale bridge, the wind whistled in your faces, the moon hung low in the sky above the chain of hills, you ran into hardly anyone, you talked about Remarque.

I sat in my apartment in the MS. VICTORIA, there was a movie on TV about two formidable women who had devoted themselves to studying chimpanzees and gorillas, I followed their patient attempts to get close to a troop of gorillas, and another train of thought took me into other seminar rooms where, forty years earlier, your docent, who had had to leave Germany in the thirties as a Communist and a Jew and had returned there, to you, to work with you, was so alive and convincing that I never forgot her class on the so-called Sturm und Drang movement, an early-bourgeois antifeudal movement. You identified with the young men of back then who rejected the demands of absolutism, their watchwords were Nature! Freedom! and they cunningly defended themselves against censorship, for example, the young Goethe had had his "Prometheus" bound into his volume of poetry in such a way that they could remove the poem, if the censor insisted, without damaging the rest of the book. "I know of nothing poorer under the sun than you, you Gods"—ha, that atheist! that loather of princes! this Goethe was your man, and your blossoming dreams grew ripe. Yes, said the docent you worshipped, maybe he wasn't quite a revolutionary, our Goethe, but still, he had always exerted a little pressure on a faraway end of the lever—he said so himself. You, though, in your advanced era of progress, held the lever in both hands and would never let it go.

This docent, who had opened your eyes to the fact that even the most delicate love poem was embedded in a social fabric—thirty years later, when she had grown old and was teaching in another city, she had her students draw up a resolution in which you were accused of ideological capitulation. You could not brush that one aside as easily as some of the others.

Eventually, after a long time, both of these women researching and getting to know the behavior of chimpanzees and gorillas on opposite sides of the world were trusted enough by the respective primate groups that they could get very close to them without producing a flight response or aggressive reaction. I watched them sympathetically, almost with envy.

In the other train of thought that continued to run without stopping, I saw the exhibition in the Weimar Castle, "Society and Culture in the Age of Goethe," that you used to lead groups of visitors through during school holidays. I saw you and G. sitting in the assemblies, I heard the speakers, who said that the class struggle was intensifying, you had to prepare to face critical situations. However much we hated the war, he said, pacifism was practically suicidal nowadays; your readiness to defend the Republic must not be mere lip service; in short: you had to learn how to use a gun. Suddenly it was totally silent in the room.

That night, you and a comrade of yours went back up the hill to the Nietzsche House, where you were living. She said: I never wanted to hold a gun in my life. Then you could see before your eyes the heaps of guns that the defeated soldiers of the German army had thrown into ditches in the streets, in April 1945, streets your fugitive caravan passed by; none of you touched any of the weapons but the concentration camp inmates who were being marched north along some of the same roads, on a death march from the Sachsenhausen camp, picked up guns they were barely strong enough to carry and took up positions on the high ground above the valleys through which you were walking.

You said to the leader of the assembly: I have a child. He said: I know. Don't you want to protect your child? Think carefully. You phoned your mother and said you had to hear your child's voice even though she couldn't talk yet. The following day, every one of you said to the leader: Yes, you would take part in the weapons training. I don't remember if you were ever actually required to. That was in 1953. You were twenty-four years old.

The ancient gestures of the apes, suggesting human gestures, moved me and I was gripped as I followed the story on-screen of how "Melissa," a stray female ape with a child, tried to gain entry into the group, making the meek, submissive gestures that we, I thought, knew only too well—how she carefully touched the senior group member, the alpha male, on his shoulder after they had sat quietly together for a long time, then finally reached for his hand and brought it to her mouth several times, "kissed" it, and then, with infinite patience, sought the acceptance of the group of females too, until at last, I was touched and relieved to see, she was peacefully squatting between the others with her child on her lap.

I called Peter Gutman, I had to ask him if he knew that apes could kiss. He said no, he had not known that. What he did know, he said, was that he had unlearned the ability to kiss. Or did I think that kisses over the phone could replace real kisses?

No, I said, I certainly don't, and Peter Gutman was pleased that we were in agreement. It's not a real life, he said. And yet it's the one we're all forced to live. Unreal even in our private lives.

Hello, Monsieur? I cried. Don't go overboard. You think that some original has been lost on the long road from the apes to *Homo sapiens*? The original form of life? Of love?

It seems that way sometimes, Peter Gutman said. For example: If this wonderful woman across the ocean that I talk to longingly on the phone for hours were suddenly here in front of me, would I even know what to do? Who could promise me that? Isn't it possible that I need this absurd situation, this absurd suffering at our inability to be together, in order to keep her at arm's length? The same way I need my insane perfectionism to keep me from finishing the book about my philosopher.

Well, that is all rather *sophisticated*, Monsieur, I said, and I thought: What are we talking about here?

Sophisticated? Peter Gutman sighed and admitted it. Otherwise I don't talk about it at all, he said, and I asked: Why with me?

Because you are unhappy yourself and you understand unhappiness.

Me? Unhappy? What makes you think that? I've never said anything of the sort.

Exactly, Peter Gutman said. Do you have something to drink there? Okay. Sleep well.

I turned off the TV, then the lights. I sat in the dark and heard the MS. VICTORIA breathe. After a long time I went to the kitchen and made myself a margarita, I took it and put it on the narrow shelf next to the telephone, I did not bother to calculate the time difference since there was nothing I needed more urgently now than to hear that voice, so I dialed the Berlin number I knew so well. Of course there was no answer right away, he was asleep, but I let it ring for a long time until I heard his half-asleep "Hello?" At which I complained that he would never learn to answer with his name like you're supposed to, and he asked if I even knew what time it was there, and I said, No, I don't know. Five thirty in the morning, he said, and I said Oh, I was just about to go to bed. We said nothing, the ocean roared its quiet roar, then he asked, Is something wrong? and I said: No, what could be wrong? Do you hear the roar of the ocean? Did you know that the MS. VICTORIA breathes at night and rocks like a ship on the sea? —I didn't know that, he said. But say hello to your MS. VICTORIA for me, it needs to look out for you. I asked: Are you saying you think I need looking out for? and he said: You never know. No, I said, you never do. We hung up. I felt better.

I got up late, it was the weekend after all, and made a hearty breakfast. What was I singing, unconsciously, as I did it? I had learned to pay attention to that information. I was singing "I Had a Comrade Once," the version sung by the International Brigades in the Spanish Civil War after Hans Beimler fell in the Battle of Madrid. "A bullet came a-flying / It came from Germany / The aim was true / The course was too / A German gun, you see." Tears used to come to my eyes sometimes when I sang those words, that was back in the naive days when we still believed in fairy tales. A friend of mine, himself a fighter in Spain, who had recently gained access to the secret Spanish military archive, told me that the version of Hans Beimler's death in our history books was not true either. "Happy the nation that needs no heroes." Anyway, I realized, there had been no more songs in the German Communist movement since Spain. Its soul had been ripped from its body with sharp instruments and the pain was nothing to sing about, for a long time it was not supposed to be felt at all. Artificially transplanted substitute songs were struck up at public occasions but they did not stand the test of time. And why should songs outlive the people who sang them, I thought. "The Spanish sky spreads its stars / Above our defensive trenches . . ." We sang the songs of the old people, we sang "Die Moorsoldaten": "Everywhere you cast your eye / Bog and heath lay all around." But we also sang the new Thälmann Song, "Thälmann, Thälmann, out in front / Germany's immortal son," or we sang "The Roses Bloom in August" at the World Festival of Youth, but something was missing, we stopped singing those songs, they sounded wrong.

Now what was going on here, I had to pull myself together, I said to myself, I couldn't spend my everyday life so wrapped up in my thoughts, earlier I had forgotten to take my purchases with me at two different stalls at the wonderful vegetable market on Second Street, someone had had to come running after me with the bags. Then suddenly my shopping cart had disappeared, which I could not do without—now it's happened, I thought, now someone's stolen my cart with my leather jacket in it—and then there it was suddenly standing right in front of me, blocking the aisle, people had to squeeze past it.

My mind is elsewhere, I thought. When I went to the *office* that afternoon I crossed at a red light, a car had to slam on the brakes. A stack of newspaper clippings faxed from Berlin was sitting in my mailbox, I put them in a folder and stuffed the folder into my bag without looking at them, I was not up to it.

I went back to the MS. VICTORIA, sat down at the little machine in my apartment, and wrote, to my surprise:

In the City of Angels my skin is being peeled back. They want to know what lies beneath, and they find, as in every normal human being, muscles tendons bones veins blood heart stomach liver spleen. They are disappointed, they were hoping for the entrails of a monster.

Really, I heard myself say to myself, don't go overboard. I let the sentences stand.

I called Peter Gutman. How does it happen, I asked him, that our civilization brings forth monsters?

Thwarted life, he said. What else. Thwarted lives.

I don't know, I said. Maybe we're born monsters?

A storm is blowing from paradise, Peter Gutman said. It pushes the angel of history backward ahead of it. But it doesn't turn him into a monster.

But he doesn't have eyes in the back of his head, I said.

No, he doesn't, Peter Gutman said. That's just it: he's blind.

Blind to history, I said.

Blind to horrors, if you prefer, Madame.

Thank you very much, I said and hung up. I thought: Being blind to horrors would be a good thing, who could live keeping all the horrors in mind. There has to be something like an expelling, extruding, exorcising of horror, I thought. I remembered how you couldn't stop picturing your cleaning woman's young son who had gotten stuck under a raft while swimming in the Warta and drowned, and how his mother had had to watch when they pulled the dead boy out of the water, and you wondered how she could live with that, and I remembered that you, as a child, wondered how you were supposed to endure hearing about the suffering constantly inflicted on other people, and the fear of being hurt yourself, for your whole long life long, but you didn't then know, and would not have believed, that people, without realizing it or wanting it, develop protective techniques against self-destructive sympathy.

A line came to mind from the old poem I had kept on top in my desk drawer for a long time because I needed it every day, a poem I once knew by heart and had forgotten by then, but these lines came back to me: "Accept your fate, regret nothing."

That dreary Sunday morning in my apartment. It was raining. *Television*. A preacher in a colorful robe in front of the altar of an enormous church hall filled with hundreds of people, and next to him: General Schwarzkopf. The famous preacher read out loud to the general, in a fainting voice, the letter the general had written to his family at the start of the Gulf War. Both men had tears in their eyes. What has changed in the country since then? the preacher asked the general. Lots of people still write to him and thank him for what he did for his country, he said. Maybe we succeeded too well, he went on. Communism had collapsed. President Bush, the *"magnificent leader,"* made the right decisions in the Gulf War. The general was campaigning for Bush.

Drums beat, trumpets blared. Everyone in the enormous auditorium stood up and gave the general a standing ovation. Enthusiastic, devoted faces. The preacher prayed in a resounding voice: *God, give us men. What we need are leaders. Strong minds, great hearts, true faces who will not lie.* —Yeah! cried the hundreds of people in the hall. Their preacher called upon them to pray long and hard before they cast their vote. *Yeah!*

The thought came to me that the last intervention you undertook as a public intellectual was before the Gulf War started, an open letter to the UN asking it to do everything in its power to approve the French resolution to postpone the use of force in the Gulf region, you relayed the text by phone and fax to everyone you could, asked people to sign it, received the signatures, and sent the document to the UN—my face blushes in shame when I think about it—and then, a few days later, you sat in front of the TV at 4:00 a.m. and watched the American troops land on the coast of the Persian Gulf, where they were met by the TV cameras they had requested in advance, and tears ran down your face because you couldn't help but picture the unquenchable enmity on the part of the Arab world that would be stirred up against the West at that moment. All due to false eyewitness reports, as we now know.

How are you? It was Sally on the phone. She had quit her job with at-risk youth and signed up for a class she was taking to prepare for a degree program. —What field? —Architecture. *Interior design.*

What? I said, and I thought: You were born to be a dancer.

I saw before me, I can still see before me today, how Sally was when I met her in the mid-seventies, in a small college town in Ohio— how young she was, with beautiful posture, in peak physical shape, how happy she was when a performance of her dance troupe was shown on TV, I saw and I still see her birdlike head with her hair short as match-sticks, how relaxed, how artistic she was when she moved, how much in love with her Ron was, everyone turned their heads to look at them when they boisterously ran from the German-Jewish bakery across the big parking lot back to their car, Ron couldn't stop looking at Sally and touching her. She glowed. She had her whole life ahead of her.

Sally, Sally, I said, I never would have thought your confidence could be shaken so easily.

You have no idea, Sally said, my mother saw to that. And now she feels almost glad that I've failed, that life with Ron didn't work out. —I don't believe that, I said. —So why is she being so generous, paying for this class, when she's usually so cheap? And aside from that, don't you think a man can tell when a woman is weak? He quivers like a hunting dog when it picks up the scent of blood, and then follows that scent even more aggressively. Do you know the Frida Kahlo painting, she asked me, a doe pierced with arrows that has a woman's head, her own head? —I know that one. —And don't you know that the chase really starts in earnest when you've been hit? —Oh yes, Sally. I know.

Hey, tell me, Sally asked, what's really on your mind.

Oh, Sally, that's a long story.

So tell me.

Later. Soon.

But I didn't tell Sally the story first. I told Francesco, but only later. I wasn't ready yet.

Monday morning in the lounge, almost everyone was there, hidden behind pages from their home countries. Just in time, before the election, the news media had reported that the American GDP had unexpectedly risen 2.7 percent that year, so that President Bush could proclaim to the nation: *The recession is over!* The local media countered that the recession was still going strong in California: there was high unemployment, and various businesses that had been leading military manufacturers were near collapse. Well, of course, said Lutz, who understood politics just as well as he did art history: no one had any idea what to do after the unforeseen end of the Cold War. He read us an editorial from a German newspaper arguing that the Cold War had been a gift to democratic societies: it had pushed several industries into high gear and at the same time, by brutally reinforcing an ideological image of the enemy, restricted the validity of the democratic rules of the game. The Cold War also made possible the unchecked, cancerous growth of the secret police. Would modern societies be able to cope with the collapse of the enemy, that is, the disappearance of the image of an enemy? Without constructing new images of the enemy, new targets for military aggression and rivals in an arms race?

Clinton's electoral prospects were said to have worsened overnight.

The landscape of memory spreads out far and wide, I think, and the beam of our thoughts scans across it. In my notebooks, I come across these sentences by the nun, from the book Sally gave me:

I've begun to see the value of everybody's wisdom and the fact that people discover the same truths through many avenues. Open up your life so that you're not caught in self-concern. Then you will no longer think you're at the center of the world, because you're so concerned with your worries, pains, limitations, desires, and fears that you are blind to the beauty of existence. You will see that life is such a miracle, and we spend so much time doing nothing except figuring out the ways life is being unfair to us.

It doesn't surprise me to find Doctor Kim singing the same tune as the nun. When I told him the pain was getting pretty bad over the past few weeks, he calmly explained *It depends on what you eat*, and said not to eat sweets either. What was I supposed to eat, then? Rice and vegetables. Ah. I was sure that he followed his own advice. I didn't tell him that I was taking pain pills. He advised me to make a mental image of the condition of my hips, as precisely as I could, and to bathe the affected cartilage areas in a beneficent flow of healing thoughts. He pricked me with his needles and assured me: *I will rebuild your hip.* I could not believe him, I felt guilty, and I knew that his prognosis would not be valid for an unbeliever. He also warned me not to eat so much bread, and had an assistant measure out for me a bag full of strange ingredients, including what seemed to be bones along with the leaves and herbs and tubers, that I was supposed to boil for a very long time every morning to make a broth I was supposed to drink, and I did it too, it made my apartment reek, I held my nose and drank it, but it couldn't help me, I thought, if I hated it. I knew that Doctor Kim fasted one day a week and ate very moderately the rest of the time, and I thought, when I was back on the bus, about how he must despise us dissolute inhabitants of the Western world given over to our unchecked desires.

New Year's was approaching, it was dark already at five, I got off the bus to go into a bicycle shop and buy one of the bike locks considered secure, for the new bike I had acquired at Woolworth's for a hundred and six dollars. The old one, inherited from Bill, had been stolen from the garage, together with two other bikes parked there, locked, of course. They must have come by with a truck! —Yes, said the young and pretty policewoman who showed up at the *office* to take a detailed report, that's likely, they're organized gangs who switch a few parts and resell the bicycles right away, every day there are at least twenty reports of lost bikes in Santa Monica alone. And what are my chances of getting the bicycle back? She shrugged her shoulders. Basically zero, especially if the victim doesn't know the bicycle's serial number, as in my case.

I said *Thank you* to the young policewoman, in spite of the bad news. She answered *You're welcome*, and I bought a new bicycle. I rode it down the coastal road to Venice exactly once, more out of a sense of duty than because I wanted to: it was something one had to experience. I realized that it was very difficult for me to climb on or off the bike because the crossbar was too high, so I took it to the garage and conscientiously locked it up with the new lock, which a week later was still hanging trustily on the rail while the bike itself had been cleanly removed and stolen again. I did not want to trouble the police again with such a trifle—they were busy enough. The realization that I was not meant to ride a bicycle in this part of the world cost me one hundred and six dollars, and I left it at that.

Bob Roberts: A timely film, you might say. The viewers in the small movie theater on Second Street followed with grim pleasure the path of a corrupt, deceitful senatorial candidate, a folksinger, casting a spell over the masses with Bob Dylan–like songs given false lyrics. At the end, when it looks bad for the candidate, he and his team fake a shooting and he wins the election as a candidate in a wheelchair, but then the camera shows the man's supposedly paralyzed leg happily tapping in time at a concert. Meanwhile, the man who was paid to fake the shooting is killed by Roberts's fanatical followers.

Movies don't get any more pointed than that, I said, while the whole clan walked up lively Second Street as it got dark, to the MS. VICTORIA, to Francesco's apartment, where he had invited us for risotto. The references to the current electoral campaign were obvious, I said. I might have known that Peter Gutman, who had made an exception to his usual habit and come along with us, would contradict me. All well and good, he said. But movies like that do not make the slightest difference. It wasn't just me, the others didn't want to believe him either. Anyone who saw this movie, which was well made too, could not have as naive and gullible a view of the current election as someone who hadn't seen it, we said. I appreciate the argument, Peter Gutman said. His sarcasm sometimes got on my nerves. Now, do you think that any of the followers of our three candidates today, who go into raptures of enthusiasm when their star comes out on stage, will see this movie? Not a single one will see it, that's what I say, he said. But the Sunday preacher's speeches inciting his followers on TV, they see and hear those. And they get the message that it's normal, it's God's will, to turn off the rational mind when it's time to decide who should lead this country for four years.

Francesco and Ines's apartment was homey, furnished with Italian tablecloths, pillows, and wall hangings. Francesco took command in the kitchen and had to concentrate on the risotto, so a few comments he threw in here and there were his only contribution to our discussion. Lutz, though, didn't want to let Peter Gutman off the hook for his

cultural pessimism, as he termed it. At least a movie like that is courageous, he said, and you couldn't convince him that it would have no
effect, even if that effect could not be measured. What do you think,
Emily?

Emily, the film studies professor who had recommended the movie
to us, shook her head. Effect? she said. *No. Nichts. Nothing. Niente.*

You see, it's just for the chosen few, Peter Gutman concluded with
satisfaction.

I was furious at him, for whatever reason, and accused him of
enjoying it when his dark predictions were proven right.

Peter Gutman raised his eyebrows.

A sizzle came from the kitchen as Francesco threw the fish filets
into the pan of hot oil. Ines asked what kind of dressing we wanted on
our salad, we said *Italian dressing* of course, and Francesco left the all-
important final minutes of the risotto to Ria (still wearing her leather
cap): stirring, carefully pouring the hot broth over the risotto, measuring out the butter, folding in the Parmesan she had grated. Francesco
arranged the fish filets garnished with lemon slices and dill in layers on
a large platter, Ines served the salad in little bowls. We all had the same
white dishes in our respective kitchen cupboards. The white wine was
chilled, we were hungry, it tasted delicious, we were in a good mood.

By the way, Pintus asked, hadn't we noticed that the nation was
much less gripped by the election than by the final retirement of their
idol, the basketball player Magic Johnson, who was unfortunately HIV
positive and, after a short, celebrated return to his team, now had to
throw in the towel because the players on other teams did not want to
run the risk that he and one of them could be injured at the same time
and his infected blood might contaminate their healthy blood. This sequence of events had divided the nation, not the platforms of the presi-
dential candidates, which were, in the end, so similar.

We said nothing.

I try to think back to that bygone time, which now lies spread out
before us, or actually behind us, like a well-lit field where everything
is clearly visible, and I wonder if, for all our skepticism and cynicism,
we really foresaw so clearly and with such certainty how things would
be today. That we would be at war again. Probably only Peter Gutman
thought anything was possible. It was after that risotto dinner at Francesco and Ines's that he took me up to his apartment, for the first time

actually—he said he wasn't ready to call it a night, and I said me nei-ther, so I had to follow him up another flight of stairs and walk into an apartment laid out exactly the same as mine and yet more different from mine than I could possibly have imagined. It was untouched; nothing suggested that anyone lived there. No books, no pictures, no news-papers on the table, no flowers, even the chairs looked like they hadn't been touched. So bare and austere, it was stifling. Peter Gutman saw me standing in the doorway, he knew that the sight of his apartment was a shock to me; he said nothing and I said nothing. He offered me the comfortable armchair and went to the kitchen, where I heard the refrigerator door open and close and he came back with a good white wine, he knew his wine. At some point he said that comfort disgusted him because of its hypocrisy. He had a goal in mind that night, I think, he wanted to get to something in me. And he started by going on the offensive: They knocked the fight right out of you all, didn't they? he said.

I understood what he meant but played dumb. Who? Out of whom? What fight?

He didn't respond to that at all. You've lost only when you see your-self as having lost, he said.

So he didn't believe in objective criteria?

It's about whether you let yourself be defined by the other side, the winning side.

In short, Peter Gutman had taken it upon himself to defend me from something like a loss of self. He explained to me much later that he thought he had detected in me a kind of depression beneath the surface that he wanted to fight back against. But at the time, he had no way of knowing its real cause.

It must have been on that same night that I told Peter Gutman about an experience I'd had at the theater a long time before. It must have been back in the fifties, I said. *Lyubov Yarovaya*, a play by a Soviet author. The title heroine is fighting in the civil war in 1919, as an officer in the Red Army. Her husband, whom she loves, is an officer for the Whites and he plans an attack on the Reds. A furious argument with Lyubov does not dissuade him from his plans, so she shoots him. She has to shoot him, the playwright suggests. And I thought, I told Peter Gutman, that that's how a revolutionary has to be. Able to do that. And at the same time, I knew I could never be like that.

And? he said.

And it took me a long time before I realized that any moral system that puts people into such conflicts takes something away from their humanity. The New Man is a reduced man.

But people fight to the death for their ideas everywhere, to this day, Peter Gutman said. Even today.

It must not be easy to write down something like that, he said then. No.

Do it anyway. You can take it out later.

It strikes me that we never called each other by our first names. "Monsieur" and "Sir" were all I needed for him; he called me "Madame" or used no form of address at all.

Adieu, Monsieur.

Sleep well, Madame.

Looking back from today, it seems to me that the time before New Year's 1992/93 felt so long because I had so much new to see, hear, think about in those few months. So many new faces too, crowding around me in that short span of time. Some appeared once, with a piece of information, a question, a message, news, and then disappeared again, while others became "*Bekannte*," "acquaintances"—a word that doesn't really translate into American English because "acquaintances" there turn so quickly into "friends," in a different sense from the German word for "friends" too. Bob Rice, for example, the architecture historian. It is now finally time for him to appear.

It was almost Christmas, in stifling heat, the *Christmas* psychosis was in full swing even though you weren't allowed to talk about "*Christmas*," so as not to insult the non-Christian religions, instead people wished each other "*Happy Holidays*." The streets were aglitter with elaborate decorations, there were masses of Christmas trees everywhere, often trimmed to exact pyramid shapes, and in the CENTER's hall a giant, lavishly decorated Christmas tree greeted us. We rode up in the elevator to the tune of "A Great and Mighty Wonder"; meanwhile, Mrs. Ascott had invited us to a tree-trimming party in the *lobby* of our beloved MS. VICTORIA, at which Peter Gutman and I agreed that she, Mrs. Ascott, would make a perfect *lady* for a comic mystery novel.

Buildings! Neutra buildings! was the motto of our architectural guide, Bob Rice. He knew everything there was to know about the famous architect who had emigrated from Germany to America in the twenties. Francesco and Ines crowded into the back of Bob's tiny Honda, which, as though alive, picked up the scent and was off to the next destination of its own volition, back and forth across the megacity, on freeways, boulevards, up the canyon on steep rocky roads to the *"grandmother's house"* on the top of the topmost peak, a tiny little house that Neutra had built as a guesthouse for the mother of the family who lived far down the hillside—an ambiguous success, since the grandmother liked it so much in the little house that she stayed. The old lady who lived there now knew the story and showed us the stunning view of the city in all directions.

That's how it was everywhere we went. We were let in everywhere, everyone living in the various houses knew Bob. In one of them, originally built for a famous actress, a woman lay sick in bed upstairs but even so we were allowed to walk around the ground floor, in the large, bright rooms, appreciating their proportions and interrelations.

It seemed only natural that Neutra would want to experiment not only with new ways of building, but also with new ways of living. Bob drove us to the Schindler House, built by the other great émigré architect who had left his unmistakable mark on this faceless city. That was where the Neutras and the Schindlers had lived together. A Japanese-style building, very low, flat, with moveable walls and numerous doors to the bright, open air outside, where, we learned, they could sleep outdoors all year round. We stood on the flat roof and Bob took a bottle of red wine, six small silver tumblers, and a little tin of salted peanuts out of his leather briefcase—here was where he wanted to toast with us, here and nowhere else, he had a knack for symbolic gestures.

There was at least one more building we had to see, he said. It was at the edge of Koreatown, the neighborhood where the most businesses had been set on fire during the *riots* in April, by blacks who felt discriminated against due to the rapid social advancement of the Asians. The house Bob showed us had been built by Neutra in the thirties as a prototype apartment building for affordable social housing. We were not let in there; poor people lived there now, mostly Hispanics. Five stories tall, symmetrical rows of windows, half-drawn curtains, bottles on the windowsills, women's and children's heads peeping out, laundry hung over the window ledges. Across the street were small single-family houses, also poor, with unemployed men in straw hats hanging around in groups outside the front doors. They observed us in silence.

With the climate here, Bob said, even the slums aren't as miserable as in New York or Detroit.

Francesco and Ines had moved off and were strolling along next to the Neutra house; Francesco was taking pictures. A car approached them from behind with a black man driving and a black woman in the passenger seat. She rolled down her window and shouted a curse word at them, thinking they were idle curiosity-seekers. Francesco, instead of keeping his mouth shut, answered aggressively and the driver braked right next to our car; the woman jumped out, an imposing woman, maybe thirty years old, very confident, unleashing a loud barrage of curses on us. Bob grabbed my arm and quickly shoved me to the car, saying to the woman in a soothing voice, *We're just looking at the architecture*, and we probably both realized how ridiculous this explanation must have sounded to the black woman, who got back into her car, which then sped off, tires squealing. Francesco and Ines got in the car with us. The men in the straw hats in front of the houses showed no reaction at all. Bob said: *She's just angry*, and I thought: Well, that was something we had to experience too.

Karl, a photographer friend of Bob's, was waiting with a few other guests in Bob's apartment and he mixed us drinks. *Gin and tonic*, I drank it too fast and felt better. With glasses in hand we strolled through Bob's house, a Neutra house of course, *like a shrine*, one of the women visitors said softly. There was the bookshelf filled with books by and about Neutra. Handwritten letters from Neutra under glass in the study. But the piece that was most important to Bob, the only thing he and his wife had fought over during their divorce, was the poster for an old movie called *I Married a Communist*. Tom wanted to know if we in the GDR would have been allowed to make a film called *I Married a Capitalist*. It totally depends on the ending, I said. If the contradiction breaks up the marriage, why not?!

There was a lady there, a professor's wife, all done up—professional hairdo, a lot of attention to her clothes, and too much makeup on the same kind of wrinkly, suntanned face that so many older American women had. She wanted me to tell her if it was right to let the German Communist leader, what was his name again, escape abroad, where was it, I said: Chile, and: His name is Honecker. *Right*, the lady said, and where was it I lived? Berlin, I said, adding: *East Berlin. Oh*, the lady said, and had I always lived there? *Yes*, I said, taking slightly perverse pleasure in it, and the lady didn't know what else to say, but I would have given quite a bit to be able to see what pictures were running through her head.

Bob Rice, always attuned to what was going on around him, started to tell us a story: the story of how he acquired Freud's overcoat and lost it again. It was Richard Neutra's widow who had given him, her husband's faithful chronicler, Neutra's overcoat as a memento after Neutra's death. Originally, she assured him, it had been *the overcoat of Dr. Freud*— they were both Austrians, both from Vienna, and had known each other well. The coat was old by that point but not shabby: good prewar manufacture. Bob was certain that he would be able to handle any situation in life in this coat, and we knew that he could definitely end up in situations where he desperately needed such protection. Bob said he had not worn it but had hung it on the door of his *office* at the university so that he could always see it. Then, he had had to go away for a few days, and he had locked his door, contrary to normal practice and to what he usually did. He could swear to that. When he came back, he couldn't believe his eyes: The coat was gone. In desperation, he asked around and launched a massive search, in vain of course. He was and remained inconsolable. All he had was the thought that, through a chain of implausible coincidences, the coat had ended up on the back of one of the *homeless people* and was keeping him warm through the cold, wet winter.

What do you think of my story, Bob asked me later.

Listen, I said, tomorrow I am going to start writing a book that will be called:

THE CITY OF ANGELS, OR, THE OVERCOAT OF DR. FREUD

Do it, Bob said, and then came his generous offer: Take everything you can use.

Everything? I said.

Everything, he said.

That will be a book, I said, I can never publish.

It's a working hypothesis you use to get closer to things, Bob said.

That won't be enough this time, I said. I'm scared, of course.

I know, Bob said. *Take care of yourself.*

He brought a book of poems to the table, bilingual German and

English, for me to pick one and recite it in German. I looked under "Baroque" and found Paul Fleming (1609–40), a rhymed and metered sonnet in German and a prose translation in English. I read in German:

TO HIMSELF

Be undismayed in spite of everything; do not give up, despite everything; give way to no twist of fortune; stand above envy; be content with yourself and think it no disaster even if fortune, place, and time have conspired against you.

I read it, happy to have found it again, I felt my way along the words that rose up once more, the words you used to know by heart, and right next to the poem in your desk drawer were the little green sedative pills you took because you wanted to make yourself insensitive to the conflicts you had with the people you still thought were your people. You still hoped it would all turn out to be some kind of misunderstanding.

What saddens or refreshes you, think it chosen for you; accept your fate, regret nothing, do what must be done and before you are told to do it. What you can hope for may happen any day.

But then, I remembered, in one of the serious conflicts you had with them—all at once the whole course it took, its cause and its outcome, were there in my mind—you were supposed to admit something you couldn't admit, and they refused to budge, and you refused too, and all of a sudden you knew: No. I do not want to be the same as them. It was a bitter insight, a liberating insight.

What is it that we lament, or that we praise? Each man is his own fortune and misfortune. Look round at everything—all this is within you; leave your empty delusion,

and, before you go any further, go back into yourself. The man who is master of himself and can control himself has the whole wide world and what is in it at his feet.

The last lines in German hung in the air: *"Wer sein selbst Meister ist und sich beherrschen kann, / Dem ist die weite Welt und alles untertan."* For the man who is master of himself and can control himself, the whole world and everything in it is *untertan*: subjugated, underfoot. That can't be how it is, I thought. Nobody uses words like "*untertan*" anymore.

Typical German, Francesco said. First you Germans want to master yourself and then the whole world. Karl, the photographer, said that "*untertan*" was the one German word he hated most—that single word might well have been the reason he'd left Germany. I wouldn't have guessed that Karl was originally from Germany: even when he spoke German he had a faint American accent and sometimes he had to stop and hunt for the right word. He said that in English there's no way to say the word "*untertan*." We turned to the translation, which said: he "has the whole wide world and what is in it at his feet."

There, you see, Francesco said. That's the crucial difference: whether you want to master the world or whether the world lays itself at your feet. Yes, but, I said, there's nothing wrong with self-mastery! There is, there absolutely is! Francesco shouted. Suppressing yourselves is what causes the whole disaster! And you don't even see that it's your undoing! We had been drinking quite a bit. Eager for a fight, we went through the poem line by line, some of the lines passed muster in Francesco's eyes and others not. I insisted you couldn't have one without the other—misery and grief were the lining of Dr. Freud's *overcoat*—but Francesco wanted his joie de vivre and optimism and assertiveness pure, without the shadow of melancholy, defeat, and failure. Without the background of German history, in other words, I said. Francesco said I was playing games with the German Misère, and he wouldn't stand for it! Our argument got louder. The voice of the *lady* from earlier sounded in a sudden silence: But when the Wall came down, you all celebrated, didn't you? And she couldn't understand why her simple question unleashed a burst of laughter. I said: Oh yes! to the lady, and looked cheekily at her. *I was so happy!*

Bob, I said, I need that poem. *I'll fax it to you*, he said. I would find it the next morning in my mailbox at the *office*, I would need it, and soon I would know it by heart again. And Bob would watch over me, he would be there when old friends gathered or when I met new friends, *How are you?* he'd ask, and I wouldn't have to say *Fine*, I could sometimes say *Bad*, sometimes *It's very hard*, and he would say *I know*, and one day he would take me to a very meaningful dinner at Gladstone's, but that came later.

First, after the long day with the Neutra houses, I dreamed about emigration again. We were sitting in a car that had rotted away, it was clear that "new money" would come and then we would emigrate. A man with a wide face and a nose overgrown with fur, who was authorized to make the decision, confirmed that we had to "go." We wanted to know if a lot of people had to "go." No, the man said, most of them wanted the new money. In my dream I was very aware of my position as an outsider. It pained me that we had to "go." Apparently we could bring a few things with us, some women stowed items of clothing in the car for us and then more passengers crowded in. The car got more and more full. But we still had to say goodbye to our daughters, we said. Apparently they already knew, and they were going to stay.

When I woke up I remembered our drives in the country when you held the road atlas on your knees and looked and looked for the country you could find refuge in, and you never found it, and you and G. mockingly recalled Brecht's poem "The Buddha's Parable of the Burning House" ("Truly, friends, / Unless a man feels the ground so hot underfoot that he'd gladly / Exchange it for any other, rather than stay, / I have nothing to say to him"), and then one day, after flipping through the atlas for a while, you finally cried: Strassburg! Not in Germany but they speak German! But secretly you knew it was just a game.

Wasn't it almost Christmas then too, in that dark winter of 1976 that sharpened the outlines of the situation and put the thumbscrews on you and G. But now, after more than a quarter century and so far removed from the origins of that calamity, I could calmly ask myself what it actually was that unleashed this pain that took your breath away: at first you didn't recognize the pain, you tried to run away from it through the dim, badly lit streets, up Friedrichstrasse to Chausseestrasse, the unassuming drugstore on the corner, a bright shop window with toothpaste tubes, sponges, detergent, and a many-pointed Christmas star hanging there lit up pink from within, an ordinary little display that it clenched your heart to look at, until you suddenly recognized and felt with a sense of liberation: So, this is pain. An almost unbearable pain at a loss.

You can regret false feelings, you can curse them if
you want, but you cannot deny them or change them. Or
at least it takes years, even decades, before what
used to be a false feeling is only false, no longer a

feeling. Maybe that's precisely what we mean when we say a person has changed. Of course you can coddle your false feelings too.

Or maybe it was just fear? I asked myself, when I looked up from my machine. You certainly knew what fear was. You certainly were afraid, that November of 1976 which is under discussion here, when you all were driving home from that meeting at a friend's and mentally tracing the path of the protest letter you had drawn up together, which, at that very moment, as you arrived back in your apartment, might well have already been passed up the various steps of the "apparatus" to "Number One" and also, as a copy, transmitted wirelessly out of the divided city, via the Western news agency you had given it to, to various radio stations, broadcasts that, even if the stations obeyed the delay period imposed on them, would unleash a firestorm that you could only vaguely imagine. They'll throw us in jail, said the comrade of yours sitting in the backseat. And you didn't really believe that the singer they had expatriated would really be allowed to return to the country because of your protest, did you? That was the question people kept asking you—some of them furious, some despondent, some cowardly—and all of you said "Yes, we did," or "No," depending who was asking or who had called you in for questioning, and on whether you were acting strategically or straightforwardly, and in any case, you all said that you had to do it, and that was the honest truth, and sometimes you added that this singer's expatriation recalled Germany's darkest hours and that you would not have been able to continue to write if you had accepted it without saying something. Was the word "socialist" spoken? It certainly was. It was used on both sides, as accusation and as defense, and the ones who felt worst about their own cowardice were the ones who were angriest with you and repeated the word "damage" most often: you and the others had done your country irreparable "damage." You seized on that word and threw it back. Only when an old comrade, a Jewish woman who had spent many years in the emigration, shouted at you in a trembling voice during an assembly that you wanted to bring back the concentration camps did you and the others stay silent, there was nothing to say to that, and you knew: It was hopeless. That was when the pain came. Pain and rage at the people sitting across from you, angry or cold, trying to get you to recant and to reveal the originator of the conspiracy and to play you off against each other, and the realization grew and grew that you and they were enemies, irreconcilable enemies—that there was no longer any common language between you, or any shared future.

It was early in the morning, I couldn't take it anymore in my apartment in the MS. VICTORIA and I walked to the Ocean Park Promenade. The tape player of memory kept running in my head, I thought it was really too bad about the diary in which, in a sulfur bath in Hungary a year after that winter of our discontent, you had written out an exact chronicle of the events, and which you put in your suitcase like a criminal, so that you would not have it on you in case you were searched; the suitcase was loaded into the airplane with the other suitcases but it never arrived at the Leipzig airport. You and G. waited at the lost luggage counter for a long time, submitted every possible search request designed for such cases, which almost always, they assured you, brought results. And yet you did not include in the list of the missing objects the diary you missed most. Nothing was found, but the travel insurance replaced all of the lost objects without a hitch—towels and nightgown and shoes—just not the diary, which couldn't officially exist at all. It was documented nowhere, not even by me, to be safe, and so it was easy for it to dissolve into nothingness, and now there is nothing to compel anyone to believe it ever existed since even the official files, in which I had placed a certain hope, failed in this particular case: the diary was not to be found in the big green wooden chest with the mass of other documents, and I caught myself criticizing the people who had kept themselves so well informed about everything we did for being so careless. But was it their job to be complete? Or truthful?

We also found no record in the files of that dark night when a fully manned police squad car was stationed at the corner across from your house, for hours. You and G. were standing at the window behind the curtain, which you had hung only after the young gentlemen in their cars had put your apartment under observation from the parking lot on the other side of the street. You and G. saw someone from the squad car separate from the team and walk to the phone booth on your side of the street, at which point your own telephone immediately started ringing, in the middle of the night, and when you picked up the phone no one on the other end of the line said anything, and the squad car drove off after a while, and you and G. could go to bed, though without being able to fall asleep. The next day, the official party newspaper was delivered late, not until noon.

All of it true but none of it provable, I thought, while the morning joggers ran past me and the sun on the left had already crept up high in the sky, and memory wouldn't stop: that strange night did receive a kind of explanation later, from something an actor friend told you. That same night, after an opening-night party, he had happened to walk past the print shop where newspapers, hot off the presses and bundled together on pallets, were loaded onto trucks. One of the bundles had gotten untied and a newspaper had fallen out, and he had been able to read the headline in large print on the front page, which said that all of you, the conspirators who were first to sign that protest letter, had recognized your action as damaging and had recanted. Someone else claimed to know that they had planned to arrest you that night and put pressure on you for so long that you would sign the recantation, but that another faction in the leadership had put a stop to the plan. A crazy story, impossible to prove.

You were afraid then. I have learned since then that emotional memory doesn't get calloused over but rather stays sensitive in the place where the emotion cut deep. Have I become more fearful? I refuse to answer. Meanwhile, I remember, I have since found in my files a copy of a plan that the agency actually did carry out: to discredit you with the other protesters, they spread the rumor that you had secretly recanted your signature after all in one of their "conversations" with you, and admitted your action was a mistake. They did not spread around that the only answer you ever gave them in these "conversations" was no—an answer which, as you knew with bedrock certainty, was inviolable and would never change. From motives of self-preservation.

That was one of the turning points in my life, I thought.

Ocean Park. It was getting hot out, solitary runners and walkers moved past my bench with single-minded determination, soaked in sweat. Then a man with Indian features came and leaned against the railing opposite me, said *Merry Christmas*, and asked if he could sit next to me on the bench. *Sure.*

I am an Indian, he said, *from Oklahoma.* He was here for only two days, he said, to visit a girlfriend, but when he showed up she had moved to Kentucky. He had been walking a long way, from Venice. He was wearing a bright-colored T-shirt and had a white sweater knotted around his neck. What's your name? he said. I said my first name. His was Richard. *Not an Indian name*, I said. His last name was Indian, he said, and he said it, something very complicated. He shook my hand; his was crippled. I asked him what he did for a living. He couldn't work anymore, he said, pointing to his hand and to a long scar on his forearm: car accident. *Very bad.* Then came what I was apprehensively waiting for: *Could you spare some change?* Unfortunately I had run out of the house without a wallet, without money. I said so, regretfully. He nodded. Was I married? When I said yes, he stood up: *Nice talking with you*, and he left. And that, I thought, was my first encounter with one of the original inhabitants of America.

Then the two young men in bright white shirts and slick hair with perfectly straight parts came by to push their Mormon Bible on me. I pretended I hardly spoke a word of English, barely understood it, and anyway was not a believer and would never be one, at which point one of the two gave me a piercing look and asked me how I knew. At any rate, they contented themselves with handing me a *leaflet* and informing me that God had offered up his son for me, for the forgiveness of my sins too. The truth was, I should have asked those two bright white young men (who had managed to unload their Bible on a woman a little ways farther on) how a father could be so cruel as to give over his son to a hideous sacrificial death, and why the only way for a Christian to be set free of his sins was the cross, a torture device that dislocates his arms. Whereas the circle, the symbol of Buddhism, puts humanity as a whole in the center of the universe—the circle that surrounds you, according to Pema the nun, shows you that you are always standing in the sacred space, and you can open your senses to perceive the meaning and beauty of every single detail in every moment of your life. *If you want to attain enlightenment you have to do it now.*

Back to the MS. VICTORIA, where there was no one around at that hour of the morning except Mr. Enrico and the cleaning staff. Hello, Mr. Enrico, *nice to see you, yes, I'm fine, yes, my apartment is okay, thank you,* and there was Angelina in my apartment, the only black woman among the cleaning personnel in the MS. VICTORIA, along with Alfonso, a Puerto Rican, who had just changed my sheets—for my bed and also the second bed I never used, but I couldn't say anything about that to them—and were now cleaning the kitchen. This heat, I said. Were they thirsty? They hesitantly admitted they were, but they didn't want me to offer them anything to drink. I mixed us three Campari sodas, they hesitantly took them, but only Alfonso sat down with me at the little round kitchen table and quickly drank his. Angelina didn't want to sit down, she said she was so tired that she wouldn't be able to stand back up again, but I still suspected she just didn't want to sit down in my presence. Angelina was not dark brown, like most of the people we whites call "black": Angelina was actually black. She had curves wherever a woman could have them, without being fat—her forehead, cheeks, and lips were curved too, even her chin was round, and her nostrils; the bridge of her nose was set deep between the hemispherical bulges of her flashing white eyes, and her elbows were round, and the knee that peeked out from under her wide colorful dress when she stretched for something, and her hair with its little round curls on her spherical head. How long had she been here, I asked. Six years. She was from Uganda. She had six children there, who had lived with her mother until her mother died and now lived with her sister, she was working for them. *I have to work very hard,* she said, smiling, and I learned that she sometimes worked two shifts a day, in different hotels, and barely slept. I didn't ask Angelina about the father of her children, I asked how old she was, thirty-six, she said, and her children were between six and eighteen, she hadn't seen them since 1989, three years, flights were so expensive. She shook my hand when she left and thanked me for the drink with a little curtsey.

That morning I was glad that they left my apartment soon, Angelina and Alfonso, so I could reach for the red folder on the shelf in the big room. I wasn't mistaken, one of L.'s letters was written in the winter of 1977: an answer to a letter of Emma's in which she had apparently hinted at something about recent events in our country. I was sure that large parts of this correspondence had not been sent through the official postal system, but I had little hope of discovering after the fact who had acted as courier for Emma and L. without attracting suspicion.

So, L. had written to her (and my!) friend Emma in February 1977, in that dark winter:

My dear,
   No, I don't believe history repeats itself. It's true that my dear gentleman is of the opinion that we human beings, especially we on the left, are unable to learn from our mistakes. But look:

You and I can say without any false modesty that we've learned something! You were no longer able to agree with the dogma that a class enemy lurks in anyone who thinks differently, and you paid the price, not a small one. And I, who used to make fun of you for your loyalty to the Party, I can understand now why you never left it. Today we wouldn't have any more arguments about such questions, fights where we quivered in rage, standing across from each other in your kitchen. Isn't that some kind of progress?

I can see it now, by the way—that kitchen of yours. I could describe every single thing in it. Yes, I'm sometimes sad that I will never see that kitchen again, where you are sitting now with your friends. And this girl you seem so worried about. She walks straight into every trap? Why? What is she trying to prove? That she's brave? That she can accomplish something? Or just that what she wants to believe in is worth any sacrifice?

Did my friend Emma actually ask me those exact questions? Sometimes I was moved that they had discussed me behind my back, sometimes hurt. If it's true that I walked straight into every trap, I thought, then surely it was only because I didn't think it was a trap. That changed. Why did it take so long? And so much effort?

L. wrote:

Well, let the young people do what they have to do. They won't do it any worse than you and I did, if they're worth anything. And what else are they supposed to do? Give up?

Pema, the Buddhist nun, tells the story of a woman running away from some tigers. She runs and runs and the tigers are getting closer and closer. When she comes to the edge of a cliff, she sees some vines far below her, so she climbs down and holds on to the vines. Then she looks down and sees that there are tigers below her as well. Then she notices that a mouse is gnawing away at the vine to which she is clinging. She also sees a beautiful little strawberry bush close to her, growing out of a clump of grass. She looks up, looks down, looks at the mouse, then just takes a strawberry, puts it in her mouth, and enjoys it with all of her senses . . . This struck me as inhuman, something impossible to do and impossible to want to do either.

Computer crash. After the first shock, after the attempts of various savvier friends to fix it, which even included them getting advice over the phone from even-savvier friends in the middle of the night—apparently a computer problem is self-evidently a major catastrophe that any computer person is prepared to help resolve by whatever means necessary at any hour of the day or night—after we got a general idea of how much text I had actually lost, since I was too lazy to back up the file to disk every night; after I realized, in other words, that I could refill the empty space with the material saved in my head, I feel something like a bizarre schadenfreude. Take that, computer! So what does this crash actually mean? A cry not to be ignored, from the depths of technology, telling me "Stop!"? A sudden, highly welcome release from a constant source of stress? Permission to use the heat of this unusually hot Mecklenburg summer as an excuse for my laziness? Or am I to understand this ordinary occurrence some other way, obsessed as I am with the search for meaning? Is this "crash"—what a concrete image!—trying to warn me that I am approaching the point in my writing that I was more or less consciously, more or less artificially, trying to avoid?

It's always a sign when I start losing my hair. Back then, in the New Year's heat in California, my hair started falling out again, by the handful. I passed the information along to Berlin: I'm losing hair by the handful. You can spare it, it'll grow back, came the voice from across the ocean. Not this time, I thought, and I went and found pills for hair and nail growth and tried to remember when else my hair had fallen out. After the typhus, in 1945, you were almost bald. After the births of your children, dozens of hairs lay on your pillow every morning, the same as now on the firmly stuffed pillows in my wide American bed. After that plenary meeting of the Party in 1965. After the Warsaw Pact troops marched into Prague in 1968. In that hopeless, dark winter of 1976–77, when the cars with surveillance teams took shifts outside your window and you stood behind the curtain and asked each other the question: LEAVE OR STAY? After the five operations in 1988. After the people's uprising failed in the fall of 1989—it had no platform, it had to fail, but the hormone responsible for hair growth did not seem to care about these facts, nothing we can understand seems to have any effect on it, it reacts only to the gusts of emotion that reach down to the roots of our lives.

Thomas Mann's diaries. "Pacific Palisades, Saturday, 10/15/49: . . . Letter to a German man who sent me a note declaring his love for Serenus Zeitblom . . . It does me good to see that there are still people in Germany who find something to love in the work of my old age, in my work at all—not just something to carp about. When it comes right down to it, it's a stupid German trait always to have to tear down and belittle the best they have, anything that represents them nobly and well to the world. No other nations do that."

Television. I watched *Mr. Clinton*, who would be inaugurated president of the United States the next day, with his wife, Hillary, who had had to tone down her clothes and her all-too-confident appearance during the election, and their daughter, Chelsea. They were walking across the famous bridge in Washington to the replica of the Liberty Bell, at the head of a huge stream of Americans of every age and skin color, holding hands with black children. The bell tolled. Chelsea was not going to be sent to a *public school*, even though the Clintons were obviously in favor of *public schools*, but Americans seemed to forgive her parents for that, and I wondered if I would be embarrassed in three or four months that my eyes had teared up at the sight of this relaxed, joyful crowd of people striding ahead.

Dream. I am going somewhere on the autobahn with lots of people in different cars. No one I know in "real life" is there. A bare, deserted landscape. Short stop. Sudden departure. Now I'm driving all alone in a tiny car, I stop, and I see the hood of a giant green truck looming large in the rearview mirror. I have to keep driving, but for some reason I desperately want to go back, so I boldly turn the wheel and steer my car onto the center divider. A few pale figures are standing on the other side and one says to the other: It's the anniversary of the founding of the GDR today. The other casually answers: We're skipping that. Then they anxiously shout at me: Careful! On the side of the autobahn I'm trying to drive onto, an ambulance comes racing up with a Red Cross flag flying, it turns onto the lane I'm coming from, right in front of me and my little car, and stops after a few hundred feet. Only now do I see that there are dead bodies inside, covered with blankets, some coffins too. All gray. We had stopped just a few feet before a disaster and hadn't noticed a thing! The pale light over the landscape. A surreal picture.

On the radio over breakfast, I heard a man talking about his parents, who had been put to death forty years earlier. They were honorable people, I heard him say, who were trying to make the world a better place. I realized that the man on the radio was one of Ethel and Julius Rosenberg's sons. My brother and I, he said, were ten and six years old when my parents were executed. Entirely apart from what it means to lose your parents like that, you can hardly imagine what it was like to grow up in the United States as the child of such parents. —What was it like? the woman hosting the show asked. Then Robert told the story of a nightmare childhood: the need to lie about his own name, the orphanage he called a "prison," being kicked out of school under the pretext that the parents of the other students had found out who they were. *It was quite an experience*, he said, and there are other children in America whose parents died for a better world too, but had been forgotten. He and his brother had set up a foundation to support these children.

I can still remember the day perfectly. It must have been in 1953, you were studying at the university in Leipzig, your first child had been born, you were sitting on the couch in the heated room with the baby in your arms. It was morning. You heard on the radio that Ethel and Julius Rosenberg had been put to death in the electric chair that night in the USA. You cried. You stroked your small daughter's little head. I can still feel today, in my fingertips, how soft and fragile it was. I still remember that you thought: I will never forget this day. And I never did forget it.

Time for afternoon tea at the CENTER. Everyone there knew the Rosenbergs' names, they had all thought long and hard about the moral tangle that the atomic physicists had found themselves in: Did their work on the atomic bomb help defeat the Nazis? Didn't a scientist have a fundamental obligation to refuse to work on a weapon that could, in the end, destroy the human race? Or didn't he have to do everything in his power to stop those who wanted to destroy the human race and use their own weapons against them? Guilty either way. The old tragic conflict. But why did the conflict of Orestes, of Iphigenia, seem human to me while that of our atomic scientists seemed inhuman? I asked Peter Gutman, who was walking back to the MS. VICTORIA with me. He said: When normal, well-intentioned people find themselves driven into a dilemma where they cannot do anything right, by their own standards, then the society they live in is sick.

I said nothing.

Doctor Kim suddenly asked me my impression of him. So, vanity after all, I thought with amusement, then I considered the question quickly and said that he seemed to have a strong will, was kind, knew what he wanted, had a sense of humor, could laugh at things, most of all he seemed to know the hierarchy of things and could tell the difference between essential and inessential. Doctor Kim smiled as inscrutably as ever, put six needles in, turned off the light, said *Relax!*, and I, half-asleep, thought: maybe it's not vanity, maybe he knows that everyone would ascribe to him the qualities he would like to have, and I thought about what I had not told him: That he probably liked having influence over other people, being superior to them whenever possible; but that the respect he enjoyed stemmed from a genuine authority, a superiority that wasn't an act and that he also didn't seem to take advantage of. When he came back: *Did you relax?* I looked surreptitiously at him so that I could describe him later: his long head with Asian features and dark skin, his slender, sensitive hands, his blue tracksuit with its clean white collar. Sigrid, who took my payment of sixty dollars in the waiting room, said she had been very sick with cancer and he had saved her life with a strict diet, meditation, and acupuncture. Her last exam showed no more metastases. Sigrid was German but spontaneously spoke English most of the time, even with me.

The full movie theater on Third Street one afternoon. Emily, my upstairs neighbor, our film expert, had convinced me to come with her for something everyone has to have seen: *Close Encounters of the Third Kind*. I was not prepared to see the aliens intrude right into our midst, terrifying us with glaring lights in the sky, making dolls move in a well-ordered American suburban home before the housewife's eyes, making all the appliances run, from the iron to the refrigerator, literally dragging the child away from its horrified mother out through the cat door—all her secret fears and unacknowledged wishes. And then that they would be made to land by technology and music, in a field meaningfully laid out by a François Truffaut who believed in flying saucers, giving back the humans they had borrowed, including of course the abducted child, and taking on new space travelers. Most of all, the touching image of extraterrestrials who are technologically advanced but in other ways unredeemed and who needed us—something Emily, who otherwise said little on the way home, did not want to entirely rule out. By which she indirectly revealed that the movie extraterrestrials' appeal to our sympathy had worked on her.

She invited me to her apartment for barbecued duck that night, where I found Mary, a successful, superthin radio journalist who liked to talk, and Marc, an engineer working on the space telescope that was supposed to pick up signals from other civilizations, whose existence Marc firmly believed in. It was *statistically evident*," he said. But only Mary could supply a personal experience "of the third kind," which she usually—in other words: with unbelievers—didn't discuss. Several years ago, when she was driving through Arizona with her family, including a small child and a dog, and was on a mountain with a famous lookout point, a superbright light like nothing she had ever seen appeared in the sky and she couldn't start her car. They put it in neutral and let it roll down the hill; the child was shaking in fear and started to tremble all over and the dog crawled under the seat, quaking, its paws covering its head in an unnatural position. But she, Mary, had looked out the window, she said, and seen three dark, cigar-shaped objects in close formation coming toward her. She screamed and the other adults saw them too. Then there was a kind of inaudible explosion, a very bright light, and it was all over. The sky was empty, the car was working again, and they drove on in silence. Since then, though, she was absolutely certain that the reports of people who claimed to have been abducted by aliens were based on fact.

And that's not all, Mary said. A friend of hers, a scientist with a thing about watches—his wristwatch always had to be precisely correct, down to the second—was driving to London, a trip that normally took two hours, when suddenly, again after a blindingly bright light, he saw an object approach him in the sky: polygonal, green, encased in white light like a shell. It landed next to the street he was driving on, right next to his car, in fact. That was the last thing he remembered. When he came to, he found himself in his car on the outskirts of London, and his reliable wristwatch showed that exactly five minutes had passed. And there was no question of optical illusions. Her friend never told anyone about his experience because he didn't want people to think he was crazy, but two truck drivers who had been driving through the same area at the same time had seen exactly the same thing and reported it to the police, there was a story about it in the paper that her friend read two days later.

The barbecued duck was crispy and well-seasoned, the California wine was good, news and rumors about the CENTER and university business occupied the group for a little while but then the evening's topic came to the fore again. Emily claimed to know about a woman an extraterrestrial had gotten pregnant. She was abducted for the birth so they could take her baby away from her. Later, they showed her the child again to let her see that they had used it to reinvigorate their own genetic material. Emily told us this in all seriousness, as though it were the most natural thing in the world. Anyway, she added, who could say that there were only "good" extraterrestrials, why wouldn't the division into good and evil be in force "there" too, so that "they" would be a kind of mirror image of our own world, technically more advanced and humanly less advanced.

She turned to Marc: Wasn't it rather dangerous, what he was doing? Marc said there was no way to know, but personally he would happily join any operation that set out to explore the depths of the universe and if he made it back, and if Emily was still to be found on this earth, he would give her all the information she was apparently so desperate to learn. Emily agreed, she had even tried to talk to astronauts directly and find out what they had dreamed in space. Once she had even managed to talk on the phone to someone who had been to the moon, and had had the courage to ask him. He had curtly dismissed the question: You can't squeeze blood from a stone. An awful thing to say, in Emily's opinion, but she had had the impression that he was lying. Or that they had trained them not to have dreams. Maybe it was different with Soviet cosmonauts, she said.

They were unwilling even to admit the possibility that we were the only rational creatures in the universe, as though they were afraid of the loneliness that would overwhelm them if that were true.

I still remember that I had one of my strangest dreams that night. We are driving in pairs in a rolling, grassy, partly swampy landscape, I am dragging one of those big tin milk canisters that farmers use in cow stalls, I dream that a dark goat is grazing comfortably in front of us, we go toward it, probably to feed it, it is completely tame, I dream that it lets me pet it, and then suddenly it swallows the enormous canister of milk in one fell swoop, in my dream I panic, the animal will never be able to get the canister out again, I carefully, timidly touch the goat's body and do in fact feel the sharp metal edges of the canister under its fur, the goat doesn't seem to feel sick yet, it's my fault, I say in the dream, I should have been more careful, then I remember that the ancient Greeks had a sacred goat, Amaltheia, maybe this is Amaltheia, I say, unhappily, Amaltheia is ruined and it's my fault, then the goat moves off away from us across the swampy field and before we can catch up to it and save it, it sinks into the swamp before our eyes, uncomplainingly, sucked down because of the heavy metallic canister inside it, and I woke up with a deep sense of disaster and didn't have the courage to try to interpret the dream.

Today, something I saw on TV late last night prevents me from starting in on what I had planned for today's writing. I saw men's faces, mostly older, some quite old. The stories they told, or more accurately the statements they gave, had the ring of truth. Most of them were former employees of the legendary U.S. institution whose name, CIA, provokes very different reactions in different regions of the world and different classes of society. I cannot figure out what is making them decide to revisit their heroic deeds of the sixties, seventies, and eighties just now. Is someone pressuring them to do it—they who are, after all, the historical winners? What devil is driving them to say at this point that twenty thousand Vietnamese were murdered on the CIA's orders, whether they belonged to the Vietcong or not? That there were orders to assassinate Patrice Lumumba, Martin Luther King, Fidel Castro? That the fall of Salvador Allende in Chile proceeded according to their ingenious plan? Anyone America wanted out of its way, the CIA had murdered, and every president either ordered it personally or at least knew about it, one of the old men says. Why is he saying that? Because he is overcome with regret? Because some of it has become known anyway by this point? There is a third possibility: Because they can afford to say it. Because no one can or will hold them accountable. Because they rule the world, so they are automatically in the right. Because everything necessary to secure their mastery over the world was, by definition, good. That's how it is, and these old men, by no means uncritical in looking back, know perfectly well that none of their revelations will have any consequences. Maybe they produce fear, perhaps even horror, in a few hundred television viewers, so what? That doesn't do any harm to how they feel about life, the feeling that lets them live without self-doubt on the enchanted isle of the rich, powerful, and right.

I did not expect to be able to fall asleep, but I did, and near morning a younger woman appeared, a not unpleasant stranger, and she held out to me in both hands half-transparent body parts of some amphibian-type creature formed around a delicate skeleton, and she said: You have to swallow the turtle. When I woke up, I had to laugh. She was right.

The overcoat of Dr. Freud, I thought, what in the world might be hidden in its inner lining, working its way out only bit by bit? Yes, Bob Rice said, I've wondered that too. What does it mean that I lost the magic coat? That it could be stolen from me? Did I really lock the door? And if not—which is actually impossible, but I can't entirely rule out the possibility, per Freud himself!—what might that mean? Did I somehow want to be free of it, so that it wouldn't hang on my door anymore and remind me every day of certain things I would rather forget?

You don't know who you're talking to, mister, I said, I have just recently learned a thing or two about memory and forgetting that I wouldn't have thought possible. Everything in me struggled against it but it couldn't be put off any longer, I had to go public with it, I started to write a kind of report, as truthful as possible, and I faxed it to a newspaper in Berlin. I didn't tell anyone about it until Peter Gutman took an article out of the fax machine in the office one morning, glanced at the headline spread across several columns, and passed it to me. This is for you. I read the headline, saw my name in large type, and understood. My files had been given to the media.

Hey, listen, I said to Peter Gutman. There's something I need to tell you.

You don't need to, Peter Gutman said, and left me standing there. He didn't want to hear anything. But he came back again a few minutes later: I hope you haven't forgotten that it's my birthday tomorrow. Eight o'clock, my place.

He was one of the last people I could "tell something" to, but when I could he was the person I told in the most detail, the most often.

SO WHO COULD I TELL THE STORY TO

—the story that now needed to be told, even though it wasn't a story at all? The principle of chance would have to decide for me: Who would sit next to me in the lounge for afternoon tea? It was Francesco. Alone. Not bad, as random choices go. I put the faxed newspaper article on the table in front of him, the one where my name appeared in the headline in the context of two letters of the alphabet that for months now had meant in the German media the highest degree of guilt, and I started talking, I talked the whole afternoon through, no one interrupted us, it got late, the sun set, unnoticed by us, and then I finally got to the end, and Francesco said: Shit.

Francesco had sat down by himself on that quiet, rainy Sunday, behind his newspaper, planning to complain again about the news from Italy. They've destroyed the country, he said. Our political class has destroyed the country, and we just sat and watched. That's how it always goes, I said, and since he looked up, paid attention, and seemed interested, I could put the faxed article on the table in front of him, and since he folded his newspaper and looked inquisitively at me, I could talk. Some people found Francesco insensitive, he was inclined to angry outbursts, but he listened the right way and I told him about the week, nine months before, that for me existed outside of time.

About your trip, every morning for ten days, to the part of East Berlin you knew least well. About the street that had just become famous, infamous, because it housed the offices of the agency that, of all the evils the crumbling state had stood for, was the most evil, the most demonic, contaminating everyone it touched. I tried to describe to Francesco the feeling you had when you turned into that courtyard surrounded by a square of monotonous five-story office buildings. He knew buildings like that, he said, and how could he not, as an architectural historian. The fleeting thought that this kind of agency could only be headquartered in buildings like that. Whenever you looked for a spot in the giant parking lot that was always full you were overcome with a feeling of suffocating anxiety, like you were in the wrong place. You already knew which entrance you needed to head toward, and you held your ID ready. The fact that the guard on duty gradually got to recognize you made it paradoxically easier for you to go inside. Obviously he had to write down your ID number again every time, and the different guards who had worked there before must have done the same thing, you thought as you walked upstairs, and you were well aware how much more apprehensive you would have been if you had been summoned to this building in the old days, three or four years ago before the age had "turned." Not that you even knew if outsiders—suspects?—were ever summoned to this building, or if it was only employees of the organization who set foot here. Now its deepest secrets were spread out before almost everyone's eyes, a national legacy—before my eyes too, insofar as they concerned me, I told Francesco. Can you understand, I asked him, what it took to force myself to go back there every morning, to sign in with the woman—a nice, modest, and unassuming woman, by the way—who managed the minuscule portion of the enormous mass of material that concerned you and G., which she kept in a big green wooden box you called a "sea chest," bringing out, every day, the portion of files you were to work on that day and laying them on the table in front of you in the visitors' room where others were sitting with their own stacks of files at other tables.

It was very quiet in that room. The woman handling your files told you the rules, including that she had read through every word of the files before you, but, she promised you, she was sworn to never speak about their contents.

Listen, Francesco said, you don't have to tell me any more. Yes I do, I have to, I said. There were a lot more files than you had expected. Forty-two volumes, later some additional ones too, including telephone surveillance transcriptions. You had been under observation since very early on. And the files from the eighties were not there, except for a single index card which indicated their contents. Destroyed. Or in any case, unlocatable.

And? Francesco asked. Would you have lived your lives differently if you had known?

I've thought about that a lot since then, I said. You and many of your friends had reckoned with the possibility that you were being watched. But not from such an early date. Not so uninterruptedly. You had told each other jokes on the phone, had even expressed your opinions pretty fully, just not naming names. You had to take at least that precaution. But you didn't want to take everything so seriously and make yourself paranoid. It's hard to describe, this state we lived in of simultaneous knowing and repressing, I told Francesco. Would we have lived our lives differently if we had known everything? I don't know.

That afternoon in the lounge I could not know how many evenings, how many hours, I would spend in the coming years on the never-ending conversation we called the "Stasi debate." The state of our respective files. Whether a suspicion had been confirmed or defused. In the public media, two letters of the alphabet were all-powerful: IM. An "*informeller Mitarbeiter*"—"informal collaborator"—was the Stasi term for an informer, someone not an employee of this organization who filed a report. Anyone those letters were attached to, or seemed to be attached to, was condemned, irrespective of how much or how little the letters actually said about them.

The woman helping me, I told Francesco, who of course knew what was in my files, warned me on two different mornings that I was probably going to get an unpleasant surprise that day. And? Francesco asked. Did you get an unpleasant surprise?

I did indeed: detailed reports by a friend about everything you were doing. Since you knew this friend well, this would be the first time you had the chance to ask for an explanation of how they got him to spy on you. They had had him in their clutches, it wasn't his fault. But why hadn't he given you a wink and a nod to warn you? While I was reading that report, I told Francesco, I felt like I was going to throw up, I couldn't help thinking about all the people who had read these pages before me and how many would read them later. I asked myself if it should be allowed, and I developed an obsessive idea of a giant fire being lit in the courtyard of this desolate square of buildings and me getting all the files out of the sea chest and throwing them into the fire, handful by handful. Unread. What relief I would feel.

I can imagine, Francesco said.

Instead, I said, I had to hunt down code names in the files that I wanted to make copies of—a whole trunk of copies. I had to fill out forms requesting the copies, and other forms asking to be told the real names of the people who had spied on me. Then, a couple days later, there they were in front of me, black on white, although what I mostly did was skim them, because it was too embarrassing for me. More often than not the name confirmed a suspicion, but sometimes I was painfully surprised, and then, strangely, I quickly forgot them again.

At lunch you walked—to get out of that room with all the silent people reading, each one sunk in his or her own problems and apparently unable to talk to anyone else about their problems; a particular variety of shame prevented any of you from exchanging more than a quick greeting with the others—at lunch you walked across the courtyard into one of the other buildings, ate there in a kind of canteen that had clearly been set up for the employees of this organization, a meal prepared with no love; you surveyed the other people eating and wondered how many of them had been working there three or four years ago too, and whether they had had to deny what they had earlier thought and done to get their present position. Or whether, on the other hand, they had formerly suppressed their real thoughts and now felt free. They sure didn't look free, I told Francesco. But what does that prove.

I described for him how you became more and more depressed every day and longed for the moment when you could finally hand back the files and call it a day. And how, when you drove home down the familiar strange streets, you had the feeling that a process of wilting and fading had set in and made rapid progress on both sides of the street: the facades of the buildings seemed to have aged years, in only a few days; the people on the sidewalks seemed shriveled, even though they were hauling their new purchases home in the plastic bags with brightly colored new logos on them, the new things they had wanted so badly; even the new brands of car that showed up more and more often between the old cars didn't spread the joy that they had been expected to spread, back when they were objects of longing on television. My own judgment might have been biased, I said to Francesco—maybe I was living through another one of those historical moments which I was unable to celebrate the way other people celebrated them. I had to admit that my desires and most other people's didn't point in the same direction. And that that was the cause of many of my mistakes. Sometimes, driving back home, you had to stop, step inside one or another of the new shops, and buy a blouse or some other article of clothing that you then never wore. When you got back home you had to take a shower right away and change all your clothes.

Looking into these files completely undermined and defiled the past, you know, and poisoned the present along with it. Francesco said he didn't entirely understand that. Facts suddenly bursting in on you can have a destructive effect too, I said, which made Francesco angry. Facts? he barked at me. Did I really think that what I found in those files was the truth about any facts?

That's what the public was made to think, I said.

Exactly, Francesco said. Ask yourself why.

I have thought about that a lot, I said. I asked myself many times, when I got back from that place where the damage was documented but was also spread and deepened, if that kind of knowledge could lead to the healing of any wounds.

Yes, of course, we knew we were under observation, I said. The cars parked in front of the house for weeks. The broken mirror in the bath-

room. The footprints in the hall. The obviously opened and resealed letters. The many bad connections over the phone, the constant crackling.
Of course. That was how the organizations responsible for these things
functioned normally.

Weren't you afraid? Francesco asked. Of course we were. We had
the normal fear you have about any enemy with more effective methods
at its disposal than you. And it helped that you could call it "enemy" without qualification: the relationship was clear. That had taken some
time. —I know, Francesco said, I know all about that. —As for the
categories they had pigeonholed you in, you got that from the files too:
"*feindlich-negativ*," "hostile-negative." Well, really, you could have
thought that up yourself.

You are a PUT and a PID, the woman helping with your files told
you—Underground Political Activity and Political-Ideological Subver-
siveness. But what was the insidious poison you breathed in from these
files that left you so paralyzed? You couldn't put it into words at the
time, but now I know: It was the brutal way they took your lives and
made them trite, over hundreds and hundreds of pages. How comfortably these people fit your lives into their own way of seeing the world.
Even if the facts that the observers reported on and a senior official occasionally summarized were true—which was by no means always the
case; they had to be tailored to fit the interests and expectations of the
people giving the assignments—even then, not one of them matched
how I felt. If there's anything I learned in reading those reports, I said,
it's what language can do to the truth. Those files were in the language
of the secret police, completely incapable of capturing real life. An in-
sect collector who wants to pin his find has to kill it first; the tunnel
vision of the informer unavoidably manipulates what it finds and he
soils it with his miserable language. Yes, I told Francesco, that was what
I felt: soiled.

Francesco again suggested a break. We got ourselves some more
tea; it had grown dark and we went over to the big window and saw
the last glimmers of light on the ocean. Does that make sense? I asked
Francesco. It wasn't the mass of material, not the huge number of IMs
assigned to us, not even their unmasking with their real names—none
of that was what plunged me into a depression and gave me the feeling
that I could not let myself go any deeper into these files or else I would
be pinned to a board by the demon pouring out of them. No, not pinned:

infested. I could not allow them to triumph over us after the fact. Which is then what happened in the media after all.

So, you would have liked it better if you had intelligent, sensitive informers spying on you? Francesco said.

"Liked" or "preferred" are words that truly do not belong in this context, I said. They never showed up in the reports either, of course. These informers must have laughed up their sleeves when they saw how seriously people were taking these often sloppy and careless documents of theirs, how people were combing through them for incriminating material, giving them evidentiary power again, and using them to decide people's fates. How people used these reports to deprive others of their livelihoods or keep them out of jobs that they themselves wanted. No one can open Pandora's Box and go unpunished, I said.

Francesco said it made him feel sick to imagine what would happen if all the secret files were ever opened to the public in Italy.

Not all of them, I said. Only from part of the country: only the northern files, for example, or the southern files.

It's inconceivable! Francesco said.

I laughed. Night had fallen, I could see that Francesco had had enough, he wanted to leave, but I had to keep him there. Now I was getting to what I really had to tell him—the whole long story so far had just been the necessary background. The last day in the agency's building, finally. You had more or less thoroughly read through the forty-two volumes of files, learned the informers' real names and forgotten them again, you thought it was over, thought it was behind you, and then the woman helping you, with whom you had become almost friendly and who knew your files better than you did yourself, cleared her throat: There was something else. A feeling of looming disaster instantly came over you, without your having any idea of what there still might be in store, but you had to find out, right away. She hesitated. She was not allowed to show you your "Perpetrator File"—for the first time, this term! She had sworn not to. You insisted. Finally, she got you to promise that you would never tell anyone she had broken the rule.

Then she left the room for a moment, where you and she had been sitting alone since it was after closing time, and came back in with a thin green file folder that she put on the table in front of you. Even then you didn't understand. She stood behind you and paged through the file for several minutes, during which she constantly looked around to make sure that no one would catch her in this forbidden act. It's your handwriting, isn't it, she asked you, quietly, as though worried, and it *was* my handwriting, I said to Francesco, and that was when I learned that hair standing up on the back of your neck is not just an empty phrase, it really happens. But you didn't sign anything, no official agreement, nothing, the woman said. It would look very different if you had.

You didn't have time, you couldn't read anything carefully, just skim a couple pages: A clearly harmless report on a colleague, in your handwriting; reports from two contacts about three or four "meets" with you; and the fact that they had managed you under a code name. These were what made this folder a "Perpetrator File" and what hurled you, without warning, into another category of human being.

The woman helping you, who hastily took the file away again, said: It was all more than thirty years ago, practically nothing happened, and there are meters and meters of "Victim Files," surely everyone will realize how insignificant this ancient history is, but still, she had not wanted to let me fall completely unprepared into the trap that was about to open up under my feet. She read the newspapers too. Any journalist who asked her would get access to this file—as the law ordered! In her opinion, it was just a matter of time before someone received a tip and was on my tracks.

As for me, I said to Francesco, I heard myself say for the first time: I had forgotten all about that. And I noticed myself how implausible it sounded. The woman sighed: We hear that here a lot! And she rushed to take the file back out of the room.

Francesco said: Shit. Then, after a while: What are you going to do?

I said: I'm going to publish it all.

Think it over first, Francesco said. I read your German newspapers too. You need to ask yourself if you can stand up to what's going to happen.

I have no choice, I said. In any case, I couldn't speak publicly about this file without causing problems for the woman who broke the rules by showing it to me. But I've just heard that she has died, very young, of cancer. So now I can talk about it.

Kafka, Francesco said. Kafka could have come up with something like that.

You're right, I said. No one is innocent in his work either. As in life. I turned in from Second Street, crossed the Spanish front lawn, saw the staring masks of the three raccoons in the bushes, walked into the hall, waved at Mr. Enrico just clearing off his table and finishing work for the day, set foot in my strange, foreign apartment as though I were getting home, poured myself a glass of water, drank it like I was about to die of thirst, and sat down in front of my machine on the table. I wrote:

```
How can I avoid ending up feeling compelled to jus-
tify myself? That would be the most idiotic way to act
of all. But is there any correct, appropriate way to
act in this situation? And am I falling back into the
trap of asking what other people want from me?
```

I lay down on my wide bed. It was dark outside but not time to go to sleep yet, and I said to Pema the nun, whose book lay on my night-stand: The tigers are here, but where is the strawberry? I fell into a half-sleep with lines of poetry floating past, "accept your fate," oh my dear Fleming, what could you know of the disasters of fate. I drifted into a fleeting dream where a face appeared before me, the face of my friend Emma who was also dead and whom I needed now, but I thought I knew what she would have told me: Don't let anything show! That's what she would have said.

The same way she said it back then, in 1965—my God, more than a quarter century had passed since then!—after the so-called "spectacle" of that Plenum of the Central Committee where culture was once again made the scapegoat for everything going wrong. Where you felt it was necessary to defend those who were under attack, and ran up against a brick wall, of course, came under attack yourself, and finally left the auditorium, thinking: Got my hands chopped off there! Now now, Emma said, don't take yourself so seriously. It was good that you said some-thing, otherwise you would have felt lousy. And hands grow back. —So, you believe in miracles, you said. —How could I not, Emma said. The fact that I'm sitting here with you is due to a whole string of miracles.

You knew what she meant: That she had survived the years in prison under the Third Reich; that she had found shelter in this allot-ment garden when fleeing from bombed-out Berlin, before she was thrown in prison again. That she had shed tears when "our side" threw her back in jail, "under false charges"—and the news reached her of Stalin's death. Her joints were frail from arthritis, from the damp cold jail cell. She walked with a stick, had aches and pains that she ignored. Had I asked her urgently enough why even being jailed by "our side" wasn't enough to cure her of her belief in Stalin? I could have used her answer now. Ach, girl, she said once, do you have any idea what people cling to when they're as deep in the shit as we were then? If we had given up hope in the wise Steersman of Peoples we might as well have given up on ourselves . . . And you understood that this half-Germany, this state—even if it treated her harshly, even if it had many faults—was her only refuge. That she had to cling to the belief that it would develop into the humane society she so longed for. That she had to defend it.

Emma, who, unlike others, was not afraid to look facts in the face, became one of my most trusted advisors. But back then, I remembered, after that disastrous Plenum, you needed more than advice. You needed what people call professional help.

The doctor told you: Every system of power in the world has a vested interest in weakening the individuality of its subjects and tries to weaken or if possible completely extinguish it. The best thing to do is not to confront these powers, which are always stronger than the individual, but rather to retreat and live your life in peace and quiet, psychologically unharmed. It is not beyond the realm of possibility that a day might come when people can live openly again: if that day comes, we will see that the repression of their individuality has not caused any genetic mutations, that their DNA has remained untouched, and that a new generation will be capable of living without spiritual chains.

I remembered that the medicines the doctor prescribed for you didn't work; I also remembered the weeks in the clinic where the doctor finally sent you because he no longer wanted to take responsibility for your case. ("You don't send a wounded soldier back into battle either!") It was a tiny room with a barred window overgrown with vines, but you didn't need the bars there, you would not have chosen to jump out the window; keeping your body intact was important to you. Much later, a doctor told me how many pills a person needs, and of what kind, he was probably just trying to make himself feel important. The only thing you told the supervising doctor at the clinic was that you had a phobia about newspapers—they were full of speeches to the committee agreeing with everything, speeches in favor of the measures you had

fought against. There were names at the bottom of the articles and letters that you had never expected to see under such articles and letters.
Whenever you saw a newspaper you broke out in a sweat.

I felt that the new newspaper campaign already getting under way
had brought the old trauma back to life. You took the newspapers
that they delivered daily to your room in the clinic (as therapy!) and
quickly stuck them under the blankets. Since you couldn't sleep—again,
I couldn't sleep—you roamed up and down the hospital hallway at night
and often ran into another patient, the wife of a border patrol officer
whose job was to lead foreign visitors to the Wall built four years earlier
and explain to them the GDR's border control measures. Ever since, his
wife received phone calls day and night, with threats and curses, again
and again, no matter how often they changed their phone number. Finally she developed a phobia about the telephone and could no longer
sleep. Her supervising doctor, also yours, was convinced that false habits or information in the brain could be erased and replaced by learning
the correct ones, with a correct training program. He had her sleep on
the couch in the examination room and had the nurse on night duty
phone her several times a night, which made the woman panic and spend
the nights in the hallway. You eventually managed to read the headlines
in the newspapers, which was the first sign of improvement; the second
sign, according to the highly pleased assistant who was under her
professor's spell, was when she noticed me wearing new shoes I had
bought—shoes with a prominent black-and-white grid pattern that I
wore for a long time.

Peter Gutman's fiftieth birthday. There were four of us at the party,
as befitted his ascetic lifestyle and tendency to keep to himself. Aside
from me were, to my surprise, Johanna—one of our young fellowship
holders, working on the treatment of social themes in recent American
literature (but that was just an alibi for the CENTER, Peter Gutman
thought)—and Malinka, a slim, dark-haired, attractive, prickly woman in
her late thirties. She came from former Yugoslavia and had lived in this
city for several years. I don't remember anymore where Peter Gutman
knew her from; she didn't have any connection with the CENTER, co-
ordinating some kind of research tasks at a scientific institute.

Peter Gutman insisted on serving us without any help: first came
melons and prosciutto with a good wine, then he disappeared into the
kitchen area to whip up a quick Chinese dish with chicken and vegeta-

bles in a wok while we women continued to weave the threads of the conversation. Namely, that compassion for the "underprivileged" on the part of relatively prosperous people was increasingly disappearing; that people did make sure to go out of their way to express themselves politely toward them and with the correct terminology but increasingly refused any concrete help that might affect their own wallets. We all had seen affluent people hurrying past the homeless as though deaf and blind, their faces twisted into a grimace of disgust, withholding the dollar they could so easily have afforded to give.

Malinka flew into a rage. She said she understood it completely: she didn't give charity either. No one who hasn't experienced it themselves could possibly understand how hard life is in this country for someone who has to start with nothing. It had been so unspeakably horrible when she herself had first arrived that she had killed off any sentimentality she had about those who were on the bottom today. She had gotten into the habit of sitting behind her steering wheel and driving past everything without emotion: car crashes, corpses on the side of the road, the worst poverty, and the worst crimes that so often went along with immense riches. Her mantra, she said, was: *I don't care, I don't care.* And she didn't pity the *homeless people* like we did. Didn't give them any money either. She kept every goddamn cent she had for herself. In fact, she was furious at them. What she most wanted to do was shake them and shout: Don't let yourselves go like that! Keep your dignity, at least! They should pull themselves out of the swamp on their own. No one had helped her!

Peter Gutman stuck his head out of the kitchen door to look at Malinka but none of us said a word. We exchanged glances, a bit at a loss about how to respond.

Johanna told the story of how she had given money to a man in New York once and he had thanked her by saying *God bless you!* in the usual pathetic tone. She had shouted at him that he shouldn't say *God bless you*, he should curse her! He had stared at her in amazement, then calmly said: *That's my business, ma'am.*

Oh, Brecht! we laughed.

I could tell that a lot of what Peter Gutman had to say in the conversation that night (we had started discussing the vanishing, or actually vanished, role of reason in Western culture) was directed at me—it was his commentary on the article he had taken out of the fax for me the day before. He knew what was going on, but did not want to talk to me about it yet. He wanted to give me space. When we said good night, he said: *Be careful!*

What else? There is a pause, it gets longer. I have the usual suspicion that my writing has ground to a halt because I have not succeeded in breaking through the barrier labeled "Do not touch!" and because writing is pointless unless you do break through it. *The overcoat of Dr. Freud* can also be abused to protect vulnerable sore spots, I think with a mental sneer.

SOMETIMES THE PAST REACHES UP AND GRABS AT YOU

I think, and then the established, well-known course of events kicks in. The public reacts with joy and lightning speed to the word "morality" and, for good reason, flays the skin from the body of the person accused of immorality.

And the truth they all purport to serve?

What else? How to keep going? Everything does always have to keep going. In the MS. VICTORIA, everything kept going. I had to keep walking on the same paths. *How are you doing today?* This time it was the uniformed doorman at the fancy restaurant on Second Street that the guidebook listed as one of the ten best places to eat in Los Angeles. People drove up in the biggest stretch limousines imaginable, which they then entrusted to the doorman with his blinding white gloves. He had no reason to ask me, of all people, how I was doing: he must have seen right away that I was not among his clientele. *Oh fine*, I said, surprised, *and you?* —*Terrific!* he said, convinced and convincingly, a word that I used to confuse with *terrifying*, which led to some misunderstandings until I finally found the two words next to each other in the dictionary, *terrific* translated as "great," "fantastic," also "cool," while *to terrify* meant "to give someone a frightful shock," a phrase that immediately started to tumble around and around in my head—"to give a cool shock," "fantastic to be sent into shock," "a great, frightful shock" ... Stop! I ordered myself. Stop. Stop. But it was no longer in my power to make the tape recording stop.

Now the three raccoons sitting in front of the MS. VICTORIA, or hunting in the bushes for something to eat, were getting bold: apparently the garbage bins in the narrow side street were good hunting grounds. When I came home at night they were squatting in the dark in front of the circular flower bed with the bitter orange tree and staring at me. *Hi!* I said, in a friendly voice, which didn't seem to impress them. All right, so let me pass, I said in German, but they didn't know German. So I walked toward them, step by step, toward their masklike faces with eyes always open wide, and they squatted there without moving, *Don't worry,* I said, more to myself than to them since they were obviously in no way worried, and now was I supposed to just squeeze past them or what? Then the door of the MS. VICTORIA was flung open, the tall resident with the Indian face stepped out, clapped his hands, and gave a loud and aggressive yell. The raccoons scurried into the bushes. *Come inside!* the man called to me, *Hurry up, please, they're dangerous.* I ran into the building and when I turned around in the door I was looking into three pairs of wide-open eyes. *They're crazy,* the man said, *they are not acting normal.*

In the following days I saw the ragged gray cat creeping around the building, but *NO PETS!* stood on the door in big letters and no one dared bring the animal into the building past Mrs. Ascott, and when we put edible items out in the bushes we didn't know what we were actually feeding, the shaggy cat or the feral raccoons, but after only a few days its fur had gotten smoother, and then it was wearing a brown leather collar, and then one day I saw the cat on the lap of the man with the Indian face, who was sitting under the sun umbrella on the front lawn, a little dish of milk at his feet, and he was petting the cat. It trusted him and was snuggling with him. He saw the look I gave him and said *I adopted it,* and from then on the cat lay curled up in the sun, in front of the MS. VICTORIA's door, completely at peace, and it let the people it trusted pet it. Peter Gutman said that the guy was a little *crazy* himself. Have you heard him sing? He puts on old, scratchy records and sings along. —Does he sing well? I asked. —Abominably. But it's okay, I like the ordinary sounds around me, especially the ones I wouldn't hear on a luxury liner.

Diversionary tactics, we both knew it. We talked about everything under the sun except the contents of the faxes that arrived for me at the CENTER's office in ever increasing number, which Kätchen put in my mailbox without comment. There seemed to be no topic more interesting to large swaths of the German media than my actions. I didn't read every article right away when it came in: there was a limit, a daily quota of accusations that I could bear. Now it turned out that, against my original wishes, I needed a car for even the simplest daily errands, like shopping. It was a difficult undertaking that took days to take care of, distracted me, and let me get to know a sharp, capable salesman. Finally, he was delighted to see me buy a Geo, fire-engine red, which admittedly made a strange grinding noise whenever the car made a sharp left turn, but then again, when would I really need to make a sharp left turn? It was cheap and it fit in the space in the MS. VICTORIA's garage, number 7.

I warned Peter Gutman never to drive with me but he insisted on our going in this car, with me behind the wheel, to an area of Los Angeles neither of us had been to, where Malinka wanted to show us the house she was planning to buy.

It was a hideous house in a hideous neighborhood. We looked at each other, communicated our agreement, and refrained from passing judgment. Malinka said that she knew perfectly well there were better houses out there, but this was one she could afford. And it would be her own. And it was located far enough away from any possible place where new *riots* might break out. She remembered with perfect clarity her ambivalent feelings during the *riots* in April: One person inside her had stood up and crowed in triumph: Ha! Finally! while the other one anxiously followed the fires coming closer and said: You may be right, you may have a right to revolt, but dammit, don't touch my house! That's how it is, she said. The more you own, the less you can let yourself see the world the way it really is—much less the way it should be.

That's Marxism, I said.

So? Malinka said. Ur-Marxism, if you want to put it that way. Not far at all from primitive Christianity.

When I hear you two talk, Peter Gutman said, it makes me think that maybe Communism isn't dead after all.

Always these words, I said. Can't we get by for even a little while without these words?

No, Malinka said, words are so important. For example, *"riots,"* or at most *"unrests"*: those are set in stone now. It's obvious whose interests are being served by saying that these uprisings were "turmoil," "disturbances," "riots," and nothing like *"revolt," "rebellion," "insurrection,"* or "*uprising*," much less "*revolution.*" It was said to be naked, unbridled violence that had terrified South Central Los Angeles in April—no political or social motives were to be attributed to the rioters, certainly no economic motives. They had laid hands on the holiest of holies, this society's bedrock: private property. Yes, Malinka said, of course I felt sorry for the Korean shopkeepers, they didn't deserve to bear the brunt of it, but the other person in me, the one from before, understood the rioters. That's how revolutions have always started: the most disadvantaged take from the rich what they weren't allowed to have until then.

And when a revolution has failed to reach its goal and has come to an end, I say, its heirs are the first to reestablish the old property relations.

I asked Malinka—it was a compulsion, I had to ask everyone I met—if she had ever completely forgotten a crucially important event in her life. Oh yes, she said, I run into that all the time, whenever I go home and see my family. They remember lots of things that happened when I was there but which I don't have the slightest memory of. These memories are a precious possession for them; for me, they're a burden I have to throw off.

That must be a loss too?

Malinka said she had trained herself with iron resolve not to feel any regret about that kind of loss.

She didn't manage it completely, I said to Peter Gutman on the drive back. Otherwise she wouldn't have gotten worked up like that about the names given to the April uprising. By the way, that's a long-standing concern of mine: the intensity and speed with which the political class and its media push a name that suits them onto events that have surprised, maybe even overwhelmed them. Most recent example: the people's uprising in the fall of 1989, around the end of the GDR. The label "*Wende*," the "Turn," got itself firmly established. And then, interestingly, the state's name had to vanish as quickly as possible, along with the thing itself: all you saw in the papers was "the SED dictatorship," after the name of the Party, or "illegitimate state," or "unjust regime." In personal conversations today, people say "in GDR-times."

But I remember, I said to Peter Gutman, who was sitting next to me in my red Geo—mute and, I thought, rather tense, tolerating without comment my sometimes risky driving style—I remember how, many

years earlier, back on June 17, 1953, the first time I saw masses demon-
strating in the streets, it was a headache for the politicians and newspapers how to name the event then too: in the first few days there was
talk of "worker's protests" and "justified criticisms," and then we were
informed that we had witnessed a "counterrevolution," which naturally
made public discussion of the events much easier. Malinka had talked
about the split in herself—I can remember very well, I said, the split in
myself back then.

How scared you were, riding the streetcar back from the national
library in Leipzig—a whisper behind you had already alarmed you—
when you saw workers unfurling a banner on a construction site as you
rode past: We are on strike! How you ran through the center of Leipzig,
to the Germanistics Institute in the old, half-destroyed university, but
almost no one was there—no one who knew what was going on outside,
in any case, since the GDR stations were broadcasting light music and
people didn't listen to West German stations in the institute. How you
ran around the corner to Ritterstrasse, to the FDJ district committee,
and saw them throwing files and typewriters and office supplies and
furniture out the windows and the people standing down below were
enthusiastically screaming and applauding. Well, those aren't workers,
you thought, relieved. How you wandered around in the city center
among an ever thicker crowd of people, trying to find someone you knew.
How you saw "Down with Pointy-Beard!" (meaning Walter Ulbricht, the
Party's first secretary) written in chalk on a streetcar and wiped it off
with your handkerchief, and, strangely, I still remember today the face
of the older man you thought was some kind of official as he grabbed
your sleeve, brought his face right up next to yours, proclaimed the end
of this shit government, and told you to take off your party badge. How
a ring of people formed in a second around the two of you, demanding
the same thing from you, and how you said to the man in an ice-cold
voice: Over my dead body!

That was ridiculous, of course, but at the time it seemed to me the
only appropriate thing to answer, I don't know if you can understand
that, I said to Peter Gutman. He listened and said nothing. Then suddenly a comrade was standing next to you, a historian, and he pulled
you away, the two of you ran to the Historical Institute where you saw
groups of people you had never seen anything like before, wild people,

you thought, in the first row of one bunch was a muscular man with a beard and no shirt on with something like a cudgel in his hand. What if they work us over with that! the man with you said, and then you felt queasy too. But they were there at the Historical Institute to organize the defense of the premises, go ahead and laugh but what else should I call it. They had barricaded the entrance door from the inside, with desks, and a guard was placed there to let in only people he knew or who could prove they were all right. Still no orders from the Party, they said. That failure kept repeating itself in crisis situations, I said.

For the first time a feeling that there was no way out of the situation came over you, but you forgot it again. I have not forgotten how it was light out late that night and you picked up at least ten Party badges on the way home that timid comrades had thrown away. And how you were both horrified and relieved when the tanks rolled past. And how, a few days later, when you sat down in a restaurant with your Party badge on, the other people at the table pointedly stood up. And how it made you uncomfortable when it was only you and one Christian fellow student who insisted, at an assembly of student groups, that the Party should pay attention not only to the actions of its inevitable enemies, but also, and above all, to the workers' justified demands. But the line was: Don't give an inch of ground to the class enemy. And I was told that I should be careful about the company I kept.

I fell silent. Peter Gutman was silent too. Then he said: You must know Brecht's remark when he gave up his plan to write a play about Rosa Luxemburg. He said, "I'm not going to hack off my own foot just to prove that I'm a good hacker."

Yes, I knew that remark. But don't we really need to ask ourselves why it should lead to self-mutilation simply to speak or write the truth?

Oho! Peter Gutman cried. Madame! Simply speak the truth! No more and no less!

We had arrived safe back at the MS. VICTORIA's garage door. Peter Gutman got out of the car. Then he stuck his head in the car again: So, when are you finally going to ask me?

Ask you what? What am I supposed to ask you?

Whether I've ever forgotten crucially important things in my life.

You? I said. You're the person I'll ask last.

He slammed the passenger door shut.

Doctor Kim was on vacation in Korea. A friendly, moon-faced man named Wu Sun would take care of me, but first Doctor Pan had to take my blood pressure. They both shook their heads, they said numbers I couldn't believe, then they put their heads together and whispered, in English, since Doctor Pan was Chinese and didn't speak Korean—he wanted to know *"whether there are any troubles in your life just now"* and I had to laugh, oh yes, I said, there are, they were discreet and didn't ask anything more, just discussed the points into which Wu Sun should insert the needles, including now a few against my extremely high blood pressure. *Relax!* they implored me in stereo, *relax!* but I couldn't relax, and I didn't yet know that I would not be coming back there again, because I was in the grip of an anxiety that made it impossible for me to lie down calmly for half an hour.

Sally called. *How are you today.* —Oh, Sally, I said, *something's wrong.* She said she could tell from my voice.

And what about you, I asked her. *How are you?*

Very bad. She came over. We walked along the coast, up on Ocean Park Promenade, back and forth, back and forth, holding nothing back as I talked in a foreign language, in the California winter light, it had been raining for weeks, *heavy rain,* there were eight years of drought to make up for, on TV you could still see people lugging sandbags through the dark, firefighters pumping out basements, or houses sliding down the unreinforced hillsides. The ocean was brown and it beat in high waves against the empty beach.

Sally said: *It's hopeless,* that's the first and most fundamental thing you have to remember. There is no hope, *you know,* there is only the duty to keep going, to try to get through it. That's all we can do.

I know that, sometimes, I said, and then I forget it again.

She said she forgot it every day.

Sally was my test subject. I tried out on her how I felt, I spoke unspeakable words out loud under the cover of the foreign language and the foreign ocean, I saw myself standing there leaning against the trunk of a eucalyptus tree and explaining to her the various types of files, *the bad files and the good files,* and she had to laugh: Oh, you Germans!

No, I said, don't laugh, it's nothing to laugh about! Sally is Jewish, she'll understand me, I thought, illogically. Listen, I said, can't you imagine how you would feel if suddenly, looking at these files, two letters of the alphabet jumped out at you that were like a judge's sentence, a moral death sentence. IM: Do you even know what that means?

No, Sally said quite naturally, *I have no idea.*

Oh, happy America! "Stasi"? Yes, she had heard of that. Everyone knew about that.

"*Informeller Mitarbeiter*," how can I say that in English.

Oh, I see. Some kind of agent? Or spy?

Oh, Sally, you're killing me. Why couldn't she speak a single word of German? Everything was even more direct and raw and sickening in a foreign language, of course, where qualifications and distinctions fell away because I simply didn't have them available. But what good were qualifications anyway.

I'll tell you what happened, okay?

But that's exactly what wasn't so simple. All right: In my memory, which I had struggled to bring to the surface, there were two young men who dropped by your office one day, at the newspaper where you worked, and they wanted some inconsequential information from you about your job. In the files it says that they intercepted you on the street. I don't remember that. They told you what they were: personnel of the Ministry of State Security, the Stasi.

When was this? Sally asked.

1959.

My goodness, you were a different person then!

Never mind that, Sally. It's not about that. It's about memories, about how we remember: my topic for decades, you understand? And somehow I could have forgotten *that*. It came to me that you had met these two men two more times, they called themselves Heinz and Kurt or something like that. One time, I just now recall, I said, was probably near the Thälmann-platz subway station, I don't remember anymore what you talked about with them, I told Sally, in my memory they were short and insignificant encounters, which I did talk about at home, by the way, and I had told them that right off the bat. You weren't comfortable with them, I still remember that, but everyone knew that these people came to see almost everyone playing any kind of role, that was their job, it didn't incriminate you. And then, after the "Turn," when this hunt for IMs in the files began in Germany, I had not one second of thinking that I might be affected too. I didn't feel the slightest guilt. Do you understand that, Sally?

Oh yes, I understand, she said. She had been just as certain that she would never find a letter from Ron's mistress in his jacket pocket. Not that she wanted to compare the two cases, only our false certainties.

There it stood, "IM," I didn't want to believe it but my body believed it right away—my heart started pounding, I was soaked in sweat, emergency! emergency! alarm bells, flight reflexes, I would have been glad to run away all the way to the edge of the world. Is Santa Monica the edge of the world?

Yes, Sally said. When you look at it that way, it is.

It doesn't help, though. Running away doesn't help, old folk saying. Standing your ground doesn't help either. I don't know anymore what the first thing was that I thought, when I could think again. But I do know the first thing I felt, without words. Translated into words, it was: You can't tell anyone. At the beginning I knew I would keep it to myself, while I also knew that that was the wrong thing to do, and useless in the long run, and to understand that, Sally, you had to be there back then. You had already been through the first wave of the witch hunt— you had written a book describing a day of your life under surveillance, which had already been the occasion to subject you to a level of condescension and presumption you could never have imagined, even in a dream. I couldn't withstand another wave right then, Sally. Again I was faced with the choice between two impossibilities and I chose the one that seemed to hurt me less at the time.

That's what we all do, Sally said with a sigh. But did you have any obligation to talk about it at all?

That is exactly what I asked myself too, I said, when I was able to ask myself questions again, and my answer was no. No, I said to myself, I did not have a duty to talk about it. Anyway, I was scared.

You can't let any of that show here, Sally said. When they smell the scent of fear on you they pounce. Like wild animals, I'm telling you.

The overcoat of Dr. Freud came to my mind. I wished it could protect me.

On the contrary, Sally said. It's there to take your self-defense mechanisms away from you.

In a dream I was being driven down a deserted street on the top deck of a dilapidated freight truck. Apparently my task was to unload the freight from the top of the truck to get down to the actual truck bed, it was very difficult, and treacherous while the moving truck was shaking back and forth, but finally I did it, I was on the truck bed, but then, to my disappointment, it was totally empty. I woke in darkness with a feeling of hopelessness, which the dream alone was not enough to explain, and it came as no surprise when I then, in the middle of the night, asked myself: What am I doing here? I had given myself over, almost greedily, to the excitement of the first few weeks, I had almost consciously avoided taking stock of my time here; now that I thought about it, I had accepted it as something I'd earned, without that word ever occurring to me, I thought, deeply breathing in the mild California night air that came in through the big open window, filtered, like all the air in all the rooms, by the small-mesh screen windows, which were there to defend the clean, pure, immunized interior spaces against any insects that might contaminate them, or worse: make them unsafe. This bottomless need Americans have for safety, certainty, security.

But what did I know about Americans. I should just admit to myself that I was homesick. I listened in on myself, prepared to find the pain of homesickness, but it wasn't there, it had left me in the lurch. The truck bed is empty, I thought with a little self-mocking laugh.

Why wasn't I homesick? It wasn't natural, in a foreign country, the thought came to me. I hadn't wanted to live in a Greater Germany again, the thoughts went on, unreasonably, but night thoughts have a different color than day thoughts, a different slant, more than anything else they know all the secret paths and chinks in the armor they can take advantage of to force their way into consciousness, which defends itself, feebly, with the counterquestions I knew all too well. Would I really have preferred that smaller Germany in the long run, with all its shortages and deprivations—what am I saying: with its afflictions and faults—with the seed of collapse inside it, which I had, after all, been feeling for a long time? I was moving again, back on well-worn tracks, all I had to do was keep quiet and let the argument and counterargument inside me run their course, I wouldn't learn anything new, but on the other hand I wouldn't be able to fall back to sleep, this was tried and tested, there was no point in hopefully shutting my eyes.

Until, half-asleep, I heard the soft tinkling of bottles, it was the *homeless* man who lived on the corner of the alley behind the building and spent the nights scouring the garbage containers for bottles he could redeem for the deposits. I listened to the tinkling and didn't notice myself falling asleep.

A new day with the old tape recorder in my head, running on endless loop and bringing up the same question again and again: How could I have forgotten that? I knew, of course, that no one would ever believe I had forgotten it—they threw it in my face as my own offense. *Vergehen*, what a beautiful German word, both "misdemeanor" and "the fading into the past"!

I called my friend in Zurich. You're a psychologist, you must know: Can someone forget something like that? That they gave me a code name? That I wrote a report? He kept calm. And? he said. What else? And by the way: A person can forget anything. They need to, in fact. Don't you know the line from Freud: We cannot live without forgetting? —Repressing! I said. And he said: Not necessarily. We also forget what we don't think is very important. —But that can't be what happened to me in this case. —Who knows? It was such a long time ago. —Thirty-three years. —Oh dear God. And what makes you think you know what was important to you back then? —That's what I want to find out. —How? —I'm crawling back down into the mineshaft. —Good luck. But please, be careful. Right now you're the only one looking after yourself, remember that. No one will take that responsibility off your shoulders. And also, excuse me for saying so, you are going through a psychological crisis. —So what do you think I should do? Go into therapy? —That would probably be the best thing.

But there was no question of that. I didn't need help, I wasn't allowed to need help, I had to "get through it" alone. Only much, much later, maybe only today, do I understand that this stubborn insistence had more than a little in common with the old way of thinking, the one that, as Peter Gutman later said, had gotten me "into this mess." I paged through books in search of relief. I found Brecht's lines about the city I was living in myself:

> Reflecting, so I hear, on hell
> My brother Shelley found it to be a place
> Much like the city of London. I
> Who live not in London but in Los Angeles
> Find, reflecting on hell, that it must be
> Even more like Los Angeles.

City of Angels, I thought, amused. I got my fire-engine-red Geo out of the garage—a test of courage and skill every time, though I tried to make sure that no one could tell by looking—and drove to Twenty-sixth Street again. Brecht's cube-shaped house, where he had had long discussions with Adorno and Eisler and Laughton and reflected on the insoluble ethical problems of the Galileo play, was now occupied by a man I sometimes saw on his front lawn and who definitely did not know who had lived there before him. How many times would Brecht have left this house to drive downtown? Or to visit the Feuchtwangers at Villa Aurora, high above the Pacific cliffs at Paseo Miramar, which my Geo brought me to as well? Where once, years before, on an unforgettable afternoon, Marta Feuchtwanger had shown you and G. her husband's library and where there were now contractors in clouds of stone dust busy in the emptied rooms. Where Brecht could discuss political and literary problems, and agree about them, with the "little master" who, with iron discipline, dedicated all his days to his work. While Brecht avoided the other master, Thomas Mann, as much as possible. Had it ever happened in modern Europe that a country's intellectual elite, almost without exception, had had to flee? Weimar Under the Palms. Where did I hear that term?

Oh, an old actor said to me on the green lawn behind the Schoenberg house on North Rockingham Avenue, where we were standing together, each holding a margarita glass, *I'm Norman*, and he introduced me to his wife, Peggy, who looked straight out of a Chekhov play: white hair pinned up in a hairdo from the turn of the century; long, old-fashioned strings of pearls around her neck; heavily made up with deep purple lipstick; her blouse and dress also typical of that era. Norman, with blue, amphibian eyes and white hair with a precise part, and a rather small face, still unlined, was dressed in a correct suit and tie, even in the heat of this winter day. He didn't look like an actor, but that changed the moment he started to talk. His voice still carried and he delivered his stories accompanied by well-chosen gestures. He had something he needed to tell me: He had worked with Brecht. He was one of the managers of the theater in Beverly Hills where the second version of *Galileo* was premiered. He knew stories about the rehearsals with Laughton, not entirely suitable for polite company, that he enthusiastically told me anyway: How Laughton, as Galileo at the dress rehearsal, his hands in the deep pockets of his roomy robe, "*was playing with his genitals.*" How Brecht then instructed him, Norman, over the phone to make Laughton stop, which he, Norman, refused to do, even when Helene

Weigel joined Brecht in making the request. The next day, though, before the performance, a furious Laughton was seen chasing the costume director, who insisted that it wasn't his fault: The pockets had been removed from Galileo's robe. And, Norman asked, do you know who was responsible for the costumes? Helene Weigel!

Oh, madam, he said, how grateful we are to you for sending us all that German culture! Such men and women they were! Brecht. Feuchtwanger. Thomas Mann. Heinrich Mann. Hanns Eisler. Arnold Schoenberg. Bruno Frank. Leonhard Frank. Franz Werfel. Adorno. Berthold Viertel. And on and on. *Oh, madam, what seeds they planted!* And the best thing about them was their sense of humor. How they made you laugh! Hanns Eisler, for example, Norman's neighbor on the Malibu coast, once had a circulatory collapse and Lou Eisler, worried, called them to come over. Eisler was lying on the ground, Norman said, and I asked him, *Hey, what's wrong? How do you feel?* Eisler told me: I feel like a thousand frogs are having sex on my tongue! That man's life is not in danger, we thought.

Norman still admired Brecht's appearance before the McCarthy committee and Eisler's statement refusing to denounce anyone, with the remark: *They are my colleagues.*

The guests had all arrived and we were called to the table. The house, where Arnold Schoenberg had lived for fifteen years worshipped by his student, Eisler, was now occupied by Schoenberg's son Ronald and Ronald's wife, Barbara. Walking into their dining room was like walking into a Vienna salon: Nothing has changed here! Norman exclaimed. They served beef soup with bread dumplings and boiled beef with baby carrots and various sauces and boiled potatoes, and for dessert Sacher torte with whipped cream and strawberries, of course. Guests were led past a display case where Barbara had preserved the few remaining mementoes of her father, the Austrian émigré composer Eric Zeisl; she said with a certain melancholy—the daughter in the famous father-in-law's house—that her own father had been forgotten.

I remember how, near the end of the dinner, I worked up the courage to bring the conversation around to the argument between Thomas Mann and Schoenberg about Mann's use of elements of Schoenberg's twelve-tone music in the twenty-second chapter of *Doctor Faustus*, which Schoenberg had sharply criticized. Had they been able to get past their disagreements in the end? Well, Schoenberg's sons said, the two men had exchanged some letters, in other words come to an understanding, as it were. Had they met again afterward? Barbara, the peacemaker, said: Schoenberg did die in 1951, only a short time later.

The reasons why *Doctor Faustus* had so enraged Schoenberg were cataloged once again; the sons reported that the Author's Note in the later editions of the book had hurt their father's feelings too. Both the German and the English versions were brought out for Barbara to read aloud from. Schoenberg had even said, in fact, that if Mann had talked to him beforehand he would have composed a piece especially for him and the book.

I unexpectedly ended up in another argument that evening, with a German literature professor who called *Doctor Faustus* an "allegory of the Nazi state." I insisted that the book was an analysis that went much deeper, of the German character through history and the way German intellectuals and artists became entangled in the catastrophe that this history had led to. The professor did not understand what I was saying and wanted to prove he was right with quotations from the book; I was amazed at how flat and superficial his interpretation was. I forced myself to stay polite but didn't back down.

The same thing happened when the professor said he was in favor of the death penalty, after Norman described a case where some teenagers had brutally killed three children. Why should we let these teenagers live? The others at the table were in favor of the death penalty too. Here I could not stay neutral. For our own sakes, I said, that is why we should let them live. Locked up, of course, so that they can't hurt anyone else. But not killed. Would I talk that way if it had been my own child? Then someone else at the table said you can't ask that . . . Where was the dividing line, actually? I would sanction the execution of Nazi mass murderers. Still, I said: But we can imagine a society where these three teenagers would not have ended up so deeply perverted. Was I imagining things, or did this comment earn me mocking looks? I realized that most Americans see such crimes as part of human nature, not circumstance: there is simply a moral code everyone has to follow.

The very next day, I remember, I drove up to San Remo Drive again to look at Thomas Mann's house from the entrance, "where," he writes, "I lived and worked for more than a decade. I was exposed to the pressures of the often strangling afflictions of the time, of course—the same there as I would have been anywhere else—but still, under relatively mild and bearable circumstances." I decided to once again drive down the road he often walked, to the Ocean Park Promenade, to Hotel Miramar, where his wife, Katia, would pick him up in the car. On the other hand, he would torture himself with the news from Germany. December 5, 1944: "Irritating and crude article by Marcuse about my *Atlantic* essay . . . Foolishness." The article where Marcuse challenged Mann "just once, at some point, to write the unvarnished truth about his own past—as mercilessly as all great converts did." He meant the "past" that Mann had documented in his World War I essay "Reflections of an Unpolitical Man." It had caught up to him too, as an admonition even after his emigration, after all his radio speeches to the German people, in the middle of his work on arguably the most unsparing analysis of the "guilt of the German intellectuals" ever written, *Doctor Faustus.*

Memory images: The color in fashion for female *officials* seems to be crimson. It sometimes happens that Hillary Clinton and Barbara Bush and Al Gore's wife and other female congressional candidates appear on one and the same stage before the American television public in that same color. But the red that CBS used on election night, to indicate the states that had already gone to Clinton, is darker. Actually, by five in the afternoon when I get back to my apartment, everything has already been decided, the polling places have closed on the East Coast, the results are supposed to be withheld until it is eight o'clock here on the West Coast too but of course there is no question of that in this media society. We are sitting, more than fifteen of us, at Pintus and Ria's place, with red wine, bread, chicken, and cheese, and we hardly glance at the TV screen anymore, it's chaos, everyone is shouting, the Americans are trying to explain to us Europeans the indirect elections in the American system, with electoral votes, and only when the victorious protagonists appear before their followers do we become interested again. The cheer when Clinton and Hillary come out on stage; my delight when Hillary pulls Clinton's speech out of her suit pocket. The decisive blow against Bush was said to have come on the Friday before the election, when it came out that he had not only known about the shipment of weapons to Iran but had in fact approved them; when he had then brushed aside the question with a wave of his hand and gone so far as to say that his dog knew more about foreign policy than "these two bozos," Clinton and Al Gore: that was the nail in the coffin . . . We celebrate.

But as early as the following day, I heard a Christian caller to a radio program urge all Americans not to pay any more taxes until this fiend has left the White House. Reagan, yes, when he was still there everyone knew he was a father. *"Maybe he made mistakes. But we all felt his energy: He was our father . . ."* "Robert," the radio host, who was actually a preacher, had exactly the same opinion. Then someone named Sharon called, a woman who had been abused by her husband, and "Robert" curtly informed her that she has to be patient and loving with this husband, above all she always has to make him feel like a MAN, and when Sharon tried to get a word in edgewise, "Robert" screamed at her: I'm talking, you need to listen to what I'm saying! He managed to work some hate-filled remarks about Clinton into his tirade, and he told a later caller, apropos of nothing, what a good, religious person he was, he had never done anything bad in his forty-five years, but even he was hated. *Shut up!* he shouted down a woman who was trying to raise objections, until she hung up. A deeply paranoid man, who was allowed to come before the radio audience once a week and let off steam.

To continue. I reached for the red folder, the letters from this L. whom I would never meet and who was nonetheless so close to me. I saw her before my eyes, her figure, her face, her haircut—I heard the way she talked, her voice, emanating from the letters to my friend Emma with no date, but probably from sometime in the late seventies:

My dear,

Don't pressure me. I know you want someone at your side who can give you back a little of your lost sense of home. I can well imagine that people can feel homeless even when they're not in other countries, in the emigration, and that it might be even worse to have to feel that way in your own country. When we were still in France—before the war, when most of the French still clung to their belief in appeasement and stayed away from us with our frightened, threatening prophecies—my dear gentleman said once: It's so painful to see the old continent go under, even if it probably deserves it. And it did go under, didn't it, old Europe? Yes, I know—it was largely destroyed but is working to rebuild itself, and maybe, with the help of God and the Americans, it will succeed.

But I am an old woman and I'd rather the people there were maybe not so industrious, I want to see them reflecting on how that catastrophe came about and the role they themselves played in it. People who dig down into themselves to try to leave a better, more humane country to their children.

Can you promise me that that's what I'd find?

You see. I'm not coming back, Emma. Do you know what my dear gentleman is working on at the moment? He is collecting everyday observations. He asks me and everyone else he meets about their daily habits, and he reads as many German newspapers as he can get and clips out whatever he finds about the daily life of his former countrymen. So that he won't be surprised again, if they ever decide to plunge back from harmless everyday life into madness.

Oh, Emma, don't be sad.

So my friend Emma was sad: she felt like a stranger among her countrymen and women and longed for her friend L. She hadn't told me anything about that, of course. She never let her darker moods show. The experiment to which she had dedicated her life had failed. A few months before she died, when we were leaving one of those disheartening assemblies where the critics of the present conditions were punished, she said with a smile that I will never forget: Our grandchildren will fight it out better than us. —And if they don't? I said. —Hmm, she said with a shrug.

Yes, well, Peter Gutman said. He was being forced to listen to more and more of what was going through my head. I know. But actually, you could start to see this whole story from another angle. —Like what? —As an opportunity, for one thing.

YOU WERE THERE. YOU SURVIVED

It didn't destroy you. You can say what happened.

Actually, I don't know, I said to Peter Gutman—it was one of the rare afternoons when I found him in his office, where he seemed to be busy with various important papers. Who is this reporting "I" supposed to be? It's not just how much I've forgotten. What is maybe more troubling is that I'm not sure who's doing the remembering. One of the many I's who have taken shifts in me decided to take up residence in me, replacing one another in sequence, slowly or quickly. From which one of these I's is the memory instrument extracting the memories? Well, Peter Gutman said, we all live with that fear—don't we?—the fear that we won't recognize ourselves.

Just take the postwar period, I said. The Führer was dead. An emptiness opened up and spread within you. You had a good pastor in the small town where your flight from the east had brought you, he was smart and appealing for you high school students, and he invited you to approach Christian belief in a new way under his guidance: as a religion of struggle. He banged the piano hard and said that was how you had to play and sing "A Mighty Fortress Is Our God," that was what Luther meant by the joyous struggle to get through life as a Christian. You went to church on Sundays for a while, sat in the gallery, and listened to him preach, he was happy and brave and intelligent, and you thought: Why not? But then, after a few months, you had no choice but to go to him and tell him that you wouldn't be coming anymore, there was too much in his religion that you couldn't believe: the immaculate conception, the resurrection, life after death. That's a shame, he said, but you should be patient, he too had found his belief late, you had no way of knowing yet what God had planned for you.

I told this to Peter Gutman as proof that I was no longer susceptible to faith. The new faith must have found another way in. It snuck in through the head.

Yes, Peter Gutman said. Do you think you're the only one who ever believed that reason is all-powerful?

I thought we were going to stay away from rhetorical questions . . . It was obvious, the old society whose ruling classes had caused the disaster had to be completely transformed. Obviously those who had been oppressed should now get their chance. And they did. The state supported the poor people, the families that up until then had brought forth factory workers and cleaning ladies; it made it possible for their sons and daughters to go to college; there was a new wind blowing in the universities, was that a bad thing?

No, Peter Gutman said. Who said it was?

—

THE SECRET LIFE OF J. EDGAR HOOVER. Right at the start of the Clinton era—in which it turned out to be impossible to do what Clinton had promised and tried to do: end the discrimination against gays in the military—revelations were made public about J. Edgar Hoover, who for forty-eight years, until 1972, had been head of the American secret police, the FBI. We learned that he had led a sexual life that was far from "normal" and thus could be blackmailed: the relevant photos were in the Mafia's hands, which led, among other things, to the FBI becoming central in escalating the Cold War, since it could not focus its attention on organized crime so instead focused on the American Communist Party. By 1956 that party had already dissolved, for all practical purposes, but Hoover still assigned fifteen hundred agents to what little remained of it when Robert Kennedy was attorney general, whereas the organized crime unit had to make do with a mere four agents, the newspaper reported. Mr. Hoover, not without a certain pride, once informed a shocked home secretary of the British Labour government as late as 1966 that he "possessed detailed and devastating material on every major U.S. politician, especially the Democrats, so his position was unassailable." With the help of this material, he had set up a giant network of secret extortion and blackmail operations which continued into the early seventies and underlay his campaign against the New Left, the civil rights movement, and the anti-Vietnam movement. I now had a better understanding of the sighs of relief from some of my American friends after the Clinton election: Finally, a president who didn't come out of the secret police.

Nowadays, of course, retired FBI and CIA agents talk on TV without a care in the world about how they kept émigrés under surveillance during the war—there are pictures of them sitting in cars outside Brecht's house, for instance, looking exactly the way you'd imagined they would look and wearing the same hats that they wore in the movies. The dossiers assembled from their reports, with most of the names and whole paragraphs blacked out, are now handed over to scholars who request to see them. They could have been dangerous for the people under observation back then but by now they have lost their explosive charge.

Another advantage of a government existing a long time, I thought: the archives of their secret police must be far more extensive than the famous kilometers of files from the Stasi, which had only forty years to be paranoid, while the FBI has had since World War One to promote and respond to what at times was a national hysteria. John Steinbeck had only to speak out for social justice, or Faulkner to support civil rights for the black population, to justify a dossier of his own with the authorities. Ernest Hemingway's persecution mania, as one of the few artists among his mostly carefree peers to sense that he was under surveillance, appears in a different light, and Thomas Mann's fears also find their confirmation in the files: He came under observation due to his "premature anti-Fascism."

It's all a question of upbringing, said Horst, your seminar group leader. That was back in 1950: you were leaving Professor W.'s pedagogy lecture and Horst said that all this talk of predisposition, genetic basis, and inheritance of given characteristics was all nonsense. Give me thirty newborns born on the same day in the same hospital, he said, and one home where I can raise them, cut off from outside influence, and I can guarantee there will be no difference between their characters, they will all act in exactly the same way out in the world. It was a gray autumn day, on the street in the university city of Jena, and what Horst was saying made you uncomfortable although you couldn't refute it.

Language. I was slowly starting to be able to reflect on the differences between English and German, even though I could still use English only in limited ways. I thought how much easier it was for me to say *I am ashamed* than *Ich schäme mich*—how much closer the German came to the roots of my feeling, despite the similar syntax and the same meaning. The German crept right up to those roots, lapped at them, nourished them, but was also painful for them, the same way the English word *pain* could never signify the pain I was feeling, I could say *it is painful* quite calmly and casually, like a lie, I thought, while I break out in a sweat at the thought of having to say *Es tut weh* and thereby having to think about the cause of my pain. How could *"conscience"* ever replace our German word *"Gewissen,"* a word that practically carries with its bite, *"Bisse"*: the prick of bad conscience, or *Gewissensbisse*, when your conscience is wounded; or the unscrupulous amorality of a lack of conscience, *Gewissenslosigkeit*, there's no way to fool yourself about that, I thought. And what good would it do me to translate repentance into regret, say *I regret* instead of *ich bereue: He (or she) regrets what he (or she) has done. Ich bereue, was ich getan habe. Oder nicht getan habe*—or not done. It only works in German. Maybe because it's about

German actions or inactions, I thought. The foreign language as shield, or hiding place.

And then there was how I unexpectedly encountered the word "*honest*" in the store that sold Indian clothes on Second Street: after an excessively long process of shopping and trying on clothes with the only person working there, an older woman who spoke English with a thick Indian accent, I finally went to pay and was prepared to be asked to show my *driver's license* again, which here in the United States is the ID you need when you want to pay with a check instead of *cash*, so I mentioned up front that I only had an international driver's license, which was usually not accepted as totally valid, but I could also show various ID-like cards with the same name and identical address as my checks—every one of my checks had my name and address printed on it already, of course—and I immediately started to do so, which only plunged her into an utterly unresolvable conflict. I had had the experience many times already, of a saleswoman in this situation phoning some higher authority, describing in detail what a strange and unique customer she had in front of her here, and passing the buck to her superior, but this poor saleswoman owned the store. If I turned out to be one of the apparently numerous check-forgers that she was apparently worried about, it would come out of her own pocket. I saw the struggle she had to fight within herself, then saw her make an effort and take the check: *You look honest*, she said, resolutely, and I assured her, *Yes, I am*. And silently added to myself: At least when it comes to money.

On my way back to the MS. VICTORIA I thought about how this word "*honest*" could fit the German word "*ehrlich*" (candid, straightforward), but also "*redlich*" (fair) and "*aufrichtig*" (genuine), and I might add to the series the English word "*upright*" or the beautiful word "*sincere*." On the other hand, "*to do one's best*" couldn't really hold a candle to our "*sich redliche Mühe geben*," could it. Don't these English-speakers shoulder the burden of "doing their best" rather easily, which is simply impossible for our German "*redliche Mühe*" (honest toil)? Maybe it's because our "*Schuld*," linguistically speaking, seems to weigh more heavily than their "*guilt*" or "*blame*," or at least so it seemed to me. And it couldn't be a total coincidence, I thought, that it was a German poet who, at the end of his "drama of humanity" rife with guilt and disgrace, conceived the lines "He who strives on and lives to strive / Can earn redemption still." And while I walked straight at the three raccoons, who were staring back at me as usual, I suppressed a slight feeling of dissatisfaction that this poet had neglected to give the hint he perhaps should have given: how that struggle should look, the one that would result in a normal person (not a "noble spirit") enjoying the "redemption" in question.

How much easier it is, I thought, to come to terms with the temptations of youth than with the errors of your later years. All right then, at some point that has to make it into this book too: the jail story. Maybe I've told it too many times, my perspective on it has gone stale. What I see is a bare office in the Unter den Linden union building; today a large Western car company has its showroom there. Unfortunately I no longer have the election-worker ID that a functionary handed out to you election workers. Because you later destroyed it, as per instructions. Your task was to support the West Berlin SEW party, the Communists, in the elections. You were legal election workers, he insisted; there was an agreement with the West Berlin authorities, he told you. The materials you were supposed to hand out had stamps on them that proved they were legal. It went without saying that you were supposed to strike up conversations with the people receiving these materials, as much as you could, and try to convince them to vote for the Communists. These IDs with your names on them, he said, must by no means fall into the class enemy's hands. No one asked why not, you didn't either. It was the mid-1950s. Unter den Linden was still filled with construction ditches you had to walk across on planks in order to get to the Friedrichstrasse streetcar station. Lorchen, a young comrade, was assigned to go with you.

I remember the short streetcar ride to the West—a direction you otherwise tended to avoid. Three or four stops. You paged through the propaganda material and found it terribly primitive. But that didn't matter: it would never have crossed your mind to do what the other agitators did, namely throw the pamphlets in the nearest trash can, spend a few hours strolling around the Ku'damm, and take the streetcar back to the Democratic Sector. You had butterflies in your stomach, I still remember, but you couldn't let anything show because you had to be a good model for Lorchen, the young comrade. You were twenty-six. I don't remember the address you were assigned to or even the district—West Berlin was a different world for you. I can darkly see in my mind's eye a treeless street with solidly middle-class, four-story apartment buildings on either side, whose occupants, the awareness glimmered even in you, might not be the most fruitful objects of your propaganda activities.

At the instruction session, no one had thought to tell you the basic rule of illegal activity: never to hand out your fliers in a building from the ground floor up, but always from the top floor down. Emma told me this rule much later, roaring with laughter, when I told her about my failed efforts. You and Lorchen started on the bottom right. It was a dark-stained door, you rang the bell, and nobody opened the door, to your secret relief. So you pushed the materials intended for that apartment through the mail slot in the hall. And on it went, from bottom to top, since not a single apartment door in the building opened to you. Then, when you came downstairs and were back in the ground-floor hallway, a policeman wearing the West Berlin uniform was waiting there for you. I remember that your heart started pounding, but that you re-assured yourself: He can't do anything to us.

He could take you in. You had to go with him to the station, to check your papers. I have forgotten if he ever even looked at your election-worker IDs. I remember perfectly the light that greeted you outside the front door of the apartment building: the light after a rain shower, when the sky is just clearing up and the sun casts an afternoon glow onto the streets and the buildings. And I remember perfectly the young boy, five or six years old, crouching by the gutter and sailing paper boats in the water there. How he looked up at you, grasped the situation lightning-fast, and shouted: Communists! Hang 'em all! And how you proudly said to him as you walked past: You'd have your work cut out for you.

You calmed down after that. The next memory image shows me in a police station, one of the old-fashioned ones with wood-paneled walls and a kind of counter, behind which sat the sergeant on duty. He was an older man and not responsible for your case. He phoned a superior. Then he looked through your papers and actually found a page missing the stamp that made it legal—so now, unexpectedly, you were illegal. He showed you the page and explained the situation, very precisely, objec-tively, and without a sense of triumph. You felt furious at the comrades in the union headquarters who should have told you the plain truth, you were being sent to hand out propaganda after all. If only you'd known that some of your materials weren't legal. You realized your situation was not exactly rosy and that you had to stay on your best behavior.

They told you to sit down on the obligatory wooden police bench against the wall. Lorchen was scared. I remember you tried to calm her down with sentences spoken under your breath. The sergeant felt the need to argue with you about the disadvantages of dictatorship and the advantages of the free democratic system. You tried your best to straighten out his false worldview. Finally he groaned and said: How can such a clever, well-educated woman be such an idiot? Your answers were short and to the point, proud, and unyielding. In the end, he told you to look at the map hanging on the wall above your bench: a big purple map of the Soviet Union with a series of small yellow rectangles on it, scattered irregularly around the country but gathered especially close together in a few areas, especially the northeast. You see those rectangles? the policeman on duty said. They're work camps, camps for political prisoners. Every one. You felt sorry for him if he seriously thought you'd believe that. I still remember how he looked at you thoughtfully for a little while and then asked you what you would say if he could prove to you that he had been in one of those camps himself. Oh, so you're one of those! A war criminal! You wouldn't say another word to him.

And you stuck to your resolution. In fact, you were someone who longed for harmonious interactions, you had to force yourself to be rude, but it was often unavoidable in the class struggle. So you kept silent until the young superior officer you were waiting for came, and a policewoman who called first Lorchen and then you into the side room.

You had to get undressed for a strip search. Here? you said. With no curtain on the windows? No way!

The policewoman opened a closet door and told you to get undressed behind it. She found the election-worker ID you'd hidden in your sock, you grabbed it out of her hands, she tried to get it back and scratched your hand in the process. So this is how you treat people here! you snapped at her, and you started tearing the paper up into little pieces before her eyes. That's what people did in that situation, you knew it from books and movies and hadn't forgotten what they'd told you over and over in the union headquarters. You destroyed the very document you could have used to legitimate yourself. The policewoman, furious by now, screamed at you: Are you all like this? and you, calmly but shaking inside, answered: Not all of us, but a lot.

Such great dialogue, already perfect for a book. I cannot count how many times that purple map of the Soviet Union later appeared before my mind's eye but first you ended up in a squad car, separated from Lorchen, who was legally a juvenile, and you had to spend the night in a four-person cell at the Moabit detention center—even today when I drive past its long wall, guarded with barbed wire, I give it my regards with my eyes. Naturally the three women who were already in the cell gathered around you: Why are you here? —Fliers, you said. They turned away, almost disgusted. Oh, just political! They had more serious problems.

One of them paced back and forth in the cell and burst out with the same sentence every minute: Over a toothbrush! When asked, she expanded this one phrase into a long flowery story that started with an evening stroll with her "spouse," continued with a trip to a drugstore to buy some soap, where the underhanded pharmacist had thoughtlessly left a whole glass of toothbrushes unobserved in reach of the customers, which led to the taking of one single toothbrush, but then the pharmacist had an excuse to send a cop car after them. It's incitement to theft!—

Fair enough. But even a class-based justice system would not be able to turn the theft of one single toothbrush into a serious offense, you tried to reassure the woman. Then she planted herself in front of you and asked you a question fraught with danger: Do you know men? You didn't have a quick answer ready, strictly speaking you had not known many men but it wasn't about that kind of knowing, it was about whether you could count on a man if "they" gave him the once-over. —"They" who? —You know, they. If they were really grilling him to see if he'd sing. —No idea. But what was he supposed to . . . ? —Huh! Contemptuous hand gesture. If they show up with a search warrant. If they really push him into a corner, the way they like to do. If he loses his nerve and lifts up the plank in our kitchen . . . —Then what? The woman was stunned at how naive I was. Then they'd find something, wouldn't they. Maybe find a whole lot of something. Then they'd have just what they wanted: Theft in conjunction with dealing in stolen goods, that's what they'd call it. They love to overdo it when they can play a dirty trick on the likes of us. And then they'll look in our files, of course. And then . . .

Even you understood what she was getting at. Men could keep quiet too, you promised the woman, even though you didn't actually have a single piece of evidence in mind. Or at least that's what you hoped for her, with all your heart, the same way you hoped that the other pretty young woman would get through the interrogation scheduled for tomorrow without "them" being able to get a confession out of her. Even to you, the fresh-faced novice, it was clear that she, a chambermaid in a famous fancy hotel, had stolen a rich guest's jewelry, which was what she was being charged with. They always pick on the little guy! she cried, in a Berlin accent, and you could only agree with her wholeheartedly. They had been questioning her for weeks already and she was starting to get her story mixed up. No one would ever find the hiding place, she said suddenly, not even her boyfriend. She wanted to finally have a good life, at least when she got out of jail. She deserved that much. You completely agreed. She should just keep an iron-clad silence from now on, you suggested, no one could prove anything. —You're damn right! she cried, and you said she should always keep in mind the good life that she deserved just as much as the rich. Damn right! But you could see that the woman was worn out, her hands shook; tomorrow they'll get her, you anxiously thought, tomorrow she'll blab everything. —You've got nothing to worry about with your fliers, she added, almost envious. Nothing can happen to you.

That was true. Or was it? You were put in a solitary cell in the Moabit detention center and interrogated for a week yourself, every day. Nowadays everyone knows what a jail cell looks like: a cot that folds up during the day, a wooden locker, a narrow table, a cupboard on the wall with the requisite prison utensils, soap, comb, toothbrush cup. A sink. A toilet behind a low partition.

A punctilious social service worker visited you and got not one word out of you besides the most necessary information. Religion? she asked. None, you said. At which she wrote a single word, DISSIDENT, on the thin card she then slipped into the wooden slot prepared for it on the wall cupboard. That was how I first encountered that word, the one which would, much later, reappear in my life with an entirely different meaning, and which meanwhile made the pastor who also came to see you very upset. He left before long. Since you didn't get the books you wanted—a Russian grammar and Marx's *Capital*—you browsed around, bored, in a thick book of uninspired prose, stories from Shakespeare's plays, and you thought out the deceptions and false trails you were using to try to lead your interrogator astray about your family relationships. He was an unambitious man, middle-aged, who shook his head often. He only wanted to know which institution had "in truth" sent you, which was hardly a secret, but of course he didn't hear anything about it from you. He tried to ascertain if you had been given other assignments, besides this unfortunate electoral agitation, and what relationship you had to the West Berlin members of the Communist Party— all questions you stubbornly refused to answer, even though it would have been easy enough to answer them in the negative.

He couldn't get anywhere with you, but since you had told him, totally unnecessarily, that your father was dead, while in fact he was visiting your family in Karlshorst with your mother and was in the best of health, you had to think up the most cloak-and-dagger secret codes imaginable to communicate this claim to your oblivious family and prevent them from contradicting it in the presence of the interrogator, for example at one of the visits that they were allowed. So you had to watch while your mother, faced with secret messages you were trying to convey to her in short, curt sentences that of course she couldn't decipher, started to doubt your sanity, grew more and more confused, and finally, to your fury and dismay, tried to explain your behavior to your interrogator as youthful folly.

Meanwhile you couldn't deny that jail was not agreeing with you, that you were by no means as calm and cool as you were acting, that your stomach was in knots and you could hardly swallow a bite of the prison food. You grew terribly anxious and nervous and could hardly sleep. You studiously avoided the word "afraid." Outraged colleagues and comrades sent care packages of candy and vegetables to your cell, solidarity actions were conducted "on the outside," a condemnatory article appeared in the newspaper.

You knew from books that prisoners were supposed to make conspiratorial contact with the other prisoners, so you slid your stool across the floor and stood on it under the half-open barred window, pulled yourself up with the bars, and loudly whispered to either side, asking if anyone could hear you. There was an answer from the left: a despondent woman's voice. Whispering or talking in a half-loud voice, constantly interrupted by the sounds of prison life, you eventually found out the relevant information about the woman in the neighboring cell: She was from the GDR, accused of espionage activities in West Berlin for the Stasi. You couldn't pretend not to hear it: This woman was truly afraid. So here was a mission for you: You had to encourage her, firm up her resolve, which was about to give out completely. You didn't ask her if the charges were true, obviously, you just urged her not to admit a thing. Surely there was no way they could prove anything. She didn't seem to be so sure. Once, when a policewoman took you for questioning, showing obvious contempt for you, you saw your neighbor walking ahead of you down the long hall between two American MPs who were tall as tree trunks: a short, thin person with thin colorless hair. You had pictured spies rather differently.

Then the election was over, with humiliating results for the Communists. Interest in you faded and you were released; two students you didn't know met you at the prison gates carrying flowers and smuggled you onto the streetcar with their tickets since they thought it was inexcusable to exchange your good Eastern money for Western currency to buy a streetcar ticket.

I still remember how relieved you were when you could ring the bell of your apartment door. When your young daughter looked up from the bathtub and saw you. I don't think any mental picture of her from that time has etched itself as firmly in my mind as this one, and I still remember the pang you felt at the strange look she gave you at first, and I remember that the question occurred to you of whether this whole effort was worth the fact that your child had had to be without you for more than a week.

It goes without saying that your strongly worded complaint to the comrades at the union headquarters, about the fact that they hadn't told you the whole truth about the nature of the agitation material they were giving you, was gently but firmly dismissed. The comrades in the leadership had done it for a reason, you could be sure of that. Besides, you had proven yourself in the best possible way. But precisely because you had proven yourself, you could continue to disagree with them and could also give them your opinion of the pathetic quality of the material—with all its other problems, it was terribly written. That was when you heard for the first time the charge that would accompany you from then on: aestheticism.

Would "dogmatic" be the right word, I wonder, to label the person you were then? Uncompromising. Rigorous. Radical. It's words like that that come to mind. Above all: Sure that you possessed the truth, which always makes a person intolerant. *The overcoat of Dr. Freud.* But what if

I turned the coat backward? Inside out? Described my conversion—the con-version, the turning-around—and could stop being intolerant of myself? Right now? I thought. If not now, when? But it was impossible.

I sat in the hairdresser's chair and didn't like the face in the mirror, as I usually didn't when I was forced to look at it for a long time. Everything in the salon was finely orchestrated, first an apprentice named Jerry draped a cloth around me and washed my hair, then a sort of senior designer had me describe the haircut I wanted while Caroline was there, who then quickly and skillfully took care of me without a moment's hesitation or a single superfluous movement, I thought. She had ended up here from Munich, she said, the first year was hard, without knowing the language, but now she spoke English perfectly, it seemed to me. And didn't we have to be intolerant, I thought, the tape recording in my head didn't stop for a second, against those who wanted to turn back the wheel of history while we were eliminating the reasons behind humanity's false paths, pulling them up radically, by the roots. Caroline told me about her trip to Mexico, freedom is the consciousness of necessity, what else, you were free to take the step from prehistory into the history of humanity, you freed yourself of the errors, the deeply etched habits of the old era, including not least the greed for possessions, a barely comprehensible absurdity for all of you who had nothing to possess. I saw that Caroline was cutting my hair carefully, but clearly much too short, a *summer cut*, at least in my opinion. Human beings are good and can be improved, or else what is there? Caroline's story of the American boyfriend she had found and then lost again didn't exactly touch me to the core, she said to err is human, and I said: You're right about that.

I knew that a journalist from Germany I couldn't put off was waiting for me at the MS. VICTORIA. I felt flush and I was nervous about standing up, my joints were probably blocked again. Dr. Freud could probably have explained to me why my body, or whoever was responsible for it, was trying harder and harder to prevent me from walking. He would probably have advised me to follow my instinct and not agree to the meeting with Miss Leisegang in the first place. But since I no longer trusted my instincts, and since Miss Leisegang knew how to frame the meeting with her as a kind of duty, I violently suppressed my unease and met with her.

Waiting for me was a towering blonde with a ponytail wearing red capri pants, a shiny beige blouse with bright stripes and colorful top hats all over it, and a short red-and-yellow satin bomber jacket. She immediately started talking and didn't stop for an hour. Her illness, which had brought her to America, she was trying to cure it in the desert in Palm Springs. Her father, whose fault it was that she never drank a drop of alcohol, although unfortunately she was a chain-smoker. How she met her husband. How he knew how to handle her dealings with the editorial offices, where there were intrigues against her, exactly the same as with TV, everyone there was out to get her, which made her deeply depressed, so now she only worked for the stations on short-term, concrete assignments. I understood that her concrete assignment this time was me.

I soon realized that she cared much more about her questions than my answers, which she had brought along with her, already worked out, and which there was hardly anything I could do to change by that point. She had gathered from certain publications that I had become totally disillusioned with East Germany quite early on—so why had I not acted against the regime? Why had I stayed? I must have had to constantly twist and deform my writing. No, she couldn't think of any examples at the moment. Why hadn't I written a book about the deplorable state of the GDR instead of *Cassandra*? How do people live under a dictatorship? She knew the GDR only from two visits to the Leipzig Book Fair. She had not read my most important books, but she was a huge fan of my work, really. She was going to make a movie about intellectuals in the GDR. With us in the West, she said, you can say anything you want in public.

I was speechless and helpless. I knew that no explanations I offered would be of any use. I tried to object by pointing out how the West German public and media were currently reacting to my file. Yes, of course they do have this mode of investigative journalism, it's frightful, I couldn't even begin to imagine what nasty people the editors were, real hunting dogs. She wouldn't have believed it herself. But was it really so important what people were saying about me in public? I drew her attention to the fact that journalists who had tried to present the facts objectively had been reprimanded by their bosses, and that neither she nor anyone else had had the courage to speak in public about the conditions in the editorial offices that she had just described to me; they all kept nice and quiet so they could keep their places at the trough.

Yes, well, capitalism—although actually she would call the Western world a "free market society," not "capitalism"—it was dog-eat-dog, of course, naturally that goes with competition, but she had traveled almost everywhere in the world and had never found a socioeconomic system that worked better. Next, of course, came her support for the Gulf War, the Americans had such problems these days because they were protecting threatened peoples all over the world and also had to spend their money supporting the poor. Marx didn't understand a thing about the economy, unfortunately, she had read both volumes of *Capital* and discussed it all with her husband. Then she had to leave in a hurry, if I hadn't warned her she would have missed her flight. She hugged me goodbye. I shouldn't worry if we saw the world differently in some ways. She was a huge fan of mine and would always be one.

I sat there, numb. If I had read this scene in a book, I thought, I would never have believed it. And I would never use such clichés myself. But why shouldn't someone be allowed to ask questions, even if, partly out of ignorance, they were painful questions? How would understanding ever arise if no one paid attention to these questions? Again I felt the same feeling of hopelessness: None of it had any point, we didn't have a chance. But who was this "we"?

EVERY LINE I WRITE FROM NOW ON WILL BE USED AGAINST ME

But hasn't that always been true, or in any case true for a long while? Haven't I had quite a long time in which I could, or had to, get used to that fact? What is there to stop me from simply breaking off right here?

I headed out, it was still light outside—and there it was, the normal life of the normal people walking with me or toward me on Ocean Park Promenade. Wretched, wretched, when was it that I had repeated this word over and over again to myself, like a mantra? It was when you sat looking at your files and a feeling seized you of having been poisoned, a kind of queasiness you had never felt before; when you got to the documents in your files about your works. IM "Jenny," who clearly had academic training, grew more and more concerned from book to book about your straying into negative-hostile ideological currents; eventually it happened, as happen it must, that she could find nothing in an admittedly somewhat complicated text but a tissue of secret, cleverly encoded messages inimical to the state. You let off some steam by laughing but the subtle poison forced its way inside you and had its effect: Wretched, wretched! you said out loud, driving home from that agency, and another voice inside you countered: There are worse things. Which was true.

I sat down for a while on a bench in Ocean Park, in the last moments of sunlight. I wanted to drink in the light. A chubby little man around my age sat down next to me, pointed to the ocean where the sun was just going down, and said: *That's wonderful, isn't it?* —*Yes*, I said. *Marvelous.* He saw that I had a book with me with the word "Patriarchy" in the title and respectfully asked if I was "a student"; I said: Just reading. He wanted to talk. He told me where he lived in L.A., that it took forty minutes by bus to get here, he loved this place. Oh, I lived in Santa Monica? How fortunate! —It's just for nine months, I said, *I am German.* The man thought that was interesting. He had emigrated here from Ireland, twenty years ago already. He wanted to know how it was in Germany since the reunification: *Better or worse?* I said, *Different. Difficult.* He said that whenever two different things were thrown together there was always a difficult transition period. In the end would I decide to stay here instead? —No, no, I said. My family is in Berlin too . . . He understood that. —My husband had let me come here all by myself then? —*Yes*, I said. *He did.* —I wondered: Could a scene like that ever happen in a German park?

How should I get through the night? And the next, and the one after that, and the one after that? No, I would not go back to the CENTER anymore to collect my mail, the newspapers, the faxes. I don't have to know everything right away, I thought.

Peter Gutman didn't come to the phone. He let himself not be there when you needed him. The crew of the Starship *Enterprise* on *television* couldn't hold my attention that night. There was red wine, cheese. I paced back and forth in my apartment. There were Thomas Mann's diaries, I could flip through those, picking out passages unsystematically. I was touched to read what he wrote there about his last great love, Franzl, a young waiter. How he had asked himself whether he should burn his diaries or whether he wanted posterity to know who he was. Finally: They should know who I was, but only after twenty or twenty-five years when everyone is dead. "To write about all that, admitting everything, would destroy me." I thought: Not writing about it at all would have suffocated him. Breaking off the writing, and what the writing meant—the experiment on yourself, the desire to get to know yourself down to the bottom—that would have been like stopping a life-sustaining treatment in the throes of a serious disease, I thought.

So is life a serious disease, the way we are forced to lead it? I wondered.

How do people live under a dictatorship? That word "dictatorship" in reference to our social relations came with the "Turn." I thought I knew what a dictatorship was, I had lived through one already, after all, until I was sixteen, and you couldn't compare that regime to the following forty years I had also lived through, I thought, and I resisted equating the two. But the question stayed with me: How do people live under a dictatorship?

I sit here in my study, one and a half decades after I was asked that question, in front of a thick pile of manuscript pages that has unexpectedly turned up recently, from the literary estate of a colleague I had known fairly well, who was younger than me and who died young. He drank himself to death, it was said, and we all knew why. You were there in person at the beginning of the tragedy—that is the only word for a chain of events that ends with a dead man—and you never forgot it: A gathering of authors, convened on orders from "the highest places," in the new building of the Council of State with carpets on the stairs and thick curtains that opened or closed in front of high windows with the push of a button. The government of the workers and peasants could now afford that. A gloomy and at the same time tense mood; partly informed functionaries indicated that there was danger up ahead. Once again, literature and writers were going to be blamed for societal problems, this time excesses on the part of the youth. Literature was giving young people models of behavior inimical to the state and an example was lying right there on the table: the advance publication of a chapter from an unfinished novel, *Rummelplatz* (Amusement Park), whose author had done exactly what the Party had not long ago demanded that writers do—spent time in one of the biggest companies, SAG Wismut, lived and worked with the workers, and described the development of several characters in that environment. The journal had printed a chapter describing the crazy state of affairs in the company's early years, mining uranium for the Soviet Union's armaments program and thus helping to secure world peace. Who was that supposed to be useful for? the general secretary of the Party asked. Taking all these long since overcome conditions and blowing them all out of proportion now, in a novel? Did they think the Party hadn't known what was going on? Of course it knew, but it had to work with the people it had—including old Nazis, including criminals—and it reeducated them as best it could. Some of them did have leading positions in this or that big company. Some of them finally had come down in the world, others had disappeared into the West, fine, you always have to count on taking a few losses. But what did this comrade writer accomplish by describing drinking binges to the readers of today, especially the young people? The journal was slid across the table to the general secretary, where the passages in question had been marked; he read them, clearly for the first time.

A long, embarrassed silence. The break was announced ahead of schedule, with drinks and snacks, and the lower functionaries pleaded with all of you to say something for God's sake. A transcript exists of the statement you contributed, trying to defend the fact that literature has to deal with conflicts and suggest a different way of interacting with "the young people." Other people also spoke up for the author under attack, and in the end it seemed as though the worst had been prevented.

That was in 1965. Did we still believe that we could influence the opinions and even the actions of the people in charge of the government by talking, by presenting arguments? Reality, we thought, was a powerful argument itself, if only one could hear it. Power and intellect joined together: a typical illusion of German intellectuals and one that had already run aground once on the German Misère. The author's close connection to the country he was writing about rang out from every page of the book being criticized. He had not wanted to live anywhere else. No artist in our society would be ruined the way they were in the exploiter's societies before us and all around us—this was a moral code we thought we shared with the government.

I remember a night in California. Christmas, with its temperature in the high seventies, was over. Social life was at a standstill; no one seemed to be in the mood to meet anyone after work. Or maybe it was only I who felt isolated, even rejected. I had brought a heavy package of newspapers and faxes with me back from the CENTER, refusing to protect myself, and I read through the articles and essays about my case, one after the other. By that point they were appearing in different languages; reports about my case filled the news shows and newspapers not only in Germany but in the United States too, and in almost every European country.

After hesitating a long time, I called Berlin, no one answered, and I pictured all the people I knew so well sitting in a brightly lit restaurant, clinking their glasses. I seriously wondered what I should do. How to get through the night. I paged through Pema the nun's book and she informed me that every day, every single minute of my life, was exactly the right one for me and that I should accept this fact in order to keep my spirit in balance. I turned on the television and saw a program about a group of women with cancer: they met to do exercises against fear, and died one after the other. I lay down in bed and sought long and hard for evidence I could use to defend myself. I didn't find any. There was not a single corner of Dr. Freud's *overcoat* I could cling to. I could feel myself sinking into a whirlpool and knew I was in danger. To lose myself at the bottom of the whirlpool seemed very tempting, like the only possible way. I thought about how to do it, that distracted me a little. The voice inside me saying I couldn't do this to the people who cared about me, suggesting that I should at least wait until the next day, was very soft. I took some sleeping pills and paid close attention to make sure I wasn't taking too many.

I fell asleep, or lost consciousness at least, and experienced my own death. It was not a dream, it was another kind of experience. It was my limbs growing cold, from the feet up, while I stayed fully conscious, I knew what was happening, I wasn't scared, I knew that the wave of coldness would reach my heart, I gradually got stiff, with my eyes open, I was dead, but I could still see, I saw my surroundings, the walls, the window, I also saw myself lying on a wide bed. It wasn't bad. When I woke up it was still dark, it took me a long time to realize that I wasn't dead and to start to work the stiffness out of my body. I thought: Now I know what it's like to die, and I'm not afraid of it anymore. I felt something like a small consolation.

The next few days, I remember, were very dull and ordinary. I did what there was to do, read everything I was sent, saw the flood of paper swell, didn't feel a thing. I was dead after all, and it was good, nothing mattered to me anymore. As always, I sat for hours at my little machine and wrote up everything I saw and heard. At the CENTER people looked at me sidelong and avoided me, that was good too.

A senior staff member who was responsible for taking care of us invited me out to an expensive, sterile restaurant and wanted to hear "my version of the story." He can't have found it very reassuring. I could hear from the embarrassed things he was saying that he had had to defend my presence at the CENTER to his superiors at the highest levels, who in turn had to justify themselves before a shocked public. As I must know, people took "such things" very seriously here. I asked if I should leave. He was startled by the question and said so. They stood behind their scholars here, he said. They had even had a scholar a few years ago who turned out to have been a not totally insignificant member of a Nazi organization. I had serious difficulty suppressing a wicked burst of laughter.

An instinct for self-preservation still seemed to be operating within me: I made sure to spend an hour every day around noon on my bench in Ocean Park, looking at the water. At some point, Peter Gutman found out and simply came and sat next to me. He didn't say anything. Finally he said: You are neglecting your friends, Madame. I shrugged. After another while he asked if I had any plans to take part in life again at some point. That was just what I didn't know. Did I think that there was something to be gained by this isolation, then? It wasn't about that. What was it about, then? Then I knew: It was about getting through a danger zone. Crossing it while staying as numb as possible. As a way to avoid pain. But I didn't say that.

Well, fine, Peter Gutman said. He only wanted to tell me that he had gotten up to speed. Read a few items. Probably understood a few items too. He realized that at the moment I didn't want to listen to what he wanted to tell me, but he would rather say it too early than too late. I was working myself up into an unnecessary psychosis. The cause, when you looked at it objectively, was minor. Obviously the media was blowing it out of proportion. Why did I let it get to me so much? Did I really take myself that seriously? Had I wanted to see myself as unerring and irreproachable? Isn't that a bizarre kind of vanity?

This, of all things, is what never should have happened to me, I said. It was a kind of inner refrain.

Well, in that case, Peter Gutman said, if that's how it is, I hope that one day you will be happy that it happened to you of all people.

And in fact that eventually came true, weeks later, when, to my relief, I could write, in an angry letter to someone who should have known better but who had expressed a hypocritical regret about my alleged misstep in one of the countless newspaper articles about me: You can all go to hell. But some other things had to happen before I got to that point. The telephone had to take on a life of its own and bring me voices from a world I had lost, where people were apparently still living a normal life. Grace Paley had to call me from her house in the woods on the East Coast, and she had to say: You should know *I am with you.* The world gets worse and worse but people get better and better. Lev Kopelev had to call and beg me to explain things only to myself and my children, not to the petty small-minded people everywhere. While we were talking I saw him walking around his Moscow again, with his patriarch's beard, powerfully striding ahead with his walking stick, grim about slanderous newspaper articles and worried that a new wave of anti-Semitism might be looming. I saw before me the writers' house in Leningrad, where they fed you cutlets and greasy kasha even in the morning, I saw you and G. sitting on the stairs with the old translator couple, listening to their stories about the intrigues against Akhmatova and the condemnations of her in the Party Congresses, I saw the flowers still lying on Akhmatova's nearby grave. Saw the man who kept aloof, spoke little, and was surrounded by an aura of unapproachability in which he had had to spend many years. The term "gulag" was not yet known. You and G. drank in the information, you wanted to know where you were living. I wrote on my little machine:

Sometimes I think I only have to make the right kind of effort and then the right sentences, the saving sentences, will appear. But then I learn yet again that no efforts are of any use. What I need to see does not want to show itself. I suspect it is something very simple, and that's why it is so well hidden.

After a long time I am reading the nun's book again. It says that you should not try to avoid pain and suffering. You should just sit there and calmly observe yourself. That's how a person is. We are not in this world to improve ourselves, but to open.

But it's just when you try to do that, I thought, that you're punished for it. You have to be prepared for that, the nun would say. That too is something you have to withstand.

What else had to happen? One evening, when I was going home and I had turned in my keys to security on the fifth floor, the guards were sitting in front of the little television and they turned to face me. Over their shoulders I saw the dark outlines of a city, with flashes of light from explosions. One of them said: *We're bombing Baghdad, missiles.* One of the men kept saying *Unbelievable,* and I couldn't tell if this was an expression of horror or admiration for American technology. An American reporter in Baghdad was answering questions and he said the worst was twenty-five minutes ago when the earth shook from a rocket strike. It's an indescribable feeling, he said, when the missiles fly right over your head with an eerie wail. Yes, Baghdad was under fire, *"but we don't know much."* An older woman walked past, from the photography department, and she looked at the images and asked: *What happened?* The men said: *Baghdad is being attacked. Oh my goodness,* she said, and she murmured something along the lines of how she hadn't watched the news for a couple days and now this! I felt that my role was to stay quiet, not butt in. These were Americans among themselves. A hotel for foreigners had been hit, I heard the announcer say, and also a building where the Iraqis had been working on material for building nuclear weapons, but immediately after that someone from the UN said he had been in that facility a few weeks earlier and it had long since stopped operation.

Had Bush discussed it with Clinton? we asked each other and ourselves the next day, sitting in the lounge drinking our tea. The Clinton government took power. The bells were supposed to ring throughout the country, everywhere, at the same time—a new era was supposed to begin. While the bombs were falling on Baghdad.

Francesco said: The American dream. It turned out the Americans in our group did not believe in it. A blond woman, middle-aged, a friend of Emily's, a lawyer, said that only now, from reading the book by Malcolm X, did she really understand how a black person experienced white America; she had recently moved to a neighborhood where middle-class blacks lived too, which at first really annoyed her, because she simply wasn't used to seeing black people doing normal things like white people. Her son was going to a private school where there were no black children, and he didn't play with any at home either.

That morning I had heard an interview on the radio with a black cook. She was very old now and had worked for a long time for the Rockefeller family, and later for the family of an eminent politician who was apparently involved in a case of fraud. She was asked if she had known anything about that, or if they had talked about it among themselves in the kitchen. *Oh, no!* she said, very surprised at the question. We had too much to do. Cooking three meals a day! It wasn't easy.

Hmm, Peter Gutman said. Classless society.

He had shown up again at my door one night with as harmless a look on his face as he could manage. May I? he asked. He was curious about what I was writing. I handed him a couple of pages. It was the answer to a friend's letter, a kind of self-analysis. He read it for a long time, too long I thought, and said nothing. We drank the wine he had brought and ate crackers.

As you know, Peter Gutman said after a while, I have a telephone relationship.

And what does she have to say at the moment?

She counsels moderation. Especially toward oneself. She can't stand it when she sees someone lashing out at themselves.

Who does that, you?

I do it too, Peter Gutman said. Sometimes.

At the moment?

We are not talking about me, Madame. We are talking about you. Listen to what a wise old man has to say: To love oneself is the most difficult love of all.

And you, my friend, win the prize for transparent attempts to dodge the question. But I've been asking myself recently if I didn't miss out on the greatest chance of my life.

And what might that have been? Peter Gutman asked.

To come to the West. In May 1945. To cross the Elbe. Our caravan of refugees was trying to get there, like all the other caravans and all the war-weary soldiers who had thrown down their weapons too. The officers too—they had torn off their epaulettes and stripes and medals and burned their papers in little fires at the side of the road, which I despised them for, by the way. It was a matter of hours. We thought we had made it, the Americans were the initial occupation power, they took us in, then the English controlled the corner of Mecklenburg where we were being put up. But in the end, that same summer, it was the

Soviet troops who advanced to the Elbe after all, as agreed, and who established their system in the eastern part of Germany. That was where I grew up, and where I lived as though it were a matter of course. It came down to a couple of hours: if the landowner whose carts we were crouching in had had horses that were not so worn out that even blows of the whip couldn't get them to move any faster—I would have lived an entirely different life. I would have been a different person. That's how it was in Germany then, you were in the hands of utter chance.

And? Peter Gutman asked. Would you want to go back and correct the chance? Cross the Elbe this time? Be that other person you would have become?

I would probably have become a teacher, which is what I actually wanted to be. I don't know if I would have written anything, because the conflicts I had in that society were always what drove me to write. I would not have met my husband. I would have had different children, or no children. Different aspects of my personality would have come out and others would have been the ones I had to suppress. Would I have lived in a row house at the edge of a big city? Which party would I have voted for? Would my life have been boring? I would have been too old to be a '68er. I would never have visited the East. I would have spent my vacations in Italy. Now that the Wall has come down, I would go as a foreigner to see the foreign land where German is spoken too, but I wouldn't have understood the people there. Because I would think that the life that I, that we, had led was the true one, the normal one. And I would have been blameless.

Okay, Peter Gutman said. That's enough.

He left. I wasn't tired yet, I took down the red folder. Not counting the last letter, from May 1979 and by "Ruth," not L., which informed Emma that her friend had died, there was only one letter left. In it, L. apologized that so much time had passed since the last time she'd written.

Don't think, my dear Emma, that I'm not thinking of you. On the contrary, I think about our years together more than ever. Those were also my first years together with my dear gentleman. You have probably guessed why I haven't written in so long, Emma—my dear gentleman is dead. Even now it's hard for me to write it down so simply. I long for him, for his physical presence, as powerfully as ever. I still expect to see him standing in the door when I turn around from my desk, I still feel the same pain that he isn't there, that he'll never be there again.

He was in despair. All his research for the past few years was devoted to the question of where humanity is going. He never gleefully prophesized the downfall of our species, I can attest to that. The political events of recent years—the McCarthy era, the U.S.-backed coup against Allende in Chile and everything that happened in and with that country since—they finished him off. He had grown certain that the barbarism we could still theoretically escape was spreading unstoppably all over the world. He left this world of his own free will.

I've grown old, it's no fun. Being close to death is no fun. I still work, though not as much as before, of course, because I love my work, and also because you get poor in a hurry in this country if you don't work. I see Dora more often now, she is still the same brave woman she always was, she is putting her husband's papers in order and I help sometimes. I'm tired.

My friend Emma could not answer this letter anymore. She definitely received it but she was already in the hospital. Thyroid cancer. I never saw her look defeated or afraid. She had tricked one of the nurses into revealing her diagnosis; she then prepared for her death by giving away everything she no longer needed and burning her papers. Once, when I could not conceal my grief, she said: Ach, you know, I lived through everything a person can live through in this day and age. That's enough.

I needed distraction. Ann, the CENTER's photographer, had been offering for a long time to give us a tour of the slums of Los Angeles, where, everyone told us, we should under no circumstances drive alone. I had a new friend with me: Therese, whom I had met just a few days before and already felt close to. She was a journalist who had come from Germany to report on the upcoming mayoral election in Los Angeles for a German newspaper. She had been here many times before, she craved this city. She seemed to know everyone and everyone knew her. She would certainly come with Ann and me to drive through the areas of the city off-limits to whites. Therese beamed as she caught sight of the areas we were driving through, certain intersections, various individual buildings. She was in her late forties, blond, thin, with short hair and gray eyes that seemed veiled, though the veil dissolved more and more the longer she spent in the city. When we merged onto the freeway in Ann's old Peugeot, Therese sighed with happiness. She would introduce me to a new circle of friends but I didn't know that yet.

Ann lived on Santa Fe Avenue in an artist's co-op that had been set up in a former factory. Only artists who made less than $25,000 a year were accepted. The compound was surrounded by a high, impregnable fence and secured with a complicated entry system; the heavy door could be opened only with a specific entry code. Necessary, I'm afraid, Ann said, we're in a very dangerous neighborhood here. Don't think you can just go out for a walk. —Doesn't that depress you? I asked. Ann said that a person can get used to anything. And there's nowhere else in the city you can find such big apartments and studios for such an affordable rent.

I had to admit she was right. Giant rooms with high ceilings, enough space for a kind of permanent exhibition of her photographs on the walls and on cords stretched across the room, space for a darkroom, a kitchen area, and a living space with table, chairs, and a jukebox. This is living, Therese said, and Ann and I looked at each other: Therese wished she could live like this.

The residents had put in a cactus garden in the courtyard between the buildings; a painter waved us into her studio to show us the copies of Pompeian wall paintings she had made for a paying customer. A stroke of luck.

But then we went down into the underworld. Ann showed us the giant garbage pile stretching out to the horizon right across from the artist's compound, on the other side of a wide street: it was leveled off in places into a kind of lunar landscape with the wind whistling over it, blowing clouds of dust and small pieces of garbage. I raised no further objections to living next door to something like this: the low rent for artists explained and excused everything. Two men came toward us; Ann knew them, they lived in the garbage dump, she said, in sheds they had built themselves out of wooden and metal garbage. They were both carrying something in their hands—I couldn't tell what the things were, but they were apparently offering them to us for sale. Not today, thanks, Ann said in a friendly voice, and the two men waved at her and peacefully withdrew.

Ann drove us toward downtown, through neighborhoods that were more and more run-down. She would never get out of the car here, she said. Groups of *homeless people* were crouching by the walls of the buildings, on the side of the street, only a few of them moving. All black. Ravaged streets. Ann was heading somewhere specific and arranged something with someone over her cell phone. When I stop, she said, get out and run as fast as you can to the only store that has unbroken shop windows and a normal door, someone will open it and go right inside, fast. That's how it happened. A young man was waiting for us behind the barred door, opened it briefly, and whisked us inside. Ann didn't quite make it: a man was on her heels, she got free by giving him a cigarette, then a dollar, and slipped through the door, and the man pressed his cheek against the outside of the window and pointed with his finger. Ann kissed the cheek of the black man where he was pointing, through the window, and then he was satisfied and left.

We found ourselves in an oasis: a refuge for the *homeless people*. The young man had set up the back part of the room—secured with strong bars, and where he himself painted—as a workshop where the homeless could make wooden toys, beautiful things in simple shapes that were easy to sell since the only other toys on the market were plastic. They don't buy alcohol with the proceeds, he said, that's the miracle. They buy tools and raw materials so that they can make more toys. The key thing, he said, was that no one pressured them, no one asked them anything or tried to convince them of anything, and also that they could come and go as they pleased, or go away for a long time and come back later. They were simply accepted the way they were. And they, or at least some of them, accepted what he was offering: that was the second miracle, he said.

Ann felt the need to lighten things up a little so she drove us through a Mexican neighborhood she especially liked. She shopped there; it was poor, but colorful and lively. We ate lunch at a restaurant called Serenata de Garibaldi, and Therese implied that this city, Los Angeles, was something of a refuge for her. No, she said to a half-question from Ann, she still wasn't divorced from her husband, he was still insisting that he couldn't live without her. Ann said if it was her she would take the risk.

The afternoon was drawing to a close and we drove downtown again through the poor neighborhoods. Now the *homeless people* were gathering everywhere around the *missions* and *public shelters* set up by the city, like iron filings around magnets, to get a bowl of soup and a place to sleep before night fell. Now we could see for the first time how many there were—a dark, gray-black mass in long lines. Almost all of them black, many of the faces expressionless. One couple sat next to each other in the gutter: they were young, they laughed, I took them for lovers and pointed them out to Ann. She said: Lovers? Well, maybe. But there was no way to be sure that he wasn't just her pimp. She had long since stopped taking photographs in these parts of town, by the way, because it was dangerous. I could tell that a sense of shame kept her from documenting these people in their degradation. Instead, she photographed us, the privileged guests of the CENTER, in the most flattering way possible, and showed a row of the enlarged photographs in a kind of gallery along the hall on the seventh floor. I was unable to see the gallery of photos as anything but obscene.

By the time I got back home, back to the MS. VICTORIA, I was utterly exhausted. It wore a different face now: not just an oasis but a fortress, a bastion of defense against this city's poverty and misery, which we were powerless against. I paced back and forth between the kitchen and the living room, I couldn't sit down at the word processor, couldn't write anything up; I ate little and drank two whiskeys one after the other, which I almost never did, without feeling any effect. Then I took the mail I had fetched without looking at from the CENTER that morning, took it out of my Indian bag, and paged through it. A fax was there, an article from a well-respected German magazine by a well-respected journalist, and unfortunately I forgot myself and read it. It went beyond everything so far, everything I had almost gotten used to over the past few days. I felt like I was breathing another kind of air now, I was in serious, unavoidable danger. I had to make a decision that night.

I am trying to remember what I did that night—I couldn't take any notes at the time. I went to bed. I brought dear Fleming's poem with me. "Be undismayed in spite of everything; do not give up, despite everything." I repeated the line over and over until I could say it in my sleep. But it was only midnight. What now?

THEN I STARTED SINGING

I sang the whole night through, every song I knew—and I know a lot of songs, with a lot of verses. I drank two more whiskeys straight down but I didn't get drunk. The phone rang several times, I knew who was trying so urgently to reach me but I didn't pick up. I sang "An jenem Tag im blauen Mond September," I sang "Glück auf, Glück auf, der Steiger kommt," I sang "Es leben die Soldaten so recht von Gottes Gnaden." "Du Schwert an meiner Linken." Songs from different eras of my life mingled together in my mind, suddenly I heard myself singing "Was fragt ihr dumm, was fragt ihr klein, warum wir wohl marschieren" and quickly broke off.

I still remember the feeling I had that *the overcoat of Dr. Freud* was hovering above me: it had heralded that I would learn much about myself that night and, since that was dangerous, it would protect me. We would see if I really wanted to know it, as I always claimed. It didn't surprise me that an overcoat was talking to me.

I sang "Als wir jüngst in Regensburg waren," I sang "Am Brunnen vor dem Tore," I sang "Der Mond ist aufgegangen," then I sang "Spaniens Himmel breitet seine Sterne," and "Da streiten sich die Leut herum wohl um den Wert des Glücks," and then I sang "Im schönsten Wiesengrunde ist meiner Heimat Haus," but also "We Shall Overcome" and "Au clair de la lune." I sang "Das Wandern ist des Müllers Lust," and "Grosser Gott im Himmel, sieben Heller sind mir noch geblieben," and "Stehn zwei Stern am hohen Himmel," and "Guten Abend, gute Nacht," and "Kein schöner Land in dieser Zeit," and "Wohl auf, Kameraden, aufs Pferd aufs Pferd," and "Die blauen Dragoner, sie reiten," and "O Strassburg, o Strassburg, du wunderschöne Stadt," and "Das Lieben bringt gross Freud," and "Zu Strassburg auf der Schanz," and "Ik weit enen Eikboom de steiht an de See," and "Up de Straat steiht en Djung mitn Tüdelband," and "Lasst uns froh und munter sein," and "Ich hatt' einen Kameraden," and "Es geht eine helle Flöte," and "Alle Vögel sind schon da," and I didn't let myself take a break and I brought song after song up out of an inexhaustible reservoir, I sang "Die Gedanken sind frei," and I sang "Es zogen drei Burschen wohl über den Rhein," and "Drei Lilien, drei Lilien, die pflanzt ich auf ein Grab," and "O du stille Zeit," and "Hohe Tannen weisen die Sterne," and "Im August blühn die Rosen," and "Du hast ja ein Ziel vor den Augen," and "Die Blümelein, sie schlafen," and "Fremd bin ich eingezogen," and "Sah ein Knab ein Röslein stehn," and "Der Mai ist gekommen," and "Am Weg dort hinterm Zaune," and "All mein Gedanken, die ich hab," and "Willst du dein Herz mir schenken," and "Es, es, es, und es, es ist ein harter Schluss," and "Der Frühling hat sich eingestellt," and "Winter ade," and "Hoch auf dem gelben Wagen," and "Auf der Lüneberger Heide," and "Im Frühtau zu Berge wir ziehn vallera," and "Dat du min Lewsten bist," I sang for hours and hours and lightened my heart, and sang "Wir lagen vor Madagaskar," and sang "Wo die blauen Gipfel ragen," and sang "Wir sind durch Deutschland gefahren," sang "Der Landsknecht muss die Trommel rühren," sang "Das Frühjahr kommt, wach auf, du Christ," and "Am Grunde der Moldau, da wandern die Steine," and "Wem Gott will rechte Gunst erweisen," and "Auf, auf zum fröhlichen Jagen," and "Ich ging im Walde so für mich hin," and "Ein feste Burg ist unser Gott," and "Geh aus, mein Herz, und suche Freud," and "Die Glocken stürmten vom Bernwardsturm," and "Im tiefen Keller sitz ich hier," and "Über allen Gipfeln ist Ruh," and "Kein Feuer, keine Kohle kann brennen so heiss," and "Abend wird es wieder," and "Als die goldne Abendsonne, sandte ihren letzten Schein," and "Von all unsern Kameraden, war keiner so lieb und so gut," and "Steige hoch, du roter Adler," and "Masslos gequält und gepeinigt," and "Wer recht in Freuden wandern will," and "Wie herrlich leuchtet mir die Natur," and "Sonne komm raus," and "Wo man singt, da lass dich ruhig nieder," and "Unser Zeichen ist die Sonne," and "Prinz Eugen, der edle Ritter," and "Wacht auf, Verdammte dieser Erde," and "Leise zieht durch mein Gemüt liebliches Geläute," and I sang "Ade nun zur guten Nacht," and "Es blies ein Jäger wohl in sein Horn," and "Im Märzen der Bauer die Rösslein einspannt," and "Und in dem Schneegebirge," and finally "Freude, schöner Götterfunken."

Then it was morning. The first light came through the tangle of weeds outside my window and I peacefully fell asleep. A few hours later I was sitting at the narrow end of the big table at my machine, I could see a low ridge of the roof and there was a blue bird, big and beautiful, with shimmering feathers, that I had never seen there and I never saw again. It came right up to my window, sat down on the ledge, tilted its glittering silver head to the side, and looked at me. I knew that it was a messenger, and I understood its message, which cannot be expressed in words.

I dutifully wrote down everything that came to me.

That afternoon I went to Woolworth's to buy a lamp for my desk. I already had the long cardboard box under my arm and was standing in line for the cash register when a young black man came up and spoke to me, rather rudely. He seemed unkempt, with frizzy black hair peeking out from under a small cap, bad teeth, a pockmarked face. He pressed a package of candy into my hand with a dollar, I should buy it for him, he had to go somewhere in a hurry. I could hardly understand his slang, which seemed to offend him. I said I don't need the dollar, I can buy it with my own money. No, he didn't want that. Maybe he had to find a toilet in a hurry, I thought. It took a long time before the only cashier, uneducated like all the cashiers here, had rung up the customers in front of me and put their purchases in bags. I paid separately for the package of candy and took the change. Then I stood there, my box under my arm and the candy and change in my hand, and waited. He didn't show up. Was he playing a trick on me? Trying to take revenge on a white woman for something? Should I just leave? Then, suddenly, when I turned around, he was standing behind me. *Here you are!* I cried, relieved, and handed him his candy and the change. He was as if transformed. He beamed, took the candy and money, gave me a long and heartfelt handshake, and thanked me over and over again. We parted in perfect harmony. Apparently it had been a test, and apparently I had passed it.

Along with a pile of new newspaper clippings in my mailbox at the CENTER was a letter from Ruth, inviting me to a discussion with a Jewish group that met regularly though infrequently and whose leader, if you could call him that, was a friend of hers. Kätchen, who had been tending to my incoming and outgoing mail especially carefully in recent weeks, put some new faxes in front of me, facedown. *Are you okay?* I said: *No.* She said: *I didn't think so. What's the matter?* I invited her to join me for lunch. I tried, despite the linguistic hurdles, to tell her what was happening. She tried to understand. She had read the American newspapers. She said what everyone said first: But it was such a long time ago! She liked me. She wanted to make me feel better. I knew that she was horrified by the very word "Communism," the same as almost all Americans. Suddenly the muscle in my esophagus spasmed. I couldn't swallow. I had to let my spaghetti get cold and try to hide from Kätchen that I was not eating anymore. I couldn't drink either. After ten minutes, the muscle cramp relaxed, but from then on it kept coming back and I couldn't do anything to stop it.

Toward the end of the day, the "future party" started in the CEN-TER: all the staff were invited and everyone had to dress up as someone or something from the future. All I did was look for the snake armband I had bought on a day trip to San Diego and put the brightly colored wooden snake on my shoulder. So the partygoers thought I was trying to be the Snake Woman, and some of the feminists knew that the snake was an ancient feminine symbol. Most of them had gone all out with their costumes, showing up in metallically glinting suits or draped in electronic devices, others wore hats or helmets with antennas, some came as rockets. They danced to futuristic electronic music and we ate bizarre food and drank fantasy drinks. Our cohort was represented most brilliantly by Pintus and Ria, a constellated pair: two little planets circling each other.

I was surprised to see Peter Gutman appear, late and without the slightest hint of a costume, of course. But what do you mean, he said, he had the cleverest costume of all: He had come as a human being. A human being from the twentieth century. A scholar from the distant past, when there were still scholars. His costume was a hit.

We met at the bar over a bright yellow drink called a Luna cocktail. Peter Gutman had me explain my snake to him.

Aha, he said, Madame is withdrawing into the matriarchy.

But was it a step back? I said, that's the question. Besides, in the matriarchy I would have to be responsible for the whole tribe. Pretty stressful, I should think. I kept my eyes pointed straight ahead and sipped on my straw.

Then Peter Gutman said: It's an ancient rule—when you get deadlocked you have to take a step back and start negotiations over again from the beginning.

Negotiations about what? I asked. Capital investments?

You overestimate me, Madame. I am decidedly short on funds at the moment. And I doubt that in the era we all seem to be living in here there is even such a word as "capital." The last dollar has long ago been shredded to pieces by the time machine.

Are you sure, Sir? That was Emily, who had come in a fantastic costume, as Pythia, and was soothsaying left and right.

Of course I'm *sure*, Peter Gutman said. Because if that hadn't happened, if the dollar still inundated the world, then we wouldn't be living in the future. But here we all are, nice and cozy.

Then we wouldn't, if it hadn't, I said disapprovingly. Lutz from Hamburg, a star rider who said he represented intercontinental peace, commented: But he's right. Clearly he's right, but at the same time he's a hopeless dreamer.

Had I ever heard the little word "utopia"?

Oh, man, that's all I needed. Then Francesco came over too in his lavish Venetian costume with a devil's mask—the devil would never die, Francesco had argued—and made the conspicuously gentle suggestion that maybe it was time for them to take the burden of utopia off of my Eastern shoulders and place it upon their Western ones.

Unanimous agreement. What did that mean? That meant they all started talking nonsense. We had all had quite a bit to drink, of course, and the composition of the brightly colored cocktails remained secret but they brought about unforeseeable consequences, for example—our whole cohort had gradually gathered at the bar—Ria, the small shimmering planet, started going into raptures about a world where every person, especially every girl, was given a basic guaranteed income at fourteen and could separate from his or her parents. That would dramatically reduce the suicide rate among young people.

Everyone guessed what prompted Ria to this vision but we all found it much too tame. Pintus in particular felt the need to contradict her, it struck me that he had been constantly contradicting her recently. We should be more ambitious than that, he said. Back when he was with the Maoists, they had believed that you could force people into happiness. And there was no question but that people's happiness consisted in devoting their whole lives to the betterment of society, they thought. Which of course had to be fundamentally transformed, they thought. By any means necessary, including violence.

And now? Lutz asked.

Now, since we were talking about utopia, he pinned his hopes on people developing other needs, over a very, very long time. That someday they would strive for something besides money and power and consumption.

But what? And how would it come about?

Hopefully it won't be because of a disaster, Lutz said. Hopefully we won't become smart only as a result of some catastrophe. None of us will own our own car in the future, for example.

That's too bad, Francesco said.

We will have developed alternative energy sources by then, and stopped the environmental catastrophe, said Maya, Lutz's wife, in the flowing dress of an archaic goddess. Ines, cheekily dressed as a mistress, which there would always be in any imaginable future, added: Everyone will take responsibility for children then, not only the parents. —Not that! Francesco blurted out. But Ines informed him that people in the future would no longer be small-minded and selfish, but generous and, yes, well, smarter.

You mean to say, said Hanno, our aristocratic Frenchman who had come in a kind of tuxedo as an executive of an interstellar travel company, you mean to say that people in the future will know more about themselves? And will want to?

Silence.

Knowing more about yourself can also lead to despair, said Peter Gutman, the person of the present.

Spoilsport.

Emily saved the situation. She raised her staff of wisdom, murmured her Pythian maxims, looked out our twelfth-story window far across the ocean glittering in the pale moonlight, and proclaimed: People will learn how to know everything about themselves and how to use that knowledge to help each other.

How boring! Ria cried. They assured her that conflicts would not cease to exist, that in fact only then would there be worthwhile conflicts, namely, those between diverse individual people. Not just between rich and poor, high and low, believers and unbelievers.

I knew that story already. Was everything starting over again, from the beginning?

Francesco led us to a round table that was free, a bit off to the side, right in front of the wall of windows. Suddenly we had the noise of the party behind us and could talk as though we were in a separate room. I remember the big round stage-set moon describing its whole arc above the glittering ocean while we sat there, I never let it out of my sight.

For the first time, Stewart joined us, the one black fellowship-holder, who had arrived at the CENTER later than the rest of us and had always kept himself apart, until then. I suddenly understood that we had been acting self-conscious around him exactly the way the others had recently been acting around me, out of insecurity. Suddenly I could come out and say it. Stewart seemed surprised, not insulted, almost amused; the others admitted that I was right. Stewart was working on a sociological study of the black *community* in Los Angeles and as he told us about his project he left no doubt as to his radically disapproving position on the social structures he was uncovering there. Now it was he who criticized me, from an unexpected direction: He didn't want to pretend he didn't know what was going on. He read the papers too, after all, and overheard conversations and rumors in the CENTER that didn't find their way to me. That had to stop, he thought. And most of all, my creeping around had to stop.

Everyone protested but not convincingly. Creeping around?

Yes. I was acting like I had a reason to have a bad conscience. That made him angry.

Bad conscience? That's not it. —Well, what is it? —Okay, I feel like I have a reason to reflect. —Nothing against reflecting. But about what? —I want to figure out who I was back then. Why I talked to them at all. Why I didn't send them away right at the start. The way I would have done a little later.

Okay, good. So why?

Because I don't think I saw them as "them" yet. That is probably the first thing I said. Of course I don't remember everything that was said that night, but I do remember that the ocean, the Pacific Ocean outside the window, and the moon above it were with me the whole time. I noticed how difficult it was to connect normal, everyday words to the country I came from, which the newspapers my friends were reading categorically classified under the Evil Empire. I didn't argue with a lot of what those papers said, but still, I lived in a different country than that one. And how was it possible to describe that?

Facts lined up one after the other don't give you reality, you know. Facts are not enough. There are many layers and facets to reality and the naked facts are only its surface. Revolutionary measures could be hard on the people affected by them—the Jacobins were not squeamish, nor the Bolsheviks. We would not have denied that we were living in a dictatorship, not in the least: it was the dictatorship of the proletariat. A transitional period, an incubation period for the new men and women, you understand? "We who wanted to lay the groundwork for peace / could not ourselves be peaceful": I firmly believed in that. We were bursting with utopia, since that word has already come up once this evening. We didn't like our country the way it was but the way it would be: THE WAY THINGS ARE WILL NOT CONTINUE, we were certain of that.

So, I said, back when those young men approached me and I didn't send them packing right away, I probably still believed that maybe they are necessary, maybe we need them. Just two or three years later I would not have let "them" into the room. I advised others not to talk to them either, advice they took.

What had happened in the meantime? That's what my friends wanted to know. Francesco thought that what happened was what happens to every illusion: it collapsed. Lutz countered that it was more than just an illusion, it was the framework for a new society. An alternative that we—he said "we"—desperately needed. Who had seen that more clearly than they had, the '68 generation? And who had experienced more bitterly how this "we" crumbled? It wasn't so different with you, he said.

THE ARDUOUS PATH OF RECOGNITION, I said. And before that the long path of knowledge, of perceiving and learning. What didn't we think was possible? What didn't we want to believe? The hope crumbled, utopia fell apart and started to rot. We had to learn how to live without alternatives.

Only then did I notice that our group sitting at the round table was all alone in the large room. The music had long since stopped, the bar had closed, the last couples had left, there was colored paper, plastic cups, and straws lying scattered on the floor, the decorations hung slack from the few lights that were still on. It was long past midnight. I was sorry I had talked for so long, or at all. I couldn't escape the feeling that I had fobbed them off with the layers of my memory reservoir that lay closest to the surface but had not reached the real reality, not at all.

How do you mean? Peter Gutman asked. I walked to Ocean Park with him, leaned on the railing a little while longer and looked at the nighttime ocean, the moon now all the way on the right, just above the Santa Monica Mountains, before we walked through empty streets back to the MS. VICTORIA. How do you mean?

I know, I said, it's all true, but that's not what it's actually about. —What was it about? —The question is still how I could have forgotten it. Why hadn't anyone asked me that?

YOU CAN SLAVE AWAY AT THE WRONG QUESTIONS TOO

Peter
Gutman said, and he was probably right.

The following day I started to answer the truly noble letter a friend had sent me ("We have always known that the OTHER grows out of one's own contradictory life"), which would take me a week and many sheets of paper and several nearly sleepless nights. I wrote my way down to a core that I could clearly feel but not put a name to until I was startled out of my sleep one night and saw written before my eyes the last phrase of a long speech someone had given me: THE OTHERNESS IN YOU. I was convinced on the spot; it fit. Or, I thought, maybe the foreign in me too: a foreign body I had felt the way you can feel a growth in your body. A doctor would perform a biopsy to determine the composition of this foreign tissue, or actually to ascertain just one thing about it: Is it malignant or benign? And answer the question: Operate or not? The danger being that the malignant tissue could spread to the whole body, which was itself healthy, and devour it.

What happened to me is the one thing that shouldn't have happened to me, I tell myself, and that seems right but I don't actually know if at the same time a different text is moving in the opposite direction inside me, one that doubts this thesis. Something like curiosity about the steps I will take next. Or the next thoughts I will think. Even in the word "futility," the word that rules my days and nights, I find a kind of satisfaction, the same kind I always feel when I have found the appropriate label for a condition.

Rachel, the Feldenkrais instructor: I now regularly went to her tiny house to receive instruction. She was opposed in principle to violent actions. She had me feel the effects that slight changes in movement could have on the whole system. How habits that had worked their way deep into the body could block free movement. How releasing these blockages in the body could also release blockages in the brain, since in fact we do not consist of a separate mind and body—the division, suggested to us by Christianity, is false and catastrophic, Rachel said: it means we have totally unlearned how to see ourselves as a whole, with body, mind, and soul fused together in every single cell. You, for example, she told me after my third session, have always tried to control everything with your head. You're still trying to. But you're starting to see how it really works. You're learning, and not only with your head. Your resistance is giving way.

The overcoat of Dr. Freud, I said.

Excuse me?

You know, the coat that keeps you warm but also hidden, that you have to turn inside out. To make the inside visible.

If you say so, Rachel said. It's enough for me when my thoughts, movements, and feelings are in tune with each other, the way God intended. She then told me, as though obliged not to keep it a secret, that all her other patients were Jewish. Peter Gutman had sent me to her. I didn't ask anything further, she didn't say anything further. I remember that that was one of the first bright, sunny afternoons after the long rains.

My little red Geo was waiting obediently on the street in front of Rachel's bungalow but I couldn't get in because I had left the key in the ignition and the automatic doors had locked. I found the insurance card and learned that they actually did consider my mishap as falling within their jurisdiction. After twenty minutes, a competent and friendly mechanic showed up who was able to open the car without breaking the door, who had barely a tired smile for my inappropriate joke that he was in a good position to become a successful car thief, and who answered my heartfelt *Thank you so much!* with a convincing *You're welcome!* I steered the car that was once again mine onto Wilshire Boulevard and drove into the sunset as the sun sank once again into the Pacific, in all its glory.

Everything was as it should be: the three raccoons had survived the flood, the lightbulb over the entrance to the MS. VICTORIA was flickering like always, Mr. Enrico gathered up the papers on his desk and said a blissful hello, as happy as everyone else that the sun was shining on California again. I had bought groceries on the way home and I hauled the bags up to my apartment, drank my margarita, and ate bread and cheese, while the crew of the *Enterprise* once again saved an alien civilization, for which I was sincerely grateful.

Unchecked thoughts ran through my head and suddenly the word "*Schrecken*" popped up—how do you say that in English, actually? I took down my Langenscheidt dictionary: "*shock*," yes of course, that was probably right even though it didn't exactly match *Schrecken* in German, whose meaning ranged from being startled to scared to horrified. For the first time in all those months, I happened to look at the back cover and saw that the dictionary was being marketed as "The most up-to-date, with new words from all domains"—one example listed was *Wendehals*. I wanted to see how they said that in English, so I looked it up and found: "*Wendehals* (*Wende*, Turn, the fall of the Wall, + *Hals*, neck), pol. GDR contp. [= *contemptuous*]: *quick-change artist*." And at last I was convinced of the untranslatability of words. Because the young colleague who first used that word in the fall of 1989—it was in the Church of the Redeemer in Lichtenberg, East Berlin, at the writers' convention "Against the Sleep of Reason"—was doing nothing but reading, totally objectively, the description of the bird called a *Wendehals*, a wryneck, from *Brehm's Life of Animals*, and there was nothing more he needed to do to make the behavior of the people eagerly conforming to the new revolutionary conditions look utterly ridiculous, and I myself had done nothing, I thought, but recite the same definition at the famous November 4 rally at Alexanderplatz.

You were all gathered at the Church of the Redeemer in October 1989. They still didn't assign you a large auditorium but they had stopped prohibiting your events and the church opened its doors. "Against the Sleep of Reason": the motto could hardly have been better and the hundreds of people crowding into the church felt it as they listened to the dozens of speeches and performances from writers and singers that went late into the night. Stunned joy—that was the mood that night. You spoke freely, as though what you were saying were self-evident. No caution and consideration, no looking to either side, the words that lay on everyone's tongues were unshackled—a feeling that none of you ever wanted to be without again. Your repeated demand in those days was for an independent investigatory commission to determine what had happened to the peaceful protesters on the nights when the Republic was celebrating its fortieth anniversary, and who had given the orders to use violence. ("On those nights, a sickness broke out in this society.") Not long afterward, such a commission was indeed established.

—

Peter Gutman came by, unannounced but not unexpected. It was almost midnight and I showed him the draft of my answer to the friend's letter. ("To learn from one's mistakes is the hardest way to learn; how much easier to learn from one's successes but that was not granted us.") He didn't say anything, and I gradually realized what his silence meant, but I didn't care. I said I wanted to know what was wrong with me back then.

All right, listen, Peter Gutman said. It's really very simple. You wanted to be loved. You wanted the authorities to love you too.

That very early childhood fear of the thick snake lying under your bed at night, so that you couldn't get out of bed under any circumstances without stepping on the repulsive snake and getting bitten. But what did that snake have to do with your fear of lies, or of being discovered, or of your mother, who had drummed this fear into you—the worst thing anyone could do in the world was lie to their mother, "God sees everything"—the story about the man whose hand reached up out of the grave was all it took to bring you into contact with the primordial lie, the lie to the mother, that was where horror was implanted within you, bad conscience, fears ("If I did anything wrong today / Then, dear God, please look away"), self-doubt as the breeding ground for new fears and new offshoots of fear, and also the longing or need to be whole and irreproachable and in harmony with those in charge. To be loved by them. To avoid the deepest fear, of losing the mother's love.

So, Madame, he said. You weren't the only one. By the way, you have now crawled your way rather deeply into the overcoat of Dr. Freud.

On an evening not long after that came the exciting trip up to Karl's house, a bird's nest in the hills directly under the giant letters of the HOLLYWOOD sign set up in front of the cliffs, the city's trademark. You could see it, shockingly close, from out Karl's windows: it took your breath away, just like the view from the other wall of windows, of the whole gigantic shimmering city of Los Angeles by night down below. And Karl, a photographer of German origin, had built this intricate little house himself, around the initial cell of a single room, adding on a basement and a wooden porch. It was a little miracle. Bob Rice had brought me; the others there were Allan, Bob's boyfriend, an American of Japanese descent, and an older Jewish married couple, John the lawyer and his wife, a university professor, along with their daughter. We drank gin and tonics and then sat crowded around a table in one of the small rooms that all opened into each other and whose walls were covered with photographs Karl had taken. He and Allan had cooked and "Japanese flair" was promised; we felt a level of trust and closeness as though we had all known each other a long time. I was surprised again and again how warmly people treated me, even though they must all have read the article in *The New York Times* painting a portrait of me that horrified me. John, the lawyer, quietly said to me that I should simply picture Americans as creating every country and every person in their own image—lots of people would think it was *"great"* for a major newspaper to devote so much space to me, irrespective of what the article said.

Bob asked Allan to tell us about the internment of Japanese-Americans in *concentration camps* after the attack on Pearl Harbor: his parents, and he himself as a one-year-old child, were among them. Allan didn't want to say much about it, only that it was very hard for them to find their footing again in everyday American life after their release; they were met on all sides with hostility and general mistrust. He worked for Universal Studios as a set designer, by the way—if I wanted, he could show me around the studio.

John had read a lot about the events of the fall of 1989. He turned the conversation to the question of which English word would be the best translation for the German word *"Aufbruch"*—we thought of *"uprising"* but that wasn't entirely right, we would have to consult our dictionaries.

So what was it, then? What were those weeks, a few months, for which it is so difficult to find the right name? They crept up on you slowly, almost imperceptibly, along various paths, one of which ended in a parish garden after a reading in a church, with a couple dozen people standing around arguing loudly—it was early summer, the election results had been falsified, it was documented with eyewitness accounts from the polling places. I still remember how you said: They can't be doing that again! Feelings surged up inside you—mixed feelings, absolutely, you felt worry along with the anger and outrage and amazement—where was this going to end if the leaders were still, even now, yet again, unwilling or unable to look reality in the face, see the mood of the people in the country, and react to it?

DIALOGUE! was the first demand of the first protesters. But the leaders imposed one stupid measure after another, finally even banning *Sputnik* magazine, from Moscow, which had taken the "New Thinking" spilling over you from Gorbachev's Soviet Union and spread it, unchecked, in your own country. You were there when, in one of the critical plays the theaters were scrambling to put on, an actor in the middle of a scene took a whole stack of these magazines and threw them onto the stage, and the audience jumped up and cheered, applauding wildly. The manifestos of various groups were still being passed around in secret, and the blunt, open discussions were still taking place in apartments, but the pace of events was increasing and could not be stopped.

I have just found the folder labeled "1989/90," containing the speeches and essays you wrote in those two or three months. It's astounding, actually. Back then you were asked to write pieces. First was an appeal to those in power to finally enter into dialogue with the regime's critics, which you wrote together with other women writers and then introduced at a large assembly where, to your stunned amazement, it passed, with seven No votes. Clearly the tide had turned. Then came interviews, commentaries, appeals broadcast over the radio and television stations you suddenly had access to. It strikes me that these texts were infused with hopes that, later, had to be recognized as illusions—you called one of the petitions "For Our Country," obsolete by the time it appeared. But I have learned since then that a popular movement cannot exist without these hopes, without these illusions.

The most important thing I'm trying to remember, though, is not these texts or anything that anyone wrote or broadcast: the most important thing is the condition you found yourselves in. All the crowds of people rushing through the streets, complete strangers discussing topics that had been taboo only yesterday and saying, shouting, doing what no one, including them, would have thought themselves capable of, in an intelligent and imaginative and disciplined way. Your condition was absolutely not giddy happiness, it was often a very painful experience, for example when the investigatory commission you had demanded so urgently actually met: long sessions in the Rotes Rathaus and later in a church, where the ruling powers, in the form of high-up functionaries and eventually the very highest, had to justify their abuses of power and appear before the commission in their shabby, sorry condition.

I knew, I told Peter Gutman, that I would never live through anything like that again. We were all going through a psychological crisis.

On TV: a documentary about Charlie Chaplin, with a strong focus on his persecution by Hoover, the head of the FBI. At the end of the show, text appeared on-screen saying how many miles of files this Hoover had left behind. By now, everyone knew, or could know if they wanted to, that the future president of the United States, Ronald Reagan, formerly an actor and president of the Screen Actors Guild labor union, had betrayed and informed on his colleagues as FBI Confidential Informant "T-10." *So what? Never mind.* As Mr. Hoover himself said before the House Un-American Activities Committee: "Communism is an evil and malignant way of life. It spreads like an epidemic and, like an epidemic, a quarantine is necessary to keep it from infecting the nation." Malignant life-forms that have not even crossed the threshold to subhuman status are supposed to be exterminated, of course, without a trace of bad conscience.

I walked down Second Street to distract myself, and in front of the restaurant that supposedly served the best burgers in the city I ran into the friend who had come from Europe to interview me, despite his fear of flying. We had arranged that he would be left undisturbed to prepare, on this first day of his stay, but then he invited me in to join him. That was the only burger I ate in America: it was served in a little wicker basket and was extremely good. We talked about his flight, and the wine in Lufthansa's business class, and jet lag, and the climate in Germany, both meteorological and political, and at the end he asked: Why did you continue to stand by the flag? No, don't say anything now.

We said goodbye and I walked past the Indian store to buy myself a deck of tarot cards and a detailed guide to how to use it. I saw an incredible picture on the front lawn of the MS. VICTORIA: Mrs. Ascott, the manager, who forbid nothing more strictly than bringing pets into the building, was sitting at the little white table on the right, under one of the large-leafed exotic plants, wrapped in one of her flowy pastel-colored robes, with a cat on her lap. She was petting it. It was the little cat that the tall, Indian-looking man had adopted; he had since left. *Isn't it sweet, isn't it lovely?* she asked, and, to my amazement, she even knew my name. *Yes, Mrs. Ascott, it is.* Signs and wonders.

On my table lay the incriminating file, the corpus delicti, that my friend from Germany had brought me. Tied with thick cord— CONFIDENTIAL! Dozens of journalists had seen it before me and discussed it at length, as allowed by law. I couldn't open it yet. I was tired. I lay down in bed and read Thomas Mann's diaries.

On November 22, 1949, he had written: "Adenauer, the Chancellor, told a Frenchman that Germany does not want an army. Militaristic memories must not be reawakened. And already, no sooner has the question of disarmament been resolved to G's benefit, the whole West German press has started calling for rearmament against Russia. Russia would respond by instating universal military service in East Germany.— Becher and Eisler had come up with a new German national anthem, all about peace and unity, designed not to offend any enemy nations.— I feel like a mayfly, outdated and absurd. Militarism for peace. But what is the right thing to do, and what has a future?"

Good question, I thought. Why did you stand by the flag?

Once, I remembered, someone had explicitly called upon you to "stand by the flag." It must have been in the seventies. In Leipzig. You were sitting—a group of authors—at breakfast in a hotel where you had stayed after an event the previous day. Then an older man unexpectedly came up to you, a former district attorney who had been removed from office when he refused to bring charges against Walter Janka and Wolfgang Harich: he had "neglected to pursue the necessary struggle against the enemies of the GDR." Now he was head of the department of books and publishing, in other words the head censor. He put his hand on your shoulder and said: Just stand by the flag! —By what flag? you asked, baffled. And he said: The flag of humanity.

I fell asleep. I dreamed a dream that forced its way through the defensive perimeter created by the sleeping pills, and I know it for a fact since I wrote it down—I would never invent such a transparent, easy to interpret dream. So, I dreamed I was lying on a kind of board, and in my sleep a circular saw was cutting off my limbs, slice by slice, first my legs, then my arms, finally my head, until my brain sat there by itself and then that was sawed to pieces too, and then a male voice cried: So it must be! Then my name appeared in neon lights, and finally, at the end of the dream, that went out too.

When I woke up, I had the intense feeling: I am a danger to myself.

I went to the phone early and called Berlin, and said: My body is leaving me. Time is leaving me too, in the same way, but probably not at the same speed. Maybe what Yuri Trifonov said is right, that the libido for writing weakens with age, I said, but in return I received only the harsh answer that that was just an excuse, I was apparently still thinking about an audience instead of what I needed to do, which was simply to try to get clarity about myself and write only for myself. As always in such cases, my first reaction was to want to contradict him, but then I surprised myself by simply saying yes, and I enjoyed admitting it. *The overcoat of Dr. Freud*, I said. —What? —Oh, nothing. —Did libido make you think of that? —No, but, wouldn't that be a good title? —It depends.

On what? —On whether the path goes all the way down to the underworld: the entrance to the underworld is a wound, I heard the voice say. One moves by slowly feeling one's way in the dark. A tunnel feeling. I HAVE TO CLIMB BACK DOWN INTO THIS MINESHAFT. But did I really have to? Or was it only another compulsory exercise? A STRANGE PERSON LOOKS BACK AT ME FROM THERE. But is that even true?

Why did you stand by the flag? The hotel. The interview, the anxiety, the spotlights. My answer was not ready yet but I could give a partial answer: It was hope that the people—the many people, who, I believed, thought like I did—would eventually prevail. Because it couldn't be otherwise. Because otherwise this country and everything it embodied for us would perish. Because we had no alternative . . . I knew that his question would stay with me for years.

That night we went out for Mexican food; the tension had given way to exhaustion and I couldn't hold my tongue. I reproached my friend, who, as warned, had questioned me "mercilessly," for acting high and mighty. He said: Now you have really insulted me. And I burst into tears.

The next day we drove, in pouring rain at first, to Sunset Boulevard, turned onto Paseo Miramar, and drove up to Villa Aurora: Feuchtwanger's house, which had been added on to after Marta Feuchtwanger's death. We could stand on the terrace and look out in wonder at the ocean; I could tell my friend how it used to look inside the house, with all the valuable books. Then we sat for a while on a bench by the Malibu coast, in the sun that had come out around noon, and we felt good. My friend said: They see me as a radical leftist now but I haven't changed at all, it's my country that has shifted past me to the right, unbelievably quickly. And I thought: Why should they always be the ones paying attention to our problems? Why shouldn't we also be interested in their problems for once?

Then we drove all the way up Sunset Boulevard again and started singing. We sang "Wacht auf, Verdammte dieser Erde" and "Wenn wir schreiten Seit an Seit" and "Spaniens Himmel breitet seine Sterne," "Und weil der Mensch ein Mensch ist" and "Madrid, du Wunderbare" and "Durchs Gebirge, durch die Steppe zog unsre kühne Division" and "Wohin auch das Auge blicket, Moor und Heide nur ringsum," my friend knew all the songs and I asked him where he'd learned them. Where do you think, he said. When I was living in Berlin before 1961, before the Wall, I always went over to your side and bought Ernst Busch records.

That night I sat alone in my apartment and drank the Lufthansa wine my friend had left me and read in Thomas Mann's diaries from Pacific Palisades—just a few miles away. Sunday, December 4, 1949: "Much painful longing these days, and pondering about its nature and its goals, about erotic enthusiasm in conflict with insight into its illusory nature. The highest beauty, maintained as such against a whole world—I wouldn't want to touch it . . . To write openly about all that would destroy me."

I sat down at my machine and wrote:

Now writing is just working your way toward the border that the innermost secret draws around itself, and
to cross that line would mean self-destruction. But
writing is also an attempt to respect the borderline
only for the truly innermost secret, and bit by bit
to free the taboos around that core, difficult to admit as they are, from their prison of unspeakability.
Not self-destruction but self-redemption. Not being
afraid of unavoidable suffering.

Or overcoming that fear. A young Thomas Mann today, I thought, wouldn't need to shy away from professing his homosexual inclinations, but on the other hand they don't seem to be his truly "innermost secret." The curse that lies over the life of the German composer Adrian Leverkühn, whose similarity to himself Mann never denied, is not to be able to love, not to be allowed to love. That is how he touched upon the innermost secret, of men unable to love, I thought, who are prepared to do monstrous things to fill their emptiness.

Was it a good sign that I was no longer able to write? A sign of sincerity?

I feel like the rider across Lake Constance from the Schwab poem, I told my friend in Zurich over the phone.

You're overreacting, he said.

What an idiot I was back then.

All right, fine. But that's all there is to say about it now.

And how do you explain that I could have forgotten it?

Simple: It didn't matter to you very much.

That may be true, but it's not something I can say now.

You can say anything now.

You mean, since no one believes me anyway? By the way:

I HADN'T STARTED WRITING YET

This statement was true, I knew it. And its purpose was to proclaim that afterward, after I had started writing, I would no longer have been able to have these contacts of the wrong kind. There was something like a sense of relief there—the vise-grip opening, even if only a fraction of an inch.

I remember how I allowed myself to get up late, or to start reading in bed early. My joints would be blocked either way, no treatment could rebuild a destroyed joint, wasn't that a perfectly good reason to putter around with unnecessary chores and curse the little machine on the narrow end of the table as an unreasonable scold? I remember how I caught myself talking to myself, gruffly. How I screamed at a stuck drawer: Come on already, you bastard! How I stood in the middle of the kitchen then, the dish towel in my hand, and said out loud: It doesn't have to be like this. Okay, then what? I knew perfectly well what. There was no sense in denying that this text was growing much more slowly as time went on, that time was in a hurry, it was always there, extending out, maybe I could use it to shake off this feeling of hopelessness that had dug its claws into me.

I couldn't stand to be alone anymore, I had to be around people, so

I walked to the Third Street Promenade and ran across one of the giant garbage trucks that said on the side in large letters: *If you don't start recycling your trash, Santa Monica will look like the inside of this truck.* I couldn't help thinking of the enormous number of plastic bags in which even the smallest purchase here was wrapped, and that my habit of always saying *No bag, please* and putting my purchases into a cotton bag I brought with me was my only contribution to reducing garbage. I decided to eat another sandwich from Natural Food, where you could check off the components you wanted on a list and then, when the sandwich was ready, the young waiters would call you by your first name. There was a poster on the wall outside: *In loving memory of Tony.* I started reading a newspaper someone had left at the next table, the *Daily Breeze,* I had never seen it before, and I read the headline "OSCAR FOR TRUMBO EASES YEARS OF PAIN," and there was a big color photograph of a woman in her seventies, sitting in a red blouse and subtly checked pants on a gray couch and holding a gold statuette resting on her knee in her right hand—the Oscar—and this was not a woman beaming with happiness into the camera, since the Oscar was actually for her late husband, the once-famous screenwriter Dalton Trumbo, one of the famous "Hollywood Ten," who had refused to denounce supposed Communists among their colleagues and so had ended up blacklisted along with a number of other writers, directors, and actors. With the help of a black market for blacklisted writers, he earned a little money, but he wrote, wrote, wrote, his widow said, and she bore the burden of housekeeping and raising the children since she couldn't find a job either unless she was willing to divorce her husband and change her name; she had to get used to people standing up and leaving when she sat down next to them, and the neighbors not letting their children play with hers. Her husband spent ten months in jail for contempt of the House Un-American Activities Committee; she was furious and at the same time terrified about her family's future. She typed up the final versions of her husband's manuscripts that he then smuggled into a Hollywood network, under various pseudonyms; a friend agreed to front as the *screenwriter* for a movie that Trumbo had actually written, and won an Oscar for it.

Exactly like in Czechoslovakia, I thought, after the Warsaw Pact troops marched in: Translators forbidden to publish found colleagues who would put their names on other people's work. Similar behaviors and forms of solidarity seemed to develop under similar pressures. Then I was lost in memories.

Your Czech translator friends could obviously not translate your books under their own names anymore, they were in the inner circle of dissidents. They found a Slovakian German professor who was willing to let his name be used and who didn't ask for a krone in return. The reader for the publishing house knew, of course, but other than him, you thought, it had to be kept an absolute secret, and when I could read in Prague for the first time after the "Turn," I told the story and lots of people came up to me after the reading and laughed, saying: But we all knew!

It was absolutely no consolation to me to learn that dissident opinions were punished on both sides. That what had seemed to be the most deeply divided world was, in its deepest depths, nourished from the same roots, in other words was even more menacing than most of us were willing to believe.

My name was called and I got my *chicken salad sandwich* and *sparkling apple juice*. I put down the newspaper and wanted to start eating but I felt someone looking at me: ten feet away, on the far side of the sidewalk, a very young black woman sitting on the edge of a large stone urn of flowers and staring at me. From her clothing, she could be a *homeless person*, but I wasn't sure, since a few feet away from her was one of the little carts people used in supermarkets here, with a neat stack of several bundles inside. She's hungry, I thought, and my first impulse was to offer her my sandwich but I had already taken a bite. How could I eat under this stare? Which sometimes turned upward, actually, so that only the whites of her eyes were visible. She had woven her hair into many thin braids and tied them into a bun on the back of her head; a few of the strands were dyed a little lighter than the rest of her black hair. She was wearing a thick red parka in the heat and was fussing with the string of pearls on her left wrist; every now and then she let out a mocking laugh, or you might say a mocking laugh slammed into her. I ate my sandwich and decided to give her some money when I walked past her later, but how did I know she wanted money, how did I know she wouldn't reject my money with the same mocking laugh? How did I even know that her stare saw me at all? She was clearly mentally ill. I didn't give her anything when I walked past her, or rather slipped past her. I gave the money to two men sitting on two different benches, each man holding a sign: HOMELESS AND HUNGRY; one of them had a paper cup set up in front of him for coins. On the way back I avoided the location where the woman might still be sitting on the edge of the urn of flowers with her mocking laugh. I knew I wouldn't forget her, but what good did that do her?

In the Midnight Special bookstore I looked for and found the books by Art Spiegelman that someone had told me I had to read: *Maus*. The fate of a Jewish family—the author's—depicted in cartoons, with the Jews as mice and the Germans as cats. A daring, risky move. These are the saddest mice anyone has ever drawn, the woman who had recommended the books to me had said—and she herself was one of the people the books were about. *A Survivor's Tale* was the subtitle. I had met people here who defined themselves as *survivors* of the Holocaust, including this woman, Agnes, who a few days later would take me to a meeting of members of the *"second generation."* They survived, she said, which is not the same as living. That's how some of us still see ourselves, just like our parents.

On the title page of the first volume of *Maus* was an aggressive black swastika with a cat face stylized into a Hitler caricature in the middle, and a mouse couple, clearly fugitives, cowering in the swastika's shadow down below. I stayed up late reading, crying again and again.

I crossed Wilshire Boulevard; to the right on Third Street was the little dry cleaner's where I took the silk blouses I had bought cheap. The friendly Korean woman there knew me by that point, called me by my first name, I no longer had to give her my address, she would cry when I left, she said. She worked day after day, twelve hours a day, in this dark and stifling room between cleaned clothes hanging down from the ceiling. After California Avenue was the block with the MS. VICTORIA at the end; the street was lined with exotic trees that would one day burst into thousands of intense red flowers in the shape of bottle brushes, and I was happy when I learned that the trees were actually called *bottlebrush trees*.

What else? I pause. I fight against time. In the stacks of paper that I brought back to Europe over the ocean, most of the verbs are in the present tense, of course. I keep forgetting to transpose what I take from the various documents into the past tense. Everything I am describing now is in the past: The day when we finally carried out our plan to take a day trip south, to San Diego, where I bought a wooden snake with some of its joints missing from a kiosk selling Mexican art, the snake that now sits on my little cabinet of souvenirs and reminds me of the conversation I had with the seller. She didn't want to sell me the snake: *It's broken!* she said. And I said: *It doesn't matter, I am broken too.* She gave me the snake at a discount. *Broken*—a good way to put it. My colleagues who had driven south with me noticed that my mood had cleared up, when we were sitting later at a long table at Alfonso's and enjoying his Mexican cooking: grilled shrimp and steak, or tortillas and red beans.

Then I spent a long time in the museum, standing in front of Jana Sterbak's Medea dress: a woman's body woven out of wire, wrapped in an installation of electrical wires plugged into a socket and flashing on and off and on again. Everything burned on this woman's skin—life was burning on this woman's skin—it was the dress that Medea was said to have given to Glauce, her rival, that burned her skin. A text was projected onto a screen and I wrote it down:

> *I want you to feel the way I do: There's wire wrapped all around my head and my skin grates on my flesh from the inside. How can you be so comfortable only 5" to the left of me? I don't want to hear myself think, feel myself move. It's not that I want to be numb, I want to slip under your skin: I will listen for the sound you hear, feed on your thought, wear your clothes. Now I have your attitude and you're not comfortable anymore. Making them yours you re-lieved me of my opinions, habits, impulses. I should be grateful but instead . . . you're beginning to irritate me: I am not going to live with myself inside your body, and I would rather practice being new on someone else.*

The woman with her burning skin who wanted to slip into my skin, make me feel what she was feeling, free herself from her pain, but who couldn't feel at home in someone else's body after all. A longing I knew well. A disappointment I knew well.

The *"second generation"* group met in the San Fernando Valley. Agnes, a tall, bony woman around sixty, drove me the long way north on the freeways. She had to talk. She had to tell me about her husband, a Russian writer, who had emigrated from the Soviet Union as a Jew in the pre-Gorbachev era and whom she, a child from a German-Jewish family, had met here, to her unspeakable happiness. He had written a book critical of Stalin, which she gave me. She could not get over his death three years ago. She was furious as she told me what several of her female friends had told her: that at least she could be happy that her husband had died and not left her for another woman.

We found the building where the *second generation* group had reserved one of the smaller rooms, but the room was still much too big, there were maybe forty people spread out in the first few rows. I was glad to see Ruth there; I was feeling very OTHER. These were not the same people who had met at Ruth's: these were mostly older. The head of the group, running the event, was a good-looking man in his mid-forties, a doctor, very confident, experienced as a moderator. He introduced me with a comment that shocked me and that I disagreed with: that I was "*a lone voice in the wilderness.*" He said I was the first German they had invited. He said that most of the people there had never spoken to a German person. There were hardly any old people from the "*first generation*" there, except for his own, very old mother, a Viennese woman, who was supposed to help me with translation but who was so agitated that I had to try to get by as best I could on my own with my clumsy English.

The people there took me, totally understandably, as representative of today's Germany. They asked me about the situation in "Germany"— West vs. East meant nothing to them. They asked tough questions and I tried to be clear but sympathetic in my answers. The reports they were getting from Germany today confirmed the judgment they had of that country, with which they identified me. I tried once again to assure them that most Germans today were not anti-Semitic. I could see that many of them did not believe me. I felt that it was especially important to convince one younger, attractive woman but she kept not believing my protestations and I could not convince her.

At the end of the event, the young couple who had asked me if they could take their child to Germany came up to me and told me they had decided to do it. I was glad to hear it. We were still sitting in a large group in a café; I was eating ice cream and could hardly take part in the conversation because I was exhausted and had almost completely lost my ability to speak English. Ruth said a particularly warm goodbye and Agnes drove me back. It was already dark. She was a bit embarrassed during the drive and told me that the young, attractive woman had been telling people in the group that I had collaborated intensively with the secret police in the GDR and had denounced my colleagues. That was an unexpected blow. So now I had to tell Agnes all about that too.

The room I returned to felt alien to me. My little BROTHER computer sat there spitefully on the narrow end of the long table, with its gaping lid, yearning to suck in empty sheets of paper and spit them out again covered with my confessions, an automatic process for which it no longer needed me. Diskettes with mysterious labels were filled up behind my back, again and again I would be told the disk was full and I had no idea what it could be so full of. DISK CAPACITY EXHAUSTED— finally I told the machine that I was exhausted too and it coolly replied: BACKUP FILE SAVING PLEASE WAIT. My breaks and pauses were dictated by my word processor, now it was rattling again already and spitting out what I had not typed in, it was a master at undetectable forgeries, someday it would have to answer for its crimes, when I had had enough of this unpleasant game and stopped production. Because how could I continue to put up with the manipulations it was imposing, in the depths of its unfathomable program, on my unprogrammed, comparatively harmless and credulous entries? It even confronted me with questions of conscience: SAVE? DELETE? Do whatever you want, that's what I really wanted to say; my index finger played with the tempting key. One soft little push and the text would disappear. So now I had to see what I really wanted. Had my rage and disgust reached the point where it wanted to destroy the object of this rage and disgust? I pressed the other key: SAVE. Rattling in triumph, my little machine gulped down a new portion of characters. READING DISK INDEX. Then I pressed the button that erased the screen, but the text's disappearance was deceptive. Onward.

It's strange, I don't feel guilty, can you explain to me why that is? I had recently started talking to the gray American squirrel that darted across the low wooden shingle roof and up to my window every day; when I was sitting at my little word processor, I saw it from very close up. But no matter what I felt like asking it, my squirrel never answered. It was February by that point, the buds on the trees on Third Street between Wilshire Boulevard and California Avenue had opened all at once, a lush white cherry blossom in the middle of winter. But what does "winter" mean here?

I was standing on Santa Monica Pier with Therese—I saw her

often in those days and her desperate love for this city was contagious. The pier enchanted her. It was a flawless day: the sea beat against the shore in little, foaming white waves. Malibu Bay, Therese claimed, was the most beautiful stretch of beach in the world, and I didn't argue, but had she really never noticed that the water here had no smell? This magnificent Pacific Ocean beneath us, this unforgettable translucent green with a white fringe of foam, no show nature could put on could ever be more beautiful, but did it smell like the ocean? Algae, fish, water, like the modest, gray Baltic? Therese had never noticed the lack of smell and in fact she didn't want to. She wanted to take me to see her friends in Venice, I had to meet them but first she had to introduce me to Venice with its unique charm, of course it's a bit overrun with tourists, true, the canals that were supposed to imitate or suggest the original Venice had been filled in, true, the formerly romantic buildings were a bit dilapidated now, it's true, but wasn't that precisely its appeal? Wasn't this the epitome of the spirit of California? In Venice, where it's too crowded to walk even on weekdays and where all the weird and semiweird types in Los Angeles—now including us, apparently—come pouring in on Saturdays and Sundays, squeezing past shacks with millions of T-shirts for sale and crowding around the squares where the performers are. A thin black man pulled his volunteers—or should I say: victims?—out of the crowd with snakelike movements: a black woman, a white woman, a Mexican woman, a Japanese woman. The white woman didn't want to do it, she absolutely refused to go out onto the dance area, she was a little chubby and was wearing a dress that was too short for her given her unshapely knees, the other three women were more attractive, but the black man had no mercy and pulled the white woman into the center, she slipped out of his grasp and now he got annoyed, he held her tight in his grip while her baby-faced boyfriend left her in the lurch and accepted with an embarrassed grin her handbag which the black man condescendingly held out to him, then the man turned on a tape recorder, a tango, and took the Mexican woman first and danced with her: he was an artist, he danced with each of the women according to her own music—he danced them, if that's a word, he made the puppets dance—he never got too close to them, it was all out in the open, and nonetheless it was a rape taking place that no one could prove against him, no one could even mention it without seeming ridiculous, only the black woman was a match for him and she whirled around him, laughing loud, with obscene gestures, until he laughed too and accepted it and transformed the duet from a kind of animal-training into the dance of a true pair. The white woman looked pathetic in contrast, especially since the black man treated her with exaggerated politeness: he danced out all her weak points, so to speak, to the thunderous applause of the predominantly nonwhite audience.

He's taking revenge, Therese said, and we hurried to leave.

It was an unforgettable day, the day Therese took me to meet the gang. The day I met Jane, and Toby, and Margery. I called them "the young people" and I could tell that I felt curious about them. Not Susan yet—Susan was just a rumor, a topic of conversation. Susan was one of them, and then again not. Actually, she had wanted to be there too that day, but no one who knew her had really expected her to show up. She never kept appointments. She wants to make herself seem interesting by acting ditzy, Margery said. Jane thought she really was ditzy, there was no other explanation for her baffling behavior. If they were trying to make me curious about this Susan, they certainly succeeded.

We were sitting in the blazing sun outside the famous German café on Main Street in Venice, eating authentic German apple tarts and talking as though we had known each other a long time—unlike the way it usually was in America, I thought, where people do talk right away but it stays at the level of *nice-to-see-you* conversations. This was different. I liked that they acted with each other like I wasn't there, as though I wasn't disturbing them, thereby proving that I truly wasn't. Susan, I learned, was a rich woman—No, not well-off, Therese said: really rich. She owns an island. Not a big island, but still. At the same time she was rather stingy, like many rich people. For instance, she lived on one of Venice's narrow streets in a tiny little house that was about to collapse, like all the houses here. But expensive! Margery shouted. Don't kid yourselves about that! Anyway, Susan was also about to buy a villa in Beverly Hills, she's haggling with the broker so much that she's going to let it slip through her fingers. Everyone laughed. I learned that the modern buildings forming one side of the small square where we were sitting belonged to Susan too, and that she had let Jane open a photography gallery in one. Would I like to see it? Of course.

I learned that Jane was a photographer herself—an excellent one, Margery whispered to me. She, on the other hand, gave counseling to married couples who couldn't get along, she explained with a shrug. Gotta earn your money somehow. Sometimes she really had it up to here with these rich people who made each other's lives hell out of sheer boredom. And Toby? A thin, quiet, younger man; I got the impression that no one wanted to walk too close to him. I saw him fleetingly put a hand on Therese's shoulder and saw how she rubbed her cheek against it while we were crossing to Jane's studio. Jane had discovered a very gifted young Hungarian photographer—landscapes, faces as I had never seen them before. Jane loved the Hungarian's work and was as proud of the photographs as she would have been if they were her own. I felt more and more drawn to her, but did I still have enough time to start new friendships here? Then Therese was already arranging our next get-together.

Ruth called. She absolutely had to see me and discuss the evening with the "second generation," which she couldn't stop thinking about. She was disappointed with the people there, they only wanted to wrap themselves up in their worries and prejudices about Germany and refused to make an effort to perceive new realities. They categorically refused to set foot in Germany. They had terrible problems with their parents, some of them had moved far away just so that they wouldn't have to see them so much, but they had uncritically adopted their parents' views about Germans.

That's certainly understandable, I said.

Yes and no, Ruth said. The other side of the coin was that they longed to talk to Germans about the wounds that the Germans had inflicted on them. I had probably noticed that myself. Several of them had called her after the event and said: Finally, they had been able to talk to a credible German for once in their lives.

What more could anyone expect? I said.

My mother is very sick, Ruth said. She's going to die.

My heart started pounding: The mother would die without the daughter having reconciled with her. Ruth guessed my thoughts. No, she said, they had talked things out. They had found their way back to each other. There was no trace of resentment against her mother in her anymore.

Are you crying? Peter Gutman asked when he walked in. Tears of joy, I said. You've come at a good time.

Glad to hear it, he said. And I don't hear it often.

Self-pity? I was trying to provoke him.

Sarcasm, he said. Better than self-pity.

Is your mother still alive?

No. My older brother died of cancer suddenly a couple years ago, and his death broke her will to live. We had kept his cancer a secret from my mother. My other brother, who now has cancer himself and doesn't want to acknowledge it, now blames us for that. To this day I'm not sure what the right thing to do was. She died of grief, you'd have to say.

I said nothing.

So I've managed to leave you speechless. I'm using you as a life raft, you realize.

The blind leading the blind, I said.

I sometimes wonder what could have implanted such a powerful superego inside you.

So we're back to Freud? But that's something I can tell you exactly, Monsieur: Prussian Protestantism. Work hard, be humble, loyal, and always honest. Virtues preached by my dear mother.

And forgiving oneself did not belong among these virtues.

Absolutely not, Sir!

And it's probably very hard to learn that skill later.

Yes, Sir.

But where does this sense of sin while you're writing come from?

Ah, you've noticed. It's because of the cold gaze. The writer's cold gaze upon the object. And the moment you have enough distance from your pain to write about it, the writing is no longer wholly authentic.

So when you should write, you can't, and when you can write, you shouldn't.

Correct, Sir.

Hmm. You've really worked out quite an argument there. Is Madame a closet Calvinist perhaps?

Let's talk about you, Monsieur.

What do you want to hear? That I acquired all my neuroses on my own? In puberty I started working like mad in school. My teachers actually advised me to take it easy. I even changed my handwriting, suddenly it turned all precise and finicky. No, my family didn't put any pressure on me. Although naturally—but what does "although" mean here!—anyway: Although naturally—and what does "naturally" mean here either, dammit!—there was a "guilt" that was never talked about, as in many Jewish families. My mother's parents didn't make it out of Germany, they died in Theresienstadt. An aunt who had emigrated early to America tried to explain to me once, in a round-about way, why they hadn't been able to save their parents; I repressed it right away. I don't think that this sense of guilt played a role in my immediate family. Although, it occurs to me, my mother, when she was dying and very confused, suddenly asked: Where are my parents?

I said nothing. Peter Gutman said maybe he should leave. I said: You do realize I'm German?

So now you're thinking that as a Jew I must find it hard to talk to a German about these things?

I'm asking. I've met Jews here who never want to set foot in Germany. I can understand that. I think I would probably do exactly the same thing in their place.

That's what I thought too, when I was young. Then I went to study in Germany, got excited along with my German contemporaries about the German thinkers on the left, some of whom were also Jewish. No, it wasn't hard. There was only one time something snapped in me, when the registration office kept insisting on seeing my official police certifi-cate of a clean criminal record, which they don't have in England, and they threatened not to accept my registration if I didn't supply one. Then, to my own amazement, I suddenly started screaming in the middle of this German office that they had kicked my parents out of the country and murdered my grandparents and I was not going to stand there and let any German bureaucrats threaten me. And then I ran out of the office, and I was rather satisfied with myself, although at the same time I did feel a little bit ridiculous.

There, you see.

See what?

A real German wouldn't have felt ridiculous in the least, he would have felt goddamn great. Anyway, what happened?

Oh, my registration went through after a while without the police certificate. But how did we get onto these old stories?

The German-Jewish question.

Yes, right. By the way: I have exactly the same problems talking to certain Jews as I have talking to certain Germans. The same way I've never been with a Jewish woman. Until now, now's the first time, and that's the problem.

I asked what the problem was exactly.

He said he couldn't help inflicting another Jewish story on me. It was the story of Esther, whom he had met while at the university. She was from a rich Orthodox Jewish family, worshipped by her father and also by a husband she loved very much. He, Peter Gutman, had created a terrible conflict for her, and his conscience tormented him over it, but he couldn't suppress his feelings.

For Orthodox Jews it's a permanent stain for a wife to leave her family. She'll never do it. It was all completely hopeless, he said. Sometimes he truly could not figure out what made them keep putting themselves through this torture.

Maybe it would make sense to think seriously about why you do it first, I said cautiously. Did he understand now why I had tried to get him to tell me about his family?

You mean: Unto the third and fourth generations?

Yes. And now do you also understand why trying to come up with an aesthetic form for certain kinds of content so often seems obscene to me? By the way: How long have you been depressed like this?

A year.

That's too long.

It's hell, I would say if I believed in heaven and hell.

Have you ever had suicidal thoughts?

I live with them. Don't you know how consoling it is, to know that you don't have to go on living?

I do. I do know that.

And? The tape recording in your head, is it still running?

It's running. But we were talking about you. Is there anything that helps you?

It's better when I can talk about it.

I hope you don't wake up in a panic attack tomorrow.

I will give you a full report, Madame.

The tape keeps running. HOW AM I SUPPOSED TO EXPLAIN TO THEM THAT NO OTHER PATCH OF GROUND ANYWHERE ON EARTH INTERESTS ME AS MUCH AS THIS LITTLE COUNTRY, WHICH I THOUGHT WAS UP TO THE TASK OF THIS GREAT EXPERIMENT? IT FAILED, IT HAD TO FAIL, AND WITH KNOWLEDGE CAME SUFFERING. HOW AM I SUPPOSED TO EXPLAIN

TO THEM THAT THIS SUFFERING IS A SIGN AND MEASURE OF THE HOPE I
HAD STILL BEEN HARBORING IN A LITTLE HIDING PLACE SOMEWHERE,
HIDDEN EVEN FROM MYSELF?

Shenya called from Moscow, in the middle of the night, she had mixed
up the time difference between Moscow and Los Angeles. Oh well,
doesn't matter now. Was I asleep? No? She disapproved. She read the
German newspapers, she wanted to check in. —Oh, Shenya! —What?
—Don't try to fool me, you wanted to sound me out. She sometimes
found German idioms funny—this one was literally "you wanted to feel
my teeth"—but if it has to be your teeth, okay, she said. So what's going
on? —It's hard to say in a sentence. —Well, I could take two sentences.
She had time.

Shenya, older than I was, liked to call herself "the Red sailor." She
had come to Germany with the Red Army in 1945 and been a cultural
officer in Berlin for the next few years. She kept up lasting friendships
with the writers and theater people she'd helped back then. She devoted her life to the task of promoting German literature in the Soviet
editorial and publishing offices where she worked. We were agreed, she
said that night on the phone, that we wouldn't let things get us down.
I knew how often people had tried to take her down. She was Jewish,
that was an added hurdle. I said: But that was in a different time. Ach,
she said, that's just what people think. The people who want to take you
down are always the same people, just painted different colors. You listen
to what they have to say and then you ignore it. Or had I forgotten what
I told her once? How my deepest wish was to be clear, to make myself
clear through writing? So. Who was stopping me?

You have a good memory, Shenya.

Thank God, she said. I can still see us sitting in the hotel room
with the head of the publishing house, do you remember?

Did I ever remember! It was about a book of yours, which Shenya
absolutely wanted to publish and the publisher could publish only if you
took out certain scenes mentioning the Red Army. They were too critical, he said, and the Red Army was the only thing holding their enormous empire together.

You didn't want to be responsible for the collapse of their enormous
empire but you couldn't take out the scenes, just as you couldn't take

out the scenes about the Vietnam War that the American publisher wanted cut. All that would be left of your book was a fish skeleton, you said.

Yes, he was truly sorry to hear that, and you were too, and Shenya was too. Suddenly both of us burst out laughing on the phone. When we were done, Shenya said that the real reason she was calling was to tell me that now they're going to print the book that was at issue back then, without a single sentence cut. It was the Americans, in fact, who had simply left out the passages they didn't like, against my will and without my knowledge. And she knew that.

Well, I said, now your enormous empire has collapsed even without my help.

Don't be so sure, she said. The intellect can undermine even what seems most solid.

Shenya, I said, after a short pause, would you ever have thought I could have forgotten it?

She understood the question right away. Nothing could be simpler, she said. If I didn't forget most of the things in my life, I wouldn't survive.

But that I never felt even the slightest hint of a suspicion all these years! Who would believe me?

If you still care whether or not they'll believe you then you're not yet through it, my dear. If you let the past defeat the present then they really have won.

Was our whole life for nothing?

Now that's not worthy of you. Go read a page or two of your books.

I just have. In the first one, the one you didn't translate because the Soviet officer supposedly came across as too weak compared to the German doctor, she asks the Russian she used to love about the most important characteristics of the men and women of the future, and do you know what he says? Brotherhood. The ability to be honest and open. Not mistrusting others. Being able to speak the truth. Not seeing innocence, softness, and naiveté as weaknesses. Living in a world where coping with life no longer means having to walk over dead bodies without flinching.

And? Shenya said. That would all be wonderful.

Shenya! Even the youngest, most idiotic writer in the world wouldn't write that today! I wrote it five or six years after Stalin's death. I was thirty. They were already keeping those files on me. How many times in our life do we turn into a different person, Shenya?

She said she would have to think about that. I knew, did I not, that we were living in the most diabolical century in history? That overpowering forces were tugging at every one of us in all different directions. You had to try to stand firm. There was nothing more you could do. And with that, *do svidaniya*.

Shenya is dead now. At the time, I still remember, I went back to bed, there was no question of getting back to sleep. I thought about that time in Moscow. Stalin's picture, larger than life size, hung above the hotel entrance, it hung over the desks in every office, it was almost never out of your and G.'s sight as you drove through the city in a bus or a taxi. The term "cult of personality" hadn't been invented yet, not that it would have come to your mind; Russian friends thought that pictures and banners had replaced the newspapers and pamphlets during the Revolution, for the people who could barely read, but now it was possible to forgo them after all. Anyway, those were side issues that you could work out together, they said.

But the friend who had accompanied you the whole time as an interpreter—and probably not only as an interpreter—poured a glass of vodka over the desk lamp when you were saying goodbye in your hotel room, and uttered a curse too. He clearly thought you were being bugged; you laughed but took his suspicion seriously. He was the first one who communicated to you, without words, that he no longer believed in anything. You felt uneasy when he left—but where did that anxiety come from? What did it matter to you what this Russian man believed in?

There was a movie running in my mind, I hadn't forgotten a thing. Not how you and your family had experienced the march of the Red Army into Mecklenburg, not your fear when the occupying forces changed, when the Americans left and the Russians came—but it wasn't just Russians, there were Mongolians with them too, Kalmuks, the people said with a shudder in the Mecklenburg village, you lived through the scattered bands of Soviet soldiers raping and marauding through the countryside, the torn uniforms, the sorry state of their weapons, the peasant carts that had brought them to the center of Europe, while you, in the spring of that year, 1945, had trekked in your fugitive caravan past highly valuable German war materiel just lying there thrown away, left standing, made unusable, tipped over into the ditches in the roads, and it was deeply demoralizing that these badly armed, inadequately clothed and fed, mostly dark-skinned, sometimes slit-eyed soldiers had defeated our well-armed troops who were supplied with everything, but over the course of very few years your feelings shifted, unnoticeably at first, to the point where the victory of these Soviet troops seemed not only the desirable outcome but your very salvation, and the idea that you, the Germans, the National Socialists, might have won instead of them became a horrifying vision.

A series of faces appeared before my eyes—people from Moscow, from Leningrad, people you could talk to openly without holding anything back. Some of them, former officers in the Red Army, had entered what was then the German Reich as victors, with their troops. One of them even arrived in your hometown just after you had fled. He had become a writer, was part of a delegation to Berlin, and he sat next to you at dinner one evening. Suddenly he said how much it depressed him that they had needlessly destroyed the central part of the city you were from. This part of the city has since been rebuilt with ugly new buildings, I have seen them . . . Later, someone else asked you to look for a woman in a Mecklenburg village and, if she was still alive, to find out if she had a child, born in 1946. Unfortunately there was no trace of her to be found.

Professor Yerussalimski: the historian who met you in the park of Cecilienhof Castle, of all places, where the historic Potsdam Conference had taken place and where he had come for an event. Who clarified the historical roots of Stalinism to you and beseeched you never to give up your critical attitude toward the official proclamations coming from the Soviet side. He was very sick and had trouble breathing. You were able to visit him once more, in a Moscow hospital; he insisted on walking with you in the garden, so you could talk. He died shortly thereafter. Or the colleagues who also, suspiciously often, walked with you on the streets or in the parks and told you the true stories of their country, and their own stories. So that you thought, for a while, that there were vast numbers of intelligent and critical men and women there, to reform their enormous empire from within, that that's what they wanted to do themselves, until, with "glasnost," the work they had longed to do for so many years was made possible and in fact forced upon them: To reveal the true face of their country and make their fellow citizens look at it straight on. It was a Herculean task. "Utopian," a word people say today with the corners of their mouths pulled down in contempt. But you saw their tired, determined faces in the editorial offices where, suddenly, a new spirit was in the air.

Hardly one of them is left, one name after another in my Moscow address book has dropped out. I don't dare cross them out.

OLD AGE IS THE TIME OF LOSSES

But also of seeing clearly?

When Ruth came by I could see it in her face: Her mother had died. Ruth brought me a volume of poems by Nelly Sachs that had belonged to her mother. I fought with all my might not to accept this gift: nothing could be less deserved, I said to Ruth, especially now. It would crush me to have it. Ruth didn't let up. She could see I needed it, she said, from the very fact that I was refusing it so vehemently. Maybe I wouldn't see that myself until much later, but I should just stick the book in a corner and stack some other books on top of it. Sooner or later I would crave it, and that was how it should be. I opened the book:

World, they have taken the small children like butterflies
and thrown them, beating their wings, into the fire—

I had to accept the book, and would have to read these lines again and again.

Peter Gutman's unexpected knock on the door that day was one of those coincidences that you are staggered by only after the fact, once its consequences have become apparent. He picked up on our mood and wanted to leave right away but we kept him there. I introduced them and saw that they went up to each other like old friends. While I got bread, cheese, and tomatoes from the kitchen and poured some red wine, they were already deep in conversation, talking about their lives. It was unbelievable, shy as they both were.

They barely noticed that they had started eating and I kept quiet and listened. Ruth even trusted Peter Gutman enough to tell him the story of her mother, which she normally kept locked up tight, and he spoke in hints about what he called his "life problem." And from there it wasn't far to the realization that their problems had been forced upon them by the dark history of the century. Still, Peter Gutman said, it was highly likely that the catastrophes of our time would be overtaken by the horrors of the century to come, at whose threshold we were standing.

Ruth argued strongly against him. What good did it do anyone to be purely pessimistic about the future? she said. Didn't he know that it was possible to think and wish catastrophes upon oneself?

Peter Gutman did not believe that, actually, and said so more with the expression of his face than with words. Unfortunately, he said, it's impossible to wish away hard facts no matter how much psychological energy you apply.

I realized only then that we had been speaking in German the whole time—Ruth with a slight Rhineland accent that she had never lost; she sometimes had to hunt around for the right word, which I found moving. She had worked herself up, she really wanted to convince him. She knew only too well, she cried, where it leads when a man gets himself caught in the web of his hopeless thoughts and even the most intelligent and deeply loved woman can't free him.

Then how could she explain, Peter Gutman asked, that the deepest thinkers of our time had the pessimistic worldview she was so opposed to?

Like who?

Well, Sigmund Freud, for example.

Yes, Freud! She admitted that. Of course, he was one of her intellectual leading lights. But, she said, no matter how painful the insights were that his life had forced upon him, he had never given up, he had kept working, kept pursuing his efforts to heal damaged souls. He showed, in other words, that he hadn't lost hope. A man like that had overcome his despair at humanity through his own heroic life. Whereas others . . .

Ruth suddenly broke off, as though she had said too much.

Peter Gutman pushed her to keep talking. Later, he admitted to me that from that moment on he had felt an inexplicable excitement. Yes, well, Ruth said, she knew "deep thinkers," as Peter Gutman called them, who could no longer free themselves from the whirlpool of that word "futility." Not even the most passionate efforts of the women they loved could help them. She knew that, she said, from her friend Lily.

Unbelievable, I thought. I still remember, I thought: Unbelievable.

Her friend? You haven't mentioned this friend yet, Peter Gutman said.

No? My mistake, Ruth said. She should have mentioned her friend Lily right away. A psychoanalyst. From Berlin. Where her good little colleagues had looked on without a word as Jewish psychoanalysts were expelled from their organization under pressure from the Nazis. They had had to emigrate and it was they who made psychoanalysis flourish in America. Her friend, even though she was not Jewish herself, had realized that there would be no possibility for analysis under Nazi Germany. She also refused to be separated from the man she loved, who, as a Jew, had emigrated to the United States in time, because of her.

What Ruth was saying about Lily, her life, her character—I felt like I recognized it all. From L.'s letters lying in the red folder on my shelf.

And her lover, the philosopher? I heard Peter Gutman say. What was his name?

I knew it already, he later told me. It wasn't possible, but I already knew it.

Ruth said the name Peter Gutman was waiting for.

There was silence for a few seconds, then Peter Gutman said softly: Yes. It's him.

It was the man whose life and work he had been living and breathing for years.

He was in greater and greater despair as time went on, Ruth said. He saw human beings as badly designed, willing to risk their lives for immediate gratification. He suspected that the self-destructive urge was programmed into our genes.

Coincidences like this never happen in real life, I thought. But on that evening I was filled with a feeling of absolute rightness like nothing I had felt for a long time. Everything seemed to fit together in a meaningful way. I thought I could sense the same mood in Peter Gutman—he was lively, curious.

Only right at the end, around midnight, when Ruth was about to say goodbye, did Peter Gutman ask her, quietly: How did he die? Ruth said: He killed himself. Peter Gutman did not seem surprised.

We parted quickly, suddenly very tired. We made plans to go see Ruth. Maybe she would find letters from my friend Emma in Lily's papers, which had been entrusted to her. My stay in this city acquired a new urgency. I sat down for a few minutes more at my little machine and I wrote:

The workings of chance are strange. I find it almost embarrassing that chance can change a mood so drastically, so that it suddenly seems possible that things will get better. Only now do I realize I had stopped believing they ever could.

I went to sleep; the tape recording in my head had paused. I was too tired to read. I dreamed about an enormous dark body of water that I had to cross. A red full moon hung in the sky. A voice cried out: You haven't had enough yet? No! I answered. Shine, good old moon, shine! I walked and walked through the knee-high water. I couldn't see the shore and it seemed impossible that I would ever reach it. Still, I didn't feel afraid or hopeless. When I woke up, a voice I didn't recognize said: CITY OF ANGELS. I took it as a challenge.

And since I could in fact write for hours and hours a day but not every single hour of the day, and I had to pass the remaining time somehow, and since there wasn't any way I could get the time to simply disappear—it's strange, time is always there, indestructible, immune to all our efforts to sway it—since, in other words, I needed what is called distraction (which doesn't get nearly the credit it deserves), I was glad to drive to Chinatown again and go to Mon Kee. The ten of us sat at the big round table in the simple room and right away, after we drank our first cups of tea and ate the spring rolls, the table filled up with ten oval platters: prawns in every shape and disguise, Francesco had to have sweet-and-sour fish, Pintus was in the mood for beef, I stuck with the crispy roasted duck, the bowls of rice were passed around, a bottle of beer per person was not enough, of course, we turned the large lazy Susan in the middle of the table and helped ourselves to all the dishes, Ria had on new earrings from the flea market in Pasadena, Ines complained about Francesco's inability to decide where to spend the next couple years, in Italy or here, where the famous Frank Gehry was living and building the buildings Francesco wanted to write about, Pat had had a total falling out with her landlady and had to move yet again, Hanno still didn't know what to focus on in his work, Pintus had finally finished reading the proofs for his book on the spirit of the early Middle Ages, Lutz had gotten word that his application for a teaching position in Frankfurt had been accepted, we were happy for him and toasted him and Maya. And Peter Gutman, who had come along for the first time, told us for the first time everything about his philosopher and the man's fate.

Four or five months later we would be scattered across Europe and might never see each other again, but the sympathy that bound us together was no illusion, I knew that our feelings for each other were genuine, we liked knowing so much about each other, we liked how we wanted to tell each other things, we were happy about the network of relationships that had formed. I realized that it was quiet around the table and that I had said out loud what I had only meant to think. Actually we're a good team. Then the fortune cookies were brought out, with advice from the oracle. We opened them and I read: *You are open and honest in your philosophy of love.*

And the next day, or one of the days after that, I was sitting with Bob Rice at Gladstone's. He had invited me to dinner. *How are you,* he said when we saw each other, and I said: *It is very hard,* and he answered: *I know,* and then he said something that made me laugh: *I am proud of you.* Gladstone's is a gigantic restaurant on a cliff, with an almost vertical drop down into the ocean, where hundreds of Americans can eat with their families at the same time, and big wooden tables, gigantic portions, most of the diners fat, the children already fat too. We ordered my obligatory margarita—not as good here as elsewhere—and coconut shrimp. The hamburgers are good here, Bob said.

Bob hadn't realized it would be so loud, that we would have to scream because everyone else was screaming. He had brought me there to tell me about how it had been my books, of all things, that had helped him come out. He had to cup his hand to his mouth like a megaphone to shout the quote from my own book at me and tell me how terrible it is when you have to keep an important part of yourself hidden all the time, when you have to always conceal yourself, and what a relief it is when you finally stop. You think, he shouted, now with the menu rolled up in front of his mouth like a megaphone, you think that once you've said that you can say anything, and you're free.

The overweight mothers and fathers of the families all around us had no problem adding to the general noise with their own; the portions they were polishing off were unbelievable—gigantic steaks, mountains of sausage, hamburgers bigger than the palms of their hands—and everything the children asked for was put before them. But Bob hardly seemed to notice. He told me about his boyfriend, about their life together, named various great men who were gay, and shouted at me (I didn't catch every word) how happy he was to have found a way to a kind and loving relationship with his wife, after a long, difficult time, and that his children loved him and came to stay with him sometimes.

We were sitting very near sea level, the sun had just set into a haze, and Bob said: Do you see those bright stripes on the horizon? That's what I love the most. There was a gray light that you rarely saw here. The noise got louder and louder.

Bob, who had heard me read from my text "Trial by Nail," had brought along a poem he wanted to recite for me, but it was impossible in the pandemonium. We went out onto the wooden patio, where it was damp, cold, and dark, and we were alone. We sat right next to the railing that divided us from the ocean and couldn't hear anything except the roar of the surf; it sprayed us, the wind had gotten strong, and Bob read, once again shouting, the poem about the nails of the Cross that the English poet Edith Sitwell had written in 1940:

> Still falls the rain—
> Dark as the world of man, black as our loss—
> Blind as the nineteen hundred and forty nails
> Upon the cross.

Yes, I said, the nails of the Cross come up in my text too.

That evening really stuck with me. What will stay with me from today? That it's spring again, in all its glory? That the question of whether this is my last spring, or one of my last springs, underlies everything I see? That the news reports of ten thousand Iraqis and three thousand American soldiers killed in the past four years in Iraq do not seem to have shocked anyone?

It's a nightmarish thing to imagine: being able to see into the future.

But at the time this gift was something I actively sought out. I had been foolhardy enough to show my new friends—the "gang," as we called ourselves by then: Therese, Jane, Margery, and Toby—my tarot cards. We met up outdoors, at a private airport where Manfred (Jane's boyfriend, a German painter) had set up a studio in an unused hangar. It was one of those afternoons that turn into an evening under a magnificent sky. *Country songs* were coming out of Manfred's stereo; a grill had been fired up outside and the air smelled of bratwurst. We had brought wine and beer in coolers and private jets and helicopters were taking off from the nearby airfield: the rich, they told me, flying home at the end of the day from their offices in L.A., where they made their money, to their palace-like villas in San Diego or Malibu.

Friends of friends came and went, were given food and drink, drawn into the conversations, said hello to me without showing any intrusive curiosity, praised Manfred's iron sculptures, and some of them sang along with a song or two.

You see, Manfred said, for me this is America. Once you've lived here a while there comes a dangerous point where you miss the boat and can't go back to Europe again. That had happened to him. He had spent a few weeks in Germany the previous year, he said, as a kind of test—and it didn't work anymore, he had to accept it. It's true that the friendships here are not very deep, that you find yourself moving in pretty shallow waters sometimes, but the lightness here is just so refreshing most of the time, compared to the German need to complicate everything.

I wondered when was the first time I had heard anything firsthand about America. Have you ever heard of Leonhard Frank? I asked Manfred. He hadn't.

You can see him sitting there—white-haired, thin, dressed correctly but casually too. He has come from Munich because of a book that had been published by an East German publishing house, and he is sitting in a group of fellow writers, mostly East German, who like him had had a shorter or longer stay at a writer's colony on a lake in Brandenburg; there were two German states at that point but no Wall yet, no travel restrictions. There was a currency shortage in the GDR, though, and Frank, the West German, had to stay in the GDR long enough to spend the money he received for his books sold there. The West Germans weren't exactly beating down the bookstore doors for Leonhard Frank's books, any more than for those by Heinrich Mann, or Lion Feuchtwanger, or Anna Seghers. You all knew that he had lived in the United States as an émigré, and you asked him about it; he was happy to talk about it, but he stuck to anecdotes and little stories.

When his wife, Charlotte, walked into the room his face lit up and he didn't take his eyes off her. She was an actress and had been in an American television series, he told you, as a beloved star who got sick with tuberculosis and died at the end. She had had a doctor demonstrate to her how people with lung disease cough, so she could play it more convincingly. After the death of their favorite character, the public wanted to say their farewells to her publicly, so the producer made Charlotte lie in a coffin as a dead body on the stage of a theater so that the public could file past her. Charlotte had lain there, stiff and rigid, and thought the whole time, like a mantra: A hundred dollars, a hundred dollars. Leonhard Frank admired her for that the same way he worshipped her for everything she did and every word she said.

Apparently he had spent his first few months in Los Angeles, when not serving time sitting idly in the film studio, staring out over the Pacific Ocean from a bench in Ocean Park. When someone asked him what he saw there, he said: Europe's over there. No, he was told, that's not Europe over there, that's Japan. He had shaken his head and left. And, I told Manfred, I couldn't help thinking of that myself, many times, when I was sitting in Ocean Park, maybe on the same bench he used to sit on.

And just now, more than fifteen years later, I find in Leonhard Frank's autobiography, *Heart on the Left*, this description of the condition exile imposes on the émigré: "Now there was no going back. This crippling consciousness accompanied him for seventeen long years, day after day . . . : there was no going back to Germany, to his studio, his life, his landscape, the place he felt at one with, as though he were a part of it . . . His life was not his life anymore. It had snapped in two in the middle."

Manfred said yes, he understood very well how a person could yearn for the old country. But then Jane was here too, he couldn't transplant her to Europe. I saw the look Jane gave him, I saw how attached to him she was; it surprised me and made me happy. We ate, drank, circulated between the different groups; Jane came up to me and told me she never thought she would ever find someone again who would matter to her as much as Manfred. Why not? I asked. I'll tell you later, she said.

She told me later that same night. When it got dark we left but didn't want to part company yet; we arranged to meet at Toby's in Venice later, then we split up into the different cars and I ended up with Jane in hers. We drove on the freeway in silence for a while; I had the feeling, not for the first time, that freeway driving in the dark awakened the desire to talk. Jane asked me if I thought Manfred was wrong for her, since they were so different. I said that that's what I thought at first, but after I saw them together I didn't think it anymore. She herself hadn't known, she said, that this was exactly what she needed. The only relationships she had known up to that point were difficult ones, especially between people who were close to each other. I have to tell you, she said, that both of my parents were German Jews who had survived different concentration camps and met after the war in one of the camps for *displaced persons*. Her father had had a family before, a wife and daughter, who'd been killed. I think he could never really love me, Jane said, he always saw his dead first daughter behind me. Can you imagine what that means to a child? Photography had helped her find herself, she said. Strangely, it was because when she was behind the camera she had to concentrate on other people and totally disregard herself.

I remember how glad I was to have met Jane.

Toby's rooms in his small Venice house had been almost entirely cleared out; I saw how shocked Therese was. No one had told her that Toby was about to burn his bridges again and go to Mexico. The models for buildings he had designed were standing in the corner: delicately crafted, original constructions of thin pieces of wood. No one wanted to execute the projects, as usual, Toby said with a certain bitterness. He had to try somewhere completely different again, he said. He handed around wine and *crackers* and then I had to bring out the tarot cards. Everyone had to whisper in my ear the question he or she wanted to ask the cards. I let everyone assure me that they didn't actually believe in tarot cards, that it was only a game we were playing. Then I shuffled the cards and it started.

Toby surprised me by wanting to know whether his relationship with his father would improve. I laid out the cards in the prescribed pattern and found that two male figures, very far apart, were on the path toward each other. Toby seemed happy about what the oracle had said—he had never thought that they would stay enemies forever, he said, and I didn't have the heart to repeat: It's a game, Toby, it's just a game!

Therese wanted to know which continent she would find happiness on, and the cards said that she should keep moving and seek her happiness precisely in her restlessness. Or if not her happiness, at least her destiny. Therese grew pensive and leaned against Toby.

I wanted to keep Jane from handing herself over to the cards too— you're not superstitious! I wanted to say, but I didn't know the word "superstitious" so I said *Don't believe in the cards, please, Jane!* She said: *Of course not, don't worry.* But she insisted I lay out the cards for her question too. She wanted to know whether anyone could love her. I cursed my thoughtless, foolhardy willingness to start this game and shuffled the cards for a long time, desperately determined to draw out the right answer for Jane. I was lucky: as the last card, shining out over all the rest, I turned up THE WORLD, which promised, beyond any doubt, a universe of love to everyone it appeared to, love both given and received. I certainly had a lot to say about that, in Jane's case. Satisfied? I asked her. *Thank you*, she said, and I couldn't tell if she had seen through me. Did she want to believe the cards? I realized that the cards inevitably gave me power over other people and I made the firm decision never to bring out my tarot deck for anyone again.

Until, a few days later, Peter Gutman knocked on my door and asked me, without beating around the bush, to use the cards to help him figure out how you should act when you love someone but any hope of ever being able to live with that person is a complete illusion. I no longer remember the tricks I used to force the cards to give the result I had been working toward from the beginning: Sublimate, I said. You and she have to sublimate your feelings.

Oh, yes ma'am, he said.

Incidentally, they had long since broken their vow not to talk on the phone anymore, of course. They called each other much more than they should, but it didn't make them any happier. There was nothing to say to that.

He asked about my own "symptoms." Were they behind me? Not entirely, I said. He expressed his disapproval. Couldn't I finally accept being an average person, with mistakes and misdeeds like everyone else? Good God, cut it out already! he said. You didn't hurt anyone!

Yes I did, I said defiantly. Myself.

What is this really all about? It's about clarifying to myself that this will pass. Experience says it will, even if I can't believe it myself yet. A time will come when it will be hard for me to remember this.

I wanted to do without sleeping pills for once. A glass of warm milk would be nice. I stood up and made myself a glass of warm milk with honey. It was still dark but the birds were already starting their morning concert. Who said I always had to think along with the thoughts running through my head? Where was that written? Hollowed out, that was the right word: I was hollowed out. Just drink this milk in small sips now, I told myself. Now just lie down. Now I'm tired. Now the homeless man who looks for bottles in the garbage bins under my window every morning has arrived. I heard the clinking of the bottles, then nothing more.

How are you today? A whole elevator full of oblivious, innocent people. *Oh, thank you, I'm fine. That's wonderful.* Someone had told me that the women who worked in this building were expected to wear a different outfit every day. I noticed myself starting to follow this rule. What was wrong with me? I talked with Kätchen in the office. She said she was tempted a lot of the time to just throw all these faxes arriving for me from Europe into the shredder. I could laugh about that. I had told her she could give up the search for L., and told her Lily's story. I stuffed the new stack of papers sitting in my cubbyhole into my Indian bag without looking at them.

I went to Third Street and ate a sandwich. I bought myself another inexpensive silk blouse. When I got home I heard my phone from the stairs. It kept ringing and ringing and then I heard the outraged voice from Berlin. Where were you, dammit! I couldn't reach you, I kept trying and trying! —I was just eating lunch! —Ah, okay. I thought I shouldn't have faxed you that article. —What article? —A rather unpleasant article by someone you wouldn't have expected it from . . . He named the writer's name. —Haven't read it yet. —Then don't, okay? Listen, I mean it. Don't read it. I shouldn't have sent it. —Ach, you know? What's too much is too much. —Exactly. But then I couldn't reach you and I just broke out in a cold sweat, you know? —Listen, once and for all: I'm fine. Nothing's happening to me. There's no danger. —Okay, good. I was being ridiculous, I only thought, because of that damn article . . . —No. And especially not because of that damn article. Go to sleep. Isn't it midnight there? —Yes, you're right, it's midnight here. —Here it's only four in the afternoon. It's hard to get used to that, don't you think? —Yes, I think so too, it's hard to get used to that. —Good night.

I read the article a few days later, in small gulps. It was the overdose, and I waited to see my reaction. There was almost none. Was I starting to build up defenses and immunities at last?

I know it sounds unbelievable but there were pink birds there, a smoky pink—and one such bird appeared early that morning on the edge of the roof outside my window.

For days, this whole teetering disk of a planet wavered and wobbled on the point of a needle.

The MS. VICTORIA had an underground life. When I took the elevator down to the basement to use the washing machine, I sometimes met our cleaning staff, almost all Latinos, except for Angelina from Uganda. Down there they were among themselves and free to take out their sandwiches and drink their coffee from paper cups, to make fun of each other and maybe of us too, laughing loud, in fact shrieking with laughter, they barely noticed me, they were with each other and showing around photos of their children, slapping their thighs, with joys and feelings that I would never share, and as long as they had these miserable jobs they were freer than I would ever be, I thought, they didn't worry about what else was going on in this city, they had been there only three or four years, maybe illegally, they spoke only the most necessary English and were almost impossible to understand, they never voted—whoever wanted to be in charge should be in charge—their lives were harder than I could ever even imagine but now, in these fifteen minutes in the middle of their workday, they were sitting there and were with each other and in a good mood and didn't care about the dirty, sticky basement hall and the white woman carrying her laundry bag past them, who, two hours later, when they came up to her apartment to scrub the sinks and vacuum the floors, would get the feeling from them that her well-being mattered deeply to them.

I feel a pull from the end and have to brace myself against it, have to let things I have kept my silence about until now, or at least haven't mentioned yet, rise up in me and have to put them down on paper. "A pull from the end": only now do I notice the double meaning of this metaphor, but I let it stand, even though—or because—it applies in both senses. The pull from the end of life, not just from the end of this book.

Always the same thing on every station, I said to Peter Gutman while we were driving through Los Angeles again and listening to the radio. It's the same with me, always the same old song and I can't turn it off.

You realize, of course, that you would be off the hook in an instant if you expressed regret, he said. Let your friends help you. And if they don't help, why not use your enemies? Your contempt for the journalists who say to your face that they couldn't carry out their duty to be thorough when they heard that the competition was about to publish the story, they had to get in there first? Hate can make a person strong too, believe me.

You're telling me I should hate? Monsieur?

Peter Gutman refused to take the bait. He wanted to know why I still refused to get mad, for God's sake.

It never occurred to me, I said. Then: I wonder if it was all for nothing.

You have to wonder? Of course it all was for nothing, and it was all inevitable too.

You sure know how to console a person, I said, and he said yes, he certainly did, if that's the word I want to use. Wasn't it any consolation to know that we weren't the first? And wouldn't be the last?

WE ARE STRANGELY DESIGNED CREATURES, AREN'T WE?

*You're
right, Madame, we are.*

And then I told him to turn around and look at the sun setting into the ocean at the end of Wilshire Boulevard: as always, it took the last handbreadth above the horizon incredibly fast, as though it had pulled itself together with a last burst of energy for its final sprint. And so it was again, and now it would get dark fast, and I thought that in the long run I did not want to live in a country without twilight. I am very fond of the northern twilights, I told Peter Gutman, and then we were quiet the rest of the way and before long we got to Ruth's house.

She had invited us over to talk about Lily and show us a few things.

Now, so many years later, my astonishment has only grown: Did the three of us really act as though our gathering there, for that reason, were the most natural thing in the world? I can hardly believe it. Did Peter Gutman and I never once express our nervous astonishment at the unbelievable number of extremely unlikely coincidences that had had to take place so that the riddles we each carried around with us could find their answers here? Or had we so accustomed ourselves to the state of acute psychological crisis we clearly were all living in that no miracle, no matter how unimaginable, could throw us off track? Was that how it was? If it hadn't happened like that I would have had to invent it.

Ruth bringing out a wooden box with Lily's effects. Her offering us tea and *cookies*, because hospitality demanded it. That we drank the tea and ate the *cookies* even though secretly we only had eyes for the wooden box on the side table. It was a simple chest, with a bolt to close it; Ruth had probably originally gotten something or other in it in the mail once. It contained, as we saw when she finally opened it, mostly papers.

Lily had put everything in order before she died: since she had no children and no relatives, she had to worry about her estate herself, she had told Ruth. Lily was a woman without the slightest self-pity, Ruth said, with a coarse sense of humor sometimes—totally unlike her philosopher, who had been her lover for more than forty years, Ruth said she had just recently calculated it for the first time. She would not go so far as to say that no other man ever darkened Lily's doorstep, Lily was a passionate woman, but she had told Ruth many, many times that out of the billions of people on this planet of ours she had found the one man she was meant to be with. And she had never stopped marveling at her luck.

And the philosopher? Oh, him! No, other than his wife, Dora, a paragon of fortitude, and Lily, he had not had any other women, and didn't need another one either. And believe it or not, Ruth said, there had never been the slightest hint of jealousy between the two women.

So Lily entirely subordinated herself to her love for this man? I asked, unconsciously a bit aggressively. Oh, no! Ruth cried. She said she couldn't imagine another woman less suited to a subordinate role than Lily. Sparks flew between her and the philosopher sometimes, she said. She had often thought that for someone like Lily one of the worst things about exile must have been that she had to perform a kind of mimicry just to survive. Or hadn't we noticed how conformist American society was, through and through? Lily had opened Ruth's eyes to that too. Up until then, Ruth had truly believed in the free critical spirit that the newspapers advertised as American. Lily had a little test she used: How did the person she was talking to react when she mentioned, apparently in passing, the word "Communist"?

You are the first American I've met who says that word like an ordinary, everyday word, I said.—I used the informal pronoun with her, and we stayed with it from then on.

They both taught me that, Lily and her philosopher, Ruth said. They showed me how every—or almost every—American talks around the word, total cowards, and how they—how we—cut ourselves off from an enormous and momentous field of European thought and action, and imposed a disastrous taboo on ourselves, when we define all Communists as criminals. I later asked about certain writings, certain authors, certain names. It even helps me with the patients I treat, as a matter of fact, which I hadn't expected.

How? Peter Gutman asked. Surely you don't try to instill Communist ideas in your patients!

Good heavens, no, Ruth said. She wouldn't have any patients left if she did that. But it's strange how clear-sighted you can be about the inhibitions in someone else's thoughts and feelings after you have seen through one of your own. Well: seen through it to some extent.

I was the only one of us three, I reflected, who had ever known real live Communists. At first I could count them on my fingers. The first ones were bogeymen, rumors, I remembered. You saw before your eyes the face of your maid, Anneliese, who told you, the child, how her family had cried when the Communists in your hometown had had to publicly burn their flags on Moltke Square after the Nazis' victory. Really, were you Communists? you asked in disbelief. Yes, they were Communists, she said. The next one was a man from the neighborhood, who drove a beer truck if you remembered correctly, and you could only pick up rumors about him that the grown-ups were whispering among themselves—he had come back from a concentration camp but had had to sign something saying he would never talk about it, and he really was mute as a fish now. From that point on, it was firmly imprinted in your mind that to be a Communist was just as bad as to be a Jew. Luckily, neither of these conditions applied to you or your family.

Then, your first real live Communist—I have told his story many times—was the man from the camps, doubtless a prisoner the SS were bringing north on the death march from Sachsenhausen, who, together with the other survivors hastily left behind by the team of guards, mingled with the refugees on the field that the first occupying force, the Americans, had set aside for your caravan to spend the night on. The man your mother offered a bowl of soup to. Then she asked why he had been in the concentration camp and he said: I am a Communist. Ah, your mother said. But they don't send people to concentration camps for that! The man's expression didn't change. He said: Where have you all been living?

Your second real live Communist was Sell, the shoemaker in the Mecklenburg village where you were stranded with your family in the spring of 1945, after your flight. The Russian occupying force demanded that the villagers put horses and carts at their disposal for all their transportation needs, and your job, as the mayor's assistant, was to divvy up the corvée according to the size of each villager's property. The shoemaker, who owned only one horse, burst into your office and started yelling at you: The burden you had imposed on him and other landless homeowners was absolutely too large! You were outraged and sure that you were in the right, so you denied his accusations, but he continued to storm and rage, banged his fist on the table, and slammed the door shut behind him. The mayor, who hid in his bedroom whenever there was any conflict, appeared and informed you that Sell was a Communist, the only one in the village by the way, and that from now on whatever they say goes.

I had to break off my stream of memories so as not to miss what Ruth was bringing up out of the box of Lily's belongings. First, a photograph: Lily, in the last decade of her life, leaning against one of the palm trees in Ocean Park with the Pacific in the background. However I may have imagined her before, it was immediately obvious that this is how she had to have looked: short, delicate, but powerful, with a face sensitive but at the same time bold. Her hair was lightly bunched together, not tied up, as though the wind were blowing in her face, and even though she was standing still she gave the impression of someone walking. Walking straight ahead.

Yes, Peter Gutman said. Then he inspected the second photo for a long time, apparently taken the same day in the same place, but this time Lily was sitting on a bench in Ocean Park next to a man. They weren't looking at each other or touching each other but there was no doubt that they were a couple. He was petite for a man; his hands lying on his knees could almost have been a woman's hands; his head was too big for his body. His eyes were hidden behind the thick lenses of his glasses. None of us said it, but I think we all thought it: The man in this photograph had used up almost all of the material substance of his life.

Ruth said she had taken these pictures. She remembered the afternoon exactly, because of her ambivalent feelings. The three of them had been having a particularly good time together that day, but at the same time she was overwhelmed with a grief that she couldn't put into words. It was grief over the fact that it would all be over so soon.

While Ruth was talking, she was bringing up more treasure out of the chest: Lily's passport, a bundle of documents from her time in Berlin, her doctor's diploma, and, I had hardly dared hope for it, a picture of her and my friend Emma as very young women, surrounded by other women, deep in a serious conversation, apparently during a congress. The photograph was yellowed and worn around the edges—Lily had kept it for decades, through exile in several countries, had brought it across the ocean and kept it safe.

How young they were. How beautiful. How energized. How full of hope.

What could they have been talking about so intently? Their differing opinions? Ruth said that Lily was an ardent anarchist. She had rejected—loathed—any narrowing and constraining of ideas into a dogma. A political party, she had often lectured me, Ruth said, turns into an end in itself too quickly; it can't produce real change.

The philosopher, for his part, held the view that people had to be forced to do things for their own good. In our century, he had said, humanity has come to a crossroads: for the final time, they could choose between two seemingly opposite directions—and then it turned out that both paths led them astray, to tragedy. And taking part in this process, the philosopher had said: That was our life. So? Lily had countered. Wasn't it exciting? Wasn't it interesting?

Ruth pulled an ordinary gray file folder out of the box and held it up. This is the core of Lily's legacy, she said: a debate, an exchange of opinions and arguments, between Lily and the philosopher, conducted over a long span of time, partly to try to convince the other person and partly to clarify their thoughts for themselves.

That's unbelievable, Peter Gutman said.

Ruth handed him the folder. He should use it in his work. Peter Gutman immediately started paging through it. Unbelievable, he said, again and again. I had never seen him so excited. Something like this happens to a scholar only once in a lifetime.

There, you see, Ruth said in a friendly voice. And here and now, of all places. Through me, of all people.

The image of the crossroads had taken hold of me. When had I realized that I had to learn to live without alternatives? In stages, I remembered, it's not the kind of thing you can learn overnight. You're sitting with comrades who are going through the same thing as you. Your numbers are shrinking. The older ones are in a better position than you younger ones: They have had practice clinging to hope against all reason. In their view, you don't have the right to give it up yet. The project they have dedicated their lives to is one that will take generations, it is no short-term task for our minuscule lifespans. When I think about them, I told Peter Gutman and Ruth—when I think about my friends, all dead now, I see their bright, individual faces rising up from a dark flood that is about to swallow them. When I asked one of them about it, he said: Something always remains. Just look what horrors the French Revolution ended in, and what do you think when you think about the French Revolution now? Liberty, Equality, Fraternity.

I didn't ask, I said, what posterity will think when it thinks about us.

Maybe, Peter Gutman said, people will say: In the end they lived without illusions but not without remembering their dreams. Remembering the wind of utopia in the sails of their youth.

From your lips to God's ears, I said.

I got into my red car alone, since Peter Gutman had something else he needed to do downtown, and I drove down Sunset Boulevard. I saw the crowds of people, white, black, brown, yellow, drifting down the street. No one in posterity is asking about them, I thought, and that is the fate of the vast majority, so what do you care?

I had gradually lost my reluctance to join the avalanche of metal hurtling along the network of roads through Los Angeles. My little red car was a great help in filing away the layout of the city in my brain, but suddenly something was very wrong, the car started shaking, luckily a gas station appeared up ahead and luckily I reached it. The attendant, an extremely bright Latino man, quickly figured out that I had gotten a nail lodged in my left rear tire; I watched in admiration the speed with which the man repaired my car, Los Angeles is a car city, it was obvious to everyone that everyone needed a drivable car at all times, *Thank you so much. You're welcome, ma'am, good luck!*

Onward, down Sunset Boulevard, down to the ocean, don't fight the flood of forgetting that flushes us all down this famous road into the dark sea.

I had no trouble finding our street, the door to our underground garage, and in one bold turn, without any back-and-forth maneuvering, I parked my little car in its place between Francesco's wood-paneled classic car and Pintus and Ria's elegant black coupe. Mrs. Ascott had parked her enormous white car by the entrance, as always, blocking half of the lane—as the manager of the MS. VICTORIA she gave herself permission to do so. We ran into each other by the entrance and said our friendly hellos. When had it taken hold, actually, this feeling that when I opened my apartment door I was coming home?

I must have made something to eat that night, I probably sat in front of the TV while I ate it, and only then did I open my Indian bag that I had brought to Ruth's. It was probably late. I can still see before my eyes the big white envelope with my name on it—no one besides Ruth could have stuck it in my bag. The envelope contained a page with Ruth's handwriting and an unopened airmail letter addressed to Lily. The letter, Ruth wrote to me, had arrived from Germany while her friend lay dying. She had found it with the other papers Lily had left her. She had not wanted to open it. Now, she wrote, she wanted to give it to me, because she thought that that was what both Lily and the letter writer would have wanted.

It was written by my friend Emma.

It was postmarked from a West German city, with West German stamps. I held it in my hands for a long time, turning it over and around, before I finally opened it. This letter must have almost crossed Ruth's letter with the news of Lily's death. It was written in Emma's sweeping, old woman's handwriting, on the marbleized stationery I recognized as hers.

Dear Lily,

This is going to be a long letter. I have a chance to give it to West German friends who can mail it from there, so it'll get past the censors.

I have cancer. No one knows except me. I'm sure you'll believe me when I say that it wasn't a great shock to learn that I don't have long to live: the feeling we had in the Nazi years, that we're all dead people temporarily on holiday among the living, sank its claws deep into us. During all these years since, I lived as though behind a curtain. I always kept busy and didn't want to let myself get paralyzed. When Stalin died, I was in jail here "under false accusations," and when a guard whispered the news to me, I cried. Don't say anything about that, I have already told myself everything there is to say.

You'll remember the time, right after Hitler seized power, when we were in the audience at one of the "Führer's" speeches in a giant auditorium and we heard the thunderous applause of the crowd. When we were leaving, you said: Now they have their Messiah. We have to get out of here as fast as we can. You were clear-sighted and decisive.

I stayed, I had my instructions from the Party. A suicide mission, in retrospect. We were a little group and they caught us after a year. It's only because none of us gave away any names that we made it through with our lives. Three years in jail and then kept under strict surveillance so there was no way I could do anything else. Almost no way.

I wonder what we would have done if we had known everything back in the thirties—known all about the purges in the Soviet Union, the gulag. We probably would have despaired and been unable to act. Our nightmare was a Fascist Europe, and we told ourselves Stalin had prevented it.

We ran aground. The country I live in and placed my hopes in at first is getting more and more fossilized and rigid from year to year, and the moment is in sight when it will lie there on the side of the road, a motionless corpse for anybody to plunder. Then what? A long phase of rotting and putrefaction?

Is there an obvious answer I just can't see? Oh Lily, write

back soon, your old friend Emma really doesn't know what to do anymore. Warmest regards, my dear. What did we used to say? Adieu.

Emma kept her cancer a secret from me for a long time. Then she died quite quickly. She didn't talk about death. Only once did she say that she wouldn't mind ending up on another planet, a little one, moving away from Earth quite fast, from which she could see our planet from the outside, as a whole, for the first time. She said that that would be very instructive.

I was overwhelmed with an indescribable exhaustion that night. Strangely, Emma's letter had consoled me. I fell asleep right away and slept far into the next day. I remembered one dream clearly: Plummeting through layer after layer of increasing density, first air, then water, swamp, garbage, gravel, I was in danger of getting stuck, suffocating. Suddenly there was stone beneath my feet, where I could stand, and a voice: You are on firm ground. The sentence stayed with me for a long time. I understood it.

On Sunday I wanted to go with Therese and Jane and the others in the gang to church, the First African Methodist Episcopal Church. In the neighborhood where the church was, the day of rest seemed to be honored: the streets were empty. Our gang had arranged to meet and we were there early, so we walked around the block. Therese knew her way around here too and showed us the buildings that the parish had bought and set up for social services—school, kindergarten, old-age home. The community did not seem poor; in fact, the neighborhood exuded a modest prosperity and respectability. The well-tended lawns were not extravagant but were kept in meticulous order; almost all of the houses, wooden like everywhere else in the city, had received a new coat of paint in recent years (bonbon pink, sky blue, turquoise, with blinding white window frames); there were garden swings behind the houses and lower-middle-class cars in the driveways, which the black home-owner would wash on Sunday mornings while his children, in cute clothes, came out of the house holding hands with their mother, who was done up in a big hat and an elaborate lace blouse, and together they would gracefully make their way to church.

They've made it, Therese said. Still, they're not totally secure—they're bank tellers and insurance agents and retail managers and traveling salesmen and city employees, they overdo it a little sometimes in their eagerness to imitate the whites, and they still think they can manage to be as successful as the whites and religious too, I mean truly religious, in the biblical sense. You'll see.

We signed in and were taken to the *office*, where the *ministers* gradually came in: black women and men in white robes with long silk shawls in various colors draped over them. They greeted us, hugged us, offered us something to drink, asked about our backgrounds and jobs—the room was suddenly full of people, it was a relaxed, cheerful atmosphere, and finally the reverend arrived. He was the oldest one there and his face reminded me of a dark, shriveled fruit, it was the face of a kind old clown; he beamed and hugged us too, I felt the pressure of his strong hands on my upper arms, and I thought: There is more than one kind of security, and the kind that this man exuded is probably the hardest kind to acquire.

The reverend asked one of the *ministers*, a stately middle-aged woman with a violet shawl hanging over her white robe, to show us to our places. There were seven of us: Jane, Margery, Manfred, Toby, and Susan along with me and Therese. I was glad that we were sitting in the fifth row, not the first, and we seemed to be the only whites in the crowd of at least four hundred people who had filled the church by then. It didn't make me uncomfortable, it was just that in that moment I felt many gazes upon me: watching, testing, but what did this test consist of? Should I act like a white person did in this situation? How exactly was that?

Then the floor started shaking under our feet, rhythmically, and I heard the clapping, then the singing. I turned around with everyone else and the choir was marching in; everybody stood up, including us, and everybody began to clap in time with the song. I hesitated, I always avoided clapping in time to things, but then I did it too, it wasn't embarrassing. The fifty or sixty men in the chorus rejoiced, there was no other word for it: they were so joyful they could barely contain themselves but they nonetheless kept to the song, the words, the melody, the rhythm of the clapping and the dragging, hesitating double-steps they were taking down the center aisle before dividing into two groups in front of the pulpit, still singing and clapping, and symmetrically taking their places on the platforms rising steeply up on either side of the pulpit, facing the congregation. They sang loud and long, delighting the listeners, and a female soloist stepped out from the choir to a microphone and was met with shouts and applause, her radiant voice opened our hearts, there is no other way I can say it, then the singer stepped back, waving, into the choir that continued to sing, sing, praise and rejoice. One of the *ministers* had stepped up to the pulpit, almost unnoticed, and now I saw that the other ministers were sitting on benches to either side of him, and he started the liturgy in a spoken and sung call-and-response with the congregation.

My gaze fell upon an elegant woman in the first row, in a grass-green, tight-fitting suit with a green-and-white hat on her head, white cotton gloves on her hands, and she jumped up and loudly answered the minister's questions, *yes*, He is the Lord my God, *yes*, I believe in Him and His only son, *no*, I will have no other gods before Him. The woman threw up her arms, swayed in time to the choir that had started up again, and a second minister was standing at the pulpit and joyfully pronouncing the confession of sins, and, just as joyfully, certain of being heard, the plea for forgiveness. This community's God did not seem to be a jealous God who insisted on repentance and contrition, he seemed to know that it was not possible for his children to keep his commandments, in fact there were many things in this world that even he could not change, he seemed to know that they tried their best and that they were sorry when it yet again didn't quite work out, their efforts to be good and avoid evil, maybe it would turn out better next time if Father in Heaven was willing to let it pass this time, and He certainly was willing, the *minister* knew it and thanked him for it and the whole congregation joined in his thanks with all their hearts and I felt that nothing divided me from them more categorically than this ritual of confession and forgiveness, but I couldn't indulge in this painful feeling for long, since now there was a woman *minister* introducing us, the guests, and I saw that there were a few other white people in the church, including a few people I knew from the CENTER, we all had to stand up and the congregation was asked to welcome us, and they did. First the people right next to us hugged us, then people sitting farther away came up and stood in a short line, I felt lots of black cheeks on my cheek, heard a lot of voices say *Welcome*, and I started to smile, to laugh, to feel good.

The service took its course, interspersed with crescendos of song from the choir. Now the reverend was standing at the pulpit, kindly and confidently responding to the happy welcome from the congregation. Today he wanted to talk to us about how it's up to us, every day we can change our life and start a new one. *Yeah!* many people cried, *Right!* cried the woman in the green suit, the reverend waved at her and she enthusiastically waved back. The reverend started to speak. He had a froglike face with incredibly supple lips. Almost every single sentence he spoke was met with cheers and affirmation, *Oh yes, you're right,* the ministers in the background were the chorus, but without any tragedy, expressing with mimicry and gesticulations: *Isn't he wonderful?* Sometimes one or another of them jumped up to cry out loud: *Great! Wonderful!* Sometimes one of the *ministers* was so excited that he nudged the reverend in the ribs, and the reverend took a few *sidesteps,* rock-and-roll style, the audience liked that, he danced a few more rock moves, the congregation jumped up and cheered, the woman in the green suit brilliantly performed a solo number in front of the first row, the people next to her applauded, the reverend gave a full-throated laugh and proclaimed to his people that he had no trouble imagining that every man and woman among them could see everything in a new way, just like that, starting right now, see with the eyes of love, and that it would be so easy for them with the help of the Lord to simply turn their life inside out like the old hat hanging in his closet at home, many of you know the one I mean, he said. They certainly did, oh yes, they knew that hat, they described it to each other and thought it was a brilliant idea their reverend had had, to compare their lives to that hat, but was it an unfair comparison? No, it was fair, he was right, as always, and they cried it out to him too, and they would have kept up their cries for a long time if the choir hadn't powerfully started up again, this time led by the large bass voice of one of the older singers.

At the same time, some of the *ministers* were taking the plastic sheet off the long narrow table that stretched almost the whole width of the church between the pulpit and the first row, and which now was revealed to be the communion table, with a row of believers already kneeling before it, including the woman in the green suit, who wanted to receive communion from the reverend himself and looked up at him with deep devotion.

And now came something I didn't expect: the whole church went up for communion, man after man, woman after woman, row after row, starting in the back, and the ministers skillfully and affectionately managed the access to the table of the Lord, put the women's handbags on one bench, supported the disabled, there was a great movement, but completely calm, in the church, to the long, drawn-out notes of the music, I saw white people kneeling down too, including one of the directors of the CENTER. I saw Annie, who was Jewish, receive the Christian sacrament. Now it was our turn. I couldn't be the only one to refuse. Therese pushed me, I kneeled on the little bench in front of the table, tiny wafers were lying in the little plates, and a sensibly organized row of holes held little plastic thimbles of wine. I ate the bread, I drank the wine. *God bless you*, the minister standing in front of me said.

That was my first time in fifty years, I told Therese, the first time since my confirmation, and I don't even belong to any church anymore. Therese said she had been brought up in a convent school and left the church as soon as she could, at fifteen, but here it meant something different. That was what all our friends said, gathered in a small white group in front of the church, a little embarrassed, barely able to hide how moved we all were, waving in every direction to people who said goodbye to us with nods and smiles.

It was brutally hot. We split up into our cars and I ended up in the back of Therese's car with Margery sitting in front next to her. Margery, the couples therapist, said that if her patients could feel reverence and self-renunciation like that once a week they would not need any more therapy. I was tired, I closed my eyes and slipped back into memories: of the joyless, sour confirmation classes in a bare, ugly room; of the lips of the pastor grimacing hypocritically when he spoke the name of God; of my unsuccessful efforts to avoid being confirmed; of our eagerness to scoff at the sacrament.

Not the breath of a single wing beat was granted to us then, Angelina, but today I felt a steady gentle fluttering. Who was I talking to? It was Angelina, the angel, the black woman from the MS. VICTORIA, sitting next to me in the backseat of Therese's car, perfectly naturally, relaxed (if that is an appropriate thing to say about an angel) and smiling. You have to relax every once in a while, right? I said. I didn't want to bother her with any direct questions, and in any case, according to the ideas I'd had as a child about my guardian angel, it must be able to read my thoughts. Not always, Angelina said, often she was just too tired to relax after so much work. Anyway, you know it yourself. What, I asked, what do I know myself? Here I was, nagging the angel, I couldn't help it, and she said that I know that whenever I ask a question for the first time I am already very close to the answer, so why did I want an answer from her? She was there only for emergencies, what would it come to otherwise? Was she saying I should be ashamed of my question or something? Did she really not feel that this was an emergency for me, that I needed the security of a tiny little bit of certainty? About what, she asked.

WHETHER SHE, THE ANGEL, WAS PART OF MY RECOVERY

And whether I would ever feel what it meant to be happy again, I said, to my own amazement, I'm afraid I might even forget what happiness feels like, Angelina!

The angel didn't answer, it was gone. The midday heat clobbered me and I was covered with sweat as I crawled out of the car; we had to park it in the blazing sun on Broadway. The palm-lined street was free of angels from downtown to the Pacific Ocean, empty of both cars and people in this fierce Sunday heat. There were buildings, palm trees casting no shadows—where were we stranded thirsty people supposed to go? Then the miracle happened and a narrow, sky-blue door appeared in the white wall of a building, there was Susan standing in the doorway, the door opened behind her and we stepped into a darkened lounge, empty of people, which we crossed to get to a courtyard with tables set up under shady, exotic trees where people were eating and drinking, where the table we were meant to sit at was free, of course, where a big glass of iced tea was standing in front of each of us after a minute, a refreshment we hadn't even ordered but here they seemed to know what was good for you, we liked what was on the menu too, salads in many varieties, the service was fast but not too speedy, we needed time to cool off and restart our conversations with each other.

In one of the conversations, which now, in retrospect, seem to have filled those last weeks—I can see them as one single continued conversation, but not describe them, I think with regret, conversations seem to be made out of the most fleeting material of all our experiences, more fleeting even than some thoughts, because when I tried to note down what I remembered from the previous day the next morning, already only a few key words remained with me—we talked about everything under the sun, about "God and the world" as the phrase goes in German, or, more precisely, about God and the Devil: we asked each other (and ourselves) when it was that the ancient religions had found it necessary to adopt a morality that divided human action, and eventually human thought, into "good" and "evil." When, in other words, had heaven and hell, angels and devils, been invented? And why.

Angelina, my angel, had leapt up into the branches of the eucalyptus tree we were sitting under and was listening attentively to what we were saying, a little mockingly too. I was the only one who could see her: that was normal, and that was how it would remain, I stayed rational and well-disposed to verifiable facts but I got used to having her with me. She, the angel, had me say—how else could I know, except from her?—that there was a dark mystery among the angels too, not only among human beings, namely that the dark angels had rebelled against God and for their deed had to stay in the lower heavens, within the categories of space, time, and illusion, and thus closer to human beings, unlike the bright angels who stayed in the upper dimensions, circling God's throne in eternal light and song. Angelina seemed not to need my sympathy for the fact that she was one of the banished angels: she made a dismissive, almost obscene gesture that I wouldn't have expected an angel to make.

Our group had grown bigger with the arrival of Lowis—a man with a magnificent head of curly hair flecked with gray, an anthropologist, I learned, at the university there, and passionately welcomed by everyone at the table, especially Therese. He had a young woman with him whom no one had met before and he introduced her as Sanna, a kind of director by trade. There was no doubt that they were a couple. Everyone, including me, inspected the woman, surreptitiously but very thoroughly. She was exceptionally thin. I found myself drawn to her. Everything about her was brown—her skin, her artfully tied-up hair, her chic loose clothes, and even her eyes, which I noticed only later, when she turned to face me. She had sat down next to me and for a long time I saw only her classical profile.

We put before Lowis and Sanna the question we were considering: Why did the old religions require sacrifices, human sacrifice? Not every ancient religion had human sacrifice, Lowis said, for example the Hopi, an Indian people he had studied, sacrificed a human being to their gods only very rarely. The conversation then went back and forth about the forms that the scapegoat ritual takes in the present day; apparently we couldn't do without it, apparently it would continue to be performed. Even now that crucifixion is out of fashion, there is still hounding out of the city.

Sanna leaned over to me and asked quietly: Do you think they treated you like that because you're a woman?

I couldn't be the first to say it. The only way to prove it would be to collect all the terms they used against me and compare them to the ones they used against men.

Hello, Jane said, anybody home?

She was a powerful woman with thick blond hair hanging down in snakelike coils; she had a wide, beautiful face and straightforward blue eyes, strong hands, a healthy figure.

Toby, sitting across from me next to Therese: you could see from his thin hands that they could work with the tiny pieces of wood he made his models out of—models of the constructions he wanted to build but that no one wanted to have. He had a hard time dealing with his sense of inadequacy, which was about to make him go to Mexico, and he wondered if the message history was trying to tell us wasn't precisely that material values always prevailed over spiritual ones.

Sanna said she didn't think that was true. Hadn't we simply committed ourselves to the most literal way of looking at things, so that now we could see only the hegemony of material things and were no longer in a position to perceive the decisive effects of spiritual forces?

So you don't think, Susan said, that people are genetically programmed to give precedence to material values? Then how do you explain the mass of humanity's unstoppable pursuit of cars, houses, washing machines, and money, money, money?

Some of us who knew Susan better concealed our amusement over the fact that it was she, of all people—the millionaire—who was concerned about humanity's materialism. But we were being unfair to her: she was well aware of her ambivalent situation. You should talk, she said to us. Yes, especially she, but actually all of us belonged to the fraction of humanity that lived in luxury. We had a car, other people could only dream of that, and so how could we judge her for her needs?

Margery said she thought it all depended on what we considered normal. She couldn't count how many times in her practice she saw a couple who had lived their whole lives according to certain rules: the man earns the money and the woman spends it, has children, throws parties, and supervises the help. Nothing could be more normal than that. Until the woman, approaching sixty, suddenly has a fit and starts hurling the most violent and obscene curses at her husband and every-one else—outbreaks of madness that she doesn't remember afterward, but then there the couple sit, helpless in front of her, and the woman goes off on her husband in the therapist's presence while he sits next to her like a lamb, letting it all roll off his back, understanding nothing. There are people whose downtrodden, constricted lives just burst out at some point and a revulsion comes over them at the normality they have lived in up until then.

We sat in the shady inner courtyard for a long time, and Susan told us how much she wanted us to meet up and drive into the desert at the next full moon to admire the moonrise, and we agreed to do it. At some point Lowis said that he and Sanna were about to travel through the Southwest, including a visit to the Hopi reservation, where he knew an old chief, and I heard myself say: Will you take me with you? and they said: *Yes, sure.*

So that was set. We parted. I drove with Lowis and Sanna, the heat had not let up much, but I felt wonderfully refreshed. To step into the cool hallway of the MS. VICTORIA was like pulling into my home port. Mr. Enrico had two pieces of mail for me. The first was a postcard sent by a young lawyer in Leipzig. He wrote: "Unlike you, I always hated the GDR and was thus immune to many things. You, however, were an important part of the GDR, and I hate you!"

The second was a note from Peter Gutman, who wrote that he wanted me to have a quotation he had just run across from his favorite essayist. The quotation ran: "I do not deny the horrors of the gulag and am disgusted by everyone who denies the Stalinist past, but Commu-nism was a tremendous hope. In Marxism—this is very Jewish—there is an insane overestimation of human beings. It makes us believe that we are creatures capable of social justice. A terrible mistake that count-less millions of people have paid for with their lives, but a generous idea and a great compliment to humanity."

I lay down on the bed to rest for a moment and slept for twelve hours.

What else? Danger is approaching, I hear on every channel while I write this. The politician on TV says it is not a question of whether a terrorist attack will strike Germany, but when, even though they were able to prevent it this time. Fears are rising in the population, but that is in no way what we're trying to achieve, he says, that is the wrong re- action. This era, I think, has a hinge that it pivots around—we can name the date, September 11, 2001, after which Time is different than it was before. Different how? Made of different material, a substance satu- rated with dark geological inclusions which, if they were set free, would mean our death. We weren't prepared for it, and we notice only gradually and against our will that we have realized it too late and can no longer "defeat" "it." "It" is here to destroy our roots.

Time passed, I had started to count the days. Sometimes, at night, I permitted myself a word like "homesick." There had recently actually been an earthquake too, with the epicenter farther south in California: for hours on end the TV showed the measuring device whose needle shot up past the acceptable value, and then the relaxed, competent earth- quake scientist who had to comment on this swing of the needle so that panic wouldn't break out among the population. I remembered the lec- turer, a German woman, who had sat next to me at a university *dinner* and told me that her husband, an earthquake scientist, could not preach often enough that it wasn't a question of whether, but when, there would be a major earthquake in Los Angeles: THE BIG ONE. Everyone knew it but no one wanted to believe it, no one took seriously the fact that the city had been built on tectonic plates, the San Andreas Fault, that were drifting apart ever more dangerously. She and her husband, in any case, always had gallons of drinking water ready in their house and a week's supply of nonperishable food. In an emergency situation, all hell would break loose all around them, so they hid their supplies. Carefree Americans simply refused to see what even the collapse of computer networks would mean, never mind anything else. What would happen, for instance, if the financial system collapsed? Her husband didn't dare to imagine it. They wanted to move away from this danger- ous area, and sooner rather than later, but her husband's career kept him here.

The road, nestled up against the ocean. The light, the heavenly light. The cars, bumper to bumper, my little red Geo right in there with them, one of the few afternoons when I dared the traffic to drive to the beach even though I had a headache. My thoughts had gotten fixated on the earthquake.

It went fine this time too, didn't it? —Who was talking to me? —Angelina. —So angels really can read minds? —By the way, you should turn left here, there are no more parking lots for a while. —I know, I just wasn't thinking about it. —That's the headache's fault.

The parking lot was full, like every parking lot always was. Angelina directed me to the one free spot. She let me discover the patch of beach where I could set up my folding chair with its sun umbrella and look at the ocean, not just at half-naked people. I let Angelina know that I wanted to be left alone. My headache was getting worse, in fact. When I had looked my fill and the glitter of sunlight on the water had started to hurt my eyes, I picked up the book I had neglected for so long: *The Wisdom of No Escape* by the nun, Pema.

Now I do not intend to say anything to justify or provide any sort of explanation for the Angel Angelina's appearance on the scene. According to surveys, 86 percent of Americans believe in miracles and of course in heavenly creatures too, such as angels. Or that a statue of the Madonna no one had really ever noticed before, in the house of a priest no one had ever really noticed either, could suddenly start to shed tears. And obviously I, with my unshakable belief in the Enlightenment, did not and do not believe in such occurrences, let me make that perfectly clear. I clearly remember my reaction when Emily, the American, after an excellent big *dinner*, told us openly, as though it were entirely natural, about her *"psychic,"* a woman who lived in Mexico, had paranormal abilities, and had just relayed oracular wisdom to her over the phone for more than two hours, including the information, very important to Emily, that her two cats who were being boarded in New York absolutely did not want to be moved again so soon. That information removed a terrible burden of guilt from Emily's conscience. I remember that I kept quiet and thought: This can't be happening. Emily called herself an "intellectual Marxist," was certainly a materialist, but she nonetheless thought that extrasensory phenomena were possible, we couldn't know what kinds of energy traveled through our unconscious and the universe. And actually, I thought, what about my *overcoat of Dr. Freud?* My fetish? —No, the other voice in me said, that wasn't the same at all. That was purest, crystal-clear rational science compared to Emily's *psychic.*

Angelina told me you don't have to explain everything, and by the way, I was sick. —Sick? Me? That little headache? —And the fever? —What fever?

My forehead was hot, but we were having one of the hottest days yet. I opened a newspaper that called itself the *Weekly World News* and that I had picked up at the *deli* while I was buying my Greek salad and bread. Headline: *"The Most Horrifying Photo Ever Published!"* Then, in giant letters: *FACE OF SATAN APPEARS OVER WACO!* And a photograph of a cloud of smoke rising up from the compound of this sect that had apparently set its own building on fire, in which was visible a face that looked like how a child might imagine Satan to look. The same grotesque face, I read, had appeared above several major catastrophes in recent years and was proof that the great battle between God and Satan had begun, and that it was everyone's duty to choose sides—now.

I leaned back in my chair, forgot my headache and chills, and lost myself in the life around me: the blue of the sky, the lively movements of the half-naked bodies on the beach, the fine bright sand, the wind that had picked up and was caressing my skin. All of this, the nun said, everything in this moment, is exactly the way it should be. Your whole life. *Let it be.* I understood.

That night I had chills. I slept badly, I hadn't been able to eat, I kept tossing and turning under damp sheets, my head buzzed, the aspirin hadn't helped. Instead of feeling sorry for me, Angelina followed me with her mocking gaze. Why did I always let myself get talked into things that weren't right for me? Hadn't I realized, at long last, that patient acceptance was not my thing? But people can change, I countered. Angelina saw through that, of course, and understood that I was trying to avoid suffering. Didn't I see that I was still always fleeing from something? I said she should leave me alone. She disappeared.

An older woman, Gertrud, dressed in light blue, a kind of nurse's uniform, came by and took good and attentive care of me, she said she wanted to cook me something tasty that I would definitely eat, and then suddenly she slowly fell over on her side and started to die. I knew right away what was happening, Gertrud is dying, I thought, then she metamorphosed before my eyes into a giant dying elephant, who was very sad and made me very sad too, then it was Gertrud again in her bed, and then she was dead. Then I started crying. I didn't know anyone named

Gertrud, the only person I could think of was the old queen Gertrude in *Hamlet*, who had betrayed her husband with his brother.

Then it was morning, and standing at my bedside was Angelina, her dust cloth in her hand, which didn't surprise me. I said: My angel, but she didn't let herself get drawn into any of that. She said I was sick, she wouldn't turn on the vacuum cleaner. Shouldn't she go get a doctor? I said: *No doctor*, and she said: *Yes, they're very expensive*. Angelina, I said in English: We all must die. That wasn't news to her; she smiled knowingly and said: *Yes. That's true*.

I thought: Why do I need to learn this truth in a foreign language? Maybe in my native German I couldn't endure it. How does everyone live with this knowledge? I was inconsolable. Angelina brought me tea. My fever rose, Ria came to look in on me, Therese too, Peter Gutman stuck his long skull in and used the word "crisis." It lasted two or three days, then it was over. I stood up, still swaying a little; I recovered quickly, went to see the others, took part in their lives and their conversations.

What had mattered before had lost its importance. Now I knew that I had to die. I knew how fragile we are. Old age began. *The overcoat of Dr. Freud* had gotten torn and I wanted to find out what its lining was made of. I could do that anywhere, any place on earth, why not here?

Peter Gutman didn't approve of the mood he found me in. We were in my little Geo on our way to see Karl, the German photographer, at his house in the hills right under the letters that spelled HOLLYWOOD. The streets were unexpectedly calm. That morning, the jury had announced its verdict in the Rodney King trial—the second trial against the four white policemen who had beaten a fleeing black man almost to death. Many people expected an outbreak of violence in the city, starting in the black neighborhoods and spreading from there, if the verdict came back "not guilty." The jury had delivered a Solomonic judgment: two of the defendants "*guilty*," two "*not guilty*." The whites breathed a sigh of relief while cheers broke out in the black churches.

Life in the city continued on its normal course. Karl had covered the walls of his intricate little house with large photos, portraits of residents of the city: white, black, yellow, Latino. The longer I looked at them, the more I felt the strain they were under and the effort it took to live here. Yes, Bob Rice said—he was there too, of course, and had brought along Allan, his boyfriend—how long was this supposed to keep going? We had been spared again this time, again we whites would forget how scared we all were. We would refuse to admit what thin ice we were all walking on.

Sitting next to me was an old Jewish professor who seemed to be very sick. He was a research psychologist who had dedicated much of his life to studying Hitler's psyche; I got the impression that he felt it to be a kind of obligation he was keeping to the murdered Jews. There was one thing he could be certain of: the man was impotent. And his blindness during World War One was a hysterical blindness. The professor's wife, an elegant, elderly lady, signaled me that I shouldn't continue with this conversation. Later she whispered to me that it made her husband too anxious. Only then did I notice that we had been speaking German the whole time.

Karl said he wanted to go back to Germany as soon as he could. He wanted to photograph the faces in East Berlin and West Berlin, wanted to try to capture this unique moment. I saw before me a series of shattered faces from the year of the Turn. You better hurry, I said. They're shutting down again. They have already started to feel ashamed of having had hope for a few weeks, and having shown that hope too.

Hope for what?

I realized I found it hard to answer: it was as though answering would mean denouncing the hopeful people of the time, since what they—what we—had hoped for was so far from reality, so embarrassing, so ridiculous. I barely remember what I said to Karl. Maybe I pronounced words like "self-determination," or "justice," or "solidarity."

"Freedom," someone suggested.

That wasn't the word I heard at the time. Free elections, yes. Freedom of travel. The goals were mostly very concrete.

People mean so many different things by "freedom," don't they, Peter Gutman said.

He came along the next morning to see the places where the émigrés had lived—Therese wanted to show them to us. She had rented a nice car, she was working on her assignment to report on the mayoral election campaign. Our first stop was Mabery Road, the house where Salka Viertel lived for twenty-five years, raised her children, wrote screenplays that were mostly not produced, talked to Greta Garbo about plans for movies, and wrote scripts for her. The house became a meeting point for German émigrés in the thirties and was where she organized her extensive campaigns for colleagues in need in California, and people trapped in Nazi-occupied Europe. Her memoir, *The Kindness of Strangers*, was sitting next to me on the seat and after I read it I often drove past her house, not far from Second Street down Ocean Avenue, which curves to the right and then turns into Mabery Road. It was less than a ten-minute drive, during which I told the others about Salka Viertel, apparently in a tone that made Peter Gutman ask: You would have loved to meet her, wouldn't you?

Oh yes, I would have. It struck me that I rarely had that thought, no matter how much I admired the émigrés whose houses we were about to see. She is almost forgotten, I said. In some of the things you read about "Weimar under the Palms" she is barely mentioned.

Would I have wanted to meet Lion Feuchtwanger? We were driving up Sunset Boulevard to San Remo Drive, high above the city, and I had just reread *Jud Süss* to reassure myself that the book—obviously—contained not a hint of anti-Semitism. Unlike the Veit Harlan film, which was connected to a strange childhood memory, impossible to prove. Of course your mother would never have let you see the movie, and of course you desperately wanted to—just like *The Great King*, with Otto Gebühr, or, at the very end, *The Golden City* with Kristina Söderbaum. You were never allowed to do anything you really wanted.

Then came a memory that could not possibly be based on a real experience but that was so solid it was hard not to believe it. There were three movie theaters in our city, and one of them, the most modern, the Kyffhäuser Lichtspiele, had a side exit where you were standing one beautiful day—where I can see myself standing, in this untrustworthy memory of mine—peeking through the slit in the closed curtains into the movie hall, right at the screen. You saw different dazzling images in intense colors—a face twisted in fear, a gallows—images you wanted to keep watching at all costs but couldn't stand any longer for anything in the world. Then someone grabbed you from behind on the shoulder and dragged you away, cursing. *Jud Süss.* Longing and horror, that is what remained.

I obviously didn't tell Marta Feuchtwanger about that when we visited her a few years ago at the Villa Aurora, when it was still intact, I said. With the wonderful Spanish tiles in the entranceway; the valuable Feuchtwanger library from which Marta would pull a few volumes, incunabula; the study where Feuchtwanger's secretary, Hilde Waldo, an old invalid by then, told us about his working methods, various drafts of the manuscripts on different-colored paper, and his legendary concentration; the ancient turtle creeping around on the terrace with its incomparable view of the Pacific Ocean. All gone now, Marta Feuchtwanger was dead, the library had been donated to the university, the Villa Aurora was a construction site. Later it would give—now it gives—fellowships for German writers to live there, and it would be the only place left in the city as a reminder of the German emigration.

As always, whenever I started to follow the traces of the émigrés, I could not fight off a depressing sense of futility. Can you believe it, I said, at the end of the war I had never even heard the names of the vast majority of the people who were living here because Germany had kicked them out? Not Brecht, obviously, whose house on Twenty-sixth Street we were about to visit, not Alfred Döblin, who lived modestly in an apartment building we were driving by, as did Heinrich Mann, by the way, while Thomas Mann's villa, 1550 San Remo Drive, the next stop on our tour after taking Sunset Boulevard farther and turning off into Amalfi Drive, came across as prestigious and magnificent, although practically hidden from sight by the high hedges surrounding it. I had never dared to approach it. Therese wanted to walk onto the property; we talked her out of it. She wanted to at least see the window he had sat behind while writing *Doctor Faustus*, she said. And I had to wonder again if it was really possible that on my parents' narrow bookshelf in the "gentlemen's room," behind Hans Grimm's *Volk ohne Raum* (A People Without Space) and Karl Albrecht's *Der verratene Sozialismus* (Socialism Betrayed) and Edwin Erich Dwinger's *Die Armee hinter Stacheldraht* (The Army Behind Barbed Wire), stood *Buddenbrooks* in the second row, as I thought I remembered. I must have been mistaken, I said to myself again; because if it had been there you would have read it back then, since you read every printed piece of paper that came into your hands.

Is it possible that I didn't know the name Marlene Dietrich either? Had no one ever spoken in my presence about *The Blue Angel*? Therese knew all the houses here where Dietrich had lived. Franz Werfel? Not to mention the composers, the actors. A thick web of German culture had spread out to cover this city in the thirties. None of it was left. How many twenty-year-olds today know these names? I said.

What do you expect? Peter Gutman said. Being forgotten is the most natural thing in the world. And you, and me, and Therese—we haven't forgotten them.

We were exhausted, hungry and tired. Therese didn't care about our complaints, she had plans of her own. She took Hollywood Boulevard and brought us to Musso and Frank, where American authors such as Hemingway, Faulkner, and Fitzgerald used to meet, but also many German émigrés. Brecht, for example, was known to have eaten there. I love places like that, and we sat down in one of the booths, on the red seats that must have been there since the restaurant opened; we inspected the other guests to see if maybe a famous face might be among them. The menus had not changed either, we learned, so I ordered a cutlet—as predicted, it presupposed an enormous appetite, but in a place like this nothing could bother me.

After a while, Therese said that when she was a little girl she had wished many times that she had been born in another place, to other parents. Not locked away in that horrible Catholic boarding school. We could not imagine, she said, the forces leveled against her there, how harshly the one true faith was imposed. She had hated the church ever since, she couldn't help it. She had been given an overdose of religion. She had to laugh whenever she heard or read how children in the GDR were "indoctrinated."

I don't know why it took me so long to visit the used bookstore on Second Street for the first time. I think it was Stewart, the one black scholar in our *community*, who recommended it to me. We were sitting in front of Café Largo eating *seafood salad*. Of all the *scholars* in our year, Stewart was the one who kept the most to himself—a solitary type, who for that very reason, and despite certain guarded reactions of his in our conversations, I had long been interested in. It was possible to read mockery or criticism of our discussions in a turning down of the corners of his mouth, or a raising of his eyebrows. He was the only American in our group who lived in Los Angeles, he was further to the left than any of them, and he was the most realistic in his assessments of the conditions in this city. He came up in the labor movement, he said, but from a splinter group—the major, "white" unions didn't care about big companies exploiting Mexican workers, who were often paid absolutely nothing if they were illegal immigrants. His research as a sociologist was about how employers, with the help of the market, divided workers along ethnic and racial lines and how unions helped them do it. Or how racist the distribution of housing was, how the real estate and mortgage business worked, what they do is illegal but everyone knows about it and everyone does it. He was working toward a multicultural society and worked with groups in nonwhite neighborhoods, to politicize them. They had to understand the kind of society they lived in.

Here was someone who still wanted to change the world. So was it worth it? Stewart said: I hope you aren't giving up over there. I thought: I want to remember that a young American said those words to me, and I did remember it, and when I call this sentence to mind today I can still see the light falling from the cloudless afternoon sky down onto Third Street. I realized only later that Stewart had invited me out to lunch to say goodbye. A few days later he was gone, he had had to break off his stay at the CENTER early, they said. He hadn't said goodbye to anyone. I found a note from him in my mailbox: *Don't worry.*

So it was he who sent me to Eric Chaim Kline's used bookstore, where it was as dark as it should be in a used bookstore, and all the walls as well as several tables were covered with books. English, French, even Russian. Finally, in the back left corner, I found the German shelf and started hunting through the rows of books. I opened this or that book and read names and dates. They must have been the property of German émigrés who had died here, abroad, or were able to return but had had to leave behind the things they had originally brought from Europe. How else would a thick novel by Vicki Baum, bound in red linen, well-worn by now, have ended up here? *Liebe und Tod auf Bali* (Love and Death in Bali), published in 1937 by Querido, the émigré press in Amsterdam. I had never heard of the title but had just recently driven past Vicki Baum's gigantic house on Amalfi Drive. She had emigrated from Germany early, astutely gauging the nature of National Socialism, and she was one of the few who had found equal success in the United States and could live well. I was flipping through the book when a very polite young black man came up to me with the obligatory question: *Can I help you?* I tried to explain to him what I was looking for. *One moment, please*, he said, and a few minutes later a sprightly older man with white hair and a black yarmulke on his head came over, clearly the owner. He listened patiently to my request for literature by German émigrés who had lived here. He understood. I should come back tomorrow afternoon, he said, he thought he had some items that would interest me. I put the Vicki Baum book on hold until then.

The next day, a June day, it was unseasonably hot again. The old bookseller, Mr. Kline, took me up a wooden staircase into a long narrow storage room right under the roof beams where thousands of books were piled along the walls, on the floor, and on long tables. The heat was unbearable; I was covered with sweat in an instant. It smelled of hot paper and hot wood. What if there was a fire in here! I thought. The bookseller had cleared off a corner of one table and laid out the books that he wanted to offer me. He left me alone.

The books that I saw then for the first time are piled all around me now. I pick them up and something of the mood that came over me then returns. On the top of the pile is the little book *Der Mensch ist gut* (Man Is Good), by Leonhard Frank, a red paperback with a linen back cover, obviously old, worn, with yellowed paper, published by Gustav Kiepenheuer Press in Potsdam, with no date but with a note, "Written 1916–Spring 1917," and the dedication "To the generations to come," a solemnity that would not appear again in World War II, I thought, and the first time I flipped through the pages I could already tell that the author, in the first flush of youth back then, had written, with mocking sarcasm toward his title, a brilliant antiwar book portraying the horrors no less graphically and vividly than the later, more famous books of the 1920s. Why had this book been forgotten? It was at least as exciting and moving as Remarque's *All Quiet on the Western Front*, which lay there too, a damaged copy, without its binding or the publisher's information, but clearly the same edition as the one you mysteriously had found at your grandmother's house and read on her sofa. I have often told myself that it's impossible, you never saw your grandmother reading anything other than the *Landsberger Generalanzeiger* and how would a banned book have found its way to her? But nevertheless I can still feel the rough armrests of her sofa under my hand while you took in, from reading that book, the images of atrocity that I still, today, feel sure I remember. Just like the aphorism, printed in gothic letters and hung in a black frame on the wall, which you read over and over again, which always sounded sad to you, and from which I retained one line. Only much later would I find out the source of the line "I once had a beautiful fatherland." Heinrich Heine, I now know. How did a poem by Heinrich Heine end up at my grandmother's? "I once had a beautiful fatherland. / The oak tree / Grew so tall there, the violets gently nodded. / It was a dream." Did the poet's name appear at the bottom? It couldn't have . . . Also an émigré. Another person who felt homesick. Like the person who, in the book by Erich Kästner, *Ein Mann gibt Auskunft* (A Man Provides Information), which lay on the corner of that long table, wrote a dedication to one of his companions in misfortune: "Dearest Paul, *Merry X-Mas*— This book will help you remember our old language. Affectionately yours, Walter."

THOSE BOOKS SUCKED ME IN

And I am back in the whirlpool again when I immerse myself in the books that the émigrés, remembering, wrote after their return to postwar Germany or their nonreturn. Ludwig Marcuse and Leonhard Frank and Curt Goetz and Carl Zuckmayer, Marta Feuchtwanger and Erich Maria Remarque—books that can still be found with an Internet search, used, since most of them have not been reprinted for decades. My work grinds to a halt while I burrow into these texts. I seek out the passages where the authors describe what exile has done to them. What it means to be rootless. And what it means to realize that no one, no native of their land of exile and certainly none of their former countrymen, can appreciate how the years of this shadow existence have changed them. And I reread the story I also found in Mr. Kline's used bookstore, which I hadn't heard of before, published in a series called Pazifische Presse (Pacific Press), founded by émigrés: "Mein ist die Rache" (Revenge Is Mine), by Friedrich Torberg.

I remember every detail about the American night I spent sleepless as a result of this story—one of the first stories to describe the conditions in a German concentration camp. The sadistic tortures inflicted on Jewish prisoners by SS-Führer Wagenseil were described more harshly and bluntly there than in almost any narrative I have ever read. On a philosophical level, if one may put it that way, the story is about the question of whether a pious Jew is justified in taking revenge against his tormentor, even though the Lord says revenge is His. The first-person narrator has done just that: shot the SS man and managed the improbable feat of escaping to Holland and from there to the United States. Now he is standing on the pier in New York City, waiting for every ship from Germany to see whether any of the seventy-five comrades he left behind in the barracks is on board. Whether anyone else survived. He is haunted by the thought that they might have all been killed in reprisal for his having killed the SS commander.

Something else that is deeply disturbing in my copy: In the yellowed margins of the narrow book, the printed text is supplemented with penciled notations that must have come from a Jewish reader, an émigré. They accompany the dark events of the story with commentary, exclamations, belated advice. And under the last line, this reader wrote: "America is full of Jews who love Germany and are nostalgic."

I can still see myself in Mr. Kline's hot attic of books: the tower of books that I wanted to buy grew—known names, unknown titles by Arnold Zweig, Leonhard Frank, Vicki Baum again, Bruno Frank—but what awakened the greatest longing in me were three inconspicuous gray issues of a journal, almost read to pieces: three issues of *Das Wort* (The Word), the émigré journal published in Moscow in the thirties. I'd like these, I said to Mr. Kline when he came back. He laughed with satisfaction: I bet you would, he said. But they are not for sale, he said, he had acquired them used himself as a student in Boston and wanted to keep them. We discussed the other books—prices, shipping, everything went off without a hitch. Then I came back to the topic of the journal issues: Whether there was any way he might be willing? . . . Mr. Kline shook his head. He shouldn't have shown them to me, he said. I said I could use them in my work right away, maybe he could take that into consideration. There were precious memories connected to these volumes for him, he said. I sensed a hint of indecision in his tone and kept pushing. There was a pause. Finally Mr. Kline turned to me and said: *But they are very expensive!*

Of course they are. *How much?* I asked. Mr. Kline looked at me thoughtfully as he said: *One thousand dollars.*

He didn't want to sell them. He wanted to test me.

I knew that I had to pay the price, for many, many different reasons. I said: *I'll take them. They are more important than a new car.*

Mr. Kline seemed taken by surprise. There was a pause. *I agree*, Mr. Kline finally said. He laughed and hugged me tight. I had to go to the bank. Mr. Kline gave me the three issues to take with me and I didn't have him ship them back home with the other books. I have never once regretted the purchase.

I lay down on the bed in my apartment and flipped through the issues of *Das Wort*. I read forewords by Thomas Mann and Hemingway. I read Erich Weinert's memoirs of the faces of his fallen comrades in Spain. Who thinks about them anymore? I said to Ruth and Peter Gutman when I saw them the next day. In this new Germany, they will be consigned to oblivion. But that was exactly the point, that was why I had clung to the smaller Germany: I saw it as the legitimate successor to this Other Germany, the one that, in all the prisons and concentration camps, in Spain, in the various countries of emigration—persecuted, tortured, horribly decimated—nevertheless resisted.

I needed to turn over the pages of the thickest issue of *Das Wort* for them, the one with a gray worn cover with red letters, badly yellowed pages: a double issue from April/May 1937. I was especially lucky to have found this one. The editors had asked all the anti-Fascist émigré German writers they could find for "biographical and bibliographical information" and had printed their answers—fifty pages, one hundred authors, twenty-eight of whom I had known personally, I said to Peter Gutman and Ruth. Their faces, their fates, their writings passed before my eyes. "These books were burned in Germany"; "These books are banned in Germany" appeared under every one of the paragraphs. When this issue came out, I said, I was eight years old, a passionate reader of Grimm's and Andersen's and Hauff's fairy tales, maybe that is what saved me from the worst. Can fairy tales lay the foundation for joining the fight against injustice? For the ability to tell the difference between good and evil?

You never once heard an openly spoken word of criticism against the Führer, you only noticed the doubtful, worried expressions on your mother's face, more and more despairing toward the end of the war. She had said to a customer she trusted—it must have been 1943 or '44—We've lost the war! And she was reported. After that she was visited and interrogated several times by two men in trench coats. Your parents were filled with fear, which they wanted to keep secret from you, though they didn't succeed.

Sitting on the table in front of us was a volume of Paul Merker's book, which I had also found at my bookseller's: 574 pages, with a brown linen hardcover, the publisher stated as "Editorial El Libro Libre, Mexico,

1945." Title: *Deutschland—Sein oder nicht sein?* (Germany: To Be or Not to Be?). I knew the head of this publishing house, I told my guests: an ardent Communist from a working-class family, who worked illegally after 1933, spent time in a Nazi prison, fought as a commanding officer with the Spanish People's Army in Spain, and was interned in French camps after Franco's victory. In Les Milles among others.

You went there yourself, from Marseilles, where you and G. tried to retrace the path that Anna Seghers laid out in her novel *Transit*. There was no one at Les Milles and the building that had once housed the prisoners was locked; you and G. peered through dusty windows into the large interior room and could make out parts of the frieze on the wall—fruits, other foodstuffs—that the prisoners, among them Max Ernst, had painted to cheer up their starving comrades. The whole area was covered with pulverized stone, both finely powdered and more coarsely shattered: bricks used to be manufactured here. Every rainfall must have turned the whole plot of land into a red swamp.

It was quite an accomplishment, I said, for an émigré press to publish that book by Paul Merker in two thick volumes. And that's after the accomplishment of writing the work in the emigration. What prompted him to write it was no doubt the burning question among the leftist émigrés of what should become of Germany after the victory over Hitler—there were controversial debates on the topic, for example between Brecht and Mann, here in California, where eight outstanding writers, including Brecht and both Thomas and Heinrich Mann, considered it "their duty" in August 1943, "at the moment when Allied victory approaches," to welcome "the announcement of the German prisoners of war and émigrés in the Soviet Union" that "called upon the German people to force their oppressors to unconditionally surrender and to fight for a strong democracy in Germany." Then came the all-important sentence, anything but self-evident: "We also consider it necessary to sharply distinguish between, on the one hand, the Hitler regime and the social strata connected with him and, on the other hand, the German people."

And the next day, Brecht noted grimly in his "Work Journal," Thomas Mann dropped by Feuchtwanger's and withdrew his signature, saying that it would be "stabbing the allies in the back." He said he would not consider it unreasonable for "the allies to punish germany for ten or twenty years."

All the more did I, and do I, admire Paul Merker's farsightedness.

His book, after its trip across the ocean, now lies before me again, and I flip through it to the last page, where he proposes an eleven-point platform to the Central Committee of the Communist Party. Point One: "Establishing an anti-Fascist democratic regime and a parliamentary republic with all the democratic freedoms."

What happened to this man? Peter Gutman asked me back then.

He died in 1969, "physically and emotionally broken" as they say, I said. First he was expelled from the Party because he had been in contact with Noel Field, an American, who had helped him in his flight from occupied France and helped many other émigrés. To tell you his unbelievable story too would take us too far afield, I said. Then Merker ended up in the GDR offshoot of the Prague Slánský trials and was sentenced to eight years in prison—after Stalin was already dead! He served four years. After that, he was released and rehabilitated, by the same judge who had earlier sentenced him. And sidelined with trivial assignments.

Walter Janka, who had shared his exile with him in Mexico and been his assistant for a time after their return, was the one who had told you and G. about him. Janka also had three years of GDR prison behind him, for "forming a counterrevolutionary group." He didn't come out of it broken, he stayed militant. He worked for the movie studio and advised you and G. on film projects.

When someone becomes interested in something, it seems like everything related to that interest suddenly appears, apparently by chance, for instance I now come across a newspaper article, "Bright Spot from the Dark Past," summarizing recent research on how Berlin workers acted during the Nazi period. The resistance of Social Democrats and Communists took a particularly heavy toll: thousands jailed and tortured, hundreds executed. The argument that the Nazi social order led to social corruption in the population could not be proven in the case of the Berlin working class, the newspaper said.—Where is the monument honoring them?

I felt that I had to give myself a break from thinking, from writing. I lay down, I tried to empty my mind the way the nun recommended, but I heard the telephone ring and could not just let it ring. The voice came from far away: a friend wanting to tell me the news that the Bosnians were now blockaded in a city where, they announced, they had a chlorine factory, and if they blew it up it would release enough chemicals to poison all of Europe.

Sometimes I wish I knew how the layers of time through which I have traveled, that I penetrate so easily in my thoughts, are actually arranged inside me: as actual layers, each one stacked carefully on top of the other? Or as a chaotic mass of neurons from which a power we do not understand can draw out whichever thread we want? Will neuroscientists ever find out?

I was looking for distraction and I felt my departure date breathing down the back of my neck; I had to admit that I had paid too little attention, or none at all, to the important sightseeing attractions that everyone thinks of in connection with the magical name Los Angeles. Bob Rice agreed—you can't come to L.A. without going to see at least one of the famous Hollywood studios, he said. Allan, his Japanese boyfriend, who worked "behind the scenes" at Universal Studios, would be my guide. The date and time were arranged without my doing a thing—it was one of those undertakings where my urge to do it and my inhibition against it remained in conflict to the end, but, finally, being polite to the other person won out. A Swiss colleague joined us, a literary critic, and I saw in his face when we met up the same skepticism that I felt. Allan himself seemed to feel something almost like embarrassment as he brought us to the entrance, the several tunnellike glass-roofed moving walkways that transported tourists nonstop to the *tour* that we joined. *"Welcome to the largest film and television studio in the world. Here you don't just watch the movies—you live them. The real star is you."* Fifty minutes in a gondola, through stage-set cities spread over a giant area, past the sets for famous movies—just the movies, I said to Allan, that I wouldn't call "my genre." I'm sorry to hear that, Allan said, but I was only trying to prepare him for the fact that I might not recognize the movies and their sets. Or that I might leave the *tour* early, it was already getting on my nerves, more because of the insanely enthusiastic tourists than because of the silent witnesses on either side of the route.

But you must be interested in *Psycho*! And there it stood, spookily lit, the house of horror, and later they would show us how they had shot the famous shower scene, but first there was more: E.T. appeared, making his yearning sounds. *"Quick! Hop aboard a starbound bike! And fly home with E.T.,"* and so we did, we flew into space and then landed in various dangerous situations imitating scenes from movies I didn't know and didn't want to know. A bridge collapsed under us, we felt an earthquake in a subway station, cars tumbled into chasms, passengers shrieked, the threatening fin of a shark appeared in a pond. The best one was the snow tunnel where you suddenly started spinning around, but actually it was the walls spinning. That was something worth keeping in mind: that when you think you're in the middle of the whirlpool, being dragged down into the depths, it might be only the walls that are spinning around you and you yourself might be in the eye of the hurricane.

But how will we ever be able to tell the difference between deception and reality again? I asked.

The whole point of everything here is to make you unlearn just that, our Swiss man said. But the feelings that the deception unleashes in us are real. We pay to have these feelings.

We had also paid for a whole series of demonstrations from stuntmen, on land and on water, with gun smoke and fireballs and explosions, and an Asian swordfight in front of a dragon, but finally there was an auditorium where all the tricks were explained, for instance how you have to set things up so that someone can climb around on the Statue of Liberty and then in the end fall off, as Hitchcock did once.

Then it was already evening and we were sitting, exhausted, up on the hill in the wonderful Japanese restaurant with a view of the whole city spread out below, where the lights were gradually coming on, that's incredible, we said, unforgettable, and Allan, our host, smiled with satisfaction. First we drank a cocktail called a *kamikaze*, made of vodka, triple sec, and lime juice—it deserved the name, we thought, and before long we were very chatty; we ate sushi and *combination dinners*, a lot of food, delicious, including raw fish, and we talked about the contrast between the Japanese conscience and Protestant conscience: how one was driven by the fear of losing face in public, the other by the fear of failing before God. About how, in our opinion, it was probably progress in human history when personal conscience appeared. It was strange how well this conversation went with the day's experiences, and the view of the city, just starting to show its nighttime lights by then.

When I got back to the MS. VICTORIA, paying no attention to the

three raccoons who were keeping watch as always, I saw that Peter Gutman had once again slipped a note under my door. A sentence of Kleist
had seemed to him worth communicating: "But paradise is bolted shut
and the cherub is after us; we have to circle the globe and go around to
the other side to see if perhaps there is a back way in."

It was not yet midnight; I called him. What if we want to do without paradise?

You don't believe that yourself, he said. We are already hurtling
along in this voyage around the world. But differently than Kleist could
have imagined. Not in a carriage. With rockets. We're looking for the
back way in, and if it is closed to us too, we'll blow it open. With nuclear
bombs if necessary.

Thank you very much, I said. That'll help me get to sleep.

The next day we drove to see his friend Malinka again, drove across
half the city in my little red Geo. Malinka had made lunch and afterward we sat outside in her tiny little yard under a fragrant lemon tree
and we talked about language. Malinka said she had grown up speaking Serbo-Croatian and had quickly learned English when she came to
America ten years ago—accent-free, so as not to stand out. She wrote
in two languages. But when she had something personal to write, she
avoided Serbo-Croatian so as not to feel "*sticky.*"

My personhood was tied to language, language was my real
homeland—that sounded trite, but I could sense that the other two
heard it with a certain envy. Peter Gutman told us his view, that there
was a second person inside him who wrote in a language that, he often
thought, was not his.

We walked around Malinka's *neighborhood:* on Fairfax, a Jewish area
with Jewish restaurants, kosher grocery stores where Malinka bought
certain kinds of cheese, Jewish fathers with yarmulkes, holding hands
with their two very serious young sons, each with a yarmulke on his
own head, on the way to synagogue. A lot of older people—there were
old-age homes nearby. It wasn't affluent, this neighborhood, these people:
on the poor side, actually. But they moved at a slower pace than elsewhere in the city. It was a peaceful, almost translucent image. This city
as a patchwork.

Peter Gutman seemed to enjoy being between us, two women who
were both fond of him. He admitted to having a "*sweet tooth*" and bought
a big bag of very sweet cookies.

When I drove back down the long Wilshire Boulevard, it was already dark.

By now I was familiar with the tiny little house in the courtyard of a big apartment complex, where Rachel, my Feldenkrais therapist, had her practice. I could report to her that I was doing better, that I hadn't taken any pills, but that I was somewhat blocked again at the moment. Rachel held certain small joints in the hip area responsible and pointed them out to me on an anatomical chart. The treatment helped me but was not painless. At one point she put my leg on a pillow and gave it an order in Yiddish: Relax!

I told her about our conversation about our different languages. Rachel said: Feldenkrais is my language, and it will take me my whole life to learn it properly.

I brought the conversation around to William Randolph Hearst. We had just been shown the famous film *Citizen Kane* by Orson Welles because we were planning a trip to Hearst Castle. For reasons I could not fathom, this was said to be the best movie ever made. Rachel said: *Men like Hearst and Carnegie and J. Paul Getty must have been evil men.* We agreed on that point. She would never get rich doing what she did. The only way people got rich was by betraying and exploiting others.

When I left, she said: *You are a clever student.* It had been a long time since any praise had made me so happy.

It was time for the glass elevator up the outside of the Huntley Hotel again—Peter Gutman and I wanted to ride up it once more, drink the watery margaritas, enjoy the spectacular view, sit next to the *high school teens*—three girls with long hair acting provocative, five boys showing off to various extents, all around seventeen years old and unbelievably loud, the girls squealing at every opportunity and all of them behaving like the world belonged to them, middle-class white young people. Not one of them noticed the sunset.

Peter Gutman said: What if you wrote up your observations someday, about your stay in this America? A once-in-a-lifetime chance, he thought. That's what you think, Monsieur. Defamiliarized, of course, Peter Gutman said, I don't have to tell you that! But totally ruthless about anything personal. Wouldn't he be afraid of my ruthlessness himself? Doesn't matter, Peter Gutman said. He didn't think a writer could ever impose caution or consideration upon him- or herself when writing. I said that it was an unresolvable conflict, and to minimize it I had made it my rule to show less mercy to myself than to anyone else. But what if I was fooling myself there too?

The same conversations over and over again, with changing interlocutors.

I have realized that I take myself as exemplary; in other words, by seeming to focus entirely on myself I leave myself out. A strange motion in opposite directions.

You know, don't you, that Orson Welles had the rug yanked out from under him precisely because he was a little too ruthless in his movie about the powerful Mr. Hearst? He has Kane say on his deathbed the word that becomes the key to the whole movie—"Rosebud." Apparently—listen to this, I have it from an American source—that is what Hearst himself liked to call *a certain part of his lover's anatomy,* she was a famous actress, and he was beside himself that the movie went on and on about this intimate secret of his. He made sure that the movie was not shown in theaters, he bought up and destroyed what he thought were all the copies, and none of the Hearst newspapers was allowed to even mention the movie. Orson Welles had made himself an all-powerful enemy and he never made anything as good again.

I asked Peter Gutman whether he could imagine people who were eager to learn as much as they could about human nature, and to accept all the negative consequences that would arise as a result. To cut up the inner lining of the *overcoat of Dr. Freud* into all its component parts, you know what I mean? The way there are scientists who cannot rest until they figure out all the smaller and smaller particles our universe is made of.

I can imagine that, Peter Gutman said.

Maybe everything that's happened to me recently had to happen so that I could get closer to this knowledge. Directly, through my own skin.

We looked out through the giant windows at the twilight falling and quickly turning into darkness. It seemed to me that a shape was slipping past, I wanted to see Angelina, my angel, in it, it wouldn't have surprised me, but I wasn't sure.

But as we rode down in the glass elevator, Angelina was standing (or floating?) next to me. How did she always know when she was needed? She seemed especially mocking today.

Do you believe in angels? I asked Peter Gutman.

Excuse me, Madame? he said. What's this about?

Just answer.

Okay, fine. I believe in the mind's power to have real effects. That what someone firmly believes becomes reality. If you believe in God then that makes a God and prayers to him can work.

Faith can move mountains?

It gives the faithful confidence that they can move mountains, in any case. And it's certainly possible that the City of Angels is teeming with angels.

Black angels too, Monsieur?

What a question! There's no racism where angels come from.

There was a tried-and-true ritual that played out whenever our community of *scholars* planned a trip. Hearst Castle was scheduled. The bus stopped in front of the MS. VICTORIA, the travelers showed up, always in the same order—the people from the *staff* very punctual, of course, because for them the trip was work; I was usually in the middle; Ria and Pintus came last, without a shred of guilt, or else Peter Gutman, strolling up with an indifferent look on his face, no one dared to criticize him. The driver stowed our bags in the luggage compartment under the bus. I observed who sat next to whom—the married couples stayed together, and at first all the *singles* sat in their own rows, including me, which I preferred anyway, I wanted to see again the views to both the left and the right of the famous Route 101, where the Christian missionaries had erected their *missions* in intervals of a day's journey, to convert the peaceable Indians of the hinterlands to the Christian faith by any means necessary. Malibu sped by out the windows, where at the time, as I read in my old notes, almost uncontrollable fires were raging. Santa Barbara.

Detour: The ranch owned by the director of *Dallas* and *Dynasty*, who had bought himself a beautiful plot of land from his insane wealth—a state-of-the-art ranch, in fact, as we learned from Greg, our tour guide, who was sitting as always next to the driver's seat with a microphone in his hand. Ronald Reagan's ranch was nearby too, and when he landed there in his government plane while he was president, Greg said, all the garage doors in the area opened and closed and the other electronic devices in the houses went crazy because the airplane was so *high tech*.

My old-fashioned taste in art was not news to me; I didn't care at all about the postmodern art that the director of *Dallas* had collected and showed in a bunker-like high-security building—giant canvases, garish colors laid on with wide brushes. Sometimes only a single color. Monochromes, said Lutz, our art historian, who was showing me around. They were *"in"* at the moment. They fit the taste of the times and fetched fantastic prices. There were, of course, several uniformed guards closely watching our steps, along with two art historians on loan from the nearest university to do their master's bidding. *Once or twice a month he spends a weekend at his ranch.*

You know what this reminds me of? Lutz said. The final phase of the Roman Empire. They didn't know they were living in a final phase either. —They didn't want to know it when everything was going so well for them, I said. Why should they ruin their beautiful lives thinking about a bleak future that they couldn't change anyway?

Back on the bus. You're sleeping and missing the best views, Peter Gutman said. We had arrived at the day's destination: the Cavalier Inn in San Simeon, a reasonable hotel near the ocean with nice rooms. I unpacked my bathing suit and nothing else, and went swimming in the comfortable, heated hotel swimming pool. At first I could hardly move my limbs from the pain but slowly my joints relaxed and moved more easily. When I let myself glide on my back through the water, I was looking directly up into the sky, which was then, in the late afternoon, still an unbelievable blue. The crowns of a few palm trees jutted into my field of view. I was alone in the pool and I crossed it, traversed it, on the surface of the water, underwater: it was like a purification ritual.

How I'd always loved to swim. Your river back home was already pretty wide by the time it got to your city, not far from where it flowed into the bigger river called the Oder and from there into the Baltic. It had an incomparable smell—never again did a river smell like that. The public swimming area where old Wegner the attendant taught you to swim was built out of wood directly in the river. Wegner held you under the arms and pulled you against the current, I can feel the flow on my ribs to this day. Swimming around for fifteen minutes, precisely timed, in the deep pool was called "swimming yourself free," a beautiful expression. Then you put your towel carelessly by the other swimmers' towels on the hot wooden planks and lay down on your belly in the sun. In the winter, there were regular swimming lessons in the community pool, which had a strong smell of chlorine; there the swimming was timed, and sturdy Christel, your age, hopeless in all the other classes, was unbeatable. The two thin, awkward girls who were afraid of the water, Brigitte and Ilse, were teased.

Why have I never realized until now that for years, after you were sixteen and settled elsewhere, you had no water? You lived in areas without lakes, without rivers, without swimming pools. After that, your sea was the Eastern Sea, as the Baltic is called there. In the morning, before breakfast, it was ice cold—60 degrees at the very most, a swim of only a couple minutes. The primitive accommodations where you froze and your things barely dried whenever you had ended up there in another rainy summer. But then, in the sun, the glittering water to the horizon, the foaming white crests of the waves that you let yourself be carried by, the big breakers you threw yourself into, swimming all the way out to the buoy, the salt on your skin, wicker beach chairs packed close together, the children with their complicated sand castles, passionate conversations with your friend up on the bluffs about the future of your country—anything was possible. After all, this little Eastern Sea, an ocean of peace, was linked to all the waters in the world, you were "washed with all waters," as the German saying goes—shrewd about everything—why not? Year after year the island, free of cars, flat as the palm of your hand, tea and card games in the glass veranda on days when the rain wouldn't stop outside and evenings with red wine and guitar-playing in the hollows behind the dunes. Carefree, oh how carefree it was. The following year, the guitar was not with you anymore; the famous singer later killed himself, in a lake as it happens.

WASHED WITH ALL WATERS

Why not? But when we went back to the coastal town again last year, we stayed in a chic little hotel and could barely cross the street to the beach since the cars were parked there bumper to bumper, their license plates not just from the area, or Berlin or Dresden, but also from Hamburg and Cologne, and we had to be glad about that, the country is poor and needs tourists on its coast, but we knew we would never go back.

And one time, it comes to me now, you were on the Eastern Sea where it is called the Baltic: in Lithuania, when the country was still part of the Soviet Union. You and G. had come from Leningrad, when the city was not yet named St. Petersburg again. There you had stood on the riverbanks and looked out at the battleship *Aurora*, but here, in Lithuania, you went to see friends you had first met by the Black Sea, on the stony beach of Gagra, and the blond young man there told you he was a writer who was currently working on a piece about Jonah and the whale—you understand, he said, the whale swallows Jonah. You hadn't understood, and he could hardly believe it, the whale was Russia, he said, and Jonah was little Lithuania being swallowed up by it, and you hadn't known that that was how the Lithuanians saw it, and when you and G. visited them they brought you along to some friends' house where they used to meet, and you were not to let it be known that they had brought you there, and they told you about their Lithuanian traditions and gave you a present, cloths woven in their old patterns, cloths that still cover our table today, and they took you with them to the Baltic Sea, which, it seemed to you, they loved in another, more heartfelt way than you loved your Eastern Sea.

And the Scandinavians' way was different still. Out from Stockholm in a ship full of writers, through the archipelago, with Germany East and Germany West down below, and the tentative, polite, attentive conversations. Or else on the crunching ice, at the edge of Copenhagen, discussing with a representative from your country your and his concerns about that country. I had no idea how much would surface within me when I thought the word "sea."

Yes, you swam in the Black Sea too—it was your first encounter with the South, the oranges glowed in the gardens against the deep green leaves. On the beach you belonged to a group in the blink of an eye, a group centered around and led by Marya Sergeyevna, a lawyer from Moscow whom you and G. later had to go see in her high-rise on the Moskva, but here, on the Black Sea, she took you newcomers under her wing and initiated you, in her rough, low, penetrating voice, into the customs of the place and the jurisprudence of the country. These were indeed impenetrable for a foreigner, but Marya Sergeyevna understood them down to the core and left no doubt in her Russian clients' minds that the best she could do for them as their defender was get them off with a milder sentence of five years instead of ten, there was nothing in between, her voice blared out across the beach, and if she did manage five years then the relatives of the sentenced person brought her presents, she thought that was "swell." She had picked up slang like that when she lived in Berlin in the twenties, the greatest time in her life, she said, and my memories of the Black Sea mingle with Marya Sergeyevna's voice and a generous supply of caviar, wrapped in wax paper and an issue of *Pravda*, that she had collected for you at the back doors of the big Moscow restaurants, from cooks who owed her a favor, so that she could give it to you and G. for the plane to Berlin.

Or Brittany. Raw, rainy days by a raw, gray sea, lovely colors and bright warm beaches in Normandy. Looking out from Lisbon and Cannes, and from the edge of Sicily, at the Mediterranean. And now the Pacific Ocean. Was it enough?

And I haven't even mentioned the lakes, where you loved to go swimming—the lake near your childhood home, the lakes around Berlin, the wonderful Mecklenburg lakes. The one lake that became a kind of home for you, on whose shore, far away from the bathing area, the cows came and drank—formerly the co-operative's cows, now the corporation's cows—and whose other shore had a trout farm that has now been given up too. That lake is so clean and so deep that vendace live at the bottom, the sensitive, delicious fish that cannot be transported. The children went crayfish hunting there one summer.

Oh, and yes, Lake Zurich, along whose shore you and G. decided to go back to where you came from. Was it enough?

I had not known that I could link the story of my life to that of the waters in which I swam or by which I stood—and now, inexorably, the rivers of several countries emerge from my memory. Who will have heard of the Wipper, a stream in the Thuringia town where you found a place to live after the war, but almost everyone knows the Pleisse, carrying its stinking whitecaps past you while you were a student in Leipzig; later, in Halle, you lived on the bright bank of the Saale. Then, already, the Spree, Berlin's river, again and again to this day, with the Weidendammer Bridge you crossed again and again at various times: sometimes expectant, sometimes cheerful, sad, hounded, scared. Should I mention the jolly Panke? Definitely the Elbe near Dresden, in the evening light, incomparable, when the light from the low sun in the west fell straight into its riverbed. The Danube, which is not blue and no longer flows through Vienna, though it does flow through Budapest, your first foreign city. But the Vltava, with stones shifting around on its riverbed, which has seen and heard so many things that were important in your life. The majestic Rhine, a foreign river you admired. The quick, smiling Seine; the stolid, hardworking Thames. The Tiber in Rome. And the unforgettable Neva in Leningrad during the white nights, when the graduates processed along the embankments, singing, the girls in white dresses and the boys in dark suits. The Moskva of course, the sullen, taciturn Moskva—one time you even took a ship called *Gogol* along it all the way to Nizhni Novgorod. You never went farther east, never saw the great rivers of Asia and Africa, and never wanted to either. Just one more, the Hudson River, with skyscrapers reflected in it.

Is it enough? Maybe it was too much? Too many good things, that had to come to an end sometime?

I still remember it: Someone gently shook my shoulder. It was Ria, with Ines and Kätchen standing behind her. They had worried looks on their faces and asked me if I was sick. I was lying in bed in the hotel. What do you mean, sick? Well, no one had seen or heard from me since yesterday afternoon; I hadn't come down for dinner, or for breakfast either, and it was already noon.

I was swimming in the pool, I said stupidly, and I realized that that was the last thing I remembered. How I had gotten back to the room, unpacked my nightgown, gone to bed—I had no memory of any of it. I laughed when I told them that. They didn't laugh along with me.

Greg, who was asked for advice despite my protests, pronounced the diagnosis: a blackout. He wanted to take me to a doctor. I refused so violently that he let it go, but he made me promise to tell them immediately about any symptom I had, no matter how small. In any case, there was no time for a long discussion because the group was already gathering for the drive to Hearst Castle. Peter Gutman sat down next to me in the bus and looked sidelong at me.

So there was something your subconscious was trying to tell you, he said.

Yes, I said, there was. That I am a water person and shouldn't always stay on dry land.

I've never seen you in such a good mood, he said.

And that makes you suspicious, or what?

I sat next to Peter Gutman in my good mood, in the bus that drove us up the mountain in a magnificent hilly landscape with barely any trees. We were dropped off in front of a building that resembled more than anything else a small airport's departure hall, where you had to stand in line for tickets. I was in a mood to find everything funny, especially the welcome the visitors received from a man, no longer young, in a proper sea-blue suit, white shirt, and tie, wearing a straw hat, an employee of the state of California but one who deeply identified with William Randolph and led us through the site, from the outdoor pool ringed with Greek columns and statues—some genuine, some less genuine, the guide said straight out—through the magnificent garden, tended by eight gardeners, up a swooping staircase into one of the guesthouses, whose rooms were stuffed full of old furniture and were mostly dark and lugubrious—we wouldn't want to stay there, we assured each other—but everyone had stayed there, from Garbo to Chaplin, and whenever any of the guests misbehaved and fell from their host's good graces, they might get back from an excursion and find their suitcases packed and standing in front of the door, next to a waiting taxi: goodbye for good.

It all made me laugh, including the fact that Mr. Hearst let his guests sleep in double rooms only if they were married, while he himself was bringing Marion Davies here, his *mistress* of many years, because his Catholic wife would not agree to a divorce. In some sort of compensation, he had Marion's bedroom hung full of genuine paintings of the Madonna, and kept the alcohol locked away from her in a metal safe.

I thoroughly disliked the main building in the complex, where the owner lived, the one whose facade was like a cathedral—I hated everything about it: the gloomy room where the guests had to appear for dinner punctually thirty minutes before the master of the house, the massive flower-pattern armchairs, the refectory more like a medieval knight's hall than anything else, with rows of flags along the top of the walls, dark wainscoting, gigantic expensive tapestries, every inch of wall space filled with art that had been bought up around the world during the Depression, when everything was cheap. Original Renaissance ceilings in every room. And then, as the showstopping high point, the phenomenal "Roman Pool," which not a few cities would surely have loved to have for their residents, bathed in a mysterious light from a row of milky lanterns.

Rome in its final days. I rest my case, said Lutz standing next to me. This can't end well. It's always a bad sign when the top stratum of a society does not want to live in its own era anymore, but prefers to imagine itself back in an earlier age.

Then I realized, I remember, that I was happy to live in my own era. I could not wish I had lived in any other time. Despite everything? Despite everything. I felt a certain curiosity about whether that would remain true. Maybe the explosions in the corridors of capitalism are signs of the end times, at least for our Western culture, but I enjoy the advantages of this culture like almost everyone else.

The trip to Hearst Castle was a turning point: after it my goodbyes began, although they stretched out for weeks, during which I had the feeling of living in an ever more fragmented reality. It was as though the substance of the world, whatever that might mean, were eluding me. I lived between two realities: one of them sunk beneath the sea, no longer in need of any interventions from me, and the other, supposedly future reality, seeming to pull farther and farther away and not have anything to do with me

Maybe it doesn't touch me yet, I said to Peter Gutman during our last long conversation. We were sitting one more time on our bench on Ocean Park Promenade, talking and falling silent, watching the joggers and walkers and strollers go by individually and in groups, talking to each other in their various languages. We would miss that. We spent one more long afternoon waiting for the sun to go down.

He now knew, he said, that he would be able to finish his book about his philosopher. He said he had not had the courage until then to pose questions as radically as this man demanded: always keeping the sentence "But a storm is blowing from paradise" in mind, and always exposing himself to the storm.

Once again we cannot hope for what will happen, I said to Peter Gutman. A patchwork life, I said. The different pieces sloppily stitched together.

Write that down, Peter Gutman said.

The air grew gentler toward evening, the heat receded over the ocean, we didn't want to leave. I thought: I will always remember this light. But now I remember only that that is what I thought—the light itself, hanging over the Pacific Ocean shortly before sunset, I have forgotten. The smell of the eucalyptus trees too. But I know that it's there, so I haven't entirely lost it.

Did you know that Freud asked for an assisted suicide at the end of his life? I asked.

Naturally he knew.

By the way, he said after a while, do you still have it memorized?

I knew right away what he meant and I quoted it back to him almost without missing a beat: "Be undismayed in spite of everything; do not give up, despite everything."

We agreed that he could request the full text from me at any time, in case he should ever need it. He never did request it.

By the way, he said after another while. We're not phoning each other anymore. It's going all right. Not great, but all right.

I had thought so.

The sun quickly vanished. It was quickly dark. We stood in front of our bench and formally bowed: *Nice to meet you, Monsieur.*

The pleasure is mine, Madame.

Rachel, in her tiny shack on the corner of Twenty-sixth and Broadway: Feldenkrais teaches us, she said, to achieve greater effects with less effort through small movements. I lay down on a table and she had me find the most comfortable position and then she started to move my legs in various ways, very little and very gently. *Your mind will tell you: That's a Feldenkrais therapist, she wouldn't hurt me. But your system is not so sure. I respect your system.* She had me find the right distance apart to place my feet, and showed me a way to stand up that was less of a strain. What a person has learned badly can be relearned properly, she said, it was all about gently readjusting one's inefficient movements. After the treatment my joints really were "*softer*," my mood was brighter, I felt eager to do something good for myself, for instance to make myself some hot chocolate and "*let it be.*" Was that my last hour with her? Did she give me that advice to take with me when I left?

—

The nun would have said the same thing. I took her book with me when I drove out to see Sally, who had begged me to come see her one more time. She wanted to show me a video, a movie she had shot herself, with herself as the only actress. I scanned her face for signs of a change and didn't find them. She may have looked even older. There was one bit of progress at least: she had filed for a divorce, stating as her grounds for divorce: hate. Hatred of Ron and of herself. She was so out of touch with reality that she was hoping this step would hurt him. And I did not have the courage to tell her.

She was seeing her therapist four times a week, she said, and had of course discovered that her feelings of worthlessness were connected with her mother—who, by the way, was paying for the therapy. Sally made a salad while she talked without stopping, heated up some fish and vegetables in the microwave, made pasta, and talked and talked. About how lonely she was, how jealous she was. That she couldn't stop digging deeper and deeper in her imagination into Ron and his lover's love life. That she was unable to do what her analyst kept waiting for her to do—feel a normal straightforward pain at her loss. Instead, she had only this endless self-torture.

We ate. The light in her small apartment was pretty that evening—a northern light that picked up the reflections of the evening sun from different surfaces outside before it entered her room.

Then Sally showed me the video she had been working on for a while: a ruthless piece of self-expression, a naked display of pure suffering. First, herself as a younger, beautiful woman, putting on makeup and getting dressed. Then herself as she was now: looking much older, with gray hair, crying, talking to the camera, asking questions. Herself driving a car, talking as she drove. Herself in a bra and panties, in her apartment, moving, trying out a few dance steps. Ron's voice, something that she happened to have on tape, and her own voice saying the same words, intercut with each other. Fade in to toys, clowns, penguins in their full puppetlike nature, a dog that couldn't stop rubbing his sexual organ against a rock. Then more of herself, again and again. Her face, her body, sometimes naked too. Suitable music as a soundtrack.

I was surprised at first but then touched and moved. None of it was embarrassing or sentimental, it was all professional without being the least bit professionalized, it was courageous, going right up to a borderline and then crossing it. Why do such artistic expressions always have to be caused by suffering? But why did I even ask, I knew the answer myself.

I told Sally how good I thought the piece was, what she had done, and we talked about the final lines that she still had to add. I knew my praise would not ease her pain. We hugged each other a long time when we said goodbye. Will you come back? she asked. —I don't know, I said, and I thought: Not likely. But maybe you'll come to Europe? —*I don't think so*, she said. Finally I gave her back the nun's book. I had underlined a sentence for her—and for myself: *My whole life is a process of learning how to make friends with myself.*

The goodbyes. I try to recall them—such an appropriate word in German for "recall": *vergegenwärtigen*, "bring them into the present"! The "*gang*" was sitting in the MS. VICTORIA's inner courtyard, everyone had brought along "something to eat," by which was meant mainly something to drink. We had to say goodbye to Therese, who had finished her assignment on the mayoral election in this city. The candidate we liked had lost, of course. It takes some effort now to put myself back into the mood of that evening, which by the way was as if bathed in a long, bright twilight—the word fits, for once, as though the darkness had not simply fallen all at once as it usually did in that country; as though there were no moon or stars, just our circle grouped around a couple of camping tables on patched-up chairs with bottles of the most various sorts and colors in front of us. We topped off each other's glasses—any old glass we had snatched up—and ate sandwiches, a big wheel of cheese, bread, crackers, vegetables. If only someone had turned on a tape recorder! Or at least preserved in memory what the hours-long conversation was about. We were amazed to realize that we already had memories in common, which were perfect for letting us give the sturdy, basic conversational formula—"You remember . . . ?"—and cascades of laughter, as though we had only experienced utterly hilarious things together. Susan had in fact missed out on buying the house she had been in negotiations for—weeks ago by that point. Typical Susan. She laughed along with us. Or Therese, with her L.A. mania. How she was excited about everything, even the homeless man who had shamelessly robbed her. Laughter. Or even Margery, who had in fact flown to Berlin and come back in raptures—it's the center of the world these days!—

with the idea, in all seriousness, of opening an American Western restaurant in Prenzlauer Berg: they don't have one of those yet. For that she would give up her rich American married couples in need of therapy in a heartbeat. Sympathetic laughter. Toby offered to design her restaurant's interior for her. So his plans to head off to Mexico weren't set in stone? Therese perked up, felt hope. Well, if we're turning it into an expedition, Jane said, maybe you need a photojournalist there too? To document the whole thing, from the planning and construction phase on? Wild cheers. You can stay with me, I said.

Yes, of course! We were all a bit drunk but that can't have been all it was. It was also the moment in time that was well suited to such fantasies. A year earlier, they would not have come up; a year later, they would no longer come up. For a very short time, what we called "reality" hung suspended, and we unconsciously adapted to this condition of suspension.

The word "Iraq" used as a threat didn't exist yet; certain photographs had not yet appeared on the front pages of the newspapers. In retrospect it seems that, whatever we liked to believe about ourselves—that we were hard-headed cool customers, ready for anything—we were still, even then, a little naive. Still a little too innocent, measured by today's standards. "Innocent": an unjustifiable word at the end of a century of extremes, of violence, rivers of blood, waves of betrayal, denunciations, every possible kind of mean and dirty trick, which no one alive in that century escaped. But still, but still . . . These people sitting here on a bright twilit evening, I felt, seemed to be placing an almost culpable hope in the future.

Someone suggested we sing. Again I had the experience of seeing that Americans don't know any songs. Finally we decided on "We Shall Overcome." They had sung it with enthusiasm back in the day. They wanted to hear "Am Brunnen vor dem Tore" from us two Germans.

Suddenly the stars leapt out after all and we blew out our candles so that we could see them clearly. There was silence. Greg shouted down a nighttime greeting from a window on one of the upper floors. It was late when we picked up all the trash, put it in bags, and parted. Angelina too had vanished.

John and Judy had gone to Berlin, to meet John's new East Berlin relatives in person.

The time that had seemed so endless grew short.

I saw Bob Rice one more time. Hey, he said, when we were saying goodbye. *What about my overcoat?*

Oh, Bob, I said. That overcoat is indestructible. It has served me well. I believe I've given it back to you already.

Bob said he had figured as much.

The *goodbye parties* came closer and faster. One time, I drove my Geo without air-conditioning all the way down Olympic Boulevard, in melting heat, to Doheny Drive to buy sixty veal sausages from the famous German butcher shop there and then spent a whole morning making an enormous bowl of potato salad. We all brought a dish from our homeland along with all the bottles we had with any alcohol left in them. That was an especially nice party. Francesco, still with his thick accent, gave a warm speech of thanks and farewell, and the director of the *staff* told us how happy he was that we seemed to have enjoyed our time here after all, that we had not only viewed them and the whole institution with skepticism—he could say without hesitation that we seemed like the most skeptical group that they, the *staff*, had ever had, but also the most capable and independent.

Mrs. Ascott was wearing one of her big flowy dresses with a floral print, and still barely knew who any of us were, but started, under the influence of the strong drinks she seemed to prefer, to talk to various residents who crossed her path and trap them in long, meandering conversations, during which she never looked at the person she was talking to but fixed her gaze on a point behind their left shoulders. Francesco said: You know what's wrong with her? She has a complex. Mr. Enrico, meanwhile, threw caution to the winds and revealed himself to be a dashing Mexican, by no means disinclined to dance with preferred members of the female sex. Ria and Ines took turns—he's wearing us out, Ria said.

The director sat down next to me. He wanted to know what I had planned now. I'm taking a trip through the Southwest, I said. To see the Hopi Indians, among other things.

Ah, the director said. You're looking for the soul of America. *Good luck.*

Angelina stood on the stairs, watching the party. She smiled when

I walked past her. I did not say goodbye to her. *See you later*, I said. She did not seem surprised.

I remember I vacillated about whether I should really take that trip to the American Southwest with Lowis and Sanna. I finally agreed, mostly because of the friends who said I couldn't pass up a chance like that, and then I was surprised to find myself actually sitting in the plane to Albuquerque, a city I had hardly ever heard of and knew nothing about. I noticed that I entered an atmosphere of clarity, somewhere over Arizona, and that this clarity remained with me for my entire trip (which lasted not even ten days), and that the seat next to me in the plane was empty but I knew who was sitting there—Angelina had come with me, we had wordlessly agreed on that. I had understood that she would always be there when I needed her. The confusion of the period I had just been through fell away.

Was I only now, finally, arriving in this country? It was a country built on myths and it was as if the previous months, lived in the thick of reality, were melting away; as if this dusty place with the desert winds blowing in were the first American city I saw, the Indian women sitting in their taciturn row under the arcades on the main square and offering ceramics with Indian patterns for sale were the first American women I saw, and the round, beehive-shaped pueblos we visited on the road to Santa Fe were the way dwellings here should be.

Lui, a friend of Sanna's, was a psychoanalyst who had been given her name by the Indian healer who had saved her from a serious childhood illness when the other doctors had given her up for lost. She lived with her dogs in the northern part of the city, on the edge of the desert, and she let us spend the night in her bungalow filled with Indian art: colored pottery and masks, carvings, woven rugs and fabrics that Lui herself wore. She had no intention, she said, of worming her way into another culture and claiming to belong to something she didn't belong to, but it also would have felt wrong to her to live here surrounded by the insignificant everyday objects that the average American is so unable to do without.

Her bungalow cast a spell that we could not escape and didn't want to escape. We could easily imagine that patients would want to come see her here. She mentioned in passing at some point that people came to see her from Los Alamos too, seeking advice and healing, including a lot of women who could no longer bear their empty lives on the margins of the research labs where their husbands worked on the most horrible weapons under the strictest orders to keep their work top secret. When the husbands came to her for advice themselves, she said, the FBI came hot on their heels and wanted to find out what they had said, whether they were a security risk. Lui said she didn't lie but didn't tell them the whole truth either, and she discussed with her patients what she could tell the FBI agents—intelligent, psychologically trained people—without causing problems for the patients. "The soul of America," I said, and Lui told me with a resigned laugh that this soul had long since been strapped down to an operating table, to be dissected and indoctrinated under glaring surgical lights.

But then how could she do her job?

By making compromises, like everyone else, she said. And taking care that the core of her work wasn't damaged in the process.

Luckily I marked our route with a thick red pen on a map of *Indian Country*, otherwise there is no way I would have been able to remember the bizarre path we took—heading basically west but with two long detours north. And without the notes I took, in a red spiral notebook, what would I still retain from our trip, which, the whole time it lasted, I felt was unforgettable? Or without the photos showing us deeply immersed in our notebooks, surrounded by sparse, spiny desert plants, in the shade of our hardworking greenish Opel glittering in the sun?

Did we already know that we were on our way to the outermost extremes of American life?

LOS ALAMOS wasn't on our way but we had to include it, no question. So, north: from Santa Fe on a road lined with pueblos. The atomic bomb had been planned and built in the middle of one of the largest Indian reservations in the United States. The paltry, unassuming little museum—the first to be dedicated to the pioneers of Los Alamos—claimed that the Indians had gladly put part of their land at the disposal of the builders of the bomb, because they were loyal citizens of the United States who wanted to do their part for victory in the war; they were proud of their sons who served in the army and fought on the front lines together with white Americans.

If you wanted to see the museum you had to buy a ticket from an older man, possibly a veteran, who was hardly right for his job and whose unhelpfulness only increased the impression of something provisional and makeshift. We saw in illustrations that the technology developed in the labs of this scientific oasis had been literally conjured up out of the desert sands, and the top scientists who brought this miracle about had lived very modestly, almost primitively, submitting to the most rigid security precautions of a director who probably suffered from paranoia. They had had to endure living completely cut off from the outside world. The letter from one young scientist to his mother, after the atomic bomb was dropped on Hiroshima, was bursting with relief: now that their project had successfully been tried in public, he could finally reveal what he had been working on for so long. And neither he nor any other scientist who spoke up after Hiroshima had any doubt about the noble purpose and necessity of building the bomb. The whole museum told a story of heroes. It was as though, we said to each other, depressed, someone had waved a magic wand, back in 1945, and turned normal human feelings to ice.

THE BOMB: The new museum that had just opened—steel and glass, massive, built with the latest technology—was one big display of pride. Unlike the pathetic little museum next door, this one showed the various individual steps that led to the desired result: THE BOMB, replicated actual size in the middle of the central room. How can I put a name to the feeling that came over me as I circled around this bomb, stood in front of it, looked up at it? It was a mixture of shuddering horror and grief. While the Americans, who had come in their bigger and smaller groups to see Los Alamos, showed their admiration and pride.

I couldn't help thinking about Einstein, not for the first time, whose signature on a letter to the president of the United States had set in motion the production of the bomb. About the nights he spent after it was dropped on Hiroshima and Nagasaki. I thought: We have gotten used to seeing well-intentioned men like him, who had the misfortune of being geniuses in dangerous scientific fields, in strangleholds of irresolvable conflicts and unavoidable guilt.

We walked back to our car in silence. As a kind of compulsory exercise, we circled the giant no-trespassing zone, secured in an unbroken ring of barbed wire and with strict warnings posted. A cluster of ugly new buildings—labs and testing sites—had spread. We had no doubt that highly specialized scientists, under much more ideal conditions and for much more money than the first pioneers at Los Alamos had, were developing here, in strictest secrecy, much more effective means of destruction than the good old-fashioned atomic bomb. They had already destroyed the natural beauty of the region—that was an unavoidable side effect. We wanted to leave this place as fast as we could.

Then we were sitting in a somewhat gloomy Western-style restaurant, gnawing on steaks the size of the plate: the only dish on the menu. Sanna wondered out loud why our civilization had chosen the path of self-destruction, a decision Lowis considered irreversible. Was it a disposition in our genes? Newer research contradicted this hypothesis: Very small children, even before they could talk, apparently helped adults when something happened to them and they needed help, without being trained to do so. But was early man's merciless struggle for survival so deeply ingrained into us that even today the drive to be on top at any cost crushed all the other, "more human" needs? She thought about such questions all the time—she was just then preparing to put on a play about Robert Oppenheimer, with nonprofessional actors who wouldn't settle for the usual superficial answers. I had also planned to write something about an atomic physicist once, I said. A film script. Did they know the name Klaus Fuchs? They did. The famous atomic spy, right?

He came from a family of Protestant theologians, I said, and was given a classical education. When Hitler came to power, he had to leave Germany and he worked in England on developing the prerequisites that led up to building the bomb. Then he passed his knowledge along to the Soviets. He was convinced, I said, that the only way to prevent the destruction of huge swaths of the world was if the two superpowers were equally advanced in atomic research. When he was caught, he was sentenced as a British citizen to fourteen years in prison, I told Sanna and Lowis, and after his pardon he came to the GDR in 1959, where he became the deputy director of the nuclear research facility in Rossendorf, near Dresden. Neither of them had known that.

At the time, you and G. were fascinated by his moral conflict and what he saw as the only way out: creating a balance of terror. Your and G.'s friend, the director Konrad Wolf, wanted to make a movie about it. He had to pull strings "in high places" to get access to Fuchs.

Then, one day, you were actually standing in his office in Dresden. He was a tall, very thin man, reserved, almost severe. The word "Prussian" came to mind, and: "man of integrity." He listened to what you and G. had to say, then told you that he had given his word never to speak about this matter with anyone. As long as he remained bound by this promise, he would say nothing. With that, you were shown the door.

Might have known that would happen, Konrad Wolf said. Still, it was worth a try. You never forgot the impression Klaus Fuchs made on you and the aura of unapproachability that surrounded him.

Still, Sanna said, did the scientists' work on the atomic bomb really help defeat National Socialism? Didn't a scientist have a fundamental duty to refuse to work on a weapon that in the end could destroy the human species? Or did the end justify the means, and scientists had to do everything in their power to go after the destroyers of humanity with their own terrible weapons? In other words, guilty in either case? And then another, even more unimaginable turn of the screw: being asked to determine the targets on which to drop the bombs they had built.

They surely could not have imagined beforehand how Hiroshima would look afterward. It's the conflict of the ancient tragedies, Sanna said. But why does the conflict of Orestes, or Iphigenia, seem human to me, while the conflicts our atomic physicists find themselves in seem inhuman? Is it the monstrous perfection of the means of destruction? Does the fact that human existence itself hangs in the balance raise the conflict to another level? Is our history divided now into a Before and After?

Lowis said that when well-intentioned people are faced with such dilemmas, it is the society they live in that is sick. Maybe fatally sick.

I wondered what you had actually done on August 6, 1945. You had not heard anything about the bomb, in any case; I think you wouldn't hear anything about it for a long time. There was no newspaper where you were living, in a barn in a Mecklenburg village, and the occupying forces had confiscated the radios. It was a beautiful summer. You probably sat in a mayor's office and filled out forms.

In my motel room I took up the chronicle of my trip. My word processor was already on a ship crossing the ocean on its way back to Europe. I wrote by hand:

A history of irresolvable conflicts would be worth writing. Where would it have to start? With the Greeks? In any case, irresolvable conflicts are characteristic of modernity. What made stone-age people or primitive farmers unhappy was different in kind from the misfortunes of modern men and women. There is no way they

could have felt the terrible demands of conscience we
feel when we see that we cannot avoid making a decision
but that none of our choices is the right one. That no
choice we have is between right and wrong.

I was not surprised that Angelina had joined me here. Without her, the night I spent in that grim, damp-smelling motel room on a gigantic double bed would have been too horrible. From the threadbare armchair in the corner of the room, next to the television set, she surveyed all the objects in this sad dwelling. Through her actions alone, she made me understand that there was a connection between such rooms and the glowing bomb in the museum flooded with light. One was a precondition for the other. What are you doing, Angelina? I said unhappily. She straddled the bomb and flew out through the big window.

The next day we drove a long way through New Mexico in bad weather and spent the night at the Thunderbird Lodge, whose rooms were depressingly like all the other rooms we stayed in during our trip.

I dreamed: A few tourists are setting out for an expedition, we are all wearing yellow parkas and even rain hats, the leader of our group warns us about the "nasty" weather we will face. He doesn't inspire much confidence but for some reason it seems to be impossible to change our minds now that we've agreed to go. One of the two inconspicuous women in our group says: God sees all. We have to take a *"hidden way."* Then the other says: If God sees everything anyway, we can take a totally open way too. I brood about what it is we have to hide and which of the two is right, and I cannot decide. I know only that I don't want to be here, but I can't think where else I want to be. Then I think:

I want to live in a world where there are still secrets. Where it's not the case that every secret has
to be violently ripped away from everyone because that
is the only way to purify the world.

I woke up exhausted and with sore limbs. The weather was even worse than in my dream: cold, rainy, windy. We decided to spend an additional day in the Thunderbird Lodge and we let ourselves be talked into joining a tour group taking a trip to the Canyon de Chelly that afternoon, despite the nasty weather. We pulled on all the warm clothes we had. We would be driving in an open truck. Rain gear was handed out—that is what saved us. The wind had dropped off a bit too, but still, we got miserably cold as the day went on.

Timothy, a Navajo Indian—the Navajo are the largest Indian tribe in Arizona—was our driver and guide. He introduced himself as having been born in the canyon, it was his *playground,* and he had been leading tours through the canyon for nine years, twice a day. He stopped the truck at the tourist attractions. We stood in driving snow at a lookout point on the northern rim of the canyon, from which we could not only look down into the deep ravine but see the Anasazi ruins farther below: dwellings nested into one another, built into caves—the remains of a mysterious ancient people who had lived there for centuries and then inexplicably vanished, Timothy said. They must have been short, judging from the size of their homes. We saw their pictograms on the steep opposite cliff—white drawings of antelopes, dancing men, two swastikas too, and the sun and moon as two circles, one bigger and one smaller, beautiful and moving. Timothy thought the Anasazi had prayed every morning to "*Sunny Moon.*" He did not say how he knew it, how he could have known it, but I wanted to believe it. I could feel the mystery of this ancient people taking hold of me, and it would never let me go.

The later Navajo people had added other pictograms in red next to the Anasazi's white ones: more antelopes, but also horses, which they must have seen when the Spanish came. We kept seeing more Anasazi ruins in the caves in the steep cliff faces under overhanging rocks. They were probably ceremonial sites and could only be reached from above, by ladders. No, said Timothy (who had an Indian name too, of course, which he told us when we asked him to)—no, he couldn't tell us why these original inhabitants had left their territory, somewhere around the year 1200. Or where they had gone. The Hopi, they said that the Anasazi were among their ancestors. Timothy shrugged his shoulders.

He spoke English with a thick accent. He told us words from the Navajo language. The "little words" in Navajo were analogous to the "little words" of the Alaska Indians in Canada, he said. Not the big words. But they could understand each other's language. The Anasazi did not have a written language, he said, so we don't know much for sure about how they lived or what they believed.

It got dark and ice-cold; we were freezing. Timothy still wanted to show us the farmland at the base of the canyon, which had been in the possession of the same families since the start of the nineteenth century and had never been sold. They farmed wheat and corn. And—*what I don't like*, Timothy said, with an embarrassed laugh—is that the land belongs to the women. They pass it on to their daughters. Something's got to change there, in Timothy's opinion. And names? I asked excitedly. Children get their names from their fathers, of course, Timothy said. I would have very much liked to learn more about these remnants of matriarchy in patriarchal culture.

It happened at some point during this tour of the canyon, with its intense red and ocher tones that blazed back to life almost painfully against the bright green of the trees shortly before sunset (the sky had cleared up toward evening)—it was then that something fundamental changed within me. By the time we got out of the truck in front of our motel, the moon had risen too—big and red and aggressive. I stood there and looked at it and felt a message reach me, or an insight, I don't know what to call it. I took a deep breath. I was free.

All right then, Angelina said. —But now is when I really need you, I said. Stay with me! —Okay, Angelina said, not with much enthusiasm, but why should the first angel I meet be enthusiastic about my requests anyway? Okay, okay, my angel was a black woman who didn't take me especially seriously, I couldn't deny it, but still, she had agreed, and angels keep their promises. Angelina smiled mockingly. She would keep an eye on me. I could see that she was overextended but nonetheless I didn't hesitate to take advantage of her.

We went to a Navajo-run restaurant where the service was unfriendly and the portions were generous but the food was not to my taste. Suddenly, because of the storm, which had picked up again outside, the lights went out; the Navajo waitresses stood giggling in a corner, it was dark for a long time. The room got quieter and quieter—it had been very loud before, with tourists carrying on in ways they probably wouldn't have permitted themselves at home. Then candles were distributed to the tables, first very thin candles, then a bit later thick ones, in tall glasses. How romantic, Sanna said. Like Lowis and me, she could not get free of the images she had seen on our tour.

Maybe this was why I had come to America?

The rooms in all the motels are big and furnished the same: at least three people could spend the night in them, the beds are very wide and very soft, with the same synthetic blankets covering the sheets, the TV preset to the same channel, the same slightly musty smell that the same cleaning products try to banish. Arizona is a "dry" state, so we sat together in Sanna and Lowis's room for another fifteen minutes or so and had a sip of the good whiskey Lowis had brought along. Both of them were sensitive to the same vibrations as I was—I could tell by the way they were talking about the Anasazi. They were deeply moved, even reverent, and shaken.

Did it already come to my mind that first evening—the motto that would be a kind of guidepost for our whole trip?

A JOURNEY TO THE OTHER SIDE OF REALITY

The feeling of going outside of time grew stronger and stronger. Outside of time or outside of my own skin. At some point, the motto came to me: It was a Dream Vacation, and not only because I was taken through the strangest dreams during it, night after night. They came as less and less of a surprise as the trip went on, in fact—I prefer to avoid the word "addicted"—I started to wait for them.

Sanna came to breakfast with two beautiful ceramic drinking bowls in black and white Navajo patterns from the *gift shop*, where she had already spent an hour looking around. She gave one of the bowls to Lowis and they both drank, each from their own bowl, toasting each other with their eyes. It seemed to me that they were renewing a promise.

Lowis was studying a brochure about the life of the Anasazi—we had decided to see what we could of their traces. Their name, by the way, meant "The Oldest People": a name the Navajo had given them since no one knew what they had called themselves. We would set out for Mesa Verde, then, apparently one of the main Anasazi sites. We unexpectedly ended up back in an incredible red landscape, where the sandstone the roads and ground and cliffs were made of was every shade of red and ocher. We looked and looked; we couldn't get enough of it.

When I close my eyes, so many years later, a pale reflection of the sight rises up, providing a background for the news report that occupies my attention today: Geologists plan to declare the Holocene—the era in which we live and which, compared to earlier geological eras, is actually quite short—already at an end, and to proclaim in its place the

Anthropocene. It has been proven that the human species is now the most powerful force causing changes in and on the surface of the earth—the mass extinction of species, the emergence of new building materials (bricks, concrete), and changes that geologists will perceive only in future centuries. Some want to take Hiroshima as the start of the new epoch, others the start of the industrial age: 1800.

The Anasazi left no destruction behind them when they silently cleared out of their old settlement areas and moved to the more miserable regions that we were yet to encounter on our trip.

Since the red in the landscape is indescribable, I took an enormous number of photographs, going against my usual habit, even though I already knew that I would end up with prints that could only be disappointing. The red faded as we drove farther along the almost empty road; gray-green took its place. When we saw the signposts pointing us toward Four Corners Monument we had to follow them, until we found ourselves in front of the rock that marked the meeting place of four states: Arizona, New Mexico, Utah, and Colorado. We saw that other groups of people gathered before the monument apparently felt great respect for this place; we were unmoved, left quickly, and approached Mesa Verde, which we had read and heard so much about. We passed Sleeping Mountains, which communicated their relaxation to the landscape and whose peaks and cliffs were covered with snow.

It had taken longer to drive there than we had thought it would, and then it was another forty-five-minute drive up to the high plateau, the "green table." It was late and the friendly ranger working at the museum told us it would close in half an hour, but we didn't let that stop us, we wanted to learn about the various stages of the settlement of Mesa Verde and about the Anasazi, who had lived there for eight hundred years, built their houses in the sandstone under the overhanging rocks—under the edges of the canyons, so that they were almost impossible to reach from the outside—and dug their ceremonial chambers even deeper underground: the round kivas that you could enter only via ladder from an opening up above. It is presumed, we read on the plaques on the walls of the museum, that the women built the houses and that the tribes were matrilineal. Then we walked around the mesa and saw many of the cave ruins, and ended with the famous, many-chambered Sun Temple. There was a biting wind; it was sunny but unbelievably cold. We had not expected to spend so much time on our trip freezing.

By the museum's exit there was a large display window: *What we owe to the Indians.* It showed what the "white man" had adopted from the Indians, from medicines to plant products.

We were glad to get back in the warm car. Sanna and Lowis took turns driving and I could lie down on the backseat, wrapped in a blanket. I didn't see how the darkness overtook us. I lost myself in a labyrinth whose walls were like the walls of the Anasazi buildings; the thread that was to lead me out was not Ariadne's but, obviously, Angelina's—a thread that my angel had put in my hand, I could talk to her perfectly naturally, could ask her if these Anasazi weren't "more human" than we rich white people today. Angelina didn't answer such questions, I knew that already, and she considered guilt feelings worthless—in her view, they only kept you from living your life and being happy and going ahead and doing whatever was necessary today irrespective of whatever we had to reproach ourselves for in the past.

I said nothing. I had already secretly thought, rather often, that my angel's wisdom was a little simplistic—she probably could not fully understand the complex psyche of modern men and women. But I never expressed that out loud, and it didn't seem very important either.

We could not wait to get to the Southwestern Grand Hotel in Dolores, where we had made a reservation, and where Freddy, a short, wizened man, greeted us at the reception desk. He was a hotel owner it would have been impossible to invent as a fictional character, and he showed us to our rooms with excessive politeness and a look on his face that said we should be overcome with excitement. What we saw was a dollhouse: five rooms of a pink nightmare, tiny, dark even when the little lamps with their pink shades were on, with vases of plastic flowers on every available surface no matter how small, the blinds down, the windows unopenable, a minuscule closet, a minuscule shower with pink walls and pink towels. This, Freddy believed, was how Europeans liked their hotels—he was trying to give them what they wanted. I felt my mood growing darker and darker under his flood of talking.

The others seemed to be having a similar reaction; we needed a drink. Freddy, we learned, had not been in business for very long and did not have a liquor license. He pointed out a cramped *liquor store* across the street, where finally, after a lot of to-ing and fro-ing, an unbelievable old lady who must have escaped from a Miss Marple movie actually sold us some bottles of red wine, which she was reluctant to part with: *I told my husband to buy more red wine!* We also bought some whiskey and tequila, which of course made the Alcohol Lady highly suspicious of us. *Be careful!* she called after us as we left.

Freddy, for his part, who completely approved of our purchases, ran into difficulties. He wanted to serve us our wine in coffee cups so that the people at the other tables in the small restaurant couldn't see how he was abetting our sinful indulgence. Finally, he found a solution: Since the restaurant was divided with a lot of wood into "railroad compartments," he maneuvered us to a table in the farthest corner of the least conspicuous compartment. No one could see in. On the table there, as on every other table, stood a little wooden train, transporting salt and pepper. Freddy had the courage to bring us wineglasses there, and had a glass with us, while a young blond girl with heavily made-up eyes took our orders. *American food*, giant portions for low prices.

Freddy, though, wouldn't leave us alone. While we ate our steak, we heard everything about his family: His grandfather, a Volga German, had come over in 1906 and struggled to make it as a farmer; his father had staggered from one economic collapse to the next; he, Freddy, became a *policeman* in Ohio, a good job, *you know?*, but still gave it all up one day and moved here to Colorado with his wife and children, quickly deciding to buy this little hotel after taking a crash course in hotel management with a friend. Now he was bringing together his whole family from all over America. His brother was already there, the blond girl working as a waitress was one of his nieces, and his sister from Kansas City was coming soon. You see here before you, he said, raising his glass of red wine, a happy man. We gave him our rather faint congratulations.

The next morning, after a quick look around the place, we all agreed that Dolores was the ideal location for a thriller taking place in old-time America. There was the old Rio Grande Southern Railway station, long since out of service but preserved in its old-fashioned beauty, and there was the baker couple too, Irene and Alf, who embodied bygone times in another way. She was from Kreuzberg, in Berlin; he had brought her over after his time in the army and now they sold German antiques and baked German-style bread and cookies. They showed us their woodstove, we bought rye bread and *Bienenstich* almond-cream pastries that we would eat that night in my hotel room in Kayenta, but first we had to visit the *blacksmith*, an eighty-six-year-old man who still worked (*Why not?*), making cast-iron weathervanes for the whole village. He had come back to Dolores, he said, where, sixty-one years ago, he had found his wife—he had brought his wife back to her family. He was originally Dutch and had come to America with his parents as a young child.

For once I'd actually like to meet someone whose parents were American, Sanna said, while we drove south toward Cortez, turned off to the west, and found ourselves on a *dirt road* heading for Kayenta, back in another red landscape that eventually turned into fertile land. On the bumpy, little-used road, we passed an abandoned farm. And then, in a fenced-in ranch on the right, we saw—and it really was a vision, surpassing our wildest expectations—a cowboy, on a horse with no saddle. I don't believe it, Sanna whispered. We stopped. He herded his many cows with a lasso, exactly the way we knew from movies. Then he rode up to the fence to take a look at us, with dignity, a man in his fifties wearing torn clothes and a big cowboy hat. Next to him on another saddleless horse rode a boy about six years old, clearly the man's son, with a bright red shirt and, of course, a cowboy hat.

The man asked where we were from, and repeated back the names of the foreign countries. He had been born in this valley, he said; he took his herd into the mountains above Dolores in the summer. They were going to be branded tomorrow. He asked about our jobs, which he hadn't heard of, and then he asked: *What do you think about eternal life?* and in response to our evasive, embarrassed stammering he gave us a short speech about the "Savior." He scorned the established churches; he had been converted. He wouldn't say the name of the sect he belonged to, it wasn't about that, our Savior and Redeemer had promised us eternal life. We got the impression that the man was blessing us before we drove on. I was glad I took pictures of him: the photos would assuage my suspicions that we had met a spirit, not a man of flesh and blood. There he is in the photographs, in all his cowboy glory with his cows in the background.

I also documented the road that our *dirt road* suddenly turned into, which was one long construction site. The workers building this brand new road seemed to be exclusively Indians. We were approaching Navajo Country. There were Indians on the giant machines, Indian women on the tractors, Navajo girls holding up the stop signs; we were almost the only people driving down the road. We asked one of the girls what the road was being built for, and she said all she knew was that there needed to be a highway to Cortez, for the tourists. But we had seen oil wells on both sides of the road, and signs here and there for Texaco and Mobil Oil—one billboard for Mobil said: *We are proud to be part of the Navajo nation.* The girl we were talking to laughed an embarrassed laugh, as though we had asked her about some obscene sex act; she acted like she had never seen an oil well in her life. We had wells for company until we were back on our familiar dirt road with uncultivated nature spread out all around us.

We found a picnic site at the edge of a canyon with a fantastic view of the landscape. We ate dried beef jerky for the first time, which tasted better than we expected; we had bottles of water and the good rye bread from Dolores. After a brief detour into a landscape that left us speechless, with the San Juan River snaking along the bottom of the canyon far, far below us, we entered the domain of Monument Valley: the bizarre massif looming on the horizon like a portent. We drove a long time before we finally reached it and, after paying our five dollars each at the entrance, we could drive up to the *Visitors' Center*, where dozens of cars filled the parking lot and young Navajo men and women flocked around us, offering two-and-a-half-hour or one-and-a-half-hour tours.

We were tired but felt obligated not to miss anything, so we took the shorter tour, again on a small, open truck, this time driven by a young woman, rather heavyset, like most Navajo women. We were relieved to see that she drove the old vehicle very carefully on the bad roads of Monument Valley; we could see the valley in the best evening light, bizarre shapes lit by the setting sun, again in an unbelievable red. All the stones had names, we learned: the Mittens, the Elephant, the Camel, the Three Sisters. The second half of the drive, in the shade and against the wind, was once again bitterly cold—this time we would definitely catch a cold, and two other people in our group, an American from Washington, D.C., and his wife, shared our concern. Lowis soothed our fears somewhat by handing around some of his beloved ginger cookies, which, he was convinced, were a cure for all ills.

We got to Kayenta hungry. Wetherill Inn, a hotel run by Navajo: big rooms, spic and span. They told us at reception that we could get Navajo cuisine at a restaurant around the corner; it turned out to be, like everywhere else, a lot like Mexican food: *fried bread* with beans on top and lettuce. Disappointing.

The next morning, at breakfast, we again had the experience of waitresses not being able to understand what we were trying to order. They finally brought me *French toast* and I was satisfied. We stocked up on more jerky and set out for the Hopi reservation, which, as we knew, was located on a high plateau surrounded by the much larger Navajo Country. There was no love lost between the two tribes, we heard. This was, I later discovered, a serious understatement. The conflicts over land and property between the settled, peace-loving Hopi and the encroaching nomadic Navajo went back centuries.

I am trying to remember the feelings I had at the time. They were ambivalent: primarily interest and curiosity but I could not entirely suppress discomfort at the fact that now we too were joining the stream of spectators filing past an ancient people that had suffered under foreign conquerors and their civilization, like people looking at animals in a zoo. Lowis wanted to find the old chief who had traveled through Europe the previous year to find help and collect money for his people. That was where the chief had met the Swiss Lowis.

We drove uphill. The soil grew more and more barren—it was a riddle for anthropologists, Lowis said, why the Hopi had settled here of all places. Nothing but juniper bushes and dry grass. We spent a half hour catching up on our travel notes. Lowis told us a few pieces of information about the early settlement history of the Hopi, the battles against the Spanish conquerors and later the Americans; he quoted for us the title of a book: *When Jesus Came, the Corn Mothers Went Away.*

Then the road ran straight into Hopi country. On Second Mesa we found the Hopi Cultural Center, an ocher-colored motel consisting of several two-story buildings connected to each other as in an Arab city. There was a hideous decoration at the reception desk: *Happy Easter!* Lowis wanted to turn around on the spot and leave. But since the other place where we had reserved a room had been described to us as "*depressing*," we checked in anyway. Lovely rooms at the end of the hall on the second floor. Sanna called me into her room for a whiskey since we were exhausted, but Lowis had been interested in the history of the Hopi for a long time, especially the Hopi myths and rituals, and had never been to Hopi country himself. He was excited and urged us to keep going.

We drove toward Hotevilla, a Hopi village on Third Mesa where apparently we would find James Koots, the chief Lowis had met in Switzerland. Evening sun on the indescribably barren mesa. Views over long, endless distances, interrupted by sandstone mountains and, in the distance, Kachina Peak or the San Francisco Mountains: we later understood that two saints, of different religions, were quarreling over this mountain. The Kachinas are the godlike beings of the Hopi clans who come down from their mountain to Hopi country in January or February and spend a few months living among human beings.

We asked the first man we met in Hotevilla about James Koots and he said that James's son Denis was right there. And there he was, coming out of the *store* with a couple of shopping bags; from behind he looked like a woman, with a long, loose ponytail hanging down his back. When he heard who we were looking for, he sat down next to Lowis in the car without further ado and guided us along a *rough road* at the edge of the village. He had us stop in front of a kind of railroad car jacked up off the ground, disappeared inside, and came out again right away to wave us in. We had heard that you were supposed to bring a few things to eat as host gifts when you visited the Hopi, so we had a walnut cake and some fruit with us.

When we stepped into the railroad car, the heat and an unpleasant smell jumped out at us. An old man was standing inside; he had just been lying down and was still straightening his jacket. He had just gotten back from work, he said. He held out his delicate, slender black hand. So this was James Koots. In the dim light of the railroad car I saw that he had dark hair and a beautiful old Indian face; one of his eyes was covered with a membrane of skin. It took a while before he grasped when and where he had met Lowis, then he started to remember and loosen up. Oh, Lowis, yes, he lived on a *mountain* and they had driven together in his *truck*.

Denis, who only then told us his own name, asked us if we wanted some coffee. He had the hint of a beard, narrow eyes, and a rather reserved face. We uttered the usual European phrases and made a fuss, but Denis said it was okay.

You would have to describe the Hopi Indians' circumstances as grinding poverty. Photography was not allowed in their territory under any circumstances, and we had left our cameras in the luggage room so as not to be led astray by our reflexes, as it were. We tried to use our eyes as photo lenses. All around the homes, which we would probably call temporary shacks, lay years' worth of trash, from rusted car wrecks to mountains of empty bottles and household garbage from the past few days.

Denis took us to the house next door. It was built from large, dark stones with window frames and door frames picked up any old place; they didn't shut tight, the kitchen door kept popping open, and I could not imagine how the occupants of a house like that could possibly stay warm through the harsh winters on the mesa. Though the same was true for the occupants of the more solid buildings in the area.

The kitchen was a large square room. There was an oval table in the middle, covered with an oilcloth, and wooden chairs all around it; a sofa with busted leather cushions; a wooden armchair with pillows, for James, against the opposite wall. Denis poured the brownish drink he called coffee out of an aluminum container on the stove into cups. A young, overweight woman came in with a four-year-old girl and sat down on the leather sofa. The woman was Denis's sister, we learned, and we were sitting in her kitchen. We bantered with the girl, who was charming like all Indian children and went along with our games. They had recently started teaching children both English and the Hopi language in elementary school, we heard. There were Hopi teachers. But the Hopi did not have a written language. They disliked the written word and relied solely on an oral tradition stretching back into prehistoric times.

Denis was a young man who spoke in monosyllables. Thirty years old, he later told us. He had gone to high school in Los Angeles, when there was still no high school in Hopi country. But he had been very glad to come back, he said. Life here was *nice*, he loved this land.

I talked with the sister. When I asked her who the fields belonged to among the Hopi, she said the men, and when I told her that the fields belonged to the women among the Navajo she held her hand in front of her mouth and laughed. Did she work in the fields too? Yes. The men farmed corn and beans, the women chilies, tomatoes, and squash.

We saw the farming implements in Denis's car the next day: strong spades, with thin blades because of the hard ground. The family had had a tractor for two years; before that they had farmed only with horses. Denis had to drive three miles to his field deep in the bottom of the canyon. The Hopi, we read in a brochure, had developed a unique method of dry cultivation and apparently the "white" scientists even today did not know how it worked. I felt something like schadenfreude toward the Western scientists who were unable to penetrate the inner secret of this "primitive" civilization and I realized that I wanted the Hopi to be able to keep their secrets.

We drove with Denis to the small house where he lived. Right away a lively, especially cute little girl appeared: *My daughter,* Denis said, surprising us. Deniseya. She got right into the car with us and mastered all its technological features: opening and closing the windows, putting the key in the ignition, beeping the horn of course. When we drove on, she sat in the passenger seat with Denis, an alert and very intelligent child with a grace and lightness in all her movements that European children do not have.

Denis asked us whether we were in a hurry to get back to the hotel and when we said no he took us to Prophecy Rock, jutting up out of the landscape. We stopped in front of a cave. There used to be ceremonies there, he said, and prophecies were told. He showed us a pictogram on the cave wall: three figures in a kind of cart, with two figures letting themselves down onto it along a kind of snake line. The different parts of the drawing must have been made at different times and retouched again and again. Denis thought that the prophecy expressed by this drawing would be fulfilled: Two warriors fighting each other. This battle was still to come. Between whom? we asked. Between the Hopi and the Navajo? No, Denis said and laughed. Maybe between the Americans and the Russians.

At the cave entrance I saw a bundle of short blades of grass, tied together with another blade and charred on one end. I asked what it was and Denis said it was an offering. He pointed to a stone farther back in the cave where there were similar bundles of longer blades of grass. This was an old place of sacrifice, he said. Yes, some people still came here and brought their modest offerings to the old gods. That was the clearest proof that the old Hopi beliefs were still alive. Denis seemed to have an ambivalent relationship with these beliefs: when he sold me a hunchbacked Kachina (not cheap), a god figure he had carved out of light wood and painted, he wouldn't rule out the possibility that it would keep watch over me that very night and guard my sleep.

But I stood in front of the humble offerings for a long time. Was this the soul of America that I was looking for? I suddenly felt that I understood how the anonymous powers that create human history had ordered the world: A couple of centuries meant nothing to them

and they were driving us toward a goal that they did not make known
to us.

The Kachina did keep watch over me that night. In my sleep I felt
that Angelina was near me and I talked to her. I said that when you
go deep enough down the differences between people and between
peoples disappear. A spirit hovers around us all, I said, asleep. It was
the spirit of these offerings, which also lived in her, in Angelina. And
in Pema the nun, someone she probably didn't know. Should we call it
reverence? We whites have moved farthest away from it, I said. But now
I realized that this overcoat of Dr. Freud's had been sent to me for no
other reason than to remove my doubts about this spirit. Angelina said
nothing.

Breakfast tasted good: *blue cornmeal pancakes* with *maple syrup*.

All the villages on First Mesa, where the Hopi spring ceremonies
were to take place, were *"closed"* to non-Indians because so many whites
had failed to observe the prohibition against taking pictures or making
audio recordings. Everywhere we went, at the entrances to the mesas,
we found signs: *INTERMITTED FOR NON-INDIANS*, and we had the experience for the first time in our lives of being turned away because of our
skin color.

We met Denis in Hotevilla at two o'clock sharp, or one o'clock in
Hopi time—they had their own time, we learned: they set their clocks
back an hour by day and moved them forward again at night. We could
not find out the reason why, but Lowis told us that there was no way to
refer to time in the Hopi language, or space either, and I realized that
we were living in a different world than they were and that we could not
understand their way of thinking. Denis had put on his best, brightly
colored American shirt for us and he lifted Deniseya onto his shoulders
and set out. *Are we walking?* Lowis called after him. *Yes.* So we ran after
him for a few hundred feet to the edge of the mesa—he wanted to show
us the tiny fields far below in the canyon, surrounded by primitive fences,
which the women worked. It felt to me like looking down from above
into an earlier era of human civilization; there was something painfully
touching about these women's fields. They had to take a laborious path
down to the fields and back up, to plant, sow, and tend their crops, and
in the summer it must be unbearably hot down there. But their families
couldn't do without the meager harvests they brought back home.

We all got into the car. Denis didn't let us stop anywhere; he wasn't exactly sure what to show us. He led us to a lookout tower with the high plateau of the mesa all around. I felt obliged to look out for Deniseya, who kept wanting to escape into the street. Her *daddy* didn't give a thought to paying attention to her or telling her she couldn't do anything—she walked with us to the very edge of the mesa, where it dropped off steeply, and stood next to or even in front of her father with her toes over the edge, but he didn't feel it necessary to hold her hand. She had learned to look after herself early.

We drove back to Denis's sister's house. Old James came and joined us too. Coffee was handed out to us in plastic cups from the big aluminum pot on the stove and then we were invited to join them for a real Hopi meal, *cornbread*: a flat corn cake wrapped temptingly up in corn leaves, filled with chili (*hot* but not too *hot*) and *beef*. Good food. Denis's sister, who hadn't sat at the table with us but instead devoured her meal in an armchair off to the side, packed up three more *cornbreads* for us for the road.

All of a sudden, the taciturn Denis took an interest in our way of life. He asked Lowis and Sanna if they were married; they exchanged a look and then Sanna said, *We live together.* Denis and James gave a knowing laugh at that. I asked Denis how they got married and he said *In Las Vegas!* which made everyone laugh. Then it came out that they did have their own marriage ceremony, performed by an elder, but that the state did not recognize it. If the wife wanted to get on her husband's health insurance or inherit his property if he died, she had to get married a second time. Their life seemed very complicated to us: inadequate agreements with the whites that were not kept anyway. A little island of Hopi country in a big Navajo ocean.

Now a lively conversation got going around the kitchen table. James saw the watch on Lowis's wrist and showed us that he had the same kind, also Swiss. Those are very good watches, he said, he had lost his working in the field once and found it again two years later, still ticking. He laughed mischievously at this trick the watch had successfully played on him. Denis wanted to know where you could get a watch like that. Would he like one? Lowis asked. *Yes.* Lowis said he would give Denis his. It turned out that Denis was a member of the Blue Bird Clan. There were ten clans in Hotevilla. He, Denis, had also been to the Kachina Peaks, the holy mountains the Kachinas come down from to live among humans. Later, when we talked about how Denis didn't seem to take the Hopi beliefs entirely seriously, Lowis said: A people that no longer believes is lost. Its soul is destroyed and it is buried under the rubble of our civilization.

We had to leave. James said that he might go to London in November, for a conference. The Hopi felt cheated by the agreement that had been signed between the state and the Indian tribes in the previous century and they were working to get it revised.

He said goodbye, full of dignity.

Lowis gave Denis his watch, and Denis said only *Pretty good!* and put it calmly in his shirt pocket. The days of the week on the watch were in German, so Sanna wrote them out for him in English. When we drove off, back to the hotel, we were sore at heart. Were the Hopi a people in decline?

We sat up late in my room, maybe because I was secretly hoping that Angelina would join us. Lowis's scholarly area, as he put it, was the study of peoples and empires in decline. The riddle of their downfall could not be solved in every case, he said. In analogous circumstances, some societies collapsed and others lasted, if in diminished form, and seemed to draw strength from the ruins of the edifices that had adorned their golden age. And we have witnessed collapsing empires too, I said, and were no more prepared for their collapse than those who came earlier, it seems. But can we put ourselves in their place? Sanna said. She was about to put on a play about the fall of Troy and she needed a straightforward reporting witness's voice for it, nothing else. That's what has the greatest effect, she said.

Lowis said that decline was in the air, you could smell it. Had I "smelled" the decline and fall of my own country? Strangely, an event came to mind that I had never before put in the category of decline: a meeting with the Soviet ambassador on March 30, 1990, in his big embassy on Unter den Linden that you had often viewed as the actual government of your country and where you had not been invited for years. Then, suddenly, came a private invitation to lunch. The yawning emptiness of the cloakroom, the extrawide staircase, the enormous, empty foyers, and then an intimidatingly large dining room with a giant table in the middle, set with far too many place settings for you and G. and the ambassador and his wife sitting opposite you. A young interpreter sitting at the narrow end of the table, who didn't have time to eat anything, translated brilliantly and without an accent. A printed, gold-edged menu. Caviar and veal, baked pollock, borscht, baked chicken, served by an imposing woman with a white cap and apron. The ambassador's wife, a matron, said nothing. The ambassador felt the need to discourse at length about the advantages of perestroika and glasnost in his country. He had been specially transferred to Berlin, and now he was there in this difficult, unpredictable situation. The last elections for the GDR's People's Chamber, with the victory of the conservative coalition, had taken place less than two weeks before. But his own country's position was difficult too, you countered. And he said: Exactly. Just look at the complicated situation with Lithuania.

Why had you and G. been invited to see him? The ambassador was worried about the trouble around the Stasi files. Couldn't they make an end to it? You said no, they should archive the files and make them available to the courts and other institutions doing research on behalf of the victims.

The ambassador spoke about the total censorship of his official communications under the old SED leadership. You expressed the suspicion that Gorbachev had treated the old leadership too gently and he disagreed. He had been present six times at meetings between Gorbachev and the SED leaders in the past few years and the Soviet side had never minced words. The last time, Gorbachev said to the people with him in the hall after one of these meetings: What should we do now? The SED people had always objected that everything was going fine in the GDR, especially the economy.

You asked about the opening of the borders in November. Hadn't anyone consulted him? He only learned about it afterward; he could have spoken out against it but no one would have listened to him anyway. Everyone was in a panic and hoped that opening the borders would stop the flood of people leaving the country through Hungary.

When you asked, he assured you that the USSR would never allow the GDR to join NATO, you could be sure of that. There was no way they would give up their most important line of defense.

There would be rapid improvements in supplying the population in the USSR with what they needed, he said; the production of consumer goods as well as food had risen, the shortages everywhere were mainly due to low transportation capacity and the fact that people had too much money and bought everything up. He was either stonewalling or totally blind.

It soon became clear that he knew hardly anything about the political currents in your country, that the forces which had led to the peaceful revolution were foreign to him, and that he had apparently invited you to lunch to learn something about them. What in God's name had his secret police been doing all this time?

Without much hope of success, you tried to impress upon him that he should finally recast the role of his embassy in Berlin—that he had to see it as a connecting link between East and West, he should invite writers from the West, the GDR, and the USSR and arrange major conferences there. Show his country from its best side, the cultural side. He found everything I had to say "very important and interesting." Boilerplate.

You and G. spent three hours in the embassy. When you left, the young interpreter walked you across the front courtyard to the outer gates. In the few feet where none of the guards could hear him, he gushed that he had never heard such an interesting conversation in the embassy before. He dismissed the ambassador as an "old grandpa" who didn't have a clue. The situation was so bad in his country that many people thought a civil war was unavoidable and the question was only if it would be bloody or relatively nonbloody. You could forget about Gorbachev. He had done an awful lot for his country, if it was up to the interpreter they would build a monument to him in platinum, but now all he was good for was to be a counterweight as president. The USSR was finished anyway. The only solution would be for a social democratic party to quickly take control.

You and G. stood numb on Unter den Linden. It was a close encounter of the third kind. You had smelled the end.

Our next destination was the Grand Canyon. Thousands of tourists were going to the same place and the nearby hotels were all booked; we looked out from one of the observation platforms down into the bizarre depths of the canyon, which left me strangely indifferent—the monstrosity of nature here simply exceeded every human measure. Then we found a room at the Red Feather, some distance away from the tourist circus we did not want to be a part of. In the room, over the rest of our whiskey, we talked more about the decline and fall of ancient civilizations. Lewis thought that their disappearance almost always had to do with the people's or tribe's or clan's inability to defend itself against a technologically superior civilization. We need only remember the letters from the three Indian chiefs on display at the Hopi Cultural Center's museum, apparently sent to a government agency, describing the terrible hardship and poverty of their people and calling for assistance from the white man (machinery, seeds, technology). The whites are candid and generous, one letter said, and then went on to discuss in detail how stubborn and *narrow-minded* many of his own people were, as if deaf and blind, rejecting the advantages of the white man's way of life.

In the morning I sat in the Red Feather and wrote this down, while Sanna and Lowis wanted to take the zigzagging trail down to the base of the canyon and, especially, wanted to hike back up again. It was a strenuous physical effort that was out of the question for me. That afternoon we had a view of the whole panorama from a helicopter. A stupendous feeling.

Later we ate an excellent steak and *baked potatoes* and drank a big glass of homemade beer. We had underestimated the amount of whiskey that was still in the bottle, which we had decided we needed to finish that night, for reasons we ourselves didn't know. I felt like I was traveling in a great circle around the reality I lived in and entering it again through a back way.

My consolation was that I felt Angelina steady at my side.

That night I couldn't sleep. My grandmother's face appeared before my eyes. Angelina wanted to know why I was so depressed about it. What happened to your grandmother? —She starved to death in 1945, while fleeing. —And? —And I never really mourned her.

Didn't you like her? Angelina asked.

She was an upright woman, stingy with her feelings. She was a simple village girl, bitterly poor, who worked binding sheaves of wheat on farms in the Eastern Elbe, where she met my grandfather. He did seasonal work reaping before he joined the railroad and worked his way up to stoker on the locomotive. He learned enough reading and writing to pass the test, from a teacher that his son, my father, got for him. They lived in a basement apartment for many years. I don't know if my grandmother ever learned to write—I never saw anything she wrote. She saved her pennies and we children got a groschen from her every time we got a good grade.

And? Angelina asked. What kept you from mourning her?

I refused to let myself think that she was an innocent victim, I said. I cut off my feelings because I needed to, and wanted to, see the loss of our home and our sufferings as a just punishment for German crimes. I didn't let myself feel my pain. When she died, my grandmother was only a little older than I am now, Angelina. And now I see her face at night when I can't sleep. Why now? And why here?

Angelina didn't answer.

The next morning I wrote in my spiral notebook:

```
I have known for a long time that the real transgres-
sions are the ones that happen on the inside, not out
in the open. And that you can deny these silent trans-
gressions to yourself for a very long time, and hide
them, and never speak about them out loud. We cling
tight to this innermost secret and keep it and keep it.
```

We wanted to spend at least one night in Las Vegas. Las Vegas, we had been told, was the focal point of the America that foreigners so craved. The Mirage Hotel had tempted us with its advertising brochure, so we booked a room, amazingly cheap. You're supposed to give them your money in the gambling rooms, Lowis said. I was amazed at how restless he seemed, how eager to get to Las Vegas in a hurry. Sanna and I exchanged amused looks behind his back. Lowis said we shouldn't be so stuck up. We shouldn't try to deny that certain needs, which modern people usually have to repress, are taken seriously in places like Las Vegas and can be acted upon. And that that is what lets these modern people continue to function, without getting sick, when they get back to their everyday lives.

He waved to the people on the side of the road whose job it was to lure couples who wanted to get married to the particular one of the many small wooden buildings that they were advertising. The wedding could take place there very quickly and affordably. So? Lowis said to Sanna. Should we? —Better not at all than like that, she said. Did he see this offering as a kind of therapy too? —Why not? he answered. Compared with the strict puritanical marriage laws that held sway everywhere else.

The Mirage promised everyone who crossed its threshold an

ENTRANCE INTO A PARADISAICAL WORLD OF WONDERS

Looking back at the pictures in the brochure, I remember what I felt when we set foot in the gigantic lobby, filled with exotic plants, ingratiating music, and overpowering smells: my defenses went up. I followed the signs to the elevators unwillingly, since they led us on long, unnecessary detours to force us to walk past the gambling rooms with the roulette tables and rows of slot machines. Lowis made fun of our dislike of these cheap tricks: So, we thought that especially here at a place like this there was some kind of competition over which establishment could be most honest, could fool its guests the least, or what?

From the very beginning I felt a shortness of breath. As though someone had pumped out air from the bubble we were in, thinning the oxygen we needed to survive. I threw myself onto the bed (too soft) in the enormous, luxurious room and had to fight off a strong need to fall asleep. But I also had the feeling that I had signed a kind of contract with the power that ruled here and now I had to fulfill it. To feel such an obligation was the last thing I expected, I thought that the atmosphere there would have a narcotic effect, which in fact it did too: it muffled all my feelings so that they wouldn't be crushed by the overpowering force that had them at its mercy.

That fate must have been just what had befallen the emaciated-looking woman who sat down at our table in the Italian restaurant for a few minutes, after we refused to let her do what she made her money doing: take pictures of us. She seemed to only want to talk about her job but then her monologue turned into a delirious cry of pain, shading more and more into an indictment of the system or machine that called itself Las Vegas, which had sucked her in as a naive young woman. Her boyfriend had won at roulette and left the gambling hall with a slim young beauty, she never saw him again and he had left her completely without money, in the clutches of a monster that never had let her go, God have mercy on you, the woman said, it devours you down to the bones and then gnaws on them too. Her deathly appearance, which she tried to cover up as best she could with a lot of makeup, was a warning about precisely that. You have no idea what goes on behind the scenes here, she said. The things they dream up just to get you to leave your money here. Down to the last penny. And then, when you've lost it all and if no one comes to ransom you, they cart you off to the nearest train station and give you a one-way ticket to somewhere else. They've set up a discreet operation to handle the suicides who pile up in the hotel rooms around sunrise. No guest ever sees the dark side of this desert city.

But we didn't want to plumb the radiant city's depths, we just wanted to take a little stroll around this glittering world of pretense. We marveled at how complete the illusion was that brought us to Rome after just a short walk, the facades exactly like the real ones we knew, the sky in no way inferior to the real sky of Rome, except that the heavenly bodies traveled across the sky once an hour, imitating the course of a whole day. Suddenly we could no longer tell if the people there were visitors like us or real citizens of this mythical Rome. It scared me. I wanted to leave right away, but there was no way out except the long walk past the gaming halls.

First we wanted to try the one-armed bandits. They stood in long rows and the players sat in long rows in front of them, tightly packed together, working the machines and trying to get them to give up their money. The sound we heard—sometimes soft, sometimes loud—was the jingling and rattling of money whenever a pull of the lever forced one of the machines to empty its contents into the receptacle. Then the lucky man or woman swept their booty into the little plastic buckets they all carried, and then less lucky men and women gathered around the winner's location, for encouragement, or to recharge themselves by shyly approaching the mystical forces the winner had called down, or, best of all, to take the winner's place. If a series of wins became too conspicuous, an envoy sent by the management appeared and inconspicuously checked to make sure that everything was in order.

After we had figured out "how it goes," we found seats in front of machines far apart from each other. I halfheartedly stuck my dollars in the slot and with waning interest and pleasure saw what my one-armed bandit had to tell me. It only turned up a modest win once, not enough to make up for what I had lost. The same thing happened to the others. Lowis appeared, impatient to take me where the "real games" were played. How Lowis knew the system of roulette and could explain it to us remained a mystery; he didn't let our ignorance stop him, though, and sat down at a table and started to play. I put up modest amounts of money, lost as I had expected to, and stopped when I reached my limit: sixty dollars.

It's stupid to stop now, Lowis said, you have to give the fate lurking behind the game a chance to show itself. He turned back to the roulette table and I said goodbye to Sanna, who was not playing anymore either but had stationed herself behind Lowis. Why did I want to leave now? It was before midnight, to go to sleep now was against the customs here. I was bored, I said, which was the truth. Sanna laughed: I obviously wasn't a game-playing type, in that case. Lowis, on the other hand . . . He seems to have just discovered a part of himself he never knew he had, Sanna said.

I said that that happens to everyone at least once in their lives, it's just that in my case there were facts of my nature of a different kind that had forced their way to the surface. Anyway, Sanna said, I should go to bed. She had to stay with Lowis, whatever happened tonight. This was a special night in his life.

I could only marvel at this young woman's intelligence. Suddenly I was so tired that I could barely find my room. Before I went to sleep I tried to make contact with Angelina, but obviously no angel would follow me there. So, you were lying, I said, when you promised you would be there whenever I needed you. Angels lie too. There was something consoling about that. It would have been hard to endure something perfectly perfect.

Outside it was bright as day from the electric lights flooding the street. Excited people were screaming. I had to get back up and pull the heavy curtains shut. I found a little bottle of champagne in the minibar and drank it all down. Then I had to call Berlin.

Has something happened? cried a worried voice. —No, nothing. That's the point. —Hey, are you tipsy? —That too. But the main thing is I want to ask you something. —Ask. —Do you really realize that everything in your head will disappear when you die? —Of course. Except for what you've written down. —Oh, that tiny fraction. It doesn't seem to bother you. —I don't think about it constantly. —I do, at least recently. Nothing to say to that? The other thing I wanted to say was: We're getting older. —Thanks for letting me know. —Good night.

A distant voice. A distant place. Masses of people, a protest march, moving toward the Rotes Rathaus without needing any instructions.

They pour out of the subway stations onto Alexanderplatz, hold up their signs, unfurl their banners. They give off a mixture of merriment and pride and determination that you have never seen on so many faces, neither before nor since. It's contagious. You can feel the night's fears dissolving, they disappear in the early morning when you see the marshals with the orange sashes saying NO VIOLENCE come toward you, in the best of spirits, around Alexanderplatz. There are theater people there, you know a lot of them, one actress friend comes up to you and says: Brecht should have been here to see this. "We have now decided to fear / bad life more than death." Here to see his plays coming down off the stage onto the streets. And the miracle is that the slogan NO VIOLENCE is followed throughout the whole country, by everyone.

A makeshift platform erected on a handcart, with people taking turns on it. The unimaginable trying to become reality. And—you all sense it—it could only last a historical second. But it had happened. The flower seller standing in front of her store, handing out flyers: the need to act now. Not miss it.

Later came malice and scorn and mockery, of course. No utopia allowed. But these open, wide-open faces—they were there, I saw them. The shining eyes. The free movements. They were soon stopped, yes. The eyes were soon looking at the displays in the shop windows and not toward any distant promise. The roulette tables gained in popularity.

Noise in the hotel woke me up and I could not get back to sleep.

In the morning, there was already a light there that hurt the eyes. Lowis came down to breakfast wearing enormous sunglasses. He's a bit tired, Sanna said. They hadn't gotten to bed until four. Aha. I realized that it wouldn't be appropriate to ask how much he had won. Much later, when we were sitting in the car, he said, from deep in thought, that you really had to wonder what it meant for human evolution that in certain circumstances our brain can be overcome by a drive that is stronger than reason. At one point he had won six hundred dollars but instead of stopping he kept playing. He had lost not only his winnings but quite a bit more.

An old Japanese woman was sitting in front of the slot machines that morning at the same place as she had been the night before, playing as though possessed. We couldn't help recalling the rats in the experiment who kept pressing and pressing the button that gave them an orgasmic feeling in their brain, forgot to eat and drink, and would have died, unable to forgo this pleasurable feeling, if the experimenters hadn't stopped them.

My need to escape this place grew stronger and stronger. When we were paying our bill, we asked the older woman at the reception desk if she ever gambled here. *Oh, never!* she cried. *Those people are sick!*

We drove in silence away from the city—the shimmering, glittering oasis set down in the middle of the desert to lead us into temptation. Sanna drove, I sat next to her. We drove and drove, it got monstrously hot, and before long our car's air conditioner couldn't keep up.

Death Valley. Yes, this is how I had imagined the desert—endless, blinding sand dunes. Scorching heat. Warnings posted at the gas stations never to walk or drive into the desert alone, and never without supplies of water. Every year the desert claimed more victims.

Valley of death. Valley of the dead. There they lay, all of them, my dead, struggling out of their graves as I flew over them. Just look, Angelina said. How long had she been there next to me? How long had we been floating above the landscape? I thought: I wonder if the dead will tell me something. Angelina, who could read my thoughts, said: No. The living superstitiously believed that the dead had a message to tell them. But they were no more intelligent when they were alive than the living are today.

So, in death you don't learn anything. I found that sad.

Angelina paid no attention to moods. She had not the slightest interest in whether I was frightened by the uncanny pull exerted by the dead. We flew toward the coast. The incomparable feeling of flying. Angelina next to me. I knew that this was goodbye. A task has been finished, Angelina, but why don't I feel a sense of accomplishment? A word came to me that I had been unconsciously seeking for weeks: preliminary. A preliminary work has reached its preliminary end.

Angelina laughed: But isn't that always the case?

We flew directly into the thick smog over L.A. from the northern edge of the city. Downtown stayed on our right. Was the little country I came from too insignificant to deserve sympathy? Wasn't the writing on the wall portending its downfall—Into the void with it!—there from the beginning? Was it really possible that I could have suffered so much for a simple, ordinary mistake?

Angelina categorically stated that that wasn't the point. Only feelings count, not facts.

Maybe it was her job to be sure of that. But I had to ask: Count to whom? Counted by whom, with what units? The questions were no match for Angelina, and the way she exultantly—yes, I would almost use that unsuitable word—flew over the landscape, toward the marina with the yachts and their masts and white sails, and farther up the coastal road to the giant parking lot with its hundreds of cars, sparkling and dazzling in the sun.

My misgivings didn't bother her in the least. My suspicion that now, only in a dream—a dream, Angelina!—did I perceive a glimmer of what the real issue was. Or should be. The earth is in peril, Angelina, but we're worried about the state of our souls.

That's the only thing worth worrying about, Angelina said. Every other catastrophe comes out of that. The wind from our flight blew her hair back. Black is beautiful, I said, after looking at her from the side for a long time.

We approached Venice, I recognized the buildings, the narrow streets, the squares full of entertainers, even on that day. Before us lay the flawless curve of Santa Monica Bay (which, recent news forces me to remark, has now been damaged by storms and raging forest fires).

I don't have to fly in a big circle now, do I? I said. Back to the beginning?

Do it, she said, unmoved.

And those years of work? Just throw it all away?

Why not?

Age, Angelina, that's why not.

Age meant nothing to Angelina, she had no conception of it. She had all the time in the world. And she wanted to make me as carefree as she was. She wanted me to enjoy our flight, to look down, and, saying goodbye, etch into my mind forever the magnificent line of the bay, the white edge of foam that the ocean spilled onto the shore, the strip of sand between the water and the coastal road, the row of palm trees, and the darker mountain range in the background.

And the colors. Oh, Angelina, the colors! And this sky!

She seemed satisfied and flew on in silence, keeping me at her side.

Where are we going?

I don't know.

NOTE ON SOURCES

Much of the information in this book about Hopi mythology and history is taken from Frank Waters, *Das Buch der Hopi* (The Book of the Hopi) (Munich: Eugen Diederichs Verlag, 1980).

C.W.

Where possible, translations in *City of Angels* have been made consistent with previous translations into English. The translator would like to acknowledge in particular Christa Wolf, *Parting from Phantoms: Selected Writings, 1990–1994*, trans. Jan van Heurck (Chicago: University of Chicago Press, 1997); Bertolt Brecht, *Poems 1913–1956*, ed. John Willett and Ralph Manheim (New York: Eyre Methuen, 1976), and *Bad Time for Poetry: 152 Poems and Songs*, ed. John Willett (London: Methuen, 1995); *Selected Prose of Heinrich von Kleist*, trans. Peter Wortsman (New York: Archipelago Books, 2010); and, for the Paul Fleming poem, *The Penguin Book of German Verse: With Plain Prose Translations of Each Poem*, ed. Leonard Forster (Baltimore: Penguin, 1957).

D.S.

A NOTE ABOUT THE AUTHOR

Christa Wolf (1929–2011) was one of the most celebrated German writers of the postwar era. A central figure in East German literature and politics, she was arguably the foremost German-German writer, awarded major literature prizes in East, West, and reunified Germany. Her wide-ranging work—nonfiction, fiction, and hybrids of the two, from socialist realism (*Divided Heaven*) to feminist epic (*The Quest for Christa T.*), from ancient Greece (*Medea*) to Chernobyl (*Accident*), and from German Romanticism (*No Place on Earth*) to a real-time chronicle of life in the second half of the twentieth century (*One Day a Year*)—is marked throughout by rigorous self-examination, political engagement, and committed feminism. Her most important reexaminations of the cultural past and personal memory include *Cassandra*, a crucial text for Western feminists and a secret social critique for her readers in the East; *Patterns of Childhood*, a groundbreaking reflection on her growing up in Nazi Germany; and *City of Angels*, a sequel of sorts to *Patterns of Childhood* that takes place after the fall of the Berlin Wall.

A NOTE ABOUT THE TRANSLATOR

Damion Searls has translated books by Rainer Maria Rilke, Ingeborg Bachmann, Hermann Hesse, Marcel Proust, the Dutch writer Nescio, and others. He rediscovered the work of Hans Keilson and has translated two of Keilson's novels, *Comedy in a Minor Key* and *Life Goes On*, for FSG; *Comedy in a Minor Key* was a 2010 *New York Times* Notable Book and a National Book Critics Circle Award finalist. Searls received a Guggenheim Fellowship in 2012.